KU-495-751

# KELLEY ARMSTRONG
# THE MASKED TRUTH

www.atombooks.net

ATOM

First published in Canada by Doubleday Canada, a division of
Random House of Canada Limited, a Penguin Random House Company
First published in Great Britain in 2015 by Atom

1 3 5 7 9 10 8 6 4 2

A CIP catalogue record for this book
is available from the British Library.

ISBN 978-0-349-00223-1 (paperback)
ISBN 978-0-349-00224-8 (eBook)

Printed and bound in Great Britain by Clays Ltd, St Ives plc

Papers used by Atom are from well-managed forests
and other responsible sources.

MIX
Paper from
responsible sources
FSC
www.fsc.org    FSC® C104740

Atom
An imprint of
Little, Brown Book Group
Carmelite House
50 Victoria Embankment
London EC4Y 0DZ

An Hachette UK Company
www.hachette.co.uk

www.atombooks.net

# THE
# MASKED
# TRUTH

# BY KELLEY ARMSTRONG

*For Julia*

# THE
# MASKED
# TRUTH

**PROLOGUE** If there's anything more tragic than spending your Saturday night babysitting, it's spending your Saturday night babysitting after canceling a date with the guy you've been dreaming about all year.

"Can't you find someone else?" I say when Shannon asks me to take the gig because her grandma's sick.

"You don't think I've tried? You aren't exactly at the top of my list these days, Riley."

I wince at that. We *had* been friends. Best friends. Then, last summer, her boyfriend got loaded and made a pass at me. I shut him down, of course, but I didn't tell her, and that was my mistake, because someone else had.

"You owe me," she says.

"Can you cancel?" I ask. I know the Porters—I used to babysit their daughter, Darla, when Shannon couldn't. "They'd understand—"

"Mr. Porter is getting an award. It's a huge deal."

I take a deep breath. "Fine."

I'm walking to the Porters' when my phone buzzes. *Where r u?*

I answer, *Don't ask.*

The phone rings. When I pick up, Lucia says, "I just got

— 1

a call from Micah. Seems he was shooting hoops with Travis when Shannon walked by . . . after you canceled with Travis to cover her babysitting gig. She said her grandma's just fine, and she doesn't know *why* you'd lie to him like that."

"What? No. That's—"

"Bullshit? Uh-huh. She totally set you up."

Before I can answer, I plow into a man walking around the corner. As I apologize, I notice the butt of a gun poking from under his jacket.

"Riley?" Lucia says.

I shake it off. I'm a cop's daughter; I know people legally carry concealed weapons all the time.

"Riley?"

"Sorry, I'm at the Porters' place. I'll call you back in a few, okay?"


"I can play Candy Land now!" Darla says as her mother tries to give me last-minute instructions while applying her makeup in the main-floor bathroom.

"Claire!" Mr. Porter calls from the living room. "We needed to leave five minutes ago."

"Only because you agreed to cocktails first . . . without telling me!" Mrs. Porter rolls her eyes at me. "Men. Sorry, Riley. Tonight's a bit of a disaster. First his sister got sick and couldn't take Darla. Then an important client asked him to predinner cocktails. We'll be at the Ritz all night. Our cell numbers are on the fridge."

"You're going out?" Darla says. "*Again?*"

"That's why Riley's here, sweetheart." Mrs. Porter offers a strained smile as her daughter hangs off her arm. "If we don't go out tonight, then you can't play Candy Land with Riley."

"I have an idea," I say to Darla. "How about we set up

the board, and then we'll phone your mom and she can play on the way to dinner?"

"That's a great idea," Mrs. Porter says. "You can move for me. And if I win, you can eat my ice cream."

"Ice cream?"

"Didn't I mention that? Riley will walk you down to the Scoop after dinner."

"But if I win, you have to watch me eat mine," I say. "I think I'll get bubblegum. You don't like bubblegum anymore, do you?"

She squeals, and I laugh and propel her out as Mr. Porter calls, "Claire!" Then he sees me and says, "Sorry for shouting."

"She's almost done," I say, smiling as Darla and I pass through the living room.


"What color do you want to be?" Darla asks.

"Purple."

"There is no purple, silly. There's . . ."

She rhymes them off, but I'm busy thinking I could text Travis an explanation as we set up the board . . . except that I left my cell phone downstairs. If I go down to get it, it'll seem as if I can't even wait for the Porters to leave before I start chatting with my friends and ignoring their kid.

I look at the pieces Darla holds out. "Green, then."

"Mommy will be yellow."

Darla hums as she lays out the board. I step toward the door. It's quiet down there, and while I doubt the Porters would leave before saying goodbye, they *are* in a hurry.

"I just need to grab something from downstairs," I say to Darla.

She nods and keeps humming, her attention on the board.

I walk into the hall. I'm at the top of the stairs when a sudden *whoosh* makes me jump.

"Really, Claire?" Mr. Porter sighs and then says, "Your hair must be dry by now," and I realize I'm hearing the blow-dryer from the downstairs bathroom.

Maybe if I just grab my backpack, it won't look suspicious. I start down the stairs.

"What the hell?" Mr. Porter says.

I freeze, but I'm only three steps down, too high for him to see.

"Who the hell—?"

A resounding smack. I stumble back. A thud follows, like something hitting the floor. I inch against the wall, and when I look through the railing I can see Mr. Porter's outstretched hand on the carpet. I back up one step and crouch, my heart thumping so hard I'm struggling to breathe.

When I peer down, I see Mr. Porter's face. His mouth is bloody and he's wiping it as he sits up.

"You want money?" he says. "There isn't more than a hundred bucks, but you can take my credit cards."

The rest is drowned out by the sound of the hair dryer, still running. A door creaks behind me. It's Darla, stepping from the bedroom, her mouth opening as she sees me.

I fly up those stairs so fast I'm sure I'll be heard. I push Darla back into the room and close the door.

"The game's ready," she says, and I realize she didn't hear anything.

"Go ahead and start. I-I'll be right there."

I need to get to a phone. Is there one in her parents' room? Do they still *have* a landline?

And how long am I going to stand here wondering while a robbery unfolds below?

Robbery. Oh God, there's a robbery, and the Porters are

down there and I have Darla and I need to— I need to do something, anything.

I hurry back to Darla and drop to a crouch. "I'm going to step out and talk to your dad. You need to stay here. Start your turn. Youngest goes first, right? Now wait right—"

The hair dryer stops.

*I have to warn Mrs. Porter.*

A shriek from downstairs. A half-stifled yelp of shock has Darla's head jerking up, her eyes going wide.

"Did you hear that bird? It sounds strange, huh?" My words tumble out fast and shaky I'm not even sure she understands. "Stay right here while I—"

A shot.

I bolt up from my crouch so fast I nearly fall over. Did I just hear—? No, I couldn't have. It's a robbery. Just a robbery.

"Riley . . . ?" Fear licks through Darla's voice, and I know she heard the same thing.

"It's—it's just a car," I blurt, barely able to get the words out. "Backfiring. But . . . but . . . we're going to play a new game, Darla. Y-your mom's coming up in a few minutes to say goodbye and we're going to hide. How's that?"

The fear evaporates as she lets out the first note of a squeal. I slap one trembling hand over her mouth. "Shhh. Don't give it away. Now get under the bed."

"But that's the first place she'll—"

"We don't want to worry her. Just surprise her. Come on."

I prod her to the bed. Then I hurry to shut the door. Below, I hear Mrs. Porter's muffled sobs.

*I need to do something.*

"Riley?" Darla pokes her head from under the bed.

I quickly shut the door and run back to her.

I'm overreacting. Cop's kid—we do that. It's a simple armed robbery.

*Simple* armed robbery? At the thought, this weird bur-bling laugh sticks in my gut.

Yes, armed robbery is bad, but that's all this is. The thief wants something. He fired a shot to scare them. That's all. He wants debit cards or credit cards or jewelry, and they'll give it to him. They're smart. They aren't arguing.

Just a robbery.

*That's it, that's it, that's it.*

I crawl under the bed and strain to listen. I can still hear Mrs. Porter, her words now too faint to make out, but her tone tells me she's begging.

*Why don't I hear Mr. Porter?*

That shot.

*No, they've knocked him out. That's all. Knocked him—*

A second shot. And Mrs. Porter stops begging.

**CHAPTER 1** *If there's anything more tragic than spending your Saturday night babysitting, it's spending your Saturday night babysitting after canceling a date with the guy you've been dreaming about all year.*

How many times have those lines gone through my head in the past four months? How many nights have I lain in bed, thinking them? Stood in front of a mirror, thinking them?

*You stupid, stupid girl. You had no idea what tragedy is.*

Tragedy isn't a ruined Saturday night. It isn't a missed date. It's lying under your bed with the babysitter and listening to two shots, and then following your babysitter into the hall and seeing your parents at the bottom of the stairs, covered in blood. Tragedy is spending your life trying to understand how that could have happened, how you could have been under the bed, giggling, with your babysitter, while your parents were murdered. And your babysitter did nothing about it.

Hell is being the girl who did nothing, who has to live with that guilt. Worse, having to live as a hero, listen to people tell me how brave I was and how I saved that little girl, and all I want to do is shake them and say, "I hid under the freaking bed!"

It doesn't matter if my mother and my friends and my priest and the police and two therapists have told me I did the right thing. It doesn't even matter if my older sister Sloane says it, rolling her eyes with "God, Riley, you are such a martyr. Would you rather have been shot? Like Dad?"

Any other time Sloane brought up our father's death that casually I might have taken a swing at her for it. Maybe that's what she wanted. To smack me out of my paralysis. It didn't matter. I heard her say it, and I walked away.

After Lucia and I became friends, she admitted she used to cut. I'd been supportive and I'd tried to understand, but I couldn't really. Now I do, because the impulse to feel something, *anything*, is so incredible that there are times I dig my nails into my palms hard enough to draw blood. It doesn't help.

"Riley?" Mom says. "We're here, baby."

I look out to see a huge windowless building.

"Well, that's not just a little creepy," Sloane mutters from the backseat.

I look at the building, a hulking solid box, like a prison, and I should want to run. Tell Mom I've changed my mind, that I don't need this therapy weekend.

*I'm fine, Mom. Really. See? Big smile. Everything's fine.*

Except it isn't fine, and the surest proof of that is that when I look at this building—with a steel front door and not a single window—I don't want to run away. I want to run *to* it, race inside and slam the door behind me and lock the world out.

"It's a renovated warehouse," Mom says to Sloane. "They're remodeling it into offices, and in the meantime the builder lets community groups use it. Riley's therapist says the lack of windows is a good thing. It'll keep the kids focused. And of course, they'll be allowed out for fresh air and walks."

My sister's gaze sweeps the city block, past more brick boxes—warehouses and industrial buildings, already dark on a Friday evening, some permanently dark, judging by the boarded and broken windows.

"It's an awesome neighborhood for walking," Sloane says. "Great scenery. Probably plenty of friendly muggers and cheerful drunks." She looks at me. "Did you pack your fencing saber?"

Mom sighs. "The kids won't take their walks here, of course. There's a park where they'll go for two hours each morning."

"To use the playground equipment? Or will they lock them in the dog park and make them run laps?"

Mom sighs deeper.

Sloane mouths to me, "Tell her you don't want to do this."

"It's fine," I say.

Sloane rolls her eyes and slumps into her seat.

Mom looks at me and says, "If you don't like it, baby, you don't have to stay."

"It's only for the weekend, Mom. I'll survive."

She grips the steering wheel tighter. "I know. I just . . . I wish . . ." *I wish your father were here.* That's what she wants to say. Because as much as we love each other, she doesn't *get* me the way Dad did. But he's been gone eighteen months now. Killed in the line of duty. A hero. Just like his daughter.

I inhale sharply. *No self-pity, Riley. Chin up. Mom doesn't deserve your shit.*

I reach deep inside and pull out the part of me she *does* deserve. The old Riley. She's still there, and I can drag her out as needed, like when I'm fencing, and I can reach deep inside myself and pull out another girl, one who's more aggressive, a girl who fights to win.

A different Riley for every occasion. Right now Mom needs the cheerful one, so I pluck her out and dust her off and smile over at my mother and say, "Are we still on for next weekend?"

"You don't need to go to New York with me. I know you hate fashion shows."

"But I love Broadway musicals, and that's the deal, right? I watch your gorgeous designs paraded down the runway, and you sit through *The Lion King* for the fifth time."

"Then we'll go shopping," Sloane says. "Now that you're skinny, Riley, it'll be much easier to find you stuff."

"Sloane!" Mom says, twisting to glare at her.

"She lost weight. That's good, right?"

"Your sister lost weight because she can't eat. That is *not* good!"

"Mom . . ." I say.

"And she did not *need* to lose weight. She was a size *ten*."

I get out while Mom lights into Sloane. An old argument and not one I need right now. Mom and Sloane are both five foot two and size two. I take after my dad. When my height started shooting up in middle school, Mom dreamed that someday I'd model her designs. I do have the height now, but as my grandma says, my figure is better suited to babies than a runway strut.

I grab my bag out of the trunk. Mom catches up with me. "You know I don't think that, right, baby? I didn't *want* you losing weight. I want you to be healthy. In every way, I want you to be healthy."

"I know, Mom." I give her a one-armed hug as we walk. "So . . . New York. Where are we staying?"

I have to pass the metal detecting wand test before I can enter the building. They say that's standard practice these days, but I'm sure it also has something to do with the fact this is a group therapy weekend for kids with problems. They don't want us bringing in anything sharp—for our own safety and everyone else's.

"I'd ask you about a cell phone," Aimee says as she scans my bag, "but I know if we told you not to bring one, you wouldn't have."

It's meant to be a compliment, but at seventeen no one likes to be reminded what a rule-follower she is. I'd be tempted to smuggle a phone in if that wouldn't just make me feel petty and immature.

I say goodbye to Mom, and then Aimee takes me up to my room. She's been my therapist for a month now. She's in her late twenties and reminds me of Zooey Deschanel, with both the slightly off-kilter prettiness and the manic-pixie personality. I like her, even if I'm not sure how much good therapy is doing. She's my second counselor since the incident. Third if you count my priest. I started in teen group at church, but, well . . . I got a little tired of hearing how God would fix me. I want to fix myself.

I leave my bag in my room. I'll be sharing it with a girl I don't know. This weekend is for kids from several local groups, and there's only one guy from mine. I was supposed to get my own room, but then this other girl—Sandra—signed up at the last minute. The old me would have been happy at the prospect of meeting new people. Now I wish I could grab a sleeping bag and find a spot alone on the floor downstairs.

With Mom gone, there's no need to keep wearing my "old Riley" mask. As my mood drops, I remind myself it isn't like I had anything better to do this weekend. After the incident, there'd been no need to explain to Travis that Shannon had tricked me, though Lucia still made sure he knew. He'd come by our house that week with two volumes of *Transmetropolitan* because the first time we talked, it was about graphic novels. He paired the comics with a giant Reese's Peanut Butter Cup because he'd noticed that was my candy of choice from the school vending machines. Can a guy get any sweeter than that? No.

Two weeks later, when he asked me out again, I nearly threw up. A date with Travis would forever be linked to that night. I can barely face him in school. Hell, I can barely *go* to school. My grades are tanking, and my teachers keep saying they'll adjust them "in light of what happened." I don't want them adjusted. I don't want a free pass. I just want to pull myself together.

So I'm here, doing a weekend therapy camp. I need to make the effort, like I need to make the effort to get up every morning. If I stop moving, I'll be stuck forever under that bed, listening to the footsteps of the man who killed the Porters and praying, *Please God, don't let him find us. Don't let him hurt Darla. Don't let him hurt me.*

Aimee sends me downstairs to find the main therapy room. Easier said than done. Whoever designed this place wasn't a fan of simplicity and order. It's a warren of halls. Like someone with bipolar disorder drew the blueprints during a manic episode: "We'll put a room here! And here! Oh, and we'll connect them here!" After four months in group therapy, I've learned a lot about mental illness. Sometimes I feel like an impostor. As if I'm taking valuable therapy time from kids with *real* problems.

I'm following the maze to the main room when I pause to consider two options.

"Left," a voice says. It's a guy around sixteen. He's an inch or so taller than me. Dark hair, slicked back. Dressed in a battered leather jacket, ripped jeans and filthy sneakers. The classic bad-boy look, ruined by the fact he's wearing an Abercrombie & Fitch T-shirt and two-hundred-dollar Air Jordans.

"Aaron," he says, extending a hand.

"Riley."

His lips twitch. "You don't look like a Riley."

Four months ago I would have asked what a Riley looks

like. Now I can't work up the energy. I only shrug and mumble.

"Sorry," he says. "Didn't mean to be . . . whatever. It's just that I heard there was a Maria here, so when I saw you, I figured you were her."

He means because I'm Hispanic. Again, the old Riley would have had a comeback. Instead, I hear one— "And why would you think that?" —spoken in a British accent, heavy with sarcasm.

I turn. It's Max—Aimee's other patient. About six feet tall. Lean. Denim jacket. Jeans. Doc Martens. Dark blond hair worn long enough that he can tie it back, though today it's hanging loose.

Aaron says, "I'm not trying to be a jerk. I just meant it's weird her parents gave her an Irish name when she's Mexican."

"Are you Jewish?" Max asks.

"What? No. Why?"

"Then it's weird your parents gave you a Jewish name."

Aaron opens his mouth to answer, settles for a glare and stalks down the hall.

Max looks at me, eyebrows arched. "I don't even get a thank-you?"

"If I wanted to snark at him, I would have."

"Oh, you wanted to. You've just lost your footing, Riley." He winks. "Or should it be Ril-ia?"

I don't know Max well. No one in our group does. The rest of us have to sit in the semicircle and talk, while he stays in the back and rarely offers a word beyond a sarcastic comment. I have no idea what he's there for. I'm not even convinced his accent is real. All I know is that I have to vomit out every last anxiety and fear and self-hating thought in my head, and he gets to listen to it and give nothing in return.

"Why are you here?" I say. "You don't contribute any-thing."

"I contribute my devastating wit and charm," he says. "What more could you want?"

*Less of both*, I think, but I only say, "The point of ther-apy is to discuss your problems."

"But I don't have any problems, old girl." He cranks up the accent for that. It's his shtick, dialing the Brit-talk up to eleven, like something out of a movie from the twenties.

I give him a look. "Does anyone say 'old girl' anymore? Even in Britain?"

"No, they do not. Because I'm over here now." He grins, and I feel the overwhelming urge to shake it from his face. Well, at least I feel something. Though Aimee might prefer a less violent impulse.

"Since you *are* here," I say, "in this group, you *do* have problems. That's a prerequisite for the therapy."

"Not for me. I'm right as rain, Ril-ia Vasquez. Right as rain." He tosses me another grin and saunters down the hall toward the room.

I bend and retie a shoe that doesn't need retying, giving him time to get ahead. Then I straighten and I'm about to head in the same direction when I hear the squeak of a shoe and turn to see a girl. She's maybe fifteen, with dark curly hair, wearing a cute little dress—a bit formal for the occa-sion, but from the way she's nervously glancing down the corridors, I don't think she's a therapy regular. While the new Riley's impulse is to turn away and let someone else handle it, I know better. So I call, "It's this way."

She does a rabbit-jump and spins to face me.

"The therapy room is over here," I say, pointing.

"O-okay," she says. "I'll . . . I'll see you in there."

Again, I want to just say *whatever* and continue on. Again, there's still enough of the old me—the girl who used to serve on the student council, unofficial chick-in-charge-of-organizing-stuff—that I can't turn my back on her, no more than I could a freshman who looks ready to bolt on her first day.

"If you don't mind walking in with me, I'd appreciate that," I say as I head over. "I hate that part." I stop in front of her. "I'm Riley."

"Sandy," she says.

"My roommate? Even better. Please tell me you know more about these weekend things than I do."

A weak smile. "No, sorry. I'm a total therapy noob. I . . ." Her gaze darts to her hand, and I see her sleeve riding up just enough to show bandages around her wrist. She quickly yanks her sleeve over them.

"S-sorry," she says. "It's not— It's not as bad as it looks. I wasn't really . . . wasn't really trying to . . ." She sucks in breath. "Just a stupid thing. A boy and . . . stupid. But my parents are freaked out so I said I'd go to therapy, and we heard about this weekend, and I thought it would make them feel better if I volunteered, you know? Prove I regret it and . . ." She looks up, her eyes widening. "Oh my God, I'm babbling. I can't believe I just said all that."

I smile for her. "It's practice for the sessions. And you did very well." I look toward the therapy room, where I can hear Aaron's loud voice and then Max with some sarcastic rejoinder. "We can go in there with the guys or we can poke around out here."

"I'd rather poke around. He sounds like a jerk."

"Which one?"

She smiles, and we head off down the hall.

**CHAPTER 2** Worst thing about group therapy? The introductions.

*Hi, I'm Riley, and I . . . have a problem.*

Yeah, we all do. That's why we're here.

*Hi, I'm Riley, and I . . . need help.*

Um, well, then you're in the right place.

*Hi, I'm Riley, and I've been diagnosed with situationally related anxiety and depression leading to post-traumatic stress disorder.*

Say what?

*Hi, I'm Riley, and I was in the house while the couple I was babysitting for were murdered.*

Oh, you poor thing.

*Hi, I'm Riley, and I was under the bed while the couple I was babysitting for were murdered downstairs.*

Oh, you poor . . . Wait, you were under the bed?

No one ever says the last one. But I hear it. Over and over. Some days, it's all I hear.

Now I'm in the therapy semicircle again. Sandy sits to my right, wearing a cardigan, sleeves pulled down over her hands. Max is in the back, as usual. Aimee sits off to the side, letting the second therapist—a balding guy named Lorenzo—lead the group. The boy on the end was supposed to talk first, but he wouldn't. The girl on my left went instead. Brienne. As tiny as Sloane but blond, Brienne looks like a cheerleader. She's here for "emotional stuff." That's all she says for now, which is fine. No one will push. Yet.

I'm up next.

"I'm Riley Vasquez, and I . . ." I trail off, searching for the right words as my stomach clenches.

"Oh!" Brienne grins at me like she's about to shake her pompoms and ask for an *M*. "You were in the papers. You saved that little girl."

As I shrink into my chair, she notices my reaction and hurries on, "And you're the city girls' fencing champ. That's why I remembered the article. I thought the fencing thing was cool."

I manage a weak smile for her. "Thanks."

Aaron wrinkles his nose. "If you're the girl who saved that kid, what are you doing in therapy? Is the pressure of being a hero too much to bear?"

I flinch.

Brienne moves forward, like a tiny attack dog straining at its leash. "She saw two people die."

"No," Aaron says. "If I remember the story, she never actually witnessed—"

"Oh, for God's sake. She was there when two people *died*. She could have been killed herself."

"The point is," I cut in, "that I'm working through some things—"

"Like what?" Aaron says. "Did you even *see* them after they'd been shot?"

My annoyance from earlier flares. "No, I just presumed they were dead and called 911 without actually checking on them. Of course I saw them. I—"

"Take the tone down, please, Riley," Lorenzo says.

"What?" Brienne says. "This jerk gets to say whatever he wants, and you give Riley crap for defending herself? And if you dare tell me he's just needling her because she's cute, I swear I'll hit you. Then we'll have to spend the rest of this session talking about my anger issues, and nobody wants that."

"No, Brienne," Lorenzo says evenly. "I wasn't letting Aaron get away with that. I was about to add that we don't challenge anyone on their right to be here. Now, Aaron, you're next. Introduce yourself, please."

"Fine. I'm Aaron Highgate, and I'm here by mistake."

Brienne mutters under her breath. He glowers at her.

"Well, I am. I don't have a problem; my father has one. *With* me. That's why I'm here. I crashed my Rover, and if I don't do this weekend therapy shit, I won't get a new one."

"Tragic."

"Brienne, please. Aaron, continue."

"My dad thinks I have narcissistic personality disorder. He even bribed some shrink to agree. I'm a narcissist? He's the one screwing everything in a skirt. Mom's finally divorcing him, and she's going to take him to the cleaners. Like she should."

"All right," Lorenzo says slowly. "But why would he send you here?"

Aaron looks at Lorenzo like he's an idiot. "Um, because he hates me. Because he hates that I'm siding with Mom. Because if he can prove I'm sick and she can't handle it, then he can get custody and save a shitload of money on support . . ."

Aaron continues. While I'm not sure he has an actual disorder, there's obviously some narcissism going on there. First he doesn't want to talk about his problems. Then *all* he wants to talk about are his problems.

After about ten minutes, when he pauses for breath, I say, "I need to use the restroom."

"I think you can wait, Riley," Lorenzo says.

Aimee shakes her head. "That's okay. Let her—"

"Let her take off while I'm talking?" Aaron says. "That's rude."

"No," I say. "It's part of my anxiety issue. I have a nervous bladder, and the longer I wait, the more—"

"Whoa, TMI," Aaron says.

"You asked," I reply, and take off before anyone can stop me.

I swear, the bathroom is a quarter mile away with all the twists and turns I have to take. I stay in there longer than I need to.

When I finally open the door, I'm not surprised to hear footsteps down the next hall. Someone's come to fetch me. I'm torn between feeling guilty for hiding and wanting to snap, "Can I use the bathroom in peace?"

I won't snap at whoever it is. I've done that enough tonight with Aaron, and I feel guiltier than I should. Story of my life these days. I remember when I was little, my dad read me a story about an obsequious mouse, quailing at every sharp word, running from every scary noise, stumbling over himself to apologize for everything. I hated that mouse. Now I am him.

"Looking for me?" I say as I turn the corner, heading toward the footsteps. "Sorry. I—"

An alien blocks my path. A gray-faced alien wearing a suit and gloves and holding a gun, and the thought that flashes through my mind is a memory from the month before Dad died, the two of us on the *Men in Black* ride at Universal, going through it over and over again, laughing as we competed to see who could shoot the most aliens.

The memory comes like a fist to my gut. It disappears just as fast, and I realize I'm staring at a guy wearing a gray alien mask. Because that's what it is, obviously. A latex mask of the aliens from the old *X-Files* show. The gun, though? The gun is real.

I turn to run. I do not even *think* of jumping him and grabbing his weapon. Four months of feeling like a coward hasn't changed anything. I see a mask. I see a gun. I flee.

He grabs me by my hood. I twist and lash out, kicking and punching, and he whips me against the wall. My head hits hard enough for fireworks to explode behind my eyes. I still kick him when he gets within range and my fists aim for his gut. He wraps one hand around my throat and puts the gun at my temple. I keep struggling.

"Are you loco, girl?" he growls. "This isn't a toy."

I don't care. I'll do whatever it takes to get away because I know what happens if I don't. I can still hear the gunshots. I can see the blood. I can feel Mrs. Porter's skin cooling fast under my hands.

So I will fight and—

The gun clocks me in the temple. The same spot that struck the wall, and I black out just long enough that when I come to, I'm staring at that wall. He's behind me, with a chokehold around my neck and the cold gun barrel pressed to the back of my head.

"Riley?" a distant voice calls, a singsong: "Riley, Riley, Ri-lee-a. Come out, come out wherever you are."

Max's boots tromp along the hall. The man pulls me toward a shadowy corner. He doesn't yank me behind it, though. He leaves me standing there, exposed in the dim light, with a gun to my head and one arm wrenched behind my back.

My heart is pounding so hard I feel like I'm going to pass out. I'll lose consciousness, and I'll fall forward, and my captor will think I'm trying to escape, and he'll shoot—

"Come out, come out," Max calls. "Or don't. Actually,

let's go with that. Don't come out. You're hopelessly lost, having failed to adequately mark the trail with breadcrumbs. That way, we both have an excuse not to go back and listen to Mr. Highgate, who is, shockingly, still regaling his captive audience with all the problems he *doesn't* have."

*Oh God, go away, Max. Please, please, please go away. You don't deserve this. No one does. Just walk down another hall and let this guy take me and do whatever—*

A wave of lightheadedness washes over me.

*And do whatever.*

Kill me.

He's going to kill me.

*I don't care. Can't care. Can't escape. Just go, Max. Please, please—*

Max steps around the corner and sees me in the shadows, my expression hidden.

"Bloody hell," he says. "You can't play a proper game at all. Go hide, please, so I can spend the next hour seeking and—"

The man pushes me, and we both move into the light. Max stops. He stands there, frozen, like I was, except my shock lasted only a second or two. Max stares at us, and the look on his face . . . I'd say it's terror, but not the kind you get from seeing someone holding a gun. It's deeper than that. Raw and bone-chilling.

"It's a mask, idiot," the man says.

At least three seconds tick by. Then Max rubs his face, hard.

"Riley?" he says, uncertainty in his voice.

"Don't move," I say finally, my voice oddly steady, as if his terror swallows my own. "He's got a gun to my head and—"

Max spits a curse, and I realize he hasn't seen the gun. So what freaked him out? A guy in an alien mask?

Max breathes hard now, saying, "All right, all right." Then, "It's going to be fine, Riley. Just stay calm. It'll be fine. I'll—"

The man cuts him off with a snorted laugh. "Don't even think of playing hero, kid. All you'll do is get this girl killed. Which, by the way" —he lowers his voice to a mock whisper— "really doesn't impress the ladies."

"Don't," I say. "Please. Max doesn't have anything to do with what happened. Let him go. It's me you want."

"Really? Is your daddy rich?"

Max snaps out of it, his sarcasm slingshotting back. "Her *daddy* is dead, you tosser. You've got the wrong girl."

"Actually, we aren't looking for a girl at all. We're here for the son of Mr. Lewis Highgate, who *is* very rich indeed. As for this girlie, let's hope her daddy left a nice insurance policy. One that will help his daughter buy her freedom."

"F-freedom?" I say.

"I believe this is what you call a hostage situation. You two kiddies may not be the main prize, but you'll make perfectly fine bonuses." He prods me forward, gun still at my head. "Now, let's go meet young Mr. Highgate, phone his daddy and get this party started."

**CHAPTER 3** Our captor leads us back to the therapy room. If he speaks on the walk, I don't hear it. I just keep staring at him, thinking, *This can't be real*. Then I notice Max doing the same, an even more intense stare, his eyes like laser beams trying to cut through the mask. No, trying to incinerate it.

He blinks hard and seems surprised when he glances over to see the man still there. Surprised and dismayed. That's all—dismayed. Not panic, and maybe that's because he's decided this is all an act or a prank, but in a weird way his calm keeps me from dropping on the floor, hands over my head, breaking down, sobbing, "Not again, not again, not again."

I can hear voices from the therapy room, raised in anger and panic and fear. I don't hear words, though. It's as if there's cotton stuffed in my ears, a weird kind of deadening inside my head.

When we reach the room, there are two other men in masks, one from the *Star Wars* cantina scene, the other from *Predator*. They have everyone against the wall, faces to it, hands over their heads.

"Well, well, I see you boys started the party without me. Let me add the two final guests, then. Against the wall, kiddies. I'd tell you to assume the position, but I think you can figure that out."

I try to walk over to Sandy and Brienne, but the guy in the gray *X-Files* mask grabs my shoulder and steers me to the end, between the only two kids whose names I don't know—the boy who wouldn't introduce himself and the girl who didn't get a chance.

The girl is about my age, the guy maybe a year younger. When I meet his gaze, he turns away almost angrily, as if I were trying to get him in trouble. The girl whispers, "Maria," and I turn her way. She has dark braids and dark skin, and she's taken off her jacket and is wearing a Happy Bunny T-shirt that says *Crazy on the Inside.* I have to smile at that. I just do, even if it's only a twitch of my lips. She catches my look and nods at Aimee and then waves a scolding finger, pantomiming that my counselor had not been nearly as amused by the shirt. Which is probably why it'd been covered by a jacket earlier.

Later, I'll tell her I'm glad she wore that shirt, because for that one moment it made me forget that I was standing at a wall, hands over my head, waiting for armed captors to frisk me. And that moment's break is all I need to push out of the corner inside my head, squelch the inward panic, and take a deep breath and say, "I can do this."

I know how hostage situations work. My dad was on the SWAT team for a few years, before he decided it took him away from his family too much. But I know the stats— fatalities and even injuries are extremely rare. These guys want money from Aaron's dad. They won't get it by killing kids Mr. Highgate doesn't even know.

Does that make me relax? Just chill and wait my turn, no big deal? Absolutely not. Because no amount of logic and reasoning will change the fact that I'm against a wall, about to be frisked by armed captors. But I can suck it in enough to exchange semi-genuine smiles with Maria as our captors go the line, taking the cell phones from our counselors and checking the rest of us for contraband weapons.

When they reach the boy beside me, he turns around so sharply that the guns fly up and my breath catches.

"We already went through a metal detector," he says.

"Yeah," X-Files says. "And we're going to check you again, because metal detectors aren't perfect. Turn around and put—"

"You want to check me out? Fine. Take me to another room and I'll give you my clothes."

"This isn't airport security. You don't get options here. Turn around—"

X-Files reaches for the boy's shoulder, and he jerks away with "Don't touch me."

"Gideon . . ." Lorenzo calls from down from the line.

"Cool it, kid," Maria whispers.

"Don't tell me—"

Predator and Cantina are on Gideon before he can finish. They pin him to the wall, and he's shaking so hard, his eyes filling like he's going to cry, and I catch his gaze, but when I do, he glowers and turns the other way.

# MAX: CONCEIVABILITY

Conceivability: *the capacity of being imagined or grasped mentally.*

When Max first sees the alien with Riley, the only conceivable answer is that his meds aren't working. No. Not again. *I will not go through this again. I'll—*

*You'll what, Max?*

Nothing.

*No, really, Maximus. When you say you won't go through it again, do you mean—?*

Bugger off.

*We need to talk about this.*

No, he doesn't. Moving right along, there's an alien in the hallway, and he's quite certain he knows what that means. His latest cocktail of meds is not working. Oh, yes, he thought it was. Was so certain it was, but that was just another sign that it wasn't. Delusions of a world where his bloody meds work, and he can get back to living a bloody normal life.

*Ha-ha. Very funny, old boy. There is no normal life for you. Not anymore. Just aliens holding pretty girls hostage. Perhaps this is a new subtype of delusion—one where you get to play the knight in shining armor. Well, hop to it, then. Slay the alien. Win the girl.*

That's when the alien speaks, and Max realizes it's a man in a mask. That a perfectly ordinary criminal is holding

Riley hostage. His next thought: *Thank God, it's not the meds.* Followed by: *Bloody hell, there's a man holding Riley hostage.*

The kidnapper takes them back in the main room, and they go through the "Everybody against the wall, hands on your heads" and the pat-downs and the panic and the "Oh my God, I can't believe this is happening."

*You and me both.*

Then they're sitting on the floor, listening, and Max is trying to process what the hostage-takers are saying. It's not that he can't understand them. They came to the States a year ago, him and Mum—*I think what you need, Maximus, is a change of scenery, and what I won't mention, dear boy, is that by "change of scenery" I really mean let's both run across the ocean and find someplace where no one knows what you did.*

A year here means it isn't as if these men speak a foreign language. He understands their words just fine. The problem is that he has to keep fighting against the voice in his head that whispers this isn't real, that the meds actually *aren't* working, that, yes, the alien heads do appear to be masks but that's only because the logic center of his brain hasn't completely shut down during this particular hallucination.

Three men in alien masks. The one speaking is the man who grabbed Riley. He wears a bulbous gray head. One of the others looks like a cross between an insect and a robot . . . with braids. Max vaguely recalls seeing it before. A film, maybe? He isn't really into films. Reading is his thing. Reading and writing—wild stories that everyone always told him were so creative and vivid and how did you ever come up with that, Max my boy, and that's some serious imagination there, and you'll be a writer one day, mark my words, a famous one like Stephen King or Dean Koontz, and you'll put me in your book then, won't you, ha-ha.

No one says that to him anymore. Now it's: Hmm, there's some disturbing stuff here, son, and is this what you see in your head, and did you really dream this up or were you documenting one of your hal-oo-sin-aa-shuns. That's how his American doctor says it. Hal-oo-sin-aa-shuns. Like one of those words you read but never have to say out loud, and when you do, it's not quite right.

Bloody hell, Maximus. *Focus.*

Can't. Sorry. One of the symptoms. Disorganized thought. Look it up.

*No, Max. That's just you. Always has been. Brain flitting like a hummingbird on speed.*

Because *it* has always been there. Waiting to pop up like a funhouse skeleton. You thought you were normal, kid? Surprise!

*No, I'm quite certain no one ever called you normal, Max. Don't go blaming the crazy for everything.*

Why not? It fits the symptoms. You want to know another one? Hearing voices.

He squeezes his eyes shut. What was he thinking . . . ? Right. About the aliens.

The third guy wears a mask he recognizes from *Star Wars.* That's one film he's seen a few times, because it's an excellent lesson on story structure and the universal monomyth of the hero. He'll call that one Star Wars. The other is Braids. And the one talking? Gray.

"So the next step," Gray says, "is to contact Mr. Highgate, tell him not to phone the police and then send him a proof-of-life video and an ear. Preferably Aaron's." Gray laughs, as if this is hilarious. Even his confederates don't join in.

"Kidding," Gray says. "Well, maybe not about the ear, but we'll see how Aaron here comports himself. The rest? Hollywood bullshit. Everyone with half a brain calls the police. So that's where we start. Aaron? Smile."

Gray raises an iPhone and Aaron scowls.

"You're a natural," Gray says. "Now, let me send that to your daddy, and in about twenty minutes I expect this place to be surrounded by cops. Unless your daddy's busy tonight—screwing his girlfriend or screwing over another company—because that would be very inconvenient."

Aaron says nothing.

"There, picture sent. Video even, with a time stamp. Yes, I did the proof-of-life thing, as cliché as it is. Now, the next steps, kiddies . . ."

He keeps talking, but Max's attention slides away. This isn't real. Cannot be real. *Kidnapped at a therapy sleepover? Really, Maximus? You're losing your creative touch. You need to start writing again. Give that imagination a workout.*

Oh, believe me. It's had a workout. Just ask Justin.

*Now, Max. You weren't thinking clearly. It's not your fault.*

Sod off.

He looks over at Riley and focuses on her instead. That's easy as pie, as his gran would say. Namely because Riley Vasquez is easy to look at. Two years ago he'd have sat across the class and planned how to talk to her. *Hey, I think you're brilliant and cute, and I'd like to get to know you better, so how about we go to the cinema Friday night?*

He did fantasize about talking to Riley, but the conversation, as with most everything in his life these days, was different. *Hey, I think you're smart and sweet and a little bit messed up, and do you want to talk? Just talk? You seem like someone I could talk to, and sure, you think I'm a idiot, but that's just an act. All right, maybe not completely an act. But you seem like you need someone to talk to and I do too, so how about it? You can talk about what happened to you and— Me? Um, nothing happened to me. Nothing important. Just lost my mind and haven't found it again. Never will. Schizophrenia. Ever heard of it? Short version:*

*I'm crazy. Sorry. Not supposed to say that. Bad Max. Bad, bad Max. No using the C-word. I'm not crazy. I just see things that aren't there, hear people who aren't there . . . Huh, yeah, that does sound like crazy, but shhh, don't tell anyone. And don't worry. I'm perfectly harmless. Well, unless I mistake you for a demon and try to strangle— Wait! No, come back.*

Gray snaps his fingers in front of Max, startling him. "Am I boring you, son?"

"Yeah, kinda, mate. Can we speed this along?"

"Maximus . . ." his therapist, Aimee, says, her voice low with warning.

Gray snorts. "Maximus?"

"I prefer Max."

"I bet you do. What kind of sadists name their kid Maximus?"

"A historian specializing in ancient Rome and a lieutenant-general in the British army. And if you know anything about the salaries of academics and career soldiers, you'll realize I'm really not worth your time." Max takes out his wallet and removes three twenties. "I have sixty. Can we call it a night? Things to do and all that. It is the weekend after all."

"Max?" a voice says. "Sit down."

He turns to see Riley walking toward him. Her hands tremble, and she's obviously struggling to keep it together, and he wants to nod and say *all right* and sit down, but he wants to make her smile too, make her relax, show her this isn't a big deal, not like before, like what happened when she was babysitting.

"I'm cutting through the bull—" he begins.

"Sit. Down." She stops and lowers her voice. "Are you trying to get us killed? They have guns."

"Are you sure? Maybe we're imagining it. We are a little nuts, after all."

She gives him a look that makes him happy she's not the one with a gun.

*So no chance of that talk, then? All right. Maybe we can just make out instead.*

He chuckles, and her eyes narrow.

"Sit the hell down," she hisses.

Sorry. Not his fault. Inappropriate affect. It's a symptom.

*Bollocks. You're just an idiot. No meds for that.*

At least she doesn't look scared anymore.

Max sits cross-legged on the floor. Riley lowers herself beside him. See? Bad behavior has its reward.

*Except she kind of hates your guts right now.*

And an hour ago, she just didn't like him very much. He's making progress.

"Max?" she whispers. "Pay attention. Please. Don't make this worse."

She does have a point. If it is real, he isn't helping. If it isn't, then that's all the more reason to pay attention. Find the lies. Find the truth.

# CHAPTER 4

When they finish the pat-downs, they put us in a semicircle again, but on the floor this time. X-Files is at the front. The other two block the only exit, holding their guns casually, like a cup of coffee they've forgotten. X-Files is worse. He waves his around, gesturing as he explains the situation, the gun rising and falling, pointing this way and that, and every time it swings toward me I duck, just a little, and then I'm ashamed, not of the fear but of the way my muscles tense, ready to run. To skitter away like a scared mouse, looking for a hole to hide in.

No beds to scamper under here.

The gun points right at me, and it stays there, making me stare down the barrel. He's not doing it intentionally, and somehow that's worse, because all I can think is that his finger will slip and the gun will fire, and I'll die, not because I stood up to him, not because I tried to save anyone, but because his finger slipped. Whoops. Sorry about that, kid.

I see that gun and I keep thinking back to the moment when I was walking to the Porters', on the phone with Lucia, and I bumped into that man and spotted the gun under his jacket. That gun is emblazoned on my memory. I have described it in perfect detail to the detectives handling the Porters' murders. What I cannot describe, what would be infinitely more helpful to describe? The man's face. But I never even looked up.

I know now that man was almost certainly the killer. I bumped into the Porters' murderer that day, and all I had to do was look up. But I didn't, because my damned phone call was *so* much more important.

The gun barrel shifts aside. Then, as X-Files waves both hands, it comes my way again, and I physically jump back, but the gun keeps going. I catch my breath and then sneak a look around to see if anyone noticed. No one's paying any attention to me. Understandable, given that there's a guy with a gun at the front of the room.

We sit like we're in kindergarten, automatically crossing our legs and looking up to watch the teacher. All of us except Max. He's on the far side of the semicircle, his expression suitably somber. Then his lips twitch in a smile.

X-Files walks over and snaps his fingers in front of Max's face. *Damn it, Max. Pay attention. For once, be part of the group.*

Nope, not happening. Maximus has to give a smart-ass answer.

*Maximus.* I know enough Latin to translate that to "largest" or "greatest." Yeah, the greatest jerk.

I carefully rise, my gaze fixed on X-Files as I tell Max to sit down. When he doesn't, I keep my hands where X-Files can see them and make my way past Aaron and Brienne. I'm shaking and part of me just wants to follow my own advice and sit, but if the damned counselors aren't going to handle this, someone needs to. X-Files watches me but that's it, just watches, as if waiting to see what I'll do before he decides whether to shoot me.

As I creep over his way, Max smiles at me. The guy actually smiles, then says, jauntily, "Just cutting through the bull—"

"Sit. Down." I stop beside him and lean over to whisper, "Are you trying to get us killed? They have guns."

The smile broadens, his voice lowering, mock-conspiratorial. "Are you sure? Maybe we're imagining it. We are a little nuts, after all."

Something surges inside me. Something I haven't felt in months, and it takes a moment to identify it. Anger.

"Sit the hell down," I whisper, and to my shock, he does. I lower myself beside him, to make sure he stays there.

"Now," X-Files says, "while most of you seem to understand the seriousness of the situation, let's go over some basic rules. I promise I'll keep them simple enough that even blondie there"—he nods at Brienne, who bristles—"can follow. Are you ready?"

His gaze travels over us, as if he's waiting for agreement. I feel foolish, but I nod. Max mutters, "Get on with it," but he has the sense to keep his voice low enough that only I hear.

"Rule one: if you do anything to piss me off, I'll shoot you. Rule two: there is only one rule, and I just gave it. No excuses. No exceptions. How do you piss me off? Well, let's keep that one simple too: if in doubt, don't take a chance. We're going to be here for a few hours. Get comfortable. With any luck, you'll be home by midnight." He looks at Max. "Well, except you, Maximus. I might shoot you just on principle. Or to save you from a lifetime with that name."

Max doesn't react to the insult or the threat. He does seem to be paying attention, though. Thankfully.

"Can I say something?" Aaron asks, and I wince. *Please don't pull a Max. Please, please.*

"I don't know," X-Files says. "Can you? Seems like you can. I hear words coming out of your mouth."

"*May* I say something?"

Good lord, this really is kindergarten.

"That's better. And the answer is no." X-Files starts to

turn away, then says, "Oh, all right. But remember the rules and don't think I won't shoot you just because you're valuable. Well, no. Actually, I won't. You, Mr. Highgate, would get this." He pulls a blade from his pocket. "You have ten fingers, ten toes and other optional body parts that you might value even more. Piss me off and you lose one of them. My choice. Now ask your question."

"I'm the star here, right?" Aaron says. "The rest are just extras?"

"That is correct."

"Which means you won't get nearly as much money from their families, because they don't exactly hang out in the same social circles as mine."

"Whoa, get a grip on that ego, mate," Max says. "If it inflates any more, it'll burst."

Aaron turns toward him. "You might not like what I'm saying, but it's the truth. How many of you guys showed up tonight in a chauffeured car?"

"How many of us would *want* to?" Max says.

"The point"—Aaron turns back to X-Files—"is that they aren't worth a fraction of what I am. Therefore they shouldn't need to go through this just because *my* dad's an asshole one-percenter. I'm asking you to let them go."

X-Files laughs.

"I'm serious," Aaron says. "My dad can get you seven figures with one phone call. Their families would be scrounging all night to get you five. It's not worth the hassle. This will be much easier for you if you've got only one kid to handle."

"That's very thoughtful of you, Aaron. Very thoughtful. And the answer is: hell, no. Do you know why?"

After a moment of silence, X-Files turns to me. "Miss Riley Vasquez, answer my question."

I blink. "What?"

"Wrong answer. Come on, girl. You're a cop's daughter. And, yes, I know exactly who we have with us tonight. Miss Riley here is quite the local celebrity. Her dearly departed daddy was a detective, formerly a member of the local SWAT team, which, with any luck, is pulling up out front as we speak. Tell me, Miss Riley, why will I not let you all leave?"

"Because you're a tosser?" Max says, and I shoot him a glare.

"You need backup hostages," I say. "It's not about the money. You . . ." My heart thumps so hard I can't get the rest out. And I don't want to. I don't want to be the one to put it into words.

"Come on, Miss Riley." X-Files moves forward, waving the gun, and my gaze locks on that.

My blood rushes in my ears, voices coming as if from a mile away, barely penetrating, and Aaron's telling him to stop, leave me alone, and X-Files makes some mocking reply and then Max says, "You can't kill Aaron."

"What's that, Maximus?" X-Files swings the gun from me and a hand squeezes my arm and I jump to see Maria there, giving me a strained smile.

"You can't let us go," Max says, "because you need someone you can kill. It can't be Aaron. So we're cannon fodder."

"What the hell?" Gideon scrambles to his feet and looks ready to go after Max until Aaron grabs his arm. Gideon throws Aaron off and says, "Did you hear what he said? You're trying to get us out of this, and *he's* trying to get us killed. Giving them ideas."

Max rolls his eyes. "Yeah, mate. I'm giving them ideas, because that's not what they're thinking at all."

"Max is right," I say as I rise. "They need us to be the stick and the carrot. If things go well, they can release one of us."

"And if they don't, we shoot you," X-Files says. "Well done, Maximus and Miss Riley. At least we have two kids with brains. Which is more than I can say for Mr. Highgate, but that's what one expects of rich brats, isn't it?"

As we sit, I whisper to Aaron, "Thank you. For trying."

He frowns as if the suggestion that we be released was so obvious it doesn't require comment. It does, though. He offered to take this all on himself—let eight strangers leave him to bear the brunt of the kidnappers' wrath and frustration if their plan doesn't go well. It's not what I expected from him.

"The next thing—" X-Files begins. Then his cell phone rings. He takes it out and smiles at the screen. "Well, well, it seems we've made first contact." He clicks the speaker button and answers the phone with "Good evening. To whom am I speaking?"

"Agent William Salas," a deep voice says. "I'll be working with you to resolve this matter."

"Ooh, I score the hostage negotiator from the first call. Excellent. That will save us some time. I'm the party host tonight, and that's all you need to know about me. My guests are far more important. Let's get them to say hi. We'll start with you." He points to Maria. "State your name for the nice policeman."

"Maria Lawrence," she says, and we continue across the room.

**CHAPTER 5** Everything's going fine. At least, as fine as one might expect from a hostage negotiation. Outwardly, I think I seem calm enough. Inwardly, everything's equally quiet . . . if you don't count that little girl at the back of my brain, running in circles, shouting, "We're all going to die! Die!"

I'm a little concerned about how well I'm ignoring that girl. Just like I've been concerned about how well I handled the Porters' deaths. I suppose the fact that I'm spending the weekend in therapy camp suggests I'm not handling it well at all, but I think I'd feel more normal if I spent my days huddled in bed, sobbing and seeing their bloodied bodies every time I close my eyes. This emptiness feels callous. The anxiety and the depression feels selfish, as if a horrible tragedy befell Darla and her parents and all I can think is "me, me, me." I can't eat. I can't sleep. I jump at every noise. It's all about me.

Now, having been kidnapped, I should be a wreck. Instead, after I managed to rouse myself a couple of times, I only feel more numb than ever. As if tragedy is my new life. As if it's all I can expect. The temptation to giggle at that is almost overwhelming. First my father gets shot in the line of duty. Then I'm in the house when my babysitting clients are shot to death. Finally I get taken captive—by armed men—in the therapy camp that's supposed to help me deal with all that trauma. Ironic, huh? Not piss-my-pants terrifying. Not even but-it-isn't-fair self-centered. Just ironic.

As for the others, all I know is that they've gone quiet, and with nothing to break through my numbness, I don't rouse myself enough to look around. They're in shock or they're silent with terror or they're calmly waiting for the next step, because that's all they can do, all anyone can do. At least they aren't causing trouble anymore. That's what counts.

The hostage negotiator is asking questions. X-Files takes the phone off speaker and walks out of the room. Before he goes, he says, "You kids get a little more comfy. Talk about cute boys and cool movies and hot music and whatever else teens natter on about these days. Just don't let the word 'escape' leave your mouths. My guys have good ears and itchy trigger fingers."

After he leaves, there's two minutes of silence. Then Aimee stands and clears her throat and says, "I think we should—"

"Oh, wait," Brienne says, rising. "Are you still here? Didn't they drug you guys or something?" She looks from Aimee to Lorenzo. "I was sure you two must have been sedated, because otherwise you'd have taken charge. Calmed us down. Told us it would be okay. Got in Max's face when he started mouthing off."

"I told Max—" Aimee began.

"You said his name. That's not exactly taking charge. Riley had to handle it. Then Aaron had to handle Gideon. You two just kept your mouths shut and hoped no one noticed you. I think there are some blankets in the corner. Should we grab a couple so you can hide under them?"

My hands begin to shake. I watch her telling them off, and all I can think about is that afternoon at the Porters', how I did exactly that. I kept my mouth shut and prayed that the intruders wouldn't notice me. I let them kill two people and did nothing, because it kept me alive.

*Coward.*

That's what Brienne was calling Aimee and Lorenzo, for doing exactly what I'd done. No one says that to me. No one dares. But I want them to. I dream that someday I'll meet Darla again and she'll do exactly what Brienne is doing: call me out as a coward. It's a nightmare, but it's a fantasy too, and in the dream I break down in a puddle of regret and self-hate and relief. Thank God someone finally said the word. Thank God someone finally saw me for what I am.

Not a hero. A coward.

I clench my fists, trying to stop trembling. Then I glance up to see Max, right beside me, watching.

I turn away fast.

"Brienne," I say, and my voice trembles too.

Luckily, Aaron takes over, saying, "That's not helping, Brienne. If those two aren't taking charge, screw them." He turns to me. "So your dad really did stuff like this? Hostage negotiations?"

I nod.

"Can you walk us through it? What to expect?" He shoots a look at Max. "You can leave out the part about what happens if we mess up. I think we all get that."

"Except you," Gideon says to Aaron. "They won't kill you."

"They will if my dad doesn't pony up."

"Can we stop this?" It's Sandy. She hasn't said a word until now, and she looks like she's about to throw up. "Can we stop bickering?"

"Riley?" Lorenzo says. "If you can walk us through it, that might calm some nerves. Tell us what to expect."

"But you don't have to," Brienne adds quickly. "I know this must be harder on you than anyone else."

"How do you know that?" Gideon says. "It might be easier for her. At least she's been through something like this."

"Which is why she's here, jerk-off. *Dealing* with it. She watched people *die*. That doesn't just go away. It's called post-traumatic—"

"I'm okay," I cut in. "I'll explain for anyone who wants to listen. If you'd rather not, just move over there, and I'll keep my voice down."

No one leaves. I explain that there will be two main people out there: the commander and the negotiator. The commander is in charge of the SWAT team, leaving the negotiator to deal with our captors. The first thing Agent Salas will do is gather information. Some of that comes from X-Files and some from the officers on the team, trying to get a sense of the building and where we're located inside it and so on.

With X-Files, we aren't dealing with a mentally ill guy who randomly grabbed some kids. He knows what he is doing, so negotiations will proceed rationally, meaning there is little danger he'll suddenly start shooting us for no reason. He'll make his demands and Agent Salas will chip away at them while the team tries to figure out if there is a safe way to infiltrate the building.

I'm still talking when X-Files returns.

"All right, kiddies," he says, in that smarmy, I'm-such-a-clever-boy way that grates on my nerves. "Remember how Miss Riley said we might let a few of you go, as an act of goodwill? Wrong. Well, okay, not entirely wrong. One of you lucky children gets to go home in time to enjoy your evening. Negotiator Will is playing nice, and so will we."

Gideon jumps to his feet. "I have asthma."

"And I'm sure you didn't come to sleepover camp without your inhaler. Sit down, boy." X-Files paces in front of us and stops at Max. "I'd really like to let you go, because you're a pain in the ass. But if I do that, then all your therapy buddies here will give me grief, hoping it'll buy their ticket out. You stay. However, you are on the top of list number two: kids I'll shoot if Negotiator Will misbehaves."

Max doesn't seem the least perturbed. Hell, he doesn't seem to have even heard. He is paying attention, though, watching X-Files, *studying* the man, frowning slightly, as if he needs to read lips and he's not quite managing. It's enough to make me wonder if he has a hearing problem. It might explain the lack of attention and the smart-ass comments to cover it up.

"Who's the lucky one, then?" X-Files says.

There's a moment of silence, and I want to say Sandy. She looks closest to breaking, and given that she just survived a suicide attempt, she really doesn't need this. But before I can suggest her, Brienne says, "It should be Riley. Like I said, this is going to be harder on her than anyone, after what happened with . . . well, before."

"She's right," Aaron says. "Plus it looks good. People know who she is. She's, like, a local hero."

I flinch. Only Max seems to notice, but he just looks thoughtful. Or bored. With Max, it's impossible to tell the difference.

Lorenzo clears his throat. "They both have a point. Additionally, it will seem you're being considerate, releasing the most affected hostage."

"Which is exactly why I'm saving her as a special reward," X-Files says. "For this round, let's go with Welfare Sandy."

Sandy looks up, mortified, then stammers, "M-my dad's a seasonal worker. It's not welfare. We—"

"Really? You're arguing *against* getting to go home?"

I catch her eye and force what I hope looks like a smile as I whisper, "Go."

She closes her mouth and X-Files chuckles. "No argument, then? I didn't think so. Mr. Highgate has pointed out that most of your families would struggle to scrape up ten grand. Yours would be lucky to find a hundred bucks. But your luck just changed, Sandra. You've won the only lottery that counts: the one that keeps you alive. It helps that your little dress and sweater are adorable, in a thrift-shop kind of way. It'll play well for the cameras. See if you can squeeze out a few tears as you exit."

He waves for the Predator guy to take her. I catch her eye and give a little wave. Maria mouths something I don't catch, but Sandy does and her lips twitch in a smile. Aaron shoots her a thumbs-up and she nods, ducking her head shyly before turning away to leave.

We all sit in silence, listening to their fading footsteps. The front door is at least a hundred yards down a twisting hall, and soon we hear nothing. When I close my eyes I catch the barest sound of an opening door and a man barking commands. The door shuts. Silence falls again.

It's so quiet in here that it's easy to forget the building is surrounded by a team of professionals, all focused on getting us out alive. I think of my dad, and grief surges, but it calms me too, imagining a dozen of him out there.

When my dad was on the SWAT team, he couldn't speak highly enough of the negotiators. He said that when they were used, the rate of injury dropped to near zero. I have to remember that. As horrifying as our situation seems, it isn't nearly as dangerous as an actual kidnapping. This crime was organized and our captors are obviously professionals. Sandy is fine, and we will be too. It's just a waiting game.

I think of Sandy. Is her family out there? Has it been long enough for them to arrive? I've been trying very hard not to consider that, not to think about Mom getting that call.

*Will* she get a call? Or are they keeping this quiet, notifying only Aaron's father initially? X-Files said he wants money from everyone, but Mr. Highgate is the big fish. To keep the confusion to a minimum, they might not have contacted the other parents yet.

Maybe Mom is home, finishing a dress design, papers and swatches of fabric spread over her worktable, as she looks forward to a quiet night alone, with me here and Sloane out with her friends. I hope that's what she's doing. I hope they haven't told her and won't until they need to.

"Brienne was right." It's Max, his voice startling us out of the silence. "It should have been Riley. Letting her go early sets the right tone. Holding her hostage will turn the press against you even more."

"Umm, hello?" Brienne waves her hand in front of him. "Nice of you to join us, Max, but next time? Chime in *before* it's a done deal."

I lift my hand to back her down and say to Max, "I appreciate that, but I'm fine."

"I know it's too late for this round, but I'm saying . . ." He turns to X-Files. "You should send Riley home sooner rather than later."

"She's cute, isn't she?" X-Files mock-whispers. "You're a little slow, but you finally realized it may be in your best interests to support the cute girl's cause. Improves your chances of—what's the word you Brits use?—shagging her?"

Max's response is remarkably calm. Measured, even. "Given that I'm the least likely to leave this building alive, I doubt that's an option. Even if I do get out, something tells me none of us are going to want to see each other again. This is hardly a bonding experience. I'm only pointing out that the others are right, and there's more advantage to releasing Riley than to keeping her."

"Riley, Riley, Riley," Gideon says. "Everyone's so worried about Riley. The local hero who saved two people from— Oh, wait. No, she didn't. She was under the bed when they got shot. And now you want to give her another free pass?"

I feel everyone's gaze on me, and there's no impulse to hang my head or avert my gaze. That comes when they lie and call me a hero. This is truth.

"She *did* save someone," Brienne says. "That little girl. She did the smart thing. If she'd interfered, they would have both been killed, along with the girl's parents."

"Brienne is right," Aimee says. "Riley's response was the correct one. She didn't panic. She didn't foolishly interfere. She did what the Porters would have wanted by protecting their daughter and—"

"I think we can skip this," Max says.

Brienne turns on him. "God, you're *such* a jerk. You say one nice thing, and then you have to follow it up with assholery."

"Don't believe I said anything nice. Not really my style. I just pointed out you were right that Riley should be released. Now I'm saying Riley doesn't need you to defend her. She's heard it in therapy. Over and over. It hasn't helped then. It won't help now."

And *that* just might be the nicest thing he's ever said, even if he doesn't mean to be kind.

"If you want to pass the time," he continues, "may I suggest a game of cards to take our minds off this?"

"Do we have cards?" Maria asks.

"Are you *joking*?" Gideon says.

"No," Maria says. "We have to pass the time, and we're just getting on each other's nerves otherwise."

I look at the counselors. "She's right. Do we have cards? Board games?"

"Uh . . ." Lorenzo says. "There's a deck in the desk over there, but I don't think anyone's really in the mood . . ."

"I am," Brienne says.

"Sure, I'll play," Aaron says, and Maria goes to get the cards, and with that, we have our distraction while the waiting continues.

**CHAPTER 6** Over the next hour, X-Files takes two more phone calls outside the room. We're all trying to gauge his reaction when he comes back. We whisper and compare observations. It's Maria, Brienne, Aaron and me playing cards. Max is watching. He occasionally offers advice, which has a fifty percent chance of being useful and a fifty percent chance of totally messing us up. In other words, he's amusing himself by screwing with us. No one seems to care—it's not like we're taking the game seriously, and there are even a few chuckles when someone follows his advice and loses the hand . . . or fails to follow it and loses.

Gideon is pacing. I've got my back to him, because that pacing certainly doesn't settle my nerves. Aimee and Lorenzo are playing counselor. By that, I mean they're sitting between us and the men, alternately looking at one group and then the other, as if they're keeping the peace and ready to run interference. If anything happens, though, they'll be the last ones I turn to for help.

There's a weird feeling in that. I've never thought of myself as someone who pays undue attention to authority figures. I even helped organize a couple of protests at school, which is how I ended up on the student council—the vice-principals were trying to redirect my efforts away from reforming student policy, which only gave me a better platform for it. But I guess I still look to the adults in a room when things go wrong, and now here are two who are supposed to be keeping us safe this weekend, and at this point I'd rather rely on Max, which is saying something.

X-Files comes back in. "Miss Riley, you're up. Negotiator Will has Mr. Highgate on the line, and he's being remarkably compliant. Time to reward that by releasing the hero."

"She's not a damned hero," Gideon says. "She hid under the *bed*."

Aaron and Brienne both open their mouths to come to my rescue, but I shake my head and whisper, "Please."

"Riley's right," Max whispers. "Don't goad him or this only gets worse."

"Says the guy who specializes in making things worse," Brienne mutters.

Max only smiles. "Exactly. I don't like Gid stealing my thunder. You must admit, he's not nearly as entertaining as me."

Brienne rolls her eyes, then says, "Go on, Riley." When I hesitate, she reaches over to squeeze my hand. "Really. Go. Sure, we'd all like it to be us, but no one's going to begrudge you an early exit. We'll get ours soon enough. Aaron's dad is cooperating."

"He will," Aaron says. "He's a lousy father, but he's rich for a reason. He knows when to cut his losses and when he can turn a loss into a corporate advantage, and this is money well spent. It'll earn him good press—the poor guy who almost lost his son."

"All right," I say. "Take care, then. I know you might not want to make contact when we get out, but I'd like to know you're all okay. Aimee has my phone number and e-mail."

"We'll call," Brienne says. "Get together and celebrate with ice cream."

"I hate ice cream," Max says.

"Good, then we won't have to invite you."

I get to my feet.

"Seriously," Gideon says. "You're going to let her go? That's sexist."

Brienne sighs.

"No, really," Gideon says. "You set two girls free first. We're told we aren't supposed to do that anymore—women and children first—so I object."

"This isn't a democracy, boy," X-Files says.

"I still object. It's racist too."

"Racist?" X-Files snorts. "Releasing the Latino girl instead of the white boy?"

"Exactly. You've freed two minorities in a row."

"Um, Sandy was Italian," Maria says.

"Is there a reason we're listening to this moron?" Aaron says. "Go, Riley."

I take another step, and Gideon lunges at me. I see him out of the corner of my eye, and I react. I spin and hit him. It's not a punch. Not even a boxing jab. The only martial art I know is fencing, so my response is to swing my arm and wallop him.

Gideon stumbles. Then, with a roar, he charges me. Aaron grabs him. He yanks Gideon away and throws him aside, and when the smaller boy recovers, he's face to face with Max. Gideon swings. Max staggers back fast, his hands up, saying, "No, no, no," this look on his face . . . Max who had a gun on him earlier and never flinched, and now this boy—six inches shorter than him—is taking an awkward swing and Max reacts as if Gideon is throwing a hand grenade.

Gideon spins on Aaron, who mutters, "Thanks, buddy," to Max. Gideon charges, and I glance over at our captors, expecting them to do something, but they're standing there, watching, and I can't see their faces with the masks, but their eyes look amused. No, *entertained*. Just standing back, chilling and watching the rumble along with everyone else. Everyone except Maria, who's at the desk, going through the drawers. When she sees me watching, she motions she'll be careful.

Max has moved halfway across the room, as if to make damned sure he doesn't get pulled into the brawl. Aaron and Gideon are still going at it. It's obvious Aaron knows how to fight. Gideon does not. Aaron is only defending himself, but I can tell he's getting frustrated, and a few of his blows hit hard. Gideon is hopped up on adrenaline and just keeps going back for more, until X-Files finally moves forward and says, "Okay, kid. Fun's over." He grabs the back of Gideon's shirt. Gideon swings, and for once, his fist actually connects.

X-Files falls back with an *oomph*, then "You little brat," and I'm on Gideon in a heartbeat. I don't think. I just grab him to pull him away, and then I see the knife. X-Files pulls out a blade and the light shines off that razor-sharp edge and . . . and I drop Gideon. I don't mean to, but someone grabs me, one arm around my waist, and yanks me away from the younger boy. Before I can twist to see who it is, the hand is gone and X-Files is snarling and Aaron is running toward Gideon. I shout, "No!" but Aaron tackles Gideon, knocking him face-first to the floor. And, thankfully, X-Files eases back.

"Let him go," I say, and Aaron gives me this look of *Huh?* I say, "I mean, let Gideon leave in my place. Just get him out of here. Please."

"Is that an order, Miss Riley?" X-Files raises the knife as he turns on me.

"No," I say quickly. "I-I'm just suggesting. Asking. Can he— *May* he take my place?"

I expect him to give me the same line he did earlier with

Max, about not wanting to reward bad behavior, but he grunts, "Fine. Get out of here, boy. He'll take—"

He turns to Predator, and as he does, there's a blur behind the guy in the Cantina alien mask. It's Maria. She has something in her hand, something long and metal, and she's been slipping up behind Cantina. Now she runs toward him, weapon raised . . . and Cantina shoots her. He shoots her point-blank, and she flies back, and there's blood, just the smallest spray, and that's what I think about in that moment. *There should be more blood.*

Then I hear whimpering, and I realize it's me, and I clap both hands over my mouth to stop and someone grabs me from behind, pulling me back, the same arms as before, holding me tight as I shake so hard I can hear my teeth chatter, a voice whispering, "It's all right," but it's not all right, Maria is lying on the floor, the white lettering on her T-shirt spattered red, and she's not moving. God help me, she isn't moving.

I push off the arms and run to Maria. I hear a shout of *No!* It's Aaron and I think he's telling me not to go to her. Then I see Gideon jumping Cantina. He grabs for the gun, and everyone's shouting, Lorenzo and Aaron telling Gideon to stop, just stop, X-Files yelling that Gideon damned well better stop or he's going to get a bullet through—

The gun fires. It's a suppressed shot, like the first, but still far from silent. Cantina jerks back, his eyes wide. I see the gun, both of their hands on it, blood spreading across Cantina's stomach. Gideon is turning, and everything comes in incredible slow motion, sound off, their mouths opening, nothing coming out, nothing that penetrates my terror. Gideon turns, and Lorenzo runs between him and X-Files, and Gideon fires. Lorenzo goes down. Then X-Files aims and—

Arms grab me again. The same ones as before. I struggle madly. My brain fires in every direction, thoughts going everywhere, paralyzing me. *Get to Maria. No, stop X-Files. Do something. Just do something.*

The arms drag me backward, and I realize we're heading for the door, and I dig in my heels, but a voice says in my ear, "We need to get out of here," and I turn to see Max, and the shock of that, of realizing who has me, shuts off my brain, and I let him drag me out the door.

# CHAPTER 7

We reach the hall, and the second we do, that bubble around me bursts. I hear everything—the shouts, the cries, the scuffling, the cursing, a sob of pain. It hits me so hard I double over, hands to my ears, Max's fingers still wrapped around my wrist.

"Come on," he whispers urgently, and I know if I don't, he'll leave me here. He's grabbed me on a whim, and if I don't follow him, he'll say to hell with me and keep going.

Waves of chaos from the room pummel me, and I swear I *feel* the terror and the pain and the panic from every person there. I think of Maria, lying on the floor, and then I see her smiling at me in line, trying to calm me down, joking about her T-shirt.

I see that T-shirt splattered in blood.

Maria shot by Cantina. Lorenzo shot by Gideon. Two of us lie on the floor back there, and I heard more shots as we were running. Who else is on that floor? Gideon? Brienne? Aaron? Aimee?

My knees buckle. Max's fingers dig in, dragging me, and I want to say, *No, just leave me here*, but there's still enough of my brain working that rises above the fear and shouts, *Are you an idiot?* and I stumble after him.

Then my gut seizes, and I stop so suddenly he's jerked back with me.

"I'm running away," I whisper.

"Yes," he says. "As fast as you can."

"I-I can't." I wheel toward the room. "I won't run again. I won't hide—"

"Oh, bloody *hell*. This is not the time, Riley. *Really*, not the time."

"But I need to—"

"No, actually, you don't. You want to stand your ground? Next life-threatening situation, all right? For this one, you're getting out."

"I need to help—"

"Help *me*. I'll be your designated rescue victim for today. You can't go back, because if you do, I won't make it."

"Of course you—"

"No, I won't. Now get me out of here."

He shoves me, and I stagger a few steps and then start to run. It isn't easy. I feel the pull of those fading voices and the pull of the panic too, twin forces, one dragging me back, the other dragging me down. But I keep going. I have to. For Max. Which is madness, of course. He doesn't need me.

So why did he bring me along? He's never struck me as the sort to slow down and help someone else—especially if it might lower his own escape chances.

Yet Max hadn't just grabbed me at the last second. I'd recognized that grip and the arm around my waist as the one that pulled me back when Gideon came after me. The one that grabbed me when Maria went down too, the voice that whispered it was all right. Max's voice.

We're passing a hall juncture. I can see an exit sign ahead, pointing right. The front door is there, around the next corner, and—

Max slams his open hand into my shoulder, knocking me sideways. I start to turn, but he's pushing me toward the adjoining hall, and I realize the noise from behind us has changed—not cries and scuffling now but one of our captors shouting, "Where the hell is the girl?"

I look down the main hall, toward the exit.

"No," Max whispers. "Not unless you can outrun bullets."

He's right. The door seems so close, so damned close, but it's at least another twenty running steps away, and I can already hear footsteps thumping behind us.

I take the side corridor. I see doors. That's all I see: endless rows of closed doors in a dim hall, like something out of a nightmare.

I glance at the first door. Which is also the first place they'll look. At the second, I try the handle. Locked. Max is already racing past, and I think that's it, he's getting the hell away while the little mouse looks for a hole to hide in. But he only tries the next door and then waves to me when it opens. He holds it while I dart through. Then he closes the door behind us, as carefully as he can, while footfalls thunder down the other hall.

When that door shuts, the room goes completely dark and I stop short. Then there's a faint bluish light, and I turn to see Max holding down the glow button on his watch. He shines it around.

We're in a cleaning closet. It's big enough for me to get away from the door, picking past mops and buckets with extreme care, until I'm tucked down behind them. Max joins me.

Outside we hear footsteps. They've slowed now. A second pair joins them.

"What the hell are you doing?" It's X-Files. "Stay in the room."

"I can see the door from here," the second man—Predator—says.

"Yeah, which means we'll have to chase them if they run."

"I just thought—"

"Don't. That's my job. Now get back in there and—Shit!"

A distant shoe squeak. Then the *pfft* of a suppressed shot, and X-Files snarls, "You left them with Mark's *gun*?" Running footfalls. Several pairs, the remaining hostages fleeing the room. X-Files and Predator take off after them.

Max slips to the door, lighting his way. He holds up his finger and I see his lips move, counting to five, then he cracks it open and waves at me, still crouched behind the mops. I steady myself and follow.

We make our way to the front door. Footwear off—that was my idea, after hearing X-Files's and Predator's shoes squeaking and thumping. We move in stockinged feet to the main hall and then down it, Max walking backward behind me, both of us listening as X-Files and Predator pursue the remaining captives.

*Remaining captives.*

Maria is dead. Maybe Lorenzo too. That's not what I meant by "remaining," but as soon as I think the word I see Maria, lying on the floor, not moving, and that smell . . . Maybe there was no smell, maybe it's my memory of the Porters, but I still remember it with Maria, the stink of blood and urine and more, the smell of violent death. I can tell myself she's alive, but I know she isn't.

I stop running. Max bumps into me and turns with a whispered "What do you hear?" as he leans around and then sees my expression.

"Bloody hell," he mutters as he takes my shoulders and propels me forward. "Keep those legs moving, Riley. You can do this."

I want to throw him off. To shout at him. Why does he care, anyway? I'm suddenly furious at that care, at the burden of it. *You don't know me. You shouldn't give a damn. Get yourself out. Hell, throw me at them for a diversion. I don't care.*

Except I do care. I haven't reached rock bottom yet. Haven't even glimpsed it. As dark as the world gets some days, I still see solid ground under my feet, and I don't wish for anything else. Even if I did, I couldn't risk Max's life with mine. He's decided to rescue me, and maybe that's what keeps *him* moving. Something to focus on, to forget what we left behind in that room.

I pay little attention to my surroundings as we run. There's emergency lighting in the halls, which are builder-beige with equally nondescript flooring. What matters is the path I need to take. Down this hall and then turn left to the end, turn right and the door will be there. Freedom will be there.

We get around the corner. The exit door is just ahead. I'm reaching out, as if I can grab the knob from ten feet away. Then I see the keyhole.

The door is locked. It must be. A locked solid steel door. I slow, and Max passes me, and I think maybe he didn't notice the lock. But when he yanks on the door and it doesn't open, his expression isn't shock—it's disappointment. He saw the keyhole—he just hoped maybe Predator forgot to relock it after releasing Sandy. Did he really think the SWAT team wouldn't have checked?

He bends to examine the lock.

"Unless you smuggled picks past the metal detector . . ." I say.

He runs his fingers over the hinges.

"Or a screwdriver," I say.

He gives me a look to say I'm not helping. It isn't an angry look. Not even an annoyed one. Just a quick glance and a shake of his head before he goes back to examining the door.

"You're wasting time," I say. "We need to search for another exit."

"One they forgot to lock?"

"I'm not the one who checked this one."

"I'd be daft if I didn't."

"Then we'd be *daft* if we didn't search for another way out."

"That's plan B," he says.

"And plan A? Blow up the door?"

"You brought dynamite? Brilliant." He smiles, and somehow I hate that smile more than if he'd scowled. The smile says he's got this under control. No, not he. *We*. It says we can handle this, together. There's no arrogance in that smile, and I wish there was, because it's a smile of something worse: faith.

He puts his ear to the door.

"What are you—?" I stop. "Right. The SWAT team."

Now I get a roll of his eyes. Of course. The SWAT team is out there. All we have to do is let them know we've escaped. Communicate . . . through a solid steel door.

When I mention that part, Max only says, "We just need to let them know we're in here. They can figure out the rest. I don't hear anything, so the door must be thick. We'll need to bang on it to get their attention."

"And get the attention of X-Files and Predator too?"

He frowns, and I say, "I mean our captors. The masks. They're from—"

"Ah, right. *Predator*. That's a film. I thought I recognized it. I was calling the other Gray. Yes, I suspect they'll hear us, but it's more important to let the people *outside* hear us."

"Knock on the door and then run."

A flashed smile. "You've got it. Head that way"—he points—"and find a route for us to flee the scene."

# CHAPTER 8

There's a long corridor at the other end of the hall, with several shorter ones branching off, giving us options for an escape route. I signal Max while listening for our captors. He whales on the door and I hear only a muffled thump.

He puts his ear to the door again. I start toward him, but he lifts his hand to warn me back, while pantomiming that he can hear faint sounds outside the door.

I try to visualize what's happening out there. I've seen hostage-takings in movies and on TV, often with my dad beside me, pointing out everything that Hollywood did wrong, and I'd ask how it really worked, and Mom and Sloane would shush us, but afterward I'd ask Dad again because I knew he couldn't talk about his actual work, not really, and this gave him a way to share his job, and I think he appreciated that.

*Did you, Dad? You liked explaining it, right? You weren't just being patient with me, because I know you were always patient, always there for us, and now you're not and I miss you, Dad, miss you so much. It's not getting better. A year and a half, and it's not getting better.*

I squeeze my eyes shut. I think of those shows, and how the teams are arranged. No one hangs around the front door.

Not in real life and mostly not even in Hollywood's version, because the officers need a wider view and the only reason to be at the door is if they expect someone to come out.

Yet they *did* expect someone to come out. If Gideon hadn't opened his mouth, I'd be out there. I'd be free and the others would be waiting their turn and damn you, Gideon. Damn—

I imagine Gideon, lying on the floor. Shot.

My stomach clenches, and I remind myself I didn't see Gideon get shot. He might have escaped. Either way, he doesn't deserve any of this, no matter how much I might wish he'd just kept quiet and let me leave.

Had the negotiator known I was about to be released? It seemed not, or there'd be someone outside the door, wondering why it hadn't opened, close enough to notice that vibration when Max pounded. But there's a good chance X-Files—or Gray, which was an easier name—didn't tell them I was coming or he wouldn't have been able to swap Gideon for me, because it would raise concerns if another kid walked out that door.

Max pounds again. Then he knocks, using his knuckles. I hear that, but barely. He tries his boot next. It's a Doc Marten, vintage-style, and that's all I know, not really being my kind of fashion statement. I noticed a slight heel, and I'm hoping there's steel inside, but when he bangs it on the door it's only slightly louder than the knock.

He pats his pockets, but anything helpful would have been removed. He knocks again with his boot, whamming it as hard as he can, and the sound isn't even loud enough to catch the attention of anyone *inside* the building.

I wave him to me. He comes with reluctance, looking back at the door with every few loping steps.

"There must be a fire extinguisher or something around," he says. "Maybe I can bash it with that."

"I looked for fire alarms as we ran. I didn't see any of those or extinguishers. The building must not be up to code yet. One thing it would have, though, is a back door. It'll be locked, but it might be thinner."

He casts one last look at the door, and then he nods. We take off. We reach the first intersection and I stop short, and his hand lands on my shoulder, the first notes of irritation in his voice as he says, "You can do—"

I spin and clap my hand over his mouth. Or I try to. As soon as I raise my hand, he jerks back, his own hands flying up, as if to ward off a blow.

"Sorry," I whisper. "I just—"

"Don't do that," he says. "Don't *ever* do that."

The look on his face makes me freeze. It's anger, raw anger, and he's rolling his shoulders, trying to throw it off, but it lingers there, underlaid with something else. Fear.

I've wondered why Max is in therapy. With other kids, even if they don't talk much, I can usually figure out what is wrong: depression, anxiety, eating disorders. Max can be a jerk, but you don't go to therapy for that. I've wondered about anger management—there was a kid with that in my church group, and he'd been withdrawn, like Max, and sarcastic, like Max. But the way Max reacted in the other room, when Gideon lashed out, wasn't the response of someone with a bad temper. Now he flinched when I raised a hand.

Not a guy who lashes out in anger. A guy accustomed to being the target of that anger. Of being beaten, being abused.

"I would appreciate it if you didn't stare at me like that," he says, and his eyes and voice are so cold, I swallow.

"S-sorry," I say. "I-I stopped because I heard—"

He catches the footsteps now, from down another hall, and he pushes me toward the nearest side one, muttering, "Bloody hell," and "Can you warn me next time?"

*I would have, if you weren't freaking out because I tried to shush you.*

We hurry down the hall and into the first open room.

# MAX: CLARITY

**Clarity:** *the quality of being clear, in particular:*
*the quality of coherence and intelligibility.*

Max can remember the first time he saw the word. He was five, reading something his mother brought home in a stack of books that he could read but couldn't understand, not really, and sometimes he'd tell her so, when they'd be in a shop and he'd see some wild adventure story with a bright cartoonish cover and he'd say, "Please, Mum?" Always Mum. Never Mummy, because that was for children, just like the books with the cartoon covers, and he wasn't a child, well, yes, he was, but he shouldn't be, because children were loud and sticky and silly, and he saw the way his mother reacted in a room of them, forcing herself through a playdate, nearly plastered to the wall, lest one of the children do something mad, like speak to her.

She had a child of her own, but he wasn't like others. No, no, not at all. Max was clever, much beyond his years, thank the heavens. So she brought home the sort of books he ought to read and he *could* read them, and if he couldn't quite comprehend what he was reading, then he needed more practice, and if she caught him sneaking those adventure novels home from school again . . . well, he'd get a very stern talking-to, because Max was a clever boy and that's all he needed: a stern talking-to. Which also meant he was clever enough to hide those books, and he did, but they were not where he first read the word "clarity."

When he didn't understand the word in context, he looked it up, as he should, and only when he was quite certain he still didn't understand did he take the question to his mother. She'd tried, with growing exasperation, to explain it to him.

*Clarity: The quality of being clear, in particular, the quality of coherence and intelligibility.*

Max eventually came to understand, on an abstract level, what clarity meant, and to also understand that he'd never experienced it, not in any pure form. There were moments when the muddle in his head cleared, but that was not actual clarity, not the way he imagined it, like the perfect tone of a bell, everything else fading to silence. His head was never silent. Thoughts swam and swirled and leaped and sometimes howled, like babies in a cradle, grabbing the bars and screaming for his attention.

Clarity.

He'd come to hold the word as a talisman. Absurdly, perhaps, to focus on it as a way of hoping to gain it. His personal mantra. When the jumble in his head became too much, he'd concentrate on the word until he achieved some measure of it. Not a clear bell in the silence, but Big Ben over Westminster, loud enough to hear above the din.

Clarity, clarity, clarity.

He'd been doing well that evening. Apparently, fear for one's life is wonderful for inducing clarity—a sudden gust that knocks everything else aside. Which was not to say that his head was always too noisy for him to concentrate. Otherwise, he'd never be able to pull off top grades, thank you very much. Or he had pulled off top grades until the incident, and then, no school for you, Maximus, not just yet, let's give you time to rest, time to find some clarity, and do you know what you need? Peace and quiet, so much bloody peace and quiet that you feel as if you're about to go mad, except you can't, because you already have. Bonkers. Off his trolley. Crazy, crazy, crazy, only we don't use that word. No sir, not at all.

He'd been doing so well, so very well, until Riley tried to shush him. When he stumbled back, he'd seen the confusion in her eyes, followed by understanding, and he kept thinking, "What does she understand?" because it's not the truth, can't be the truth, that was the deal he had on coming to therapy, that his schizophrenia would remain a secret until he chose to reveal it, *if* he chose to reveal it.

But, Maximus, how do you expect group therapy to help if you won't talk about your problem?

*So I should tell them I'm crazy? That it's not some temporary bump in the path like theirs? Mine's an illness, a permanent mental illness. One that can't be cured, only managed. That's the term, isn't it? Managed? Madness under glass?*

Had someone broken the rules and told Riley he had schizophrenia? Not if she was sticking with him. If she knew, she'd be running before he lost it and started ranting like a madman.

Now, Maximus, don't think that way.

*What way should I think? Ah, yes. Clearly. Think clearly. If only I knew what that was . . .*

What does *Riley* think? She believes she understands something, so what is it?

*Does it matter? Really?*

No, it does not, and herein lies the problem. The problem of clarity. That there is a corner of his mind—No, let's be honest, Maximus, you like to play the madness card, but it's not just a corner, there's a whole floor of your mind that *is* clear. It's the floor that understands you can't be worrying what she thinks at a time like this. Also the floor that whispers, quietly and rather politely, that a boy worrying what a girl thinks of him isn't really madness, or every boy is mad sometimes.

"Max?" Riley whispers, and he blinks hard.

"Are you okay?" she asks as they crouch in the dark room, lit only by the glow of his watch.

"Right as rain," he says, smiling, and she doesn't like the smile. It annoys her in some way, perhaps because she spots the falseness. Maybe because she thinks he's mocking her. *Right as rain. Just a temporary glitch in our evening. Haven't you ever been taken hostage before?*

"We'll make it," he says solemnly, and that doesn't help, because the switch is too fast, and now she's sure he's mocking her. *Can't win, old boy. Can't win at all.*

"At least you're taking the situation seriously now," she says.

"The guns and the blood helped convince me."

He regrets the words as soon as they leave his mouth. *You truly are an imbecile, aren't you, Max?* She flinches, as if remembering the last time she saw blood and guns, the death of the couple she babysat for, and he hurries on, "I'm sorry if I was being an arse earlier. I just wasn't sure it was real."

Her brow furrows.

*Did you just say that, Max?*

Of course he did, because he was slipping and sliding like a newborn calf on ice.

*Because you're scared. Shocking, really. Given the guns and the blood and the death. Yes, it's real. Really, really real, and you aren't going to snap out, safe and sound in a padded room.*

He pushes on. "I mean that I thought perhaps it was part of your therapy. Force you to confront what happened when you were babysitting, by putting you in a similar situation, except this time you have to face the guns and the bad guys."

She stares at him, and he feels sweat trickling down his cheek. Then she gives a slow nod. "Immersion therapy. I've heard of it. I certainly hope they'd never do that without permission."

"Exactly," he says, a little too quickly. "At first, when it started, it seemed surreal. Maybe that was shock. It took me a while to think straight and realize that they'd never trick a minor that way, and it's likely unethical to do it at all without permission."

She nods, still slowly. It's not the best explanation, but she'll take it. *Confusion and shock, yes, ma'am, that's all it was. Not that I meant I thought it wasn't real because I've had hallucinations before.*

"So you're okay now?" she asks.

There's a split second where reality and his inner monologue merge, and he almost says yes, he's fine, or so they say, with the new meds, and he hasn't hallucinated in months. Which is not, of course, what she's asking at all, and he catches himself and smiles. "Right as—"

"Right as rain," she says. "Got it." And she shakes her head, but she smiles too, that slightly exasperated smile, like he's a bit daft but not really, you know, crazy.

He hears something in the hall, and he looks that way, sharply, then at her, seeing if she noticed it too, because that's the barometer these days: *If I see or hear something, is it just me?*

Except that isn't what's happening here, and he's certain of it, because the scenario has gone on too long, become too involved and too logical—as logical as a hostage situation can be. The meds have been working, and he has to trust that—trust, trust, trust—because while they have their side effects—tremors, difficulty sleeping, dry mouth—the alternative is worse. He can live like this, or so they say, though he hasn't yet decided what kind of life this is, always worrying, always wondering. But for now, the meds . . . the meds . . .

He swears under his breath.

"What's wrong?" Riley whispers.

"Do you know where they put our belongings? The things they confiscated?"

Her eyes widen and he thinks, *Bugger it, what did I say? I'm making sense, aren't I?* Because that's another symptom. He has them memorized, all the unexperienced signs that could pop up and say hello at any given moment. Like disorganized speech—more colorfully known as word salad—where what one believes one is saying has little in common with what one actually says. His doctor doubts Max will ever have that, because his thoughts aren't truly *disorganized* thoughts, not the way they could be, just, well, not exactly orderly. Organized but not orderly.

"The cell phones," she says. "Of course." Then a blazing smile. "You're brilliant."

*Why yes, yes I am, thank you for recognizing that, even if it wasn't what I meant at all. No, of course it was. Because: I. Am. Brilliant.*

"Yes, the mobiles," he says. "If we can get to them, we can make contact. Did you bring one?"

She shakes her head. "You?"

*Me? No, I don't own a mobile. Not anymore. Who would I call? Ah, yes. My friends. Perhaps my best friend, Justin. No, wait . . . Justin wants nothing to do with me. He's made that quite clear. And I'm not sure my other mates would take my calls. Not after "the incident."*

*No need for a mobile, then, not when I sit in the bloody house all day, reading and studying and pretending I'll go to uni soon. Of course I will. That's what Mum says. Just relax, Maximus. There's no rush. Take some time off. Make sure the meds are working this time.*

*You want to go out, Max? I'll take you anywhere you like. By yourself? Oh, Max, I don't think that's wise. Not yet. Yes, yes, it's been three months without an episode, but still . . .*

But still . . .

"Max?"

He shakes his head. "I didn't bring mine either. I'm sure someone did, though. We'll look for a rear door first. That will be plan B."

"Plan B? Or plan C?" A smile, not really for him, just relief at having plans, but he'll take it anyway.

"We'll make it plan B." He looks toward the door. "Do you hear anything?"

"A couple of minutes ago. Nothing since."

"Good. Off we go, then."

# CHAPTER 9

Find the back door. Find the cell phones. Back door. Cell phones.

I mentally repeat that mantra as I lead Max down the hall.

I take a better look at the warehouse now as we walk. There are, of course, no windows. Distraction-free, as Aimee promised. Which also means escape-route-free, except for those doors. The locked, thick steel doors. I just pray the rear one won't be as thick.

I have no idea where I'm heading. We're presuming the second exit is literally a back door—in the opposite direction of the front one. But it could be at the side, so I'm trying to stick to the edges. The building is a rectangle, which should make the layout obvious, but, like I thought earlier, whoever designed it must have decided a grid pattern of halls and rooms is too easy. Boring. Let's have some fun!

Halls run maybe twenty feet, past two or three doors, and then end at another corridor. Max and I will head down that one to find a branching corridor, seemingly leading to more rooms, and then it'll end too. I have no idea if I'm at the far side of the building or not because there are no windows.

And let's talk about the rooms. So many rooms. Half seem to be locked. At the rate I'm passing doors, I'm going to guess there are at least twenty rooms on this floor alone.

Either I'm turning down the third hall . . . or I've circled back and I'm turning down the first. At this point, I wouldn't be surprised. Every wall is beige. The flooring is office linoleum. The doors are standard-issue, with no numbers or other markings. I began to wish I'd brought a pen or something to mark the corners as we turned them so we didn't circle back.

When I whisper that to Max, he says, "I'm counting doors and keeping track." One step ahead of me. I'm lucky to have him. I really am.

The sounds that sent us into hiding seem to have moved on, never actually coming our way. The one noise I listened for most, I didn't hear: gunfire. Yes, that's what I listen for, as I move down the hall, the sounds not of rescue but of more death.

*You don't know Maria and Lorenzo are dead.*

Sure, they might have survived the bullets. Only to bleed out on the floor while we race around, helpless and hopeless.

*Aren't you Little Miss Sunshine?*

Used to be. Not anymore. Sorry.

The thing is, as horrible and selfish as it might be, I tell myself they're dead. I have to, or how can I justify creeping through these halls, looking for an exit, while they're dying a hundred feet away?

I think of Maria. The girl with the reassuring smile and the defiant T-shirt.

Dying alone.

Like the Porters.

No, the Porters didn't die alone. They perished together, watching their life partner die with them, both thinking of their child, their only child, in the house with killers, perhaps about to follow them into death and they wouldn't live long enough to know if she survived or shared a cold grave with them.

Little Miss Sunshine . . .

I think it's that internal sarcasm that actually keeps me going, keeps me from thinking of the Porters and Maria and Lorenzo and bottoming out right there in the hall. Wallow in the horror of their fates and then slap myself out of it with self-mockery. Whatever gets you through the night. Or through the semi-dark halls with armed killers lurking around the corner.

We turn down another hall when someone coughs up ahead.

It's not just a cough. It's . . . it's an awful gurgling, sputtering, wet sound. Max's fingers grip my shoulder. When I look back, he doesn't say anything, just keeps staring forward at that sound. Even as he glances at me, our eyes meeting, there's only a silent *Did you hear that?* Which obviously I did—the halls are quiet enough that I swear even the swish of our stockinged feet must echo.

I nod, and he looks . . . relieved? I suppose I'm not the only one who's jumpy, wondering if I'm imagining that creak down a hall or that whisper behind us. Just because Max is a guy—and a smart-ass—doesn't mean this situation doesn't scare the shit out of him.

I start toward the noise, and he grabs my shoulder again, harder this time, nearly flipping me backward as I stop. When I turn, he gives me a *What the hell?* look and pantomimes that the noise came from exactly where I'm heading. I nod, remove his hand and continue on. After an exasperated sigh, he comes after me, whispering, "We need to go back the *other* way, Riley. *Away* from the men with pistols."

I motion for him to stay where he is while I investigate. That gets me a look that's a borderline glower. I ignore him and keep going until I'm at the corner. I peer around it to see . . . blood. A snail's trail of it down the hall and through a cracked-open door. I hear breathing from inside that room.

No, it's not breathing, no more than the other sound was coughing. This is the wheezing of a life-or-death struggle for breath.

Is it Maria? She was shot in the chest. Maybe she'd only passed out and then came to after everyone was gone, presuming her dead, and she crawled in here. I pick up the pace, but Max plucks at my sleeve, and I spin on him with a glare, which he returns as he mouths, *Trap.*

*Seriously?* I mouth back, and jab a finger at the trail of blood. His mouth sets in a firm line, and I realize he has a point. Cantina was shot too. This could be him, lying in wait with a gun. Or the other two could have staged the blood and be inside, faking the labored breathing.

I motion that I'll be careful and creep forward, one ear on that door, the other on our surroundings. I can hear footsteps, but they're multiple halls away.

I inch to the partly open door and peer in to see only darkness. In that darkness, though, I hear rasping breaths, and the hairs on my neck stand on end, every horror movie rushing back. I'm leaning when Max shoulders me aside, his glowing watch in his hand now. I take it from him and shoulder *him* aside. He mock bows, granting me the honors. I ease the glowing watch to the door crack.

Lorenzo lies on the floor, his shirt soaked with blood, his face pale. He lifts his head, but his eyes won't focus. One hand is clapped over his wound. Every breath sounds like a death rattle.

I open the door.

"Brienne," he says. Then he blinks hard. "No, Riley." And I know he's far gone—even in the partial darkness there's no mistaking me for blond little Brienne, and behind me Max mutters, "Bloody hell," as if knowing what it means.

"We need a mobile—a cell phone," Max whispers as he

brushes past me into the room. He crouches beside Lorenzo. "Did you confiscate any?"

I stare at him, crouched in a dying man's blood, his final words: *Hey, can you tell us where to find a cell phone?*

That's not actually what he said. His voice is low, soft even, his wording polite, his tone apologetic. Yet all I can see is a dying man and my brain screams that we need to do something, do anything, to save him.

And how exactly would I do that? Sloane was the lifeguard. She'd studied CPR. I didn't like the water, one of those "childhood incident" things that never quite goes away. Last year, I'd signed up for a first-aid course with Shannon, back when we were still friends, but we'd skipped out to sneak into a summer concert.

I still remember giggling about that. *Hey, look at me, being all rebellious.* I remember, too, covering protests in Egypt for the school paper, and talking on Skype to someone who'd been there, and thinking *that* was real rebellion, honest rebellion, and me? I skipped a first-aid course once to go to a concert.

How many times have I thought of that missed course? Starting with kneeling beside the Porters' bodies. Now, seeing Lorenzo, the floor opens up and I'm back there, beside their bodies, thinking, *You idiot, you stupid little idiot, why didn't you take the course, and it doesn't matter if they're dead, if you have no doubt they're dead, what would you do if they weren't, and you couldn't help them because of that goddamn concert and—*

"Riley?"

That isn't Max or Lorenzo speaking. I'm not in the warehouse anymore. I'm crouching beside the bodies of two people I saw alive only moments before and there's a voice on the steps, calling, "Riley?" and I jump up, ready to shout, *No! Stay there, Darla!* but I'm not certain the killers are far enough away that they won't hear me, so I rush toward the stairs and I grip the railing and my hand slips because it's covered in blood. Their blood. Her parents' blood. And she's coming down the steps, close enough for me to hear her breathing, and I go to wipe my hands on my jeans, but that won't help and—

"Riley?"

Another voice, this one jerking me back. Fingers on my elbow. The fog clears and I see dark blue eyes, and I think, *Who has those eyes?* and I have no idea until the face comes into focus, and even then the first thing I see is freckles over a nose and a faint scar underscoring a cheekbone, and I don't recognize those either until I see the rest of the face— the arched nose, the too-sharp chin, the blond hair plastered by sweat to the side of his face.

Max.

Of course it's Max, but there's a surreal moment where I doubt myself, because I've been running for my life with the guy and I never noticed the color of his eyes or his freckles or his scar. I didn't get too close. Didn't look too hard. That's my life these days. I spent almost three hours with a group of kids—first in therapy and then as captives—and I couldn't tell you any of their eye colors. I just didn't care enough to notice.

"Riley?" Max says.

"Turn toward the wall." That's Lorenzo, rasping, his words barely more than breath. I glance down at him and he says, "It's the blood. Look away, Riley, and focus on something else." A pained chuckle. "Think about all the more exciting things you could have been doing this weekend."

I swallow, and I move toward him.

He shakes his head, grimacing with the effort. "Turn away. It'll be easier if—"

"I don't want it to be easier." *It shouldn't be easier. You're dying, and you're telling me to look away because it's triggering* my *trauma*. I skirt the blood and crouch by his head. "Is there anything we can do?"

"Survive."

I glance at Max, and he's breathing shallowly through his mouth, and maybe it's the smell of the blood, but I think he's struggling to keep calm, to not think about the fact a man is dying in front of us and there's not a damn thing we can do.

"I-I don't know first aid," I say.

A weak smile. "I believe I'm a little beyond that, Riley." He reaches to take my hand and then sees his is covered in blood, and he stops, and I teeter on the edge of that memory, of myself looking at the blood on my hands, and I squeeze my eyes shut before I topple back into it.

"We can get a mobile," Max says, his voice low. "Call for help. That's what we can do. I know they took yours and Aimee's, but are there any others?"

"Two kids brought theirs. They're with . . ." Lorenzo trails off as shoes squeak in the hall.

I dart to the door, left cracked open for that little extra light, and I start to ease it shut. Then I hear someone struggling to catch his breath and keep quiet. I peek out. It's Aimee.

I open the door, and she wheels and spots me. Her mouth forms a perfect O. Then her gaze drops to the blood on the floor. She sprints over, shoes squeaking again, and I wince, but I don't hear anyone else.

I usher her inside. She sees Lorenzo and stops with a yelp. I resist the urge to clap my hand to her mouth and instead motion frantically for her to keep her voice down.

"They need . . ." Lorenzo struggles, as if he used up his energy talking to us. "Cell phone. You have . . ."

"You have the mobiles," Max says to Aimee. "Is that right? The ones you confiscated?"

She's staring dumbly at Lorenzo. I have to take her arm and squeeze, and even then her gaze barely flicks my way.

"Unless you're a doctor," I say, "the best thing we can do for him is get those cell phones. Lorenzo said two kids brought theirs."

A slow nod. "Aaron tried to smuggle his in, but I found it while his driver was still there, and I gave it back. Maria brought hers by accident. It's with the meds."

"*Brilliant*," Max says. "Now where are the meds?"

Aimee looks at Lorenzo. "You had them."

"Right," he says slowly. "But I gave them to you. You're in charge of everything the kids brought, including the meds and that cell phone."

She blinks hard. "Yes. Of course. Sorry."

"Aimee . . ." Lorenzo says when she stops. "Take Max and Riley to the cell phone. They can handle it from there."

His lips quirk, as if there's irony in that: the messed-up therapy kids taking charge.

"I've been through something like this," I say. "I'm inoculated."

Max laughs at that, a snort that he cuts short. Lorenzo allows himself a chuckle, as if not quite willing to go as far as admitting it's funny. From Aimee's expression, she thinks I've lost it, like I'm on that brink of running screaming down the hall. Which is probably true, but I latch on to Max's laugh. It relaxes me, as does the grin he shoots as a follow-up.

"All right, then," Max says. "Let's get on with it." He cranks up his accent another notch. "Tallyho, and all that."

"What does that even mean?" I say. "Tallyho?"

"No idea," he whispers as he walks past, and I laugh then, a small one, choked back.

Before I leave, I bend at Lorenzo's side and reach for his bloodied hand, and when he resists, I take it anyway, and I squeeze it, and say, "Hang in there," and he says, "Whatever that means," and we exchange a real smile before I go.

**CHAPTER 10** Gray and Predator are stalking us. We can hear them as we creep along the hall.

I ask about the other kids as soon as we're in the corridor. Aimee confirms that Brienne and Aaron escaped the therapy room.

"Together?" I ask.

"I . . . I don't know. It all happened so fast. I was trying to help Gideon."

"Gideon? What happened?"

"He was shot. Right as you two escaped. I stayed with him, and he was still alive, along with the guy he shot. Then they—the kidnappers—went after Aaron, and I ran for help, and maybe I should have stayed with Gideon, but he was so far gone . . ."

"And Maria?" I ask.

She shakes her head, and my gut clenches and I want to say, *Are you sure? Really sure?* But her expression leaves no doubt, and I turn away, hiding my grief as we continue walking.

There's silence until we're around the next corner. Then she says, "I keep telling myself this isn't happening. That I'm hallucinating or delusional. That I've lost my mind and—" She stops short and her gaze swings to Max, who stiffens, his lips pressing together in a hard line. "I'm sorry. I didn't mean—"

"We aren't in therapy right now, Aimee," he says. "No one's concerned with word choices. But we should probably be quiet. We can talk it all out later."

"Which way, then?" I say. "Where are the meds?"

"Back in the therapy room."

"Bloody hell," Max says, exhaling a hiss through his teeth. "Could you have mentioned that?"

"I . . . I'm having trouble focusing."

"Are you sure that's where the phone is too?" I ask. "We don't want to risk going back to the therapy room if we don't have to. Not if that other guy is still alive and can raise the alarm."

"I . . . I think Maria's phone is upstairs, actually. With my things. Unless . . ." She straightens. "It's either in the therapy room or upstairs. I'm sure of that."

I resist the urge to echo Max's *bloody hell*.

"But the mobiles they took from you and Lorenzo should be in the therapy room," Max says. "With the meds."

Aimee's eyes go round. "Right, you need your—"

"Meds." He looks at me. "For my condition. Heart thing."

I look over sharply. "What?"

"Don't worry," he says. "I'm not going to keel over on you. I should just have them. In case."

"You definitely need—" Aimee begins, but he cuts her off with a look, obviously not wanting her to make a big deal of it. Which means it is a big deal. He needs his medication, almost as much as we need a phone.

"We'll go back to the therapy room, then," I say. "We'll figure something out once we're there."

We've been whispering as we move, our ears attuned to the sound of footsteps. Or mine and Max's are—I can tell by the way he keeps tilting his head, his gaze shifting, tracking distant noises. I don't think Aimee's paying attention at all. Which makes me realize, yet again, how lucky I am to have Max. Now if we just survive long enough for me to tell him that.

He's in the lead, and we're halfway down the hall when his arm shoots out. He's heard something. I do too, after he stops—a door closing down the next hall. Again he checks to see if I heard, but he's a little slower this time, as if starting to trust himself. I nod and take a step backward, bumping into Aimee, who doesn't move.

"What if it's Aaron or Brienne?" she whispers.

"We'll know that once we hear a voice," Max says.

She glares at him. "You mean, when they're shouting for help? Or pleading for their lives?"

"No need. If they're like you, they won't stop talking."

He gets a real scowl for that. I whisper that we should retreat to a room and listen. He agrees. Aimee doesn't—she's certain the sound is the other kids, that our captors would make more noise as they search. She's mid-explanation when Max lopes off, waving for me to follow. I do, and she reluctantly comes after us.

The first door we check is open. Inside is an actual office, or the beginnings of one, as if someone has started moving equipment in, preparing to take up residence. There's a desk, a printer still in the box, a bookshelf and moving cartons. And what do I see when I look at them? Nothing except obstacles to stumble over and places to hide.

We get into the room, and I scoot behind the desk, Max vaulting over it, both of us stopping as we almost crash into each other, his lips twitching as if amused that we've both managed—in a single sweep of a dark room—to spot the biggest item and race behind it.

"Good idea," Aimee whispers. "You two stay there. I'm going to get a better look."

I leap up to stop her, but she's already out the door and Max is ready to grab me back. He doesn't need to. If she's going to run headlong into danger, I can't stop her. I can only hope she doesn't lead danger back here.

I think that, and then I hate myself for it. *Ah, self-loathing, I missed you for a few moments there.*

But I'm not the only one thinking it, because Max grunts, exasperated, then hops over the desk and shuts the door all but a crack, enough to let her back in if she comes running but not wide enough to welcome her back if there's a posse on her tail.

I strain to hear her footsteps. She took off her pumps when we left Lorenzo. They're on the floor here, and wherever she is, she's moving silently.

A distant click, like a door. Then Aimee says, "Oh, it's you." I wince at the loudness of her voice, and Max mutters a curse. Then Aimee inhales, sharply enough for the sound to carry.

"N-no," she says, and I hear her then, as she backs up, and I grab the side of the desk, ready to scramble over it, knowing she's made a mistake.

"Don't. Please—"

The gun fires, and I'm over that desk before Max can stop me. Then I freeze.

Max vaults the desk, and he's at my side, not pulling me back, just standing with me, listening to Aimee whimper. My gut seizes and my legs tremble, and I want . . . I don't know what I want. To hide. To save her. To save her and to hide, to help her and yet not to do something stupid and pointless, like run out there and get myself and Max killed.

"Why?" she says. "Why me?"

"Because your job here is done, Aimee." It's Gray, his voice moving closer. "These kids aren't going to need therapy. And we don't need any loose ends."

The gun fires again. I jerk back. Max grabs me. Then I see the door, still cracked open, and I go to close it, but before I do, I look. I need to look. I peer through the crack. They're right there, ten feet away, at a junction. Aimee on the floor, dead. Gray stands over her . . .

Before I shut the door, I see that Aimee must have mistaken Gray for Aaron—he's about the same height and wearing the same color clothes. Then she'd noticed the mask.

Max's fingers close tight around my arm, and he guides me back behind the desk.

He talks to me, whispering so low I can barely hear him through my shock. I don't think it matters what he's saying. His tone is soothing but firm, and it says that we're going to get out of here, I need to trust that we'll get out of here.

After a moment, the numbness fades and I hear his words. He's not telling me vague reassurances that we'll get out. He's outlining the steps, giving me a concrete footing.

"Promise me something," I whisper when my mental feet are firmly on the ground again.

A quirk of a smile as he whispers back, "Depends on what it is."

"I need to know that if something goes wrong—if we're out there, like Aimee, and I freeze up in a flashback—you'll keep going."

He pauses. "Is that what happens? Flashbacks?"

"That's not the—"

"Is there a trigger? Blood, I suppose, obviously, and guns."

"Max . . ."

"Is there something that will snap you out of it? Talking to you? Squeezing your arm?"

"That's not the point."

"Actually, yes, it is." He pops his head over the desk. "Seems quiet. We'll talk later. With any luck, we won't need to."

"Max, I asked you—"

"I ignored the request and will continue ignoring it." He pushes to his feet. "We can circle back to avoid seeing—"

"No. We'd need to go all the way back around, because I'm not sure how else to get to the therapy room. You want to see what a flashback looks like? How I might endanger your life by freezing up? Then we're going past Aimee for a full demonstration."

I'm being sarcastic, but he nods. "Good idea. They're long gone, and this gives us a safe opportunity to test how to deal with it."

I shake my head and climb over the desk.

**CHAPTER 11** Aimee is dead. Aimee, Gideon, Maria, and if we don't get to a phone Lorenzo will join them, if he hasn't already. I don't think about that. About the likelihood that no matter how fast we move, it'll be too late for Lorenzo. I have to keep telling myself that we can save someone. Because I didn't save Maria or Gideon. Or, now, Aimee.

The sight of Aimee's body does not send me tumbling back into the horror of the Porters' murders, possibly because I'm too busy keeping my dinner down. Gray shot her in the chest the first time, but it seems that a random shot to the chest doesn't instantly kill. Like the Porters.

They had names. Claire and David. Does it make it easier to lump them together as "the Porters"? Maybe. I don't know.

Is it okay to make it easier? Or is that hiding? I don't want to hide—really, really don't want to hide—but I do want to be okay. When I hid under the bed, I was doing both, hiding and "being okay," except in the end I wasn't okay, was I? I'm alive, though, and that's more than they got, so I should be grateful.

Round and round we go, guilt nipping at my heels with every step I try to take toward "being okay," which means maybe I never will be, and I should have talked about that more with Aimee. And now she's dead, and I shouldn't think that, shouldn't think how her death affects me, because that's wrong, wrong, wrong. Like thinking that I'm sad the Porters are dead because it means I'll never get to babysit Darla again.

But all that—all that thinking, the endless thinking—it comes later, after we're past Aimee, because when I see her, I can't think anything. Can't form thought, really. Because when the chest shot didn't kill her, Gray . . .

I've heard the term before. I can even remember the first time. Dad was playing poker with three coworkers. His regular monthly game, always at our house, because "You've got a nice house, Jim. A normal house. Hell, you've got a normal life too. Good wife. Nice kids." I remember them saying that, or variations thereof, and I never quite understood what it meant, but I think now it was exactly what they said: that we seemed normal.

We *were* normal—it wasn't a facade. My parents loved each other and they loved us, and we weren't rich, but if I wanted something and it was a reasonable request, I got it. Not an extraordinary family in any way. Very ordinary, except, maybe, not so ordinary after all, because you don't get that nearly as often as you should, and maybe that's what I'm paying now, the price for normal, first my dad and then the Porters and now this.

It's like being home-schooled, never mingling with other kids, never building up your immunity to the sniffles and sneezes that everyone else takes for granted, and then you go out in the world and a common cold knocks you flat on your back. Maybe my oh-so-normal life meant I wasn't ready for trauma, that I wasn't—as I joked to Lorenzo— inoculated against it.

The poker game . . . I crept down that night after a bad dream. They were talking, and I sat on the step to listen, because it was stuff about police work that Dad never brought home. They were discussing a crime scene—a suicide—and how the man's brains were splattered on the wall, and it was then, as they said those words, that Dad spotted me on the step. He raced over with "You shouldn't be down here, baby," and I said, "What does that mean? Brains splattered on the wall?" and the look on his face, the horror that I'd overheard, wiped away fast as he scooped me up and said, "It's just an expression," and "Hey, guys, Riley's down here, okay?" and they stopped talking, and he said, "Come on in and get some chips, and then we'll take you back up to bed."

*Brains splattered on the wall.*

*It's just an expression.*

I'd heard it a dozen times since then. In a TV show, back when I could watch cop shows, before they only reminded me of my dad, every shot making me see him in front of it, the gun firing, Dad flying back, me wondering exactly how it happened—because no one tells you exactly how it happened—how long did he live, was he in pain, was someone with him? I really hope someone was with him.

Brains splattered on the wall. I'd read the line in books too, because even after Dad died, I could read those scenes—they were just words on a page, no sound, no image to trigger thoughts of my father, of the bullet hitting him.

*Was someone with you, Dad? Did they hold your hand when you died?*

I'd even heard kids at school say it, when a boy shot himself.

*Brains splattered on the wall.*

It's just an expression.

Only it's not. Not just an expression, Dad, but I know why you said that, because the truth . . . the truth . . .

When the bullet to Aimee's chest didn't kill her, Gray shot her in the head. In the forehead, a perfect hole between her wide brown eyes. And I see the wall. I see . . .

*Brains splattered on the wall.*

And it's not just an expression.

I'm staring at it, and I hear my biology teacher's voice, me madly scribbling the notes I would review again and again until the words were emblazoned in my memory.

*The brain is composed of three primary sections. First, the forebrain, which contains the hypothalamus, thalamus and cerebrum. Next, the midbrain, which is the tectum and tegmentum. Finally, the hindbrain: the pons cerebellum and medulla.*

Which parts are these? What am I seeing on the wall?

A person's life. A person's *self.* That's what I'm seeing. We can talk about the heart and the soul and "what's inside," but it comes down to this: our brains. Everything we are is in there, everything we've been and want to be, and now it's splattered on a wall like someone spit out a mouthful of oatmeal. A life reduced to this.

He shot her between the eyes. He walked over to her as she looked up and said, "Why?" and he shot her. Let her see the gun coming. Pulled the trigger and splattered her life and her self on the wall behind her. While he looked her in the eyes and watched her die.

"Riley?" Max is beside me, leaning down, temporarily blocking my view of that horrible wall. He's checking to see if I'm still there, if I've teetered over into a flashback.

I blink. He nods and moves away, and I see the wall again and say, "How can someone do that?"

"Hmm?"

"How can—?" I cut myself short and shake my head. "We need to go."

"No, we can . . ." He looks around. "There's a room over there. If you want to talk."

I'd laugh at that if I could, and if it wouldn't be horribly cruel. *We're running for our lives, but if you're feeling traumatized right now, Riley, we can talk.*

It's sweet, if inappropriate, and maybe it's a little bit of shock too, Max not thinking clearly, and when I look at him, he's staring at Aimee's body and there's a horror in his eyes that makes me realize just because I'm the one with PTSD doesn't mean he isn't suffering some *current* traumatic stress right now.

"Lorenzo," I say, and his head jerks up, gaze wrenching away from Aimee.

"Right," he says. "Lorenzo." The reminder that the clock is ticking for Lorenzo, and we need to get that phone for him, and neither of us can afford to freak out until we do. Save the therapy for later. It's time to move.

**CHAPTER 12** The therapy room door is wide open. There's been no sign of Gray or Predator. We're constantly listening for them. Even without asking Max if he is, I know the answer, because whenever we hear footsteps, he glances that way, tracking them even as we move.

A moment ago I heard footsteps on distant stairs. Heading up to the second floor.

How many sets of stairs are there? We passed near one, and I recall Aimee saying something about another when she showed me around.

I wish I'd listened more when she showed me around.

I wish I'd listened to her more in general, not just the therapy but when she tried to talk about herself, her life. The other therapist never did that. He'd drawn a clear line there. *I am your therapist, and this is all about you.* Aimee had taken a different tack. When I withdrew, she'd tease me out with talk about herself, trying to distract me from my inner monologues. It had never worked because . . .

Because I wasn't interested. Because part of me had resented her showing that personal side of herself.

*I don't want to be your friend, Aimee. I have friends. Well, I did, before the shooting.*

Some had wandered off. They didn't know what to say. And I gained a few more, the popular girls, until I realized they were only coming by hoping some of my so-called celebrity would rub off while they were being nice to the poor traumatized Riley Vasquez—double-duty pity visits for the win!

But I do still have friends, *good* friends, even if I'm not the best one in return these days. Lucia and the others, my real friends, they've stuck by.

Then there's Shannon. She came by every day that first week and I wouldn't see her, so she stopped coming, but she kept sending me care packages. Even after I was back in school, where'd we pass in the hall, she sent me comic books and novels and candy, exactly the sort she knew I liked, because we'd been best friends for so long. There'd be little notes like "Thinking of you." Except she wasn't really thinking of me. She was thinking of how she'd narrowly escaped *being* me that day at the Porters', how it was supposed to be her.

Blood money, that's what those packages are, and I want to scream at her in school, just stop in the hall and call her a two-faced bitch, and let everyone know what she did and that it should have been her, goddamn it, it should have been her. Except I don't wish it was, I don't dare, because I wouldn't have trusted her to keep Darla safe, and let's be honest here, I wouldn't have trusted her to keep herself safe, and I still care about her enough to think of that, even after what she's done.

I'd tuned out most of what Aimee had said about herself, and now I regret that. She hadn't been trying to be my friend. She'd just been trying to help. To connect. I refused that connection, like I refused a full tour of the building.

Hindsight is twenty-twenty. That's what Dad always said. *What Dad always said.*

Max and I have a plan for the therapy room. We need to, because Aimee said Cantina was still alive when she left. Step one, then, is to see if that has changed. If he has "succumbed to his injuries," as they say in polite society and English mystery novels. The English guy with me does not say that. Nor is his response at all polite when we realize Cantina has *not* succumbed.

Cantina isn't just alive—he's up and around. Maybe not exactly ready for a triathlon, but he's sitting in a chair, his shirt and mask off, chest sloppily bound with what looks like his shirt. It's bloody and he's pale, leaning on the desk for support, but he's alive and he's conscious and he's up.

Shit.

All of our plans had presumed that at least the last variable would be false. That even if he was conscious, he'd be lying on the floor in so much pain that Max could sneak up and gag him while I searched.

We peek inside the room. My gaze travels over it, looking for dropped weapons or anything we can use to bang on the door. I know where Maria lies and I don't look there. I can't. But as I'm scanning the rest of the room, I see Gideon and my knees wobble.

Max steadies me and then tugs me back down the hall muttering, "Prat," and I have no idea what that means, but I can tell it's not a compliment and I stiffen, because Gideon is dead. *Dead.* I can still see him. His open eyes fixed on the ceiling, his blood-covered hands pressed against his wound. The look on his face . . .

I reach for my crucifix. It's not there. Hasn't been there in four months. They'd taken it off in the hospital.

*No! I don't need a hospital. I'm fine. It's them. The Porters. You need to help them.*

A whispered voice, one paramedic to the other. *She's in shock, poor kid.*

I did know the Porters were dead, but I still wanted the paramedics to take care of them, to do . . . something? They were shot. They were covered in blood. I was fine. Because I'd hidden under the bed.

They took off my crucifix in the hospital, and I never put it back on. That wasn't an oversight. I'd worn it since my parents gave it to me at my first Communion. The only other time I'd removed it was after my dad died, when I flung it across the room and cursed God in every way I knew. I had it back on for the funeral, but only because it made my mother anxious to see me without it, to know that in a moment of crisis I had abandoned my faith.

But I didn't put it back on after the Porters. It isn't a crisis of faith. I'm not sure I ever had faith, not the way Mom does. Mine is more like Dad's—I believe there is a God, and I believe in honoring Him, but I'm not sure how much of a role He plays in our lives, and I don't blame Him for that, because it's up to us, isn't it? It's up to us to say we'll be a good person because that's what we believe is right, not because it'll earn us a better place in the next life.

I still reach for my crucifix, remembering the look on Gideon's face, the horror, as if he saw the Grim Reaper coming for him, scythe raised, and he could do nothing to save himself.

So yes, I stiffen at Max's insult, but when I look over, there's no hardness in his eyes, no *He brought this on himself*. He's shaking his head, his gaze downcast, and it's like when Travis broke his arm doing a stunt on his dirt bike, and Lucia and I rolled our eyes and called him an idiot, not because we blamed him, just, well, just *because*, and maybe, a little, acknowledging that it was kinda his fault.

Gideon didn't deserve to die. Gideon was afraid, maybe more than any of us. I saw that in the lineup, when he panicked at being touched. Afraid and lashing out to hide it. But despite that excuse, he still did—stupidly and senselessly and thoughtlessly—begin and perpetuate the chain of events that led to his death. His actions led to the death of Maria, lying fifteen feet away in her Happy Bunny tee, and of Aimee, in the hall—*brains splattered on the wall*—and maybe of Lorenzo, if we didn't get help soon.

Lorenzo. Don't forget Lorenzo. That's my new crucifix, my new talisman, the shining object I must keep in front of me at all times.

"You need to take him out," I whisper as we move farther down the hall to talk.

"Take him out?"

"Cantina. Subdue him. Without causing a commotion. If he's too alert, I'll distract him while you sneak up. You take him down, and we'll gag him."

He stares at me. Then he says, "I can't do that."

"You need to, and yes, I'm saying that because you're a guy. He's bigger than me. A lot bigger."

"I understand what you mean, Riley, but . . ." He shakes his head, and there's a look in his eyes, that same flinch as when I'd raised my hand, the same as when he'd avoided getting into it with Gideon.

I remember reading that the chance of abusing your spouse or child is higher if you were a victim of abuse. Is that it, then? It must be. He's heard that, in therapy, and he shies in the other direction, avoiding violence, avoiding fights, and I want to say, *But this is important! You can break your rule for this*, except that's not right. It isn't like going vegetarian and then your life depends on eating a steak. This would be a line he didn't dare cross, the proverbial slippery slope, like me making sure I'm out of bed by eight every day because I don't ever want to get out of bed these days, and if I give in, just once, because I'm really tired, I'll never get up again.

"It's my condition," he says. "My heart. Undue exertion and all that."

I nod, absently. "We need to disable him. There's no way to sneak in and grab the meds. We don't know where they are. Aimee didn't tell us . . ." Because she didn't think she needed to. She expected to be here, with us. "We need to hunt for the meds and the counselors' phones."

"All right," he says, shoulders lifting. "I'll . . . take care of him."

"No, I wasn't trying to convince—"

"I have this." Fear flickers behind his eyes, but he squares his shoulders. "I have this."

"Maybe I can—"

"No, you're right. It's not sexism. You'd do better as a distraction. I'd do better taking him out, as you put it."

"Do you know how?"

"My father is an army general, remember? He'd be a poor one if he didn't give me some military training. I can put Cantina in a choke hold . . ." He trails off and that smile evaporates fast. He pulls back, gaze going distant, as if he's seeing something I can't. A memory, like my flashbacks. It's his father, then. Or it was—I can't imagine his dad would still hit him when he's eighteen and six feet tall.

"Something," he says. "I can do something." That straightening again as he pulls on that overly British accent. "Right-i-o. Onward and upward, then. The trick, old girl, is to avoid the gun. At all costs, avoid the gun. Particularly the barrel end."

He goes still, wincing, as if realizing this might not be the right thing to say to me, but I snort a laugh for him.

"He doesn't have his gun," I say. "Remember? Aaron or Brienne got it from him. I'll still be careful, though. Now let's do this."

## MAX: TEMERITY

Temerity: *excessive confidence or boldness.*
Timidity: *showing a lack of courage or confidence.*

In his year four, Max had gotten the words confused, telling his teacher that temerity caused a friend to refuse an oral presentation. *No, Max,* she'd said. *It's timidity. Temerity is the opposite—being too cocky, too full of yourself. Timidity is Jay's problem; temerity is yours.*

His classmates had laughed. Max didn't care, which was, perhaps, a sign that his teacher was right. He'd never suffered from timidity. He'd been brought up to be confident, to be bold and even brash. The confidence from his mother—*you're smart enough to be anything you want to be, Maximus.* The boldness from his father—*show them who you are, and don't let anyone make you feel like less, Max, that's how you get somewhere in this world. Be an officer, a leader of men.*

If anyone thought Max was a little too full of himself, that was their problem. Their insecurity. Their timidity. He didn't crow over his successes or mock others for their failures. Needing to put others down suggested a lack of confidence, his mother would say. You don't climb up on the backs of others, his father would say. Eyes on your own horizon.

The truth—

*Yes, Maximus, tell us. What is the truth?*

The truth is that it's easy to hold on to temerity when you've never had cause to doubt yourself, and as soon as you do . . .

As soon as you do . . .

Max can see his target across the room. Cantina, Riley calls him. The Cantina alien in *Star Wars*, the one Han Solo shot. That's what Max had thought when he first saw him, and yet he hadn't been sure because these days, he wasn't sure of anything. Oh, he could fake it just fine. Tallyho and all that, whatever it meant, and yes, he wasn't even sure himself, but he could say it with all due confidence, the same way he'd said "temerity" in year four and he hadn't cared when he was corrected, hadn't been embarrassed to use the wrong word, because you won't learn if you don't try.

Every time one is corrected, it is not a humiliation but a learning experience. Yet even in the confines of his own mind, he hadn't allowed himself to say more than that their captor's mask came from *Star Wars*.

*Timidity. Doesn't suit you, Maximus. Not at all.*

But it has to, because he *isn't* sure, isn't sure at all, can't tell if what he sees is real, if what he hears is actually there, in the same plane the rest of the world inhabits. Temerity for him is dangerous. It lets him look at his best friend and be sure, *so sure* of what he sees that he nearly kills him.

Max forces himself to start toward Cantina. The man is resting with his head on the desk. He's alert, though. He moves too often to be asleep. Can't make this easy.

Max had crawled into the room, to avoid being a blur spotted out of the corner of Cantina's eye.

Speaking of blurs . . .

He'd seen one, in the hall. A shadow passing the end, just at the periphery of sight. Except there was no shadow, because Riley had been facing that way and she didn't see a thing. Didn't see the way he jumped like a scalded cat, either.

*Timidity: showing a lack of courage or confidence.*

Not a lack of courage in his case, though Max wasn't really sure what courage was. Oh, yes, technically, he knew:

*Courage: the ability to do something that frightens one.*

But what is courage really?

Well, boy, let me tell you about courage. Courage is being in Afghanistan, in a convoy heading through Taliban territory—

Sorry, Dad, really not the time. Can I call you Dad? It depends, doesn't it? On your mood, on what else is happening in your life, and you've never said I *can't* call you that, but there are moods, and I can read them, and sometimes it's just best to go with *sir*, isn't it? Yes, sir. I understand, sir.

I understand, sir, that perhaps you'd rather I didn't call you Dad now, after what's happened, that you're thinking a paternity test is in order. You'd never say so, but you think it. I know you do. This affliction of mine can't possibly come from you. It's your mother's side, son, you know she's always been intense.

*Intense: having or showing strong feelings or opinions; extremely earnest or serious.*

That's why we couldn't make it work, she and I. Why we never married, never even lived together. It's her fault, this fever in your brain. As for those times you've caught me talking to myself or staring into space for hours or locking myself in a room . . . that's just war—war is hell, kid, and I'm fine. I'm just fine. Too bad you aren't, son.

*Courage: the ability to do something that frightens one.*

That's what he's doing here, isn't it? Sneaking up on Cantina while his heart pounds so hard he's sure it will give him away.

*But can you carry through, Max? That's the question. That's real courage.*

It depends on what "carry through" means. Put Cantina

in a choke hold, as much as he flinches at even the thought? Yes, he can do that. For Riley, he'll do that.

Oh, that's so sweet. So chivalrous.

*Chivalry: courteous behavior, especially that of a man toward women.*

No, again, like courage, it doesn't quite apply. He'll do it for Riley, because Riley deserves to get out of here. To survive this. She's good and she's kind, and she has stuck by his side and watched out for him even though he was a jerk and made the initial situation worse, didn't come to her defense quickly enough, because maybe, if he had, she'd be out of here already.

*Ah, but you don't want that, Max, do you? You're quite happy she's still here, with you, giving you a chance to show her you're more than the idiot in the corner.*

No, he wants her to get out. She deserves to get out.

*And no one else does?*

There's Lorenzo, but Max isn't convinced he's even still alive.

*I wasn't talking about Lorenzo, and you know it.*

Max ignores the voice and continues forward, slipping up behind Cantina, trying not to think the words: choke hold.

Choke hold, choke hold, choke hold.

*Doesn't work, does it, Max? Because as soon as you tell yourself not to think a thing, it's all you do. That's part of it. Part of the madness. Part of the crazy.*

Don't use that word.

Focus on his task. On "taking out" Cantina.

*Can you do it? Can you carry through? You know what that could mean. Look around you if you need a reminder. Two bodies on the floor. If the choke hold doesn't work, he's not going to slap your bottom and call you a naughty boy. Life or death, Max. Life or death.*

*Can you do it?*

*Can you carry through?*

His breath comes harder, sweat trickling into his eye, and he blinks as the salt stings. Could he kill someone? If it was a matter of life or death? Kill or be killed? If the only life at stake was his own? No.

*And why's that, Max? Tell us, why's that?*

But it isn't just his own life at stake, is it? There's Riley, always Riley, and if he fails, Cantina will go after her. Gray and Predator will hear and come running. Bing-boom-bam. That will be the end of Riley, and that matters, Max, doesn't it? That is what matters even if the rest . . . not so much.

But the problem, yes, *the problem*, is the shadow he glimpsed out of the corner of his eye. The person who is not a person.

Unless it was really only a shadow. A movement. It's a common optical phenomenon. Entoptic phenomenon, to be exact. From the Greek for "within" and "visual." The act of seeing a shape that exists within the eye itself.

*Ah, you're a smart one, aren't you, Max? So smart. Didn't save you at all, did it? Your brain mutinies—all hands on deck, we're not taking this shit anymore—and it doesn't matter how smart you are, all the king's horses and all the king's men can't put your poor mind together again.*

But the shadow . . . What if it was a sign?

*Sign, sign, everywhere a sign, something, something, breaking my mind.*

See, the thing is, it could be a sign. Meds not working. Red alert, red alert. And if that's true, yes, if that's true, then he cannot be trusted. Absolutely cannot be trusted, because for all he knows, this man at the table isn't Cantina at all, but Gideon, struggling to stay alive, perched up here in his bloodied shirt.

*Really? You really believe that?*

No, but he believed his best friend had been possessed

by demons. The twelve Malebranche, to be precise, from Dante's *Inferno*, because Maximus Cross must be precise. No vague, nameless demons for him. That would not do.

Justin had been in trouble, and Max would save him. Because that's what friends did. So he . . .

Max stops mid-step. He sees Justin in that chair. Justin at his desk, with his back to Max. Max with his hands outstretched, his brain on fire, only he doesn't realize it's on fire, doesn't feel the flames, doesn't smell the smoke. Later, straitjacketed—

Did you know they still use straitjackets? You wouldn't think so, would you? How terribly archaic. Right up there with visits to Bedlam, which is short for the Hospital of St. Mary of Bethlehem, if you didn't know. Bedlam, Victorian London's finest insane asylum, where you could pay your shillings to see the madmen, frothing and ranting, chained to walls, covered in their own shit and piss. Most were probably schizophrenic. That's what the tour guide said, when Max visited once on a class trip.

*Most were probably schizophrenic.*

He remembers not only the words but the way she said them as if it were simply a statement of fact. Why, of course they were schizophrenic. What else would one expect?

The point . . .

*Ah, yes, you have a point, Max, buried deep in there somewhere.*

The point is that when one is mad, one is incapable of smelling the smoke, of seeing the flames, of feeling the heat. Afterward, the memory of that brain fever is clear, and the shame . . .

*Shall we talk about the shame? No, let's not today. Perhaps tomorrow, over tea and crumpets.*

The point is that a madman doesn't know he's mad at the time of madness. Which is, let's be quite blunt, the time when one really ought to know. When one needs to know, lest one attempt to expel demons without proper training. Or attempt to "take down" a supposed kidnapper who might really be—

Cantina's head jerks up. Max freezes. He's made a noise, he must have—breathing too hard or socks swishing against the floor. Cantina turns his way, twisting in his chair, and then—

And then he stops short, because his gaze falls on Riley, in the doorway, about to launch her distraction.

"You little . . ." Cantina begins. Then he shouts, "Hey, guys! She's—" and that's all he says before Max is on him, grabbing his hair and slamming his face into the desk before he can get another word out. No forethought. No time for indecision. No time for timidity. Only time to react. Which he does admirably, if he might say so himself.

It's a perfect strike, hard enough to break Cantina's nose and daze him, and then to enrage him, rearing up, like a bull spotting red—which is a myth, actually, Max notes, because he has to note it, the thought pinging through his head, but if there is an advantage to those endlessly whizzing thoughts, it is speed. The trivia zooms through his mind and does nothing to impede the signals that shoot from his brain to his fists as Cantina lumbers to his feet. Which is, if Max may humbly note, a mistake, given the fact that the man has been shot in the chest.

Max barely needs to put any power behind his swing. Cantina lunges, his brain on fire—a different sort of fire, though no less detrimental in the short run—and the man's mind might be willing, but his body says, "Bloody hell, no." Cantina doesn't even manage to lift his fist before he starts to topple, and at that point one might say Max's power-house uppercut is a wee mite of overkill, but he doesn't regret it.

Cantina flies off his feet in a way Max had always presumed was simply cinematic magic. Apparently not. He thuds down flat on his back, and that's when Max notices Riley running toward them. Running to his rescue. She stops mid-step, sliding in her socks, then she stares at Cantina, and Max braces for the look of horror, of "what have you done?"

*Remember that look, Max? On Ilsa Morton's face as she came around the corner and saw you trying to cast the demons from Justin?*

Only it's not the same look. Not at all. Riley stares in surprise, and when she looks up at him she's grinning like he is indeed in a film, the screw-up kid who knocked the bully flying. That grin is like a straight hit of oxygen, and it blasts straight to his head.

*Tell me how you don't want to save her, Max. Don't want to be her white knight.*

He did. Yes, he did. He'd made a mess of things, not helping Brienne and Aaron get Riley out when she had the chance, when the other girl—what was her name?—was released instead. He'd ballsed it up, and now he needs to make amends. To do one thing right before . . .

*Before what, Max?*

Cantina starts to rise, dazed and that snaps Max out of it. With Riley at his side, he races to subdue him.

**CHAPTER 13** Max knocks Cantina flying. Literally knocks him flying, and I can say it was just a lucky blow, but it's obvious he's had some training. Given the way he flinched when we discussed taking down Cantina, I figure it was theoretical training, his father telling him how to defend himself, Max never putting that into practice because of an inner taboo against hitting another person.

Right now, the important thing is that he can fight. Which is a relief. I'd be able to defend myself better with a saber in hand, but even without that, I think I have enough basic training to manage. I just couldn't do it for both of us.

When Cantina starts to rise, we're both on him so fast that I have to laugh a little, as we practically knock heads. Max holds him still. I pull off the guy's sock and stuff it in his mouth. Then I use Max's belt to secure his hands. Cantina's own belt works for his feet.

We search him. There's nothing to find. Brienne or Aaron has his gun, and his partners have taken anything else—radio, cell phone, wallet. We leave him on the floor and start hunting for the counselors' phones and the meds.

The room is big—at least twenty by thirty—but most is open space. There are a dozen chairs on one side, where we'd sat in our therapy semicircle. A dozen more are stacked in a corner. The only place to stash stuff is in the two desks. Max stands guard while I hunt. There's not much to pick through. Half the drawers are empty and the other half contain random assortments of office supplies. Paper, envelopes, tape . . .

The meds should be right on top. When they aren't, I shuffle through the supplies as quietly as I can, and when I still don't find anything, I take everything out and stack it on the desk. Max keeps looking over, his frown growing, eyes darkening with worry. I empty every drawer and find nothing.

I ask Max to double-check. I know he won't find anything, but I can't take the chance that in my growing anxiety I missed a bag of meds or a cell phone stuffed at the back of a drawer.

When he comes back, his mouth is a tight line, and when I say, "Are you all right?" I don't get the standard "Right as rain" and jaunty grin. He nods, but it's curt, and his gaze is distant.

"You really need those meds, don't you?" I whisper.

"We need a mobile more," he says.

Which is true—if we had a cell phone, he could get his heart medication as soon as we escaped. But he's worried about those meds too, meaning the situation is more dire than he's letting on.

"You're worried you'll need them," I say.

"I always need them," he says, and there's a sharp note of frustration there, deep frustration and bitterness and even something like shame, his gaze downcast. I understand that—no eighteen-year-old guy wants to admit to a physical weakness, especially one usually associated with senior citizens.

"Should you rest?" I whisper. "I can find you a room to wait in while I hunt for the back door."

"No," he says, adamant, that shoulder-straightening again, as if he's gearing up for battle. "I'll be fine. It wouldn't help anyway. It's more a matter of timing. The faster we get out of here, the better. We'll get out faster if we stick together."

"Are there signs? Anything I can do or not do or watch out for?"

He hesitates, and his shoulders slump, as if it's a struggle to keep that battle-ready face on.

"I'm not prying," I say. "If there's nothing I can do, okay, but if there's a sign, maybe one that you won't notice, and it means you need to rest . . . ? My grandfather has heart problems, and I know there are signs for him."

"It's . . . different for me. But . . . yes, there are signs. If I start acting . . . odd, tell me."

I'm about to say, "Odder than usual?" Tease him, lighten his mood, but discomfort jumps from him like electrical sparks, so I keep it serious and say, "Okay. Anything more specific?"

He shakes his head. "Just odd. If I say or do something that doesn't seem right. I get lightheaded and it affects my brain." He hurries on, "Nothing to worry about, but just . . . be aware and don't be afraid to say, *Hey, you're acting a bit mad.*"

I smile at that, and he tries to return it, but there's a weight there, so heavy I feel it. He shakes it off and looks over at the desk. "Before we go, we should see if there's anything we can take."

"Weapons or door knockers. Right. Maria had a letter opener . . ."


We're armed now. If you can call a letter opener and a pair of scissors "weapons." The scissors are safety ones. Max took them, but they're in his pocket, acknowledgment that they're more a tool than a weapon.

I have the opener in my hand as I walk, held like a saber, which gives me some comfort, though I keep looking for something bigger, maybe a piece of wood I could wield. I don't waste time searching for one, though. I know a piece of wood—or even an actual sword—won't help against men with guns.

I think back to when I started fencing. I was seven, and my dad came home one day and declared that Sloane and I were going to the Y on Saturday to check out martial arts classes. I thought little of it at the time, though I realize in retrospect that it must have been prompted by a case, something he'd seen that made him decide his daughters needed to take self-defense lessons, starting immediately.

Sloane settled on karate. She was already taking dance and this felt the most familiar to her, with its graceful moves. I tried karate and judo and kickboxing, and hated them all. They felt weird and unnatural. Then, after a session, we cut through the main gym to see a fencing class in progress, and I stopped, enthralled, and said, "I want to learn that."

Dad signed me up, intending for it to complement my martial arts, but after a couple of months I begged to quit karate. I'd already progressed to the next level in fencing and I absolutely loved it.

"She's a natural," Dad said to Mom one night, when he thought I was asleep. "I absolutely want her to continue. But I don't want her giving up karate. What's she going to do if some boy grabs her behind the school? Hope there's a stick nearby to whack him with?"

"Neither a stick nor a throw-down is going to save them from a real threat, Jim," Mom said. "You aren't teaching them how to protect themselves as much as you're giving them the confidence to do it. Fencing gives Riley that. Just look at her. She's already standing up to her sister. Not whacking her with a stick, but standing firm and saying no. She's also learning how to handle herself against a threat. How to stay calm and focused and plan—whether it's fighting back or knowing she can't and that she needs to get out of that situation as fast as possible, and keep her head on straight while she does."

Dad had agreed Mom was right and let me drop the karate, and he became my biggest cheerleader, rising at any hour to take me to private lessons or driving for half a day to get me to a tournament.

And Mom *was* right. I might long for a saber in my hand right now, but what I have is even better: the ability to deal with this situation. My confidence has taken a beating in the last four months, but even at its lowest, it's enough to let me believe we can get out of this, to keep going, not curl up and pray for rescue, divine or otherwise.

My parents taught me that life—and God—helps those who help themselves. If I've gotten any divine boost here, it's the guy walking beside me: Max. He's exactly the partner I need to keep my spirits and my confidence up, keep me calm and keep me moving with a clear plan in mind.

That plan is getting our asses to the back door. Finding it takes some work, but Gray and Predator seem to have retreated upstairs, possibly in pursuit of Aaron or Brienne, and I don't want to be glad of that, especially when both tried to help me. But the truth is that each time I hear a noise upstairs, I think, *Good, it's not us.*

We find the back door. It's locked.

"Bang on it?" I ask.

Max purses his lips and runs his hand over the steel. "It's thinner than the front one. It'll make more noise. But will anyone be back here?" He puts his ear to the door. "I don't hear anything. I did out front—not much, but I heard noise."

"Most of the activity will be at the front," I say. "But they'll cover all exits."

"Then we have to risk knocking. If I ask you to find a room and lie low—"

"No."

"All right, I won't ask. This time, though, I want a plan, because if it's only a couple of officers covering the back, they might not hear us. Gray and Predator will."

We whisper out a plan and then locate a safe room. Then Max bangs on the door. The boom reverberates loudly enough that I jump and so does he, and he turns with an "Oh, shit!" look on his face. We both go still, waiting to see if anyone comes to the door. When he notices I'm still standing guard, he waves frantically for me to get to the safe room, but I turn away and watch down the hall.

After five seconds of silence, there's a reaction . . . foot-falls pounding overhead.

Max's gaze swings up, tracking the sound. The footsteps are running toward the stairs. Then they're on the steps, the cadence changing to the *boom-ba-boom* of someone racing down. Max tenses, still tracking that sound, knowing we have only a few moments, but we need every second we can steal, to see if there is a response from outside, to make sure they know we're here, that it's not a random banging, that something is going on and—

The stairwell door slams shut. Max grabs the letter opener from my hand and raps it hard against the steel back door. Three quick raps, three slower, three quick, a pause, then again. I recognize the sound, but it's not until he turns back toward me that I recall a fifth-grade project and realize it's Morse code for SOS.

We get to our safe room and hide behind boxes to catch our breath. I grin at him again and whisper, "You're a genius, you know that?" and he hesitates, with this look as if not sure he's hearing right.

"Morse code," I say. "I would have never thought of that."

"I should have thought of it sooner. Now we have to hope *they* know what it means."

"They will. They'll realize something's wrong, and whatever Gray has been telling them, they're not going to believe him now. They'll insist on talking to one of us, and he can bluff all he wants, but they'll know it's all gone to hell, and this will become a rescue mission. Which means"— my grin broadens—"we just need to lie low and wait it out."


A few minutes later, we overhear Gray and Predator discovering Cantina, bound up. Their curses ricochet through the empty building. We're three halls and about a hundred paces from the therapy room, so we sneak to the door of our safe room and crack it open to listen. They're too far away for us to catch more than disjointed phrases:

" . . . the Mexican girl and the British kid . . ."

" . . . say anything . . ."

" . . . looking for my gun, I guess . . ."

" . . . taken down by a couple crazy kids?"

Crazy kids. Not wild and crazy. Nuts crazy. That's what you get when people find out you're in therapy. Most don't say it outright, but you can see it in their eyes, that wary look, as if you're going to start ranting or muttering to yourself. Some will say it, like my aunt, when she thought I couldn't hear. *Why does Riley need therapy? She's just having a rough time. She isn't crazy or anything. Take her on a vacation and let her relax and everything will be fine.*

Mom says that's just plain ignorance. She'd know—she needed grief counseling after Dad died. My aunt probably told her she just needed a vacation then too.

When Gray accuses Cantina of having been taken down by "a couple crazy kids," the injured man defends himself. Gray tells him to shut the hell up, just shut the hell—

Silence. Then Gray snorts a laugh and says, "Well, that works," and Predator says, "I thought it might. Should have done that earlier. Once this is over, I don't plan to spend my day finding him a doctor."

"I suppose you expect part of his cut."

"Fifty percent."

"That's why I like you, buddy. You're a fair man. Now let's find those kids."

Max pulls the door shut, and it's only now that I realize what happened. That Predator shot Cantina.

Put him down like a dog.

I've heard that expression too, and again it's not until now that I realize the full horror of it. I know what Cantina was. I wouldn't have given a damn if we'd walked in there earlier to find him dead. Succumbed to his injuries.

But this is different. This is cold, and it is pointless, and it is callous. It is shooting another human being just because you can.

*Well, that shut him up, didn't it? Ha ha.*

Put down like a dog.

"Riley?" Max whispers, his breath warm against my ear.

I imagine Predator casually firing his gun at his part-ner's head.

*Brains splattered on the wall.*

*Put down like a dog.*

*Should have done that earlier.*

*Ha-ha.*

"Riley . . ."

"I know." I take a deep breath and struggle to focus.

"Why does everyone call you Mexican?" he asks.

My head jerks up. "Huh?"

"I'm distracting you with an unrelated and potentially rude question. Aaron called you Mexican. So did they. But you don't have an accent, and I knew a guy at school named Vasquez who was from Spain. So as the foreigner who hasn't quite figured out your country, what tells them you're Mexican?"

I want to brush off the question. Really not the time. But that's the point, isn't it? I look down at my quavering hands, and when I squeeze my eyes shut, all I see is Predator, pulling the trigger.

I can hear Gray's and Predator's footsteps. They're far enough away and we're well enough hidden that we're safe here. For now.

I glance at Max. "I don't have an accent because my family has been here for three generations. My father's family comes from Spain. My mother's is from Cuba. That makes me Hispanic, and the presumption here—far enough from the border that there aren't a lot of Latino immigrants—is that Hispanic equals Mexican."

"So Hispanic and Latino mean the same thing?"

I shake my head. "Hispanic means you are descended from a country that speaks Spanish. Latino means you're descended from a country in Latin America. Some are both, like Cuba. But if you come from Brazil, you're Latino and not Hispanic, because the official language is Portuguese."

"And if it's Spain, it's Hispanic and not Latino. Excellent. My lesson in American terminology for the day."

We both listen. The footsteps remain distant. My heart is still thumping, though, so I whisper, "I'm presuming that accent's real and you *are* British."

"Through and through. There might be a hint of Irish thrown in, but" —he lowers his voice to a conspiratorial whisper— "we don't talk about that."

When I raise my brows, he says, "I'm joking. Mostly."

"I've heard you mention your parents. Any siblings?"

"Not a one. Mostly it's just me and Mum. My parents never married. Both on the far side of forty when I came along. Quite the surprise, I'm sure. They decided to just get on with it. Co-parenting and good friends and all that." Another conspiratorial whisper. "I try not to think about the 'all that' part, but they're responsible adults and I doubt another slip is likely at their age."

"Uh-huh."

"A very odd parenting arrangement, I know. But it works. And returning to the question about siblings, I believe you have a sister?"

"Sloane. She's a year older."

"Good friend or pain in the arse?"

"Somewhere down the middle. Closer to the latter." I think of Sloane and of Mom. Have they heard what's happened yet? I hope they haven't. As disappointing as it will be to get out there and not run into Mom's arms, I hope they know nothing of this.

"All right, then," Max says, slapping his thighs and rising. "I do believe we've chatted and stalled quite long enough. As lovely as it would be to stay here until the cavalry arrives, our intrepid captors seem to be searching the building. Best to give them a moving target. Let's head out, troops."

**CHAPTER 14** Max is right. If they're systematically hunting for us, we can't stay where we are.

"We need a cell phone," I say as we leave the room.

Max frowns over.

"Yes, I know that's why we went into the therapy room," I say. "But if Maria's phone isn't there, then Aimee left it upstairs."

"Or the bad guys found and took it."

True. "But Aimee thought she left it up there. Besides, Gray and Predator just came from upstairs, meaning it's the last place they'll look again. We can hunt for the phone and then hide while we wait for whoever heard your SOS."

"Presuming someone—"

"I know it's not a given that *anyone* heard," I say. "Which is all the more reason we need a cell phone. And your meds. You don't keep backup ones anywhere, do you?"

He shakes his head. Then his eyes go wide. "Wait. Yes. There are two in my other jeans. I was wearing them yesterday, stuffed my pills in, got distracted with a book and took two from the bottle instead. Then I found the pills later and meant to put them back but got distracted again."

"Well, it's a good thing you're easily distracted then, right?"

I'm teasing him, but his smile falters and he mumbles something as we head into the hall.

"I do that a lot," I whisper. "Get distracted when I'm reading." When his cheeks flush, I say, "And the whole I-know-what-that's-like thing is never helpful, is it? Which I should know from therapy."

He manages a smile. "I hope no one would dare say that to you."

"Actually, yes, my last therapist did. He said he had some idea of what I'd gone through, because he'd seen his dog get hit by a car."

Max's brows arch.

"I'm serious. I walked out and told my mother. She fired his ass on the spot. Mom's not the type to cause a scene, but she still knows how."

"Sounds like my mother," he says, and we both smile and then fall to silence as we make our way to the steps. There's little danger of our whispers being overheard. We can hear Gray and Predator, and they're heading the other way. Toward Aimee. Toward Lorenzo too? It'll be easy enough to find him, with the blood in the hall. And when they do, if he's still alive . . .

Put down like a dog.

I tell myself they won't waste the ammo, because their supply is limited and he'll be smart enough to fake dead.

*If he isn't already.*

I don't think about that either. We reach the stairwell and slip through the door, shutting it behind us. Then we climb to the second floor. We're still in stockinged feet. We've abandoned our footwear—too much to haul around. So we move silently, and when we come out into the hall, it is *not* silent.

There's someone in Lorenzo's bedroom.

His is the first past the stairway door. Aimee had pointed it out as we'd passed.

*You and Sandra share a room. So do Brienne and Maria. The guys are on the other side of my room, Max in one and the two other boys in the second room. And Terry—that's the other counselor—is at the end.*

She'd stopped and shaken her head.

*No, not Terry. It's Lorenzo. They swapped at the last minute. Not that you know either. But they're both good guys.*

Max hears the noise from Lorenzo's room as soon as I do, and he performs his usual shoulder-check, to be sure we both caught it. I nod almost before he looks over, my gaze fixed on the closed door. Then I do a check of my own, moving closer to whisper, "I'm sure I heard two sets of footsteps downstairs. You?"

His turn to nod now. We both ease forward. Max covers me. I turn the knob. It clicks louder than I expect, and I wince as noise erupts from inside, a scampering and scuffling. I open the door a crack, just as Aaron dives behind the twin bed.

"It's us," I whisper as I open it, and Brienne pops up from the bed, her eyes bright with terror. She blinks it back and then exhales and whispers, "We were sure they both went downstairs."

"They did," I say as I slide into the room, Max following.

Aaron's up now. He sees Max, and his eyes narrow. "Didn't get far, did you, asshole? Took off and left the rest of us to fend for ourselves."

"Actually, he took me with him," I say. "But there wasn't any other choice or I would have—"

"We know," Brienne says. "Aaron's just being cranky." She lowers her voice to a mock whisper. "Being shot at does that to him."

Aaron rolls his eyes, and she shoots him a smile, and I know that we aren't the only ones getting along better. Fighting for survival together shows you what counts and what doesn't, and all that counts, really, is *Do you have my back?*

"We're looking for a cell phone," Brienne says. She turns on a penlight. "Aaron remembered this was on his key chain. Luckily, it was still in his room. Now we just need a phone."

"Lorenzo confiscated Maria's," Aaron said. "So we were hoping he left it here."

"Aimee took it from him," I say, "and she said she put it in the therapy room or up here. But we couldn't find it downstairs."

I'm searching as I talk. Even if the phone isn't here, we should look for anything useful before we check Aimee's room. Max and Brienne join in, as Brienne says, "Aimee's still alive too? Good. I thought she'd come with us, but she must have stayed behind with Gideon. Where is she now?"

*Brains splattered on the wall.*

I don't answer. I can't. Max says, "No," and that's all he says, and Brienne says, "What?" Then, "Oh." And, "Are you sure?"

I squeeze my eyes shut and try not to remember *how* sure we are, but of course I do. I see Aimee there and open my eyes fast, dispelling the memory. I take Lorenzo's knapsack and dump it onto the floor as Max says, "We're sure."

"And Lorenzo?"

"He . . . was holding on," I manage. "I . . . I don't know if he's still . . ."

"Gideon?"

"No."

"Th-they're both dead? Plus Maria? I thought you said even injuries in hostage situations are rare."

"Hey," Aaron says.

Brienne presses her palms to her eyes. "Sorry, sorry. I just . . . I don't understand how it went so wrong."

"Ask Gideon," Aaron says. "Oh, wait, you can't. And, yeah, that's a shitty thing to say about a dead guy, but I'll say it anyway. He set them off, and once Maria was dead, everything changed. They can't walk away after that."

Brienne shakes her head vehemently. "I know guys like them. Well, not exactly like that. But guys who've been in jail or should be. My brother—" She swallows hard. "I know people who've made mistakes, and that's what this is."

"So they kidnapped us by mistake?" Max says.

"I don't mean that. I mean that shooting Maria was a mistake. Then with Gideon, it was because he shot their partner. It was panic. That's all. Once they calm down, it'll be fine."

"No," I say, as gently as I can. "It won't. I heard them when they shot Aimee. This is all about cleanup. No loose ends. No witnesses."

Her hands are shaking and I put down Lorenzo's knapsack and pull her into a hug.

"The only way we get out alive is to get ourselves out," Aaron says. "Focus on that. Finish up here fast and then check Aimee's room."

He opens the side pocket on Lorenzo's backpack. As I sift through what I dumped, Brienne and Max look elsewhere. Aaron tosses the bag aside, and I hear an odd crinkling noise. I start going through the pockets again. He says nothing, just moves to the door to stand guard.

I find what made the noise. It's a piece of paper shoved up against the side of an inner pocket, easy to miss. I take it out. It's a photocopied blueprint of the building we're in. A bunch of rooms are labeled in marker. Therapy. Aimee. Mine. Girls A. Girls B. Boys A. Boys B. Bathroom A. Bathroom B. Storage A. Storage B. Kitchen. Rec Room.

Max is looking over my shoulder. "Well, that's handy in this maze," he says.

"You'd think he'd have kept it with him."

Max shrugs. "Memorized it, put it away. That's what I'd do."

Brienne is beside me now, looking. "Kitchen." She smiles. "Where there's a kitchen, there are knives. We'll search Aimee's room for that cell and then see if we can find a weapon."

Maria's cell phone isn't in Aimee's room. Nor are Max's meds in his jeans. The moment he opens his bag, he stops and looks at Aaron and Brienne.

"Did you search my things?" he asks.

Aaron bristles. "No, asshole. I didn't rifle through your crap hoping you've got something worth stealing."

"I'm not asking if you nicked anything. I'm asking if you searched for a mobile or a weapon, which would be understandable. *Someone* has been in my bag."

He pulls out his jeans and checks the pockets. I can tell by his expression they're empty. He shakes the jeans upside down to double-check.

"They might have fallen out in your bag," I say.

He empties it as I whisper for Brienne and Aaron to go check for weapons or anything useful in the other rooms. Once they're gone, I squeeze Max's arm. It's shaking.

"I need them, Riley," he says. "I really need them. Like"—a glance at his watch—"thirty minutes ago."

"Do you feel okay?" I ask. "Do you need to lie down?"

"It's not . . ." He shakes his head sharply. "I just need them. Now."

I help him search his bag. We take out everything and shake it. Then we do it all a second time.

"Why would someone go through my bag?" He turns to me. "Check yours."

I do, but it's exactly as I packed it. Maybe one of the counselors went through Max's, suspecting he'd smuggled in contraband—a phone or a game player or a bottle of booze. If the pills fell out, they could have mistaken them for a very different kind of drug.

I suggest this to Max.

"I did make a smart comment to Lorenzo when I arrived," he says.

I sigh.

"He reminded me that all medications had to be turned in, even aspirin. I said I had some pot, but it wasn't medicinal, so that was all right."

I sigh again.

"Let this be a lesson to me about my smart mouth, right?" he says.

"I never said it."

"You're thinking it loud enough that you don't have to."

# MAX: ANXIETY

**Anxiety:** *a feeling of worry, nervousness, or unease,*
*typically about an imminent event or something*
*with an uncertain outcome.*

The English language, one might argue, has far too many words. Sometimes, though, it simply doesn't have enough. Anxiety is what one feels when walking into a test. That is, it's what a normal boy feels walking into an academic test. Max never had that problem. A year ago, though, he discovered his own special brand of test anxiety, the one where he walked into yet another doctor's or specialist's office, searching for answers that never came.

*Your son has schizophrenia, Mrs. Cross.*

That can't be. He's too young.

*Typical onset is young adulthood. Late teens is early, but not unduly so.*

*I'm precocious, Mum. Aren't you proud of me? No? Right-i-o, then. Onward and upward. Or downward, because there's really nowhere to go from here but down.*

Stop saying that.

*I'm being honest. You raised me to be honest, you and Dad. Face facts, son. And that fact is that all the king's horses and all the king's men . . .*

Stop. Just stop. We just need to get you a proper diagnosis. Max can't have schizophrenia, doctor. He's not paranoid.

He doesn't suffer from delusions of persecution. He was confused with his friend, but he never thought he was in danger personally. Therefore, it can't be paranoid schizophrenia.

*We don't use that term anymore. We now recognize schizophrenia as a spectrum of disorders, which often doesn't include paranoia for someone Max's age.*

But he doesn't have all the other symptoms either. His speech is clear. His personal hygiene is just fine. There's no flattened affect. No social withdrawal . . .

*That's why it's a spectrum, Mrs. Cross. Think of it as a buffet, not a set table.*

A buffet. Ah, that helps. Yes, indeed. I'll have the delusions and the visual hallucinations with a small side of audio hallucinations and disorganized thought. And hold the lack of bathing, please, because I'm not ever going to lead an ordinary life with that one. No bathing, no friends, no girlfriends.

Umm, wait. Better strike the friends and girlfriends anyway. Delusions and hallucinations really aren't conducive to a proper social life.

Another doctor. Another failed test.

*Fail, fail, fail. That's all you do these days, isn't it, Maximus? Make a mockery of your name. Greatest, indeed. Greatest disappointment ever.*

Then his father . . .

*Stop fighting the diagnosis, Alice.*

*But he's not—*

*Yes, he is, damn it. Stop fighting and just get him fixed up.*

Fixed up. Yes, sir, Dad. Stop messing around, Mum, and fix me up. That's your job, isn't it? Fix the mess that is your son. Get him on the proper meds, and it'll all be fine. Right as rain, old chap. You'll be right as rain. Just as soon as we get these meds sorted. Well, except for the side effects and the fact that you can never stop taking the medications and that at any point they might lose their effectiveness and you won't know it because it'll seem normal to you. Crazy is your normal, Max. Live with it. Or don't. Your choice.

Your choice.

He remembers when he agreed with his mother and fought the diagnosis and the meds, convinced they didn't understand, he was fine, better than fine, more alive than ever, everything brighter, sharper, clearer. The world had snapped into focus. It made sense in a way it rarely did to a boy still a month from his seventeenth birthday. The meds muted that world, crushed his creativity, doused his spirit. Why were they trying to control him when he was so much better now?

What saved Max, as much as he hated to think it, was attacking Justin. Once the medication stabilized him enough that he realized what he'd done, the horror of that memory kept him taking those meds, would always keep him taking them. What if that hadn't happened? If it had been a slow build to a violent break? Or no violent break at all? Would he have refused the meds once he turned eighteen? Left home if his parents tried to force them on him? Ended up like the untreated schizophrenics you see in the streets, homeless and filthy, muttering and ranting to himself? He can't think of that. It terrifies him almost as much as the memory of what he tried to do to his best friend.

*Terrified: caused to feel extreme fear.*

He will admit he's a little terrified right now, following Riley down the hall. He's overdue for his meds. Thirty minutes and ticking, and he's starting to sweat, catching a whiff of . . .

"Just a moment," he whispers, and he slips into the room, grabs his deodorant and slathers it on.

*Yes, oh, yes, wouldn't want to smell bad around a pretty girl. Can't blow your shot, Max. Even if you don't have a chance in hell.*

That's not it.

*Oh, I know. It's not about the girl. It's about the symptoms. Ignore a faint whiff of body odor during a life-threatening situation and it might be that "lack of attention to hygiene" sign you're so worried about.*

Or maybe the fact he worried about it was a sign of something else. Paranoia.

*Sign, sign, everywhere a sign.*

He's back to Riley now, and they catch up with Brienne and Aaron, who confirm they've found nothing useful. On to the kitchen, then.

Anxiety is not what he feels, walking down that hall and then the steps, every creak and shadow making him jump, certain he's not seeing actual dangers but those that exist only in his mind. Certain the meds have worn off already.

No, "anxiety" is too weak a word.

*Panic: sudden, uncontrollable fear or anxiety, often causing wildly unthinking behavior.*

Also not correct, because it is, for now, controllable. He tells himself it's not possible for the meds to wear off so fast. He's asked the doctors about that, as he asks about every possible detail, trying to make sense of it, to bring order to the chaos.

Not order. Control. That's what he needed. That's what he'd always had. It's why he'd never felt those so-called butterflies before an exam. Because he knew he had studied to the best of his ability, and he'd considered and managed all variables and therefore he would get the top mark in the class, because he always did. It was simply a matter of control.

Likewise, schizophrenia could be controlled. Or that was the theory. After months of changing medications, they finally seemed to find a cocktail that worked.

*Cocktail: an alcoholic drink consisting of a spirit or*

*several spirits mixed with other ingredients, such as fruit juice, lemonade or cream.*

Mmm, not quite right, old chap, though it'd be lovely, really. But no. Sadly, no.

*Cocktail: a mixture of substances or factors, especially when dangerous or unpleasant in its effects.*

Now that, *that*, was the proper definition. Terrifyingly accurate, though Max suspected his doctor's vocabulary was not quite as advanced as his own, and when he called it a cocktail, the man simply meant a mixture, not realizing his word choice had an added nuance.

One thing about attempting to find order—no, *control*—was that Max had asked how long he could go without the pills before he risked ill effects. The first doctor, back in Jolly Old England, had refused to answer, apparently suspecting Max was trying to stave off side effects by stretching his meds as far as possible. Which was not the case at all, so when he'd come over—crossed the pond, as they say . . . does anyone actually say that?—he'd been much more specific in his questions and backed them up with explanations. Which had still not worked with Yankee doctor number one, but his mother had recognized the problem and found him another psychiatrist, one more capable of treating her precious—and precocious—son with the respect he deserved.

The answer . . . ah, yes, there was a point here, wasn't there? The answer was that while he should endeavor to always take his pills on time, if some emergency prevented him from doing so, it would be hours before they began to lose effectiveness, and even then it was only that—a loss of effectiveness, not a complete and sudden crash into the depths of schizophrenia.

Which meant he was not panicked. Yet he was beyond anxious.

More than anxious. Less than panicked. Is there a word for that?

There didn't seem to be. They ran on a scale. Apprehensive, nervous, dismayed, frightened, anxious, panicked. There was a step missing there, the stage past stomach-clenching anxiety and before full-blown panic.

Alarm, perhaps?

*Alarm: an anxious awareness of danger.*

Yes, perhaps that was it.

"Is everything okay?" Riley whispers.

"Right as rain."

She rolls her eyes, but there's a small smile there too. Yes, right as rain. Just playing with words. Keeps my mind occupied. One has to find the proper term. Exactly the proper one.

She leans toward him, voice lowering more, and he knows she wants to say more, just for him, unheard by the others. He tries not to smile at that. It pleases him more than it ought to, because if he's being honest—*yes, by all means, be honest, Max, God knows you have little enough practice at it these days*—he will admit that he was not entirely happy to bump into Brienne and Aaron. Of course, he was relieved to know they were alive, but he'd have been quite happy if they'd made contact and then gone their separate ways again. He even thought of suggesting it.

He might still, once they find the kitchen and if he's sure, quite sure, that Riley won't say: *All right. Why don't I go with Brienne and you with Aaron?*

Riley and Max sitting in a tree . . .

That was not the case at all.

Well, perhaps "at all" was a slight exaggeration.

*Just a slight one, Maximus?*

Yes, he might—just might—have a bit of a crush on Riley Vasquez.

*Crush: deform, pulverize or force inward by compressing forcefully.*

A horrible word. Terribly inappropriate, because he had no desire to crush her, to smother her. In fact, he was most comfortable as things were, being this close to her and no closer, because he couldn't be closer, all things considered.

Yes, all things considered.

Yet it was closer than he had been before tonight. And, yes, he would admit it now, he'd already had a crush on Riley Vasquez then, listening to her in therapy sessions— ah, how romantic. Listening to her, watching her, but not *watching* in a creepy way. Well, he supposed all watching *was* creepy, to some degree, but it was simply enjoying seeing her, paying extra attention when she spoke. It wasn't as if he followed her into the toilet or anything. No, sir. He had only followed her *to* it earlier, not inside. He'd made his excuse to use the toilet in hopes of meeting up and talking to her, which was *not* creepy.

Nor was it entirely the action of an infatuated boy. No, Maximus. Honesty here, *total* honesty.

He was lonely.

There, he'd said it, somehow more shameful than admitting to a crush.

He'd never been a particularly convivial person. Gregarious but not too convivial. Yes, there was a difference.

*Gregarious: fond of company.*

*Convivial: cheerful and friendly; jovial.*

He could play at being convivial, of course, but there was an edge to it, a note that might just be a little condescending.

*Might, Max?*

In school, he'd been popular if not particularly well liked. Again, there is a difference. He could be difficult and sarcastic and argumentative, and he kept his circle of friends small, his circle of acquaintances much larger. But he was smart—if a bit of a know-it-all. Athletic, though not unduly so. Decent-looking, though only in that rather average way that both sexes seemed to find pleasant and nonthreatening. And he was a bit of a joker, a prankster, the boy most likely to both issue and accept a dare. He was bold as brass, and it seemed less that others liked him than that they liked to be around him. He'd been chosen as head boy in school, and he suspected it was not so much that his fellow students wished to honor him as that they'd grudgingly agreed he was best for the position.

At home, his calendar was always full, with other engagements waiting, should a date or a night with his mates fall through. Since he'd come to America, his social circle had shrunk to four—his mother, his father, his doctor and his therapist, and only the first was there consistently, should he want to take in a film or go to the park, which he did not because he was eighteen and his mother was a fine person, but he was eighteen.

And so, he was lonely. Which meant that when Riley stuck close to him, even after rejoining the others, when she whispered only to him, it made him flush with pleasure, as if she'd whispered some much more naughty suggestion in his ear. More even, because, well, it was hardly the time for naughty. Although, if she did . . .

"Max?" she whispers. "Are you sure you're okay?"

He nods. "A little distracted. Sorry. You said . . ."

"I was just saying I'm sure it won't be long now. I thought I heard a siren when we were upstairs, but I didn't want to mention it to the others and get their hopes up."

Her hopes are already up. He can see that in the way her eyes glow. His, sadly, are not. He suspects no one heard his SOS or there would have been some reaction by now. Whoever is covering the rear of the building had been too far away to overhear it. But he won't tell her that. Instead, he nods and smiles, and she leans in again, whispering, "You just need to hold on a little longer. We'll get you your meds."

*Ah, Riley. Sweet, sweet Riley. Always thinking of others even when you're convinced you're only thinking of yourself. You save a little girl's life and what matters is that you didn't save more. How can I not have a crush on you?*

"I'll be fine," he says, and he will be. For her, he will be.

*Speaking of sweet . . .*

Shut the bloody hell up. For once, please. Just shut up.

It does. The voice that he won't tell the doctors about, because it's a sign. A bad, bad sign. And yet he's always had the voice, and he suspects it's not a voice at all, just his busy brain arguing with itself, seeing all the angles, needling him when needling is required. Except he knows, too, that it might still be a sign, one that says he's always had this, lurking below the surface, biding its time. The schizophrenia monster, disguised as eccentricity and audacity, until it finally erupts in madness.

Riley holds out the blueprint, offering him the chance to lead the way. When he shakes his head, she keeps it, and he's relieved, because he will hold it together—for her, he'll hold it together—but it's best not to rely on him. Just to be safe.

# CHAPTER 15

There are no knives in the kitchen. Am I surprised? Not really. We're mental health patients, and I'm well aware of the suicide statistics, especially for teens, especially for those with PTSD and trauma-related depression and anxiety. I was made aware of them by my first therapist, who constantly poked and prodded for signs of "suicidal ideation." I finally made the mistake of commenting that I find it hard to get through some days, and I just want to stop. I meant school—that there were days I wanted to take more time off, but I feared if I did, I'd never go back.

He misunderstood—rather willfully, I think. He'd been so hyperalert for signs that he immediately recommended suicide watch to Mom, and when I freaked out, the therapist said that proved I was considering it. My freak-out, though, did not come close to Mom's. Directed at the therapist. Mom knew that no matter how bad I felt, it was never *that* bad, and that even in my worst moments, feeling like I didn't deserve to live when the Porters had died, I'd never considered suicide. I wouldn't do that to Mom and Sloane.

Yet there isn't just a lack of knives in the kitchen. There's a lack of a kitchen . . . or anything like a real one. The room is still under construction, with half-finished cupboards and sinks not yet connected to a water supply. We were having food delivered for the weekend, and I'd thought that was just to make it easy on the counselors, but obviously there wasn't an option. They brought in a mini-fridge and filled it with bottled water and soda, and there's fruit and granola bars on the counter, but otherwise nothing.

We search anyway. Aaron stands watch in the hall. When we are almost done, he pops his head in with "They're coming!" and we take off, all of us shoeless now, padding down the hallway at a jog, moving in the opposite direction of that relentless *thump-thump-thump*.

"You aren't getting out," Gray calls. "I know you kids are a little messed up, so let me explain it to you. There are two doors. If you have any brains at all, you've already checked and seen that they're locked tight. I heard one of you banging away, so here's a tip: it won't help. Those doors are so thick you'd need a grenade to get through them."

As he talks, we're on the move, heading away from his voice, checking rooms for a good one to lie low in. I hang back, listening to his diatribe, in case there's anything we can use.

"So you can pound and shout all you want, kiddies. I know it's frustrating, having a whole hostage negotiation team just beyond those walls. Your parents too. Well, some of them. Sorry, Brienne, but no one showed up for you. And your dad, Aaron? He's busy making financial arrangements for your release. Very slowly, though, which is why they think I'm not letting anyone else go. Personally, I think he just put in a call to his banker while he screws his new mistress. Who is, by the way, hotter than the old one, and a helluva lot hotter than your mom. Oh, she *is* outside. Your mom, I mean. At least someone cares, right? Of course, she has to play good parent if she wants all those child support payments. Your mom's there too, Maximus, and Riley's."

My mom. Oh God, I really didn't want that. She doesn't deserve this. Not after everything she's gone through. But I can't think about that. Instead, I think of something else, something that is, right now, even more important.

*And Gideon?* I want to shout back. *Maria? How about their parents? Their soon-to-be-grieving parents?*

It would do no good. I saw what he did to Aimee, and I heard him laugh when Predator shot Cantina. There's no capacity for guilt there. No conscience. He calls us crazy? He's a damn psychopath. They both are.

We keep looking, but we aren't finding a room. Most in this section are locked, and the rest are completely empty, giving us nothing to hide behind. Max whispers that we should head back to the room we were in last. I agree.

"I'd like to offer an apology." Gray's voice booms down the empty corridors. "Shocking, I know. But it's in order. Things went off the rails earlier. Blame Gideon, and if he were still alive, I'd shoot him on sight—the moron. Maria didn't help. I don't know what she expected, running at me with a damned letter opener. Of course I shot her—all I saw was someone coming at me with a weapon. But enough blame. Things went wrong. We panicked. People died. You ran. Can't blame you. That's over now, though, and I think I have a solution. You guys come back. We'll complete negotiations with Mr. Highgate. I won't ask the other parents for money. Well, I'll ask, but I won't expect it. What counts is the big dog. He pays, and you all go free. Not before that, though. You'll have to wait, because I can't risk you tattling on me and jeopardizing our payday."

No one slows. We keep checking doors and popping down side halls. And he keeps talking.

"What's done is done. Can't be fixed. But let's not add to the body count. This will all go much easier if everyone takes a deep breath, calms down and cooperates."

Max snorts. Brienne, though, slows to listen.

"Let's stop this running-around nonsense," Gray continues. "I'm sure you're as tired of it as we are. And I'm sure you must be getting hungry by now."

I catch up to Brienne and whisper, "Seriously? We're running from gun-toting killers and thinking, *Huh, I could really use a snack*?"

"Actually, I was," Max says, falling in as Aaron continues on ahead. "In fact, I may have grabbed a few granola bars when we were searching the kitchen. It's been four hours. I'm bloody famished."

"And now you have food," I say. "Meaning we don't need to stop and risk death so we can eat something."

"I don't know if I have enough to go around. Someone might need to surrender. You'll volunteer, won't you?"

"I would, but I'm not hungry. Maybe later."

We're talking past Brienne, who's quiet but listening. We banter some more—silly jokes about snacks and guns that aren't very funny, but the point is the banter itself, the shared verbal eye rolls that these guys would actually think we were stupid enough to surrender. Brienne's hesitation evaporates, and she picks up speed, joining in with a few jibes about teen guys and food as we hunt for a hiding place.

Gray is still nattering on about "stopping this nonsense." Just come out and we'll all hold hands and sing campfire songs until Mr. Highgate coughs up the cash.

"I'd like Scotch," Max says as we follow Aaron around a corner. "Sorry, ladies, but if he offers Scotch, I'm gone. It has to be at least fifteen-year single malt, though. Anything less will not do."

"I'm holding out for a pony," Brienne says.

"Too much work," I say. "I'll take a puppy."

Brienne shoots back that a puppy is more work than a pony, and she's relaxed now, paying no attention to Gray's cajoling. Max winks at me, and I smile, and I feel . . . I'll admit it, I feel good seeing that wink. As good as I can under the circumstances. That wink is a connection. We both knew that Brienne was wavering, and without a word exchanged we solved the problem together, and that feels . . . yes, it feels good, or as close to it as I'll get tonight. It's a reminder that I'm not alone in this, that there's someone I can rely on and trust, someone on my wavelength.

Dad used to say that—*we're on the same wavelength, kid*—whenever we came up with the same idea. Now I understand what he meant. I get Max, and I don't need to worry that he'll want to surrender or stop trying to escape or just say "to hell with it," and rush Gray with our letter opener and safety scissors and hope for the best. I wouldn't do any of that. So neither will he.

I'm about to say I'm going to move ahead and help Aaron search when Max motions behind Brienne's back that he's going to go ahead to search, and I laugh under my breath. He arches his brows. I shake my head, smile and wave him forward while I keep an eye on Brienne.

**CHAPTER 16** "Here!" Max whispers. He's opening a door to a room Aaron has already checked, and Aaron starts snapping something, but I see Max is gesturing, and I glance inside to spot an interior door. It's right up near the front, meaning it's obscured when the hall door opens. While Max stands watch, I dart in and check the second door. It opens into an empty room—which makes it less than perfect—but its hall door locks from the inside, which would give us an escape route.

Aaron and Brienne agree it's a good temporary hiding spot. There are boxes in the first room. None are big enough to hide behind, but once we're all in, Max grabs one and sets it right behind the closed hallway door.

"I think they can push a box aside," Aaron says.

Max ignores him and sets a second one on top of the first.

"They can push that one too," Aaron says.

"But it'll topple when the door opens," I say. "Which we'll hear from that room"—I point to the adjoining one—"and can slip out the other way."

"Oh." Aaron eyes the setup. "Okay. That's a good idea."

I brace myself against Max's smart-ass reply. He thankfully keeps his mouth shut and just fusses with the boxes.

Brienne and Aaron retreat to the next room. I stay and watch Max, intent on his task, getting it exactly right, frowning and reconfiguring when it's not. His hair falls in his face every time he leans forward, and after he makes a few increasingly impatient swipes, shoving it back behind his ear, I tug off one of my hair band bracelets and hold it out.

He takes it and smiles, and it's not his cocky grin or sardonic smirk or even his distracted no-really-I'm-fine smile. He pauses what he's doing and gives me a genuine smile. It's warm, and it's real, and it relaxes me. I suppose that's a weird reaction. *Relaxes me.* I should say "it sent a thrill through me," or "it lit up his face and I realized how cute he was." But it's like hot cocoa on a cold day, making me feel warm and happy and comforted. When he smiles, I hear, *It's okay. We'll get through this*, and that's exactly what I need.

He ties his hair back, and I gesture at the boxes, saying, "May I?" and he bows—not his usual mocking formality, but as amiable as that smile. I tweak the top box, angling it slightly, and when he tests with the door, his smile widens and he says, "Perfect," and we head into the other room with Brienne and Aaron.

Max stops beside me and lowers himself to the floor, knees up, his back against the wall. Brienne opens her mouth, as if to say sitting isn't a good idea, but I join him.

After a moment Brienne crouches beside me and whispers, "How are you holding up? Are you okay?"

"Right as rain," I say before I can stop myself, and Max chuckles.

"I'm fine," I say as Brienne looks confused. "You?"

She nods. "I was worried about you."

"Max is keeping me on track." I smile over at him, and he dips his chin and shifts, as if uncomfortable accepting credit.

Aaron finally sits, sideways facing us, his knees drawn up.

"I'm sorry," he says. "I'd say I'm sorry my dad's rich, but that just makes me sound like an entitled asshole. Which isn't to say I'm not, but . . ." He shrugs. "I'll at least apologize for having an asshole for a father, which means I come by it honestly. I'm sorry he's not getting the money faster."

"I'm not sure it would help," I say. "Even after he pays, our captors can stall for a while before the police will expect us to come out."

"He *will* pay," Aaron says. "He just doesn't want to be too quick for fear they'll raise the final price. Like I said before, he can afford it, and it's a smart business move. It'll also buy him leverage with me. Which he also needs. Get his kid to shape up and toe the party line."

"Stop crashing cars?" I say with a half smile.

"Nah, he's fine with that. I'm supposed to be a hotshot brat. Follow in Daddy's footsteps and make him proud."

When I raise my brows, he says, "I'm serious. I actually crashed the Rover on purpose. Even had a six-pack in the car and an open can in the coffee holder. Which is why I'm pissed off about this weekend. I did exactly what he expects, and he punishes me for it?"

Now Brienne and I both look at him.

"What?" he says. "Your families don't expect you to drink and drive and smash up a fifty-thousand-dollar car? Oh, right, sorry. You guys come from normal families."

"Not exactly," Brienne murmurs, looking uncomfortable.

It takes him a second to get it, but then he jostles her leg. "Sorry. Open mouth, insert foot. Especially when I'm feeling sorry for myself. Yeah, my family is screwed up. I crashed the Rover because I'm trying to convince my dad I'm just a normal bratty teen. I got in a fight with my girlfriend, dropped her off at the side of the road, bought some beer, cranked up the tunes and wrecked the car. Proving I'm the son he wants, and any evidence to the contrary was a one-time error in judgment."

"Uh-huh," I say.

He glances over. "He caught me in bed with Chris a few months ago. Chris and I have been best friends since grade school. Chris, by the way, is short for Christopher, not Christina."

"Ah."

"Yep. The world may be progressing, but in some circles, it's still the fifties. A gay kid is not what my dad wants for a son. That causes all kinds of inconveniences and complications, don't you know. So it's my job to convince my dad it was just teenage experimentation, indicating nothing but curiosity and a lack of judgment."

"Why?" Max says.

Aaron scowls at him. "Why what?"

"Why not just say this is who you are, so get stuffed, Pops. It doesn't seem as if you two get along anyway."

"Do you know what a conversion camp is?" Aaron asks. When Max frowns, he says, "You don't have them in Britain, I'm guessing. Lucky you. Mostly, they're religious, with therapy to 'straighten out' gay kids. Like this weekend, plus prayer. Lots of prayer. But there are others. There was one in South Africa a few years ago. Three kids died because they didn't get with the program. That's the sort of thing my dad was threatening. And as long as I'm under eighteen, he can do it. So I have two more years to play straight and then he really can 'get stuffed,' as you say. Just as soon as I'm sure my mom gets whatever money's coming to her."

Max nods and says, "All right. I get it," and Aaron relaxes, because Max wasn't challenging him—he really was curious.

"My father will come through," Aaron says. "He's dicking around, same as he wouldn't jump too quickly at a good investment opportunity. Which is what this is, in a way. He can't seem too eager."

"Even if it's his son's life at stake?" Brienne says.

Aaron shrugs. "You don't seize control of valuable assets and then torch them. We just need to stay out of their way long enough for him to cave."

I glance at Max. He says nothing, but I can tell by his expression he doesn't believe this, any more than I do. No more than we think Brienne's right and these are just messed-up guys who panicked and regret their mistake.

When Mr. Highgate transfers over the hundred-grand down payment, Gray will say it took too long. Highgate stalled and that wasn't a show of good faith and any agreement to resume freeing kids is null and void. He'll tell the negotiators we're all staying until the money is paid.

In a normal hostage situation, the negotiator would continue trying to arrange our early release, because that was the sure thing. He'd offer food, water, media coverage, helicopter transport, whatever it took to guarantee live bodies walked out that door. Except this is really a kidnapping dressed up as a hostage-taking. We have more than enough food and water to get through the weekend. There's no political angle, so no need for media. And I'm sure Gray has transportation all worked out. The only thing he wants is money, and I'm afraid even that isn't enough now. They'll take the hundred grand. Then they'll get the hell out, leaving nothing behind except bodies.

Pessimistic? Yes. Realistic? Yes, even as the thought makes me stifle a whimper, makes me want to curl up and put my hands over my ears and shout, "No, no, no!" But it's true and I need to remember that and not for one second give them the benefit of the doubt. Know they plan to kill us. Make damned sure they don't.

I say none of this to the others. I just take out the blueprint and study it, while Max looks over my shoulder.

"We need an escape hatch," Max says.

"Sure," Aaron says. "Or maybe a bulletproof bunker, loaded with guns and a direct line to the White House and pizza delivery."

Max doesn't even favor him with a look, just keeps studying the map with me.

After a moment, I look up sharply. "Guns. Didn't you have one, Aaron? We heard shooting."

"I grabbed one from the guy with the Star Wars mask, but it ran out of bullets."

"Where is it?"

"Back there," he says, waving vaguely. "Not much point in carrying it without ammo."

Actually, there was. I remember one of my dad's stories, about a time he'd been jumped by a kid and he'd pulled his gun—and knocked the kid out with it. I'd heard some of the guys, years later, teasing him about that.

*"And then there's Vasquez here, who mistakes his gun for a set of brass knuckles."*

*"Hey, do you know how much paperwork they make you fill out if you fire the thing?"*

*"Could have saved us some trouble if you did, Jim. One less gangbanger to worry about."*

One less gangbanger. Ha-ha. Dad always laughed along, but I knew paperwork had nothing to do with it. I remember, too, overhearing a couple of guys at a police BBQ saying Dad was soft on the gangbangers because he'd grown up with guys like that. Which was presumptuous and racist bullshit. Dad was raised in the suburbs. He didn't shoot that kid because he wouldn't shoot *any* kid. Wouldn't shoot any *person* if he didn't absolutely need to.

And, maybe, even if he needed to.

A gangbanger hadn't killed him. It'd been a forty-year-old woman in the suburbs, exactly the kind he'd grown up in. Ordinary neighborhood. Ordinary house. Ordinary family. Or so it seemed from the outside. Inside was a guy who liked to knock around his kids and his wife, and one day his wife took his gun and shot him and then barricaded herself and the kids in the house. Dad was trying to talk her into letting the children go. She shot him. Point-blank shot him. His partner jumped her, and the kids were safe and Dad was a hero. A dead hero.

"Riley?" It's Max, his fingers resting against my arm.

"We should get the gun. It makes . . ." I'd been thinking something else too, before I got distracted. Right. I turn to Aaron. "How many shots did you fire?"

"What?"

"Two," Brienne says.

"And there were two fired earlier," I say. "The gun holds more ammo than that."

"Then it wasn't full," Aaron says. "I tried a few times."

Brienne nods. "Even I did."

"Did you check the chamber?"

Blank looks.

"He's not going to come on this job with the cartridge half full," I say. "The gun's jammed."

"Can you fix it?" Max asks me.

"I can try."

Aaron points out, rightly, that there's no sense in all four of us leaving the safe room to recover the gun. He wants backup, though, and I guess it's natural that he picks the other guy in the group, but Max isn't happy about it.

"You know," Aaron says, "just when I think you're not an asshole, you go and prove me wrong."

"I could say the same about you, but I won't."

"You just did. I need backup, Maximus—"

"Really rather you didn't call me that."

"Sorry, Maximus."

"Seriously?" Brienne says, beating me to it. "This isn't the schoolyard, boys. If you two can't handle it, Riley and I will."

"I'm the one who knows where I left the gun," Aaron says. "I'm asking Max to help because I need backup."

"And only a guy can do it?" Brienne says.

"I'm not arguing about going," Max says. "It's just . . ." A quick glance at me. "Riley and I work better together. If you can tell us where the gun is, we'll go get it. Or you and Brienne can go. I would just rather . . ."

He trails off, and I know he's not keen to pair up with Aaron. I'm struggling for an excuse, a way to back him up, because the simple truth is that I don't want to be separated. Max is the one I trust. More than that, he's the one I care about. I'll do everything in my power to protect Brienne and Aaron, but Max . . . Max is different. The thought of him heading out there alone sets my heart pounding, but all I can think of to say is, "I'm fine with going. I'm the one who can unjam the gun." *I hope.*

"I think you need a break," Aaron says to me, and I'm about to argue, hotly, when his gaze slides to Brienne, and I understand what he's really saying. Of the four of us, she's still the most likely to crack, the one not completely convinced we can't go to Gray, say, "I give up," and survive. Aaron doesn't need Max with him so much as he needs me to keep Brienne calm and steady.

I glance at Max. He's figured it out, and he's not happy about it, not at all—his blue eyes darkening, his lips tight—but when I say, "All right," he only shoves his hands in his pockets and heads for the door.

I jog after him, and we pass through the interior door, Aaron hanging back to give us a moment. Max hasn't realized

I'm behind him yet, and he gets three steps into the other room before wheeling and smacking into me.

He jumps back fast.

"Sorry," I say. "I wanted to say goodbye."

"And I was just heading back to apologize for storming off in a huff."

"It didn't seem all that huffy," I say.

I offer a smile, but his return one is strained, his face still tight, and when I lay my hand on his arm, it's trembling. I squeeze it.

"Are you okay?" I ask. "And don't say, 'right as rain.'"

His lips twitch. "*Not* right as rain. Is that better?" He sobers. "I'm all right. I'd just rather not be separated."

"Are you feeling okay? Any symptoms? You *seem* okay."

"I am. Just being shirty."

"Whatever that means."

"Moody. Bad-tempered. A tad bratty too. I'm comfortable with you. I want to stay with you."

"Ditto," I say, and I lean against him, and he puts his arm around me, just a one-armed squeeze as I lay my head against his shoulder. Then the door opens, and I step back as Aaron comes out.

"Be quick," I whisper to Max. "No side trips looking for escape hatches. We'll do that once we have the gun."

He smiles, and it's a real one now. He squeezes my elbow and then takes off with Aaron.

**CHAPTER 17** "How long have you and Max been together?" Brienne asks, and I look back to see her peeking through the door.

"In therapy? A month."

"I mean *together*." When I start to protest, she lifts her hands. "It's probably against the rules, I get that. You've been keeping it a secret so you don't get in trouble."

"No, we're not—"

"That's why he was slow to say you should leave first. He was afraid if he jumped in too fast, they'd realize you guys were a couple. That's also why he grabbed you when he took off."

I shake my head. "We're not a couple. Really. We have two sessions a week together, and we've barely exchanged a dozen sentences. But when something like this happens . . ." I shrug. "You latch on to what you know. Familiar faces."

"He didn't want to leave you."

"And I didn't want him to leave. Aaron doesn't like him and . . ."

"Aaron's fine. He's not a nice guy pretending to be a prick, but he's a decent guy dealing with a lot of crap and maybe, yes, a little bit of a prick."

"We all are," I say. "Under the right circumstances."

She gives a soft laugh. "Something tells me you're the exception, Riley."

"No. I can be a total bitch. Once, I called a girl at school a really rude name, and she barely even deserved it."

She looks to see if I'm serious, and when I smile, she shakes her head. "I bet that really is the worst thing you've ever done."

"No," I say softly. "I've made mistakes."

Before she can say anything, I set up the boxes the way Max had them.

"That is smart, you know," she says. "He's a smart guy."

I smile over at her. "Even if he is a bit of a prick?"

"If I were that smart, I'd be a total prick. You're both smart. And brave." She nibbles at her thumbnail. "I don't know how you're doing it. Holding up like this. You have way more reason than anyone to be freaking out. But you're not. You're worrying about me. Worrying about Max. Taking charge. Making plans."

"Running on pure adrenaline, I think. Wait until all this is over, and I'll need a nice padded-room vacation followed by a lifetime of very expensive therapy." I glance at her. "Do you think I can sue the Highgates for counseling?"

I'm kidding, of course, but she doesn't smile. She looks away, her gaze dropping, and I shift, realizing that might have been in bad taste.

She wonders how I'm holding up. I wonder the same thing, and I'm afraid the answer really is adrenaline. That I don't have a core of inner strength—I'm just a scared little girl, cushioned by shock, ready to fall apart for good when this is all over.

I say I've never considered suicide, but that doesn't mean I don't see the abyss. It started after Dad died, when I dragged myself through my days following the carrot of bedtime. Weeks when all I could think was, *Keep going, Riley. Just a few more hours and you can run to your bedroom, close the door and curl up in the darkness, where no one can see you cry. Drop into the abyss. Wallow in grief and lose yourself there.*

It got worse after the Porters. The abyss is now wider and deeper, and it calls to me sometimes. The strangest times. I'll be walking down the hall at school, Lucia or another friend chattering away beside me, and all of a sudden I can't hear them. I imagine that the hall opens up and I just keep walking and fall into nothing. And it's a wonderful nothing, like jumping from a plane. Just letting go. Except I'm not jumping without a parachute. That isn't what I want—that hard and final stop at the end, that endless abyss. No, my fantasy is temporary. I drop into the abyss and shut off my brain and my feelings, and then I'll come back up when I'm ready.

As the abyss widens, though, I begin to fear that coming back to the surface may, someday, not be under my control. Because at the bottom of my abyss is not death—it's madness.

My greatest fear isn't that I'll kill myself; it's that I'll lose myself permanently. That it will all become too much, and my mind will snap, and I won't ever come back.

That's what I'm afraid of now. That I might think I'm on solid ground but I'm really on a bridge over the abyss, and with every step the moorings weaken, just a little, and as soon as I think I'm safely across, it'll give way beneath me.

"I'm kidding," I say finally. "About the therapy. We'll be fine."

She nods.

"What's your group like?" I say, to change the subject with the first segue I see. "I know you said you hadn't been in therapy long."

"This is my first group."

"Really?" I lean toward her and mock whisper, "It's usually not like this."

She laughs at that. Then she looks at me and says, "You are brave. I know you don't think you are. You feel like you did the wrong thing that night when you were babysitting, and it doesn't help when guys like Aaron make stupid comments. It's easy to second-guess when you haven't been there. It's like watching a movie and thinking you'd never make the heroine's mistakes, but that's because you're in the safety of your living room. You don't know what you'd do until you're there. Not really."

I nod and try to think of a way to change the subject, but she continues, "I've seen guns before. My brother isn't the only person in my family who has one. And I've probably seen more horror movies than I should. But when that guy shot Maria, all I wanted to do was drop and cover my head. Which is the stupidest and most useless thing I could have done. Then the guns kept firing and the blood was everywhere and people were screaming and . . ." She's breathing fast, bordering on hyperventilating, and I put my arm around her and she leans against me and whispers, "See? I'm the one freaking out and you're the one taking care of me."

"I'll freak out later. We can take turns."

When I look over, tears are streaming down her cheeks.

I twist to face her. "It's going to be okay. Aaron and Max will get the gun, and we'll figure a way out. We can do this."

She shakes her head so hard tears fleck my shirt. "*You* can do this. Me? I thought I was being tough. I thought I was being strong, doing the right thing even if I knew it wasn't, but it was what I needed to do. Family first, right?" There's a bitterness in her voice when she says that. Then she looks up. "Do you have a good family, Riley? I hope you do. I hope you have the best—" Her hand flies to her mouth. "Oh my

God, I can't believe I just said that. I am a total idiot. Your dad. I forgot about—"

"He was a great father," I say. "And I'm proud of what he did."

Even if I wish he hadn't. If I really wish he hadn't. No matter how horrible a person that makes me, I wish he'd just hung back with everyone else and hoped the woman didn't decide to kill herself and take her kids with her. Because that's what happens, as much as I can't imagine it. I remember talking to Dad about that once, when a guy in our city killed his wife and kids and himself, and the news said he'd left a note saying he did it because he loved them, and I'd been so mad, furious, because it made no sense.

Dad said that to some people, it makes perfect sense. The guy lost his job and was about to lose his house and all his savings over a bad investment, and he didn't see a future for himself, and he couldn't imagine how his family would survive without him. So he took them with him. Which wasn't love. It was the most horrible self-centeredness I could imagine. Dad agreed, and we'd discussed it, and I know when he went to talk to that lady, after she threatened to "end it all," that's what he was thinking—about that case and others like it—but I didn't care. Didn't care at all. I just wanted him here.

*Don't do this. Brienne needs you to be strong. Present.*

"My dad was amazing," I say. "My mom's great too. Even my sister's not bad some of the time." I try to smile for that, but I know it's a shitty smile, and then I remember what she was saying before I got distracted by thoughts of my dad.

"You said you thought you were doing the right thing. For your family. You mean therapy? They wanted you to go, and now, well, obviously . . ."

"I'm regretting it?" She tries for a smile and fails. Tears

fill her eyes again. "I don't need therapy, Riley. Or maybe I do. You know what? Honestly? I think I do. I think I need a ton of therapy if I ever agreed—"

She shakes her head sharply, and I'm not sure what to say, beyond *I don't understand*. After a moment, I say, "If there's anything you want to talk about . . ." and she gives a sharp bark of a laugh, and my cheeks heat, as I realize how lame that sounds, how trite.

"Talk?" she says. "Confess, more like. I will. Because that's as brave as I get, Riley." She takes a deep breath and says, "I didn't come for therapy this weekend. I came for you. To meet you. To talk to you. To get *you* to talk. That was the plan."

When she doesn't go on, I say, "Interview? For a school project? Or your school paper?"

"I wish." She wraps her arms around herself and sinks lower against the wall. "Believe me, Riley, I'm not the kind of girl who'd go the extra mile for a project. Or join the school paper. Or the school *anything*. And yet, I'm the good girl in my family. The black sheep who actually cares about school, not because I bust my ass to get A's but because I actually *go*, and I study enough to pass, which is as high as the bar gets for us. If I graduate high school, I'll be the first in my family in two generations. And they'll throw me a big party and tell me how proud they are of me." She laughs bitterly. "No, they'll probably set my diploma on fire to show me how worthless it is."

"I—"

"I'll tell you why I'm here, Riley. And I'll do it before you fix that gun, just in case you decide to shoot me for—" Her hands fly to her face again. "Damn it, I'm sorry. I am such a stupid—"

I take her hands and pull them down. "Don't say that. Just tell me."

It takes a moment. Then her gaze lifts to mine, slowly but resolutely, as if she is indeed peering down the barrel of a gun and trying very hard not to flinch. "My brother was one of the guys who went after that couple you babysat for."

I drop her hands. I don't mean to, but I do, instinctively, as my gut clenches and I manage a strangled "Wh-what?"

"He didn't shoot them. I swear he didn't. He isn't like that. He was standing watch. He owed these guys, and they needed a lookout. They said they were going to rough up that man—David Porter. Scare him. Only that's not what they did, and my brother didn't know what they had planned. I swear he didn't know, Riley."

"Okay . . ." I say slowly. "So you came here to talk to me . . ."

"I overheard my brother—River—talking on the phone a couple weeks ago, about the job. He caught me listening. He . . ." She inhaled. "He freaked. I tried to convince him to turn himself in, and he . . . well, he freaked out more. These guys have him scared shitless. Then, last week, he said he needed a favor from me. He'd heard a rumor that you knew more than you were letting on. That you were working with hypnotists and whatever to help you remember that day. He found out you'd be at this therapy camp, and he wanted to enroll me so I could get close to you and find out what you know. He arranged it all, pretending to be our dad."

I'm quiet, processing, wondering how he could have found out I was at this camp, but Brienne takes my silence for anger and hurries on, words tumbling out.

"I didn't know what else to do, Riley. I know that sounds cowardly. It *is* cowardly. But he's my brother, and I want to help him. What I really wanted was for him to turn himself in and cut a deal. I talked to someone who said if he told his story and identified the killers, he probably wouldn't even get jail time. But he's scared. So scared. He's not a bad person,

Riley. It's how we were raised, and it's all he knows. I was scared for him, so I agreed to help."

She continues, "I *was* going to find out what you know. I had to, so I'd know if River was really in danger. But no matter what you said, I was going to lie to River. I was going to tell him that you heard a voice—one of the killers talking to a guy outside, and you looked out the window and saw River. That way, he'd have real reason to turn himself in. Both because you saw him and because you could confirm that he was outside when it happened. That he wasn't the shooter. That . . ." She trails off. "That was my plan."

"I understand," I say.

She looks up, lips twisting in a wan smile. "No, you don't, Riley. But thanks for saying it."

"You didn't have a choice."

"Sure I did. I could have gone to the police. That's what you would have done."

"I have no idea what I would have done," I say softly. "It's like you said: you can't know until you're there."

"Maybe. But I'm sorry. I'm so sorry."

I put my arm around her. "Apology accepted. We'll figure something out once we—"

A box clatters in the other room, and we both jump as a voice says, "What the hell?" It isn't Aaron. Or Max. It's Gray.

# MAX: STUPIDITY

Stupidity: *behavior that shows a lack of good sense or judgment.*

A simple word. A vastly overused word. But in this particular instance? The perfect word.

*Mmm, not so sure there, Max. I believe the word you actually want is "dismay."*

*Dismay: to feel consternation and distress.*

*You didn't want to leave Riley behind, but it was, in fact, the proper response. The sensible one. Brienne is a bit of a mess, and she doesn't much like you—shockingly—but she does like and trust Riley. Therefore, logically, Riley should stay behind and make sure Brienne doesn't decide that what she needs—what you all need, really—is to throw yourselves at the mercy of your beneficent kidnappers.*

All right, perhaps leaving Riley was not stupidity. It still felt like it.

If he was being honest—let's, shall we?—he might admit that there was a distinct advantage to being separated from Riley. He's too busy worrying about her to think about himself.

*Is that possible? Truly, Max? Can it be?*

Not only is he worried about her, but that worry bolsters his determination to find the way out of this place.

*For her? Oh, that's so sweet. A little arrogant—that you have to be the one to save the day—but still sweet.*

There has to be another exit. There just might be. He cannot conceive of a building with front and rear doors and absolutely no other penetrable point of egress. An escape hatch, so to speak. Particularly if the building is being renovated. He doesn't expect to find a convenient construction hole in the wall—whoops, did we leave that open?—but perhaps some spot that could, with the right tools, be breached.

*You're stretching, Max. You know you are.*

It doesn't matter, because it gives him a goal. Something to focus on while trying not to worry about Riley, and between the two, he's almost too preoccupied to fret about his meds wearing off. "Almost" being the operative word, because, yes, every time he thinks that, his mind swings that way. Rather like forgetting a patch of spotty skin until you look in the mirror, and then it's all you think about.

Ah, those were the days, weren't they, old chap? When an outburst of *acne vulgaris* could put a damper on the entire day, particularly if there was some big social event on the horizon and a pretty girl you hoped to impress. Because, by heavens, if she saw spots on your chin, that would be the end of it.

Really put things in perspective, didn't it?

*Perspective: a particular attitude toward or way of regarding something.*

He really could laugh now, to think that he'd actually worried a girl might turn him down if his skin was spotty that day. Acne came and went, and by his age it had gone completely, having never been much of a problem even at the height of adolescence. Schizophrenia, though? That was a different story. Here today, here tomorrow, here forever, and it's nothing one can cure with a bit of cream. Even the meds are like the spot cover he'd once nicked from his mother's makeup drawer. They do an imperfect job of hiding the problem, and as soon as they wear off, nothing has changed.

At least with spots, a girl knows what she is getting. With schizophrenia, presuming the meds were doing their job, any remaining quirks can be chalked up to just that. Quirks.

*Quirk: a peculiar behavioral habit.*

Which he'd always had, and it never seemed to bother the girls. If anything, they found his quirks charming.

*Perhaps they'll find schizophrenia charming too.*

Yes, certainly. Who wouldn't, really? Perfectly charming, knowing your boyfriend could go off his rocker at any moment, mistake you for the victim of demonic possession and—

And that's enough of that. Focus, focus, focus. He needs to find a way out. For Riley.

*Hmm, perhaps you took my jest seriously. Dating is quite off the menu, Maximus. No matter what you do for her, once you're out that door, it's ta-ta for now. It has to be. You know that, don't you?*

Yes, he knows that. Which means that for perhaps the first time in his life, he is doing something for a girl he likes with absolutely no hope of reward beyond a smile.

But it's an amazing smile. Especially when it's real, not her smile-to-be-polite or her smile-to-be-friendly or her no-really-I'm-fine smile. When it's absolutely genuine, and it's for him. All for him, because he's done something to make her smile and maybe, for just a second, forget they are both completely snookered.

Because they aren't. There is still hope. A gun, and if he can focus, he'll find an escape hatch.

Back to the here and now . . .

Aaron has taken the lead, not surprisingly. Which is fine, because it means Max doesn't have to second-guess himself. Also that Aaron doesn't see him jump every time he catches a movement out of the corner of his eye.

Gray and Predator are still systematically searching the building. Keeping out of their way continues to be easy, because they seem to see no reason to be quiet. Men unaccustomed to being quiet. Men like his father, full of bluster and noise, because, by God, they shouldn't need to be quiet. Kings of the jungle and all that. Predators of the highest order. Only prey sneak about in silence. His father has the mind-set so ingrained that Max doubts he even notices he's doing it, thumping and banging around the house like the proverbial bull in a china shop. These men are the same. Otherwise, they'd be quieter, use subterfuge to sneak up on the kids. As it is, they're probably wondering why their prey always seems to be two steps ahead of them.

As they walk, Max has the map out. Aaron had turned once, seen him studying it and snorted, "You look like you're hunting for buried treasure."

"I am."

Aaron only rolled his eyes, but it was true. Hidden treasure, at least. The elusive extra exit point. Perhaps a door that isn't on the map. Or a room without an apparent door.

*Really, Max? This is a warehouse. Not the Castle of Otranto. Nor an episode of* Scooby-Doo. *You aren't going to lean against a fireplace and have a secret door pop open.*

He keeps looking, because he can, and because it focuses his mind on a task, and he's now doing remarkably well at that. Focusing.

*Just need an incentive, son. Some danger in your cozy life. I always worried about that with you—that you were a little soft, a little too fond of your books and your scribbled fancies. If you'd come and lived with me for a while, I'd have toughened you up. Now you see what happens. Get too comfortable in civilian life and it's not just your body that goes soft. Your mind does too. Rots.*

*Mmm, no, sir. While I hate to interrupt your pontificating, might I point out those weeks when you came to visit— just need a holiday—and spent half of it in your room, doing nothing? The nights when you came into my room and started shouting at me to start drill and Mum said you were sleepwalking? And the time you mistook me for an enemy combatant and— Oh, yes, sorry. We don't talk about that, do we? My mistake. As you were saying, sir?*

A secret door does not magically pop up as they walk.

*And where would such a door lead? You're in the middle of the building.*

Perhaps a basement?

*In a warehouse? That mind you're so proud of really is rotting a little, isn't it?*

There could be a basement, though he allows it is unlikely, given the past and present function of the structure.

*Consider the original function of the structure, Max. What was it?*

A warehouse. Used for storage. Which meant it was basically a box where one stores things. A single-story box split into two levels. They've added all the interior construction too. Walls, rooms, ceilings . . .

He slows.

Ceilings . . .

Aaron seems to sense he's fallen back and glances over his shoulder, his eyes narrowing in annoyance. Max picks up the pace and closes the gap between them as his mind whirs.

The second-story ceiling. It isn't any higher than normal. Which means there should be something above it. An attic. Or, at the very least, a crawlspace.

*Brilliant. And how will that get you out of the building? Do you expect a literal escape hatch up there, like on a holiday caravan?*

No, but it is, perhaps, a weak point. At the very least, a

spot where they can hole up indefinitely, because, as Riley said, there is only so long the police will wait before infiltrating. Grab bottled water and more granola bars, find the attic, and retreat there with their stash and their gun and wait it out.

*Mmm, forgetting something, Max?*

His meds. What if he gets everyone safely up there, and then his meds wear off and they're no longer safe, because the person who put them up there is as dangerous as the ones they escaped?

*Irony: a state of affairs or an event that seems deliberately contrary to what one expects and is often amusing as a result.*

Perhaps "amusing" is not the proper word here.

Aaron jabs a finger at a door ahead. Max catches a distant sound, one he can't quite make out, but he stops dead and turns.

"Max!" Aaron whispers.

"Did you hear . . . ?" He trails off, listening. The sound comes again. He turns sharply, but Aaron grabs his arm.

"Didn't you hear that?" Max says. "It sounded like one of the girls."

Aaron stops and listens, but Max can tell by his expression that he hears nothing. Neither does Max now. He catches slow and methodical boot thuds, coming from the other direction. Which means Gray and Predator are not near the girls or running toward them.

"They're fine," Aaron whispers. "Riley has it under control. Brienne might be conflicted, but she's not stupid. The faster we get that gun, the faster we get back to them and end this."

Max nods. They hurry into the room. Aaron looks around, as if forgetting where he left the gun. Max sees the barrel sticking from behind a box. He scoops up the gun. It's a Beretta . . . and that's about all he knows. Firearms never interested him, and his father hadn't pressed him to learn to shoot.

*Which is a good thing, isn't it? All things considered.*

Max has been around guns, though. Hard to avoid it as the son of a career soldier. While he grew up with his mother, there'd been holidays on base with his father. He'd seen guns. Seen them fired. Seen them cleaned too, the men sitting around talking and drinking a pint while they made sure their weapons would never do what this one apparently had.

As soon as Max picks up the gun, he can see the problem. The spent cartridge is jammed, sticking out of the gun.

"Shit. Why didn't I notice that?" Aaron says and takes the gun from him.

"*Careful*," Max says. "It may be jammed, but it's still a loaded weapon."

Aaron rolls his eyes. He starts cycling the gun to remove the cartridge.

"Riley can do that," Max says. "We need to get back to—"

"If it's an easy fix, we should get it working before we go."

Max shakes his head. Arguing with Aaron isn't going to make this go any faster. When the cartridge ejects, Max says, "There, now can we—"

"Just let me make sure it's clear."

Max is about to argue when Aaron starts removing the magazine, which is the smart thing to do, so he leaves him to it, moves toward the door and cracks it open.

*You didn't hear Riley, Max. It was voices in your head. It's called schizophrenia.*

I don't hear voices in my head.

*Then what am I?*

*Sod off.* He squeezes his eyes shut, and the voice goes silent. Which proves, he supposes, that it is indeed under his control. Not that he'd ever doubted it. What he doubts, as his doctor would say, is himself.

But I have to, don't I? That's the key to staying one step ahead of the monster. Question everything.

Which was bloody exhausting. Like a hamster on a wheel, endlessly running, never going anywhere. He couldn't keep on like this. He just couldn't.

*What's the alternative, Max?*

He doesn't answer. He knows the alternative, and the worse things get, the brighter it shines.

"We really need to—" He turns back to Aaron and sees him holding up the gun as he peers down the barrel. "Bloody hell," he says, and stomps toward him. "Are you mad? Give me—"

"The magazine is out, Maximus. It's not loaded. You Brits, you're all so scared of guns. It's a wonder you even have a military."

"We've had one longer than you," Max says. "And any time you'd like to compare national crime rates, I'm happy to oblige. Now put the gun away and—"

The gun fires. Max never sees how—whether Aaron's hand brushes the trigger or he turns the gun and hits it. Max doesn't even hear the gun fire, not with his thoughts half distracted, swallowing the *pfft*.

What he sees is blood. A spray of it. An impossible spray, seeming to shoot everywhere. He's hallucinating. He must be, because what he's seeing isn't possible. Aaron—the stupid blighter—was just holding the gun. Holding it and looking at it, and now . . .

And now Max is standing there, with blood dripping off his hands outstretched for the gun, the words "Just give me that" still on his lips, and Aaron . . . Aaron is gone. Vanished in an explosion of blood. Which is not possible. Not possible at all, and Max stumbles back, his hands going up, the voice in his head screaming *no, no, no*, that whatever he thinks he saw, he's imagining it because people do not explode in a spray of blood, *and you know that, Max, you know that, so just hold on, be logical and be smart. People do not explode. Just like they are not possessed by demons. Remember that and hold on. This time, you have to hold . . .*

That's when he sees that Aaron did not explode in a spray of blood. He's on the floor. With a hole through his throat, blood pumping from that hole.

Max lurches toward Aaron. His foot slides in the blood. There's so much of it. On the floor. On the walls.

Arterial spray.

*Who cares what it's called, Max?*

Arterial spray. Meaning the bullet hit an artery. He's bleeding out. That matters. That *matters*.

There's a hole through his throat, and Max knows that even if he can't see it because all he sees is blood, pumping, pumping, and there's so much—

Max is on his knees, reaching for Aaron's throat, to wrap his hands around it, because that's all he can think to do, but then he stops.

*Are you sure this is real, Max? Really, truly sure, because the last time . . .*

Max squeezes his eyes shut. Yes, the last time. Can't forget that. Can't ever forget that. But this is real. This is real, and there's a hole in Aaron's throat, and the only way he can save him is to wrap his hands around his neck . . .

*Just like Justin.*

Yes, damn you. Just like Justin, and if Max is wrong, he's wrong, but he doesn't think he is, and he sure as hell cannot sit here and reason it through, can he?

He puts his hand to the hole in Aaron's throat—or where the hole must be, where the blood gushes—and when he does, he can feel the blood pumping against his hand. Then he sees it pouring from the other side.

*Where the bullet went through, Max. Because that's what they do. They go through.*

Max yanks off his jacket and wraps the sleeves around Aaron's throat. Then he sees his face. Really sees his face. Aaron's eyes, wide. Aaron's eyes, empty. Aaron's eyes, lifeless.

*He's gone, Max. He's been gone for a while.*

No, he can't be. He's still bleeding. Look, the blood, it's still pumping—

*No, he's bleeding due to gravity. His heart has stopped.*

Bloody hell, he doesn't want facts unless they're going to help him save Aaron.

*Can't save him. Can't save anyone, Maximus. Are you sure he was the one holding the gun?*

What? Of course. Aaron was looking down the barrel—

*And you were reaching for the gun. Are you quite certain you didn't struggle for it? You have schizophrenia. You see things. Imagine things. Are you sure Aaron shot himself accidentally? Really, truly sure?*

Max squeezes his eyes shut, silences the voice and crouches there, holding the cloth against Aaron's neck, uselessly blocking the holes as the last of Aaron's lifeblood seeps through.

**CHAPTER 18** I hear Gray curse in the next room, and I'm on my feet, tugging Brienne along as she wipes away tears and follows. I crack open the hall door just enough to see Gray's back as he steps into the adjoining room.

I'm straining to hear their footsteps when Predator chuckles and whispers, "Almost missed that," and I know he's seen the second door. I don't wait for Gray's reply. I slip into the hall. Brienne follows. We tiptoe the other way. There's a corner just ahead, and I slink along the wall to it, while watching over my shoulder to be sure Gray and Predator don't come back into the hall before we make it.

Just a little farther. I can hear boots clomping around the other rooms as they hunt for us.

Three more steps. A voice. A grumble. Then Gray's "Come on out, kiddies," and I pick up the pace and dart around the corner and—

"Hello, Riley."

It's Predator. Standing right there. Smirking at me. I lunge, letter opener out, and I stab him. I don't even realize what I'm doing. It's pure reflex. A fencer's reflex.

I stab as hard as I can, and the blade sinks into his side, and he snarls, "You little bitch!" and I yell, "Run!" and when

Brienne hesitates, I yell it again as I yank the letter opener out, and I go to stab him again, but he backhands me and the opener flies into the wall, clanking, and I see the gun rise, and again I don't think, I just react. I spin, and I run.

I run as fast as I can after Brienne, already disappearing around another corner. But I'm not wearing shoes, and as good as that was for keeping quiet, it means I don't have any traction, and I slip and slide and that—*that*—is what saves my life. Predator fires, and I hear the suppressed shot, and it's too late to dive out of the way, but I'm skidding to the side, and the bullet only grazes my thigh. I keep running. By the time he fires again, I'm diving around a corner, and he misses completely, and then I see Brienne ahead, in a doorway.

I look back for Predator. I don't see him. I *do* see a trail of blood following me. I run past Brienne. She gasps and opens her mouth to stop me, but I race around the corner through the next doorway. Then I slap my hand over my bleeding thigh and run back to her, being careful to stay out of my blood trail.

I dart into the room with Brienne. She closes the door, and we retreat behind a pile of boxes. I'm limping now. It's more than a graze. Pain burns through my leg. I get behind the boxes and I sit and try to check the wound, but all I see is a rip in my jeans. A blood-drenched rip. The bullet isn't lodged in my leg—I saw it hit the wall. The wound is somewhere between a graze and a shot, leaving a gash that's bleeding steadily but isn't life-threatening.

I take off my belt and fasten it just above the wound. I have no idea if it *needs* a tourniquet—or even if I've done it right—but it seems to slow the bleeding. Then I take off my socks and stuff them into the hole in my jeans.

"Should have done that earlier," I say, waggling my bare toes. "More traction barefoot. You should take off yours too."

Brienne just stares at me. Then she blinks and, word-lessly, pulls off her socks and hands them to me.

"I don't need—" I begin.

She stuffs them into my pocket, as if for later. She doesn't say that, though. Doesn't say a word until she lifts her gaze to mine and says, "I ran."

"I know. That was the idea."

"No, I *ran*. I didn't think about anything else. I didn't think about you."

"Which is what you're supposed to do." I look her in the eyes. "This is about surviving, Brienne. About one of us get-ting out and bringing back help for the wounded. And if no one's left to help? Then the goal is for someone to get out and tell our story. Tell the police. Tell our parents."

"Yours maybe. Mine won't give a damn."

I want to tell her no, that's not right, I'm sure they will, any parent would, but that's bullshit, isn't it? It's a stranger talking from her own experience. I don't know Brienne's family, and I hope to God she just *feels* that way, as we all do sometimes, like no one cares. But I don't know the truth, and it would be condescending of me to say she's wrong.

"The goal is survival, Brienne," I say. "We're looking after each other as best we can, but you couldn't have helped me with him. If you jumped in, we might have both been shot. When I said run, I meant run."

She glances away, unconvinced.

"Please," I say. "If you want to do something for me, do this. Promise me that if I tell you to run, you'll run."

"*You* wouldn't."

"I will. If there's nothing I can do, I will."

"Promise?"

I nod. "If either of us says to run, the other will run. We'll get out. We'll get help. We'll tell our story."

"Okay."

She takes a look at my leg, saying she's taken first aid, and I tell her how I skipped it for a concert, and she laughs and says, "You really are a rebel," and I know she's teasing me, but I swear, if I get out of this, I'm taking that damned course, and maybe a few more. Which should ensure that I'll never need to use them, and if that's true, I'll never complain about wasting my time, not once.

My leg has stopped bleeding. I don't know if that's because of the belt, but I'm leaving it on to be sure. Brienne says the bullet gouged its way through, hitting muscle but nothing vital. Exactly as I expected. We plug it up with the socks while she jokes about the sanitariness of that, and I say at least it's not the guys' socks, and we both laugh, but it's a reminder, too, that the guys are out there, and they don't know where we are, and we need to get to them.

Until now it's been so easy, so damned easy. Like playing a video game where you start off winning every battle with barely a health drop, and then all of a sudden, you're hit with waves of enemies and you're dying constantly. Which is fine in games, where you don't actually die.

We've been sneaking around for hours, and every time we hear our enemy, we just need to duck into a room and wait for him to pass. This time, he's not passing.

Gray and Predator tricked us back there. They've upped their game, and my fake-out with the blood trail doesn't have them continuing along in the other direction. They're searching every room in the area, knowing we haven't gone far, and when I lean against the door, I hear them right there. The handle moves, and I'm holding it, and I frantically jerk my chin to Brienne. She grabs the knob with me, and whoever is on the other side jiggles it a little and moves on, presuming it's another locked door.

We're safe here for a few minutes. It seems best to wait and take off after they get farther away. I'm about to tell

Brienne that when the door flies open. It's Predator . . . in his stockinged feet.

I lash out. Again, I don't think, I just hit. All I have are my fists, but as I'm swinging I see blood on his shirt and aim right for it. Right for the spot I stabbed him.

As my fist makes contact, Brienne slams the door on him. It hits his arm and the gun falls. She dives after it as Predator grabs for me, and I hear Gray's booted footsteps, running from some other hall. I manage to elbow Predator in the injured spot again, and he falls back. Then Brienne fires.

I don't see where the bullet hits him. It *does* hit. I know that. I see him fall back. But we're both stumbling over him, getting into the hall as fast as we can.

We hear Gray coming, footsteps thundering along the hall. Brienne turns to me and says, "Run."

I shake my head and grab her arm and say, "No, come on," and she waves the gun and says, "I'll slow him down. Run."

"No, we—"

"You promised."

"This isn't—"

"Yes, it is." She meets my gaze. "Let me be brave, Riley. It's my turn."

I don't know if I would have run. I don't know if I *could* have. But she gives me a shove, and my wounded leg throws me off balance, and when I recover she's running the opposite way, toward the hall Gray is coming out of, and she fires and he lets out a curse, his boots squeaking as he stops short, and then she takes off, racing down the adjoining hall, and there's nothing I can do except go the other way, the way she wanted me to go, because if I follow her, then her distraction was for nothing. She has the lead. She fires again, so he'll know which way she went.

If I follow, she might shoot me by accident. If I follow,

he might shoot me on purpose. If I follow, my leg won't let me keep up, and I'll ruin everything. I'll get her killed.

So I run. I run the other way, and I barely make it around the corner when Gray appears. I peer past the edge just enough to see him going after Brienne. And there's nothing I can do except pray, and it's not enough. I know it's not enough, because God isn't there to solve my problems for me—He gave me the tools I need to do it myself, and right now those tools fail me. I can think of no solution to help Brienne. I can only run.

I get around the next corner when I hear that now-familiar *pfft* from a suppressed shot.

I catch the sound, and I hear a thump. The thump of a falling body. I swing my back to the wall, and I squeeze my eyes shut, and I pray like I've never prayed before.

Let that be Brienne's shot. Let her have killed Gray, and maybe I shouldn't think that—for her sake, because I don't want her to be responsible for a man's death, however terrible he was. Then I hear Gray mutter, "Stupid little bitch," and his boots clomp off down the hall, and I fall to the floor and cry.

# CHAPTER 19

I sit on the floor, my back against the wall, and I let the tears fall.

Brienne's dead.

Dead.

*Let me be brave, Riley.*

I hear Gray's words again, "stupid little bitch," and the tears evaporate in a wave of fury, and I leap to my feet, and I've heard the expression "I want to kill him," and I hate it, I've always hated it, never understood how anyone could say that in jest, because it wasn't jest. Never understood how anyone could say it in anger either, to feel that much hate for another person.

I do now.

If Gray were here and I had a gun in my hand—if I had *any* weapon in my hand . . . No, even without a weapon, if he came around that corner, I'd throw myself at him and I'd kill him any way I could, for what he did to Maria and Aimee and now to Brienne, for the unbelievable callousness with which he took their lives.

I clench my fists, and I want to stride down this hall, and I don't care how stupid it is, how reckless. I want to find him and kill him or die trying.

Which *is* stupid. More than stupid. Because Brienne is

dead, and she died saving my life, and now I'm going to throw it away on revenge?

I take a deep breath, stand and then sway there, my injured leg suddenly aching so much it can barely hold me up. It wants to give way, and I want to let it. Sink to the floor again and cry and wait for rescue. Pray for rescue.

Throw away Brienne's gift through revenge? Or by surrendering?

Neither, of course. I can do neither.

So I do the only thing I can: I set out in search of Max and Aaron. I suppose I should say I steel myself and wipe away my tears and set out, dry-eyed. I don't. But I do set out.

I barely notice the blood. Even when I do, there's a moment where I'm not sure what I'm seeing. It's just a thin, dark trickle of something like motor oil snaking from under a closed door. Then the emergency light reflects off the liquid, and I see that it's red, and my brain moves sluggishly, thinking, *Is this where we left Lorenzo? Or where I stabbed Predator?*

It's not, though. I know that, and the second I realize it, I'm lunging for that door so fast I fall against it. I throw it open, and I see a body on the floor, and there's blood, and oh God, there's a body on the floor and there's blood.

I stumble in, and there's light, and my gaze goes straight to it, and I see it's Aaron's penlight, in a pool of blood, shining on him. Shining on Aaron, lying on the floor, staring at the ceiling. I run to him, and I crouch beside him, but I can see it's useless. His eyes are open and his throat is covered in blood. And he's dead.

Aaron is dead.

Aaron, Brienne, Aimee, Maria, Gideon . . .

Max.

Oh God, Max. No, no, no—

I hear a noise behind me, and I turn, and there's Max, sitting on a box, staring at Aaron.

"Max?"

He looks up, and it's only then, when he moves, that *I* can move, and I throw myself at him. His arms go up to ward me off, but it's too late. I throw myself into his arms, and I hug him as hard as I can, and his arms go around me, and it's a tentative embrace, but I don't care.

I hug him and I bury my face against his shoulder and I let out a sob. He hugs me back then, squeezing me tight, and I feel him shaking against me, and when he speaks, he says, "I didn't do it," and I pull back, not sure I heard right.

"I didn't do it," he says, his voice barely above a whisper. His eyes are empty, dull with shock, and he's still trembling, and I realize what he's said and I say, "Of course you didn't—"

"He had the gun. He was trying to get it working. I told him not to. I should have—" He swallows. "I wasn't paying enough attention. He didn't listen to me, and I thought, *Sod him*, and I left him to it, and I should have stopped him. Made him stop."

"The gun went off," I say.

He nods. "I wasn't near . . ." He squeezes his eyes shut. "No. I *was* reaching for it, and I'm certain I didn't touch it, but maybe I did, maybe I knocked it or brushed it or—"

"You can't *brush* a gun and make it fire, Max," I say softly.

"But I *was* reaching. That's all I remember. I was reaching and he was looking at it, and it went off, and maybe . . . maybe I wasn't where I thought I was. Wasn't doing what I thought I was. It just went off, and I don't know how— The magazine's out, so how did it even fire?"

I cut him short with another fierce hug, and whisper,

"Stay here, okay?" and he nods. I back up, and I'm standing in the blood—it's everywhere. But I carefully back up while trying not to look at Aaron's body.

Aaron's body.

Aaron's dead.

I hear him talking about his father, the frustration in his voice, the hurt too, as much as he tried to hide it, and then I hear Brienne and—

I take a deep breath and hush the memories. I don't silence them. I can't. I shouldn't. But if I keep thinking about them, I'll go mad. Aaron and Brienne don't need my help anymore. Max does.

"You cleared a stovepipe jam, right? Cartridge sticking out?" I can see it on the floor.

"Aaron did. Then he removed the magazine."

"*After* he cleared it. *After* he chambered a live round."

He nods slowly, as if struggling to process my words. "R-right. Yes."

That explains the gun firing—and why Aaron would look down the barrel, presuming it was safe, the magazine being out. Now the question of where Max was at the time.

I look at the blood pool. Then I point to a spot just inside the door. "You were standing there."

"Maybe. I don't—"

"I'm not asking you, Max. I'm telling you. There's a void in the blood there, and then your footsteps through the spray, which means you were there when the gun went off."

"All right."

"And Aaron was standing where he fell. How tall are you?"

He blinks and I think he's going to ask why, but after a moment he says, "Six feet."

"Whew. I thought you were going to tell me in metric, and then I'd be screwed."

The corners of his lips twitch in something that can't quite be called a smile, but he relaxes, just a little. "We measure height in imperial, same as you."

"All right. You're six feet tall and Aaron was maybe two inches shorter. If arm length is roughly half of height, then the farthest you can reach each other is about six feet away. That"—I motion from the bare spot to Aaron's body—"is more like eight feet, and I'm sure he didn't have his arm extended toward yours, either. Meaning you had nothing to do with the gun firing."

Aaron is dead either way. But I do expect to see Max's shock and tension fade a little. If anything, though, his face tightens more.

"What if . . . what if it didn't happen like that?"

"Didn't it?"

"I—" He rubs his hands over his face. Aaron's blood is on them, streaking his cheek. "I don't know, Riley. Bugger it, I don't know. The meds . . . I get confused sometimes . . . I'm . . . I'm afraid . . ."

"That it didn't happen the way you think it did? That, what, you shot him?"

I'm being a little sarcastic there, maybe. Because of course he can't think that. How could he "accidentally" do that and forget it? No matter how foggy the meds might make him. For another thing, I've seen enough of Max to know there's no way he got pissed off with Aaron and shot him. But the look on his face says he isn't sure. It's shock. It must be, so I say, as carefully as I can, "Where's the gun, Max?"

"I-I don't—"

"Look. It's in Aaron's hand."

"All right. All right. All right." He's repeating the words fast, as if pushing off panic, trying to reassure himself.

"It's in his hand, and his fingers are still holding it,

and even if—I don't know—you had a psychotic break or something and shot him and tried to make it look like an accident, you couldn't get his fingers to hold it like that. Not after he was dead."

"Right. Right."

"Max? I need you to focus. You're all I have left."

As I say that, I realize what I'm saying, and his head shoots up, and I curse myself for breaking it to him that way. He says, "Brienne?" and my knees wobble. He's there in a second, grabbing me before I fall, and I collapse against him, and it's like I managed to hold it together just long enough to pull him back, and then I lose it, because she's dead. They're all dead. I can pretend Lorenzo might have lived, but it's been hours, and I know he hasn't. Everyone's gone, and once again, I'm alive.

Why me? Goddamn it, why *me*?

Survivor's guilt. That's what they call it in therapy, and I don't ever tell anyone that, because it sounds so selfish and ridiculous. *You feel bad because you survived? Think about those who didn't and stop your damned whining.*

But it's not whining. It's guilt. Horrible, suffocating guilt, because I lived and the Porters didn't. I got to go home to my family, and Darla doesn't have a family anymore. Now I'm alive in this warehouse and almost everyone else is dead, and all I can think is how unfair that is, because I don't deserve to live more than they did. If anything, I deserve it less—I already survived a tragedy once, now surely it must be someone else's turn?

"She wanted to be brave," I whisper against Max's shoulder. "She kept telling me I was brave and she wanted to be, and . . . and . . . I didn't do enough. Didn't say enough."

"What happened?"

I shake my head and pull back. "Later. We—"

"Tell me what happened, Riley. Get it out and then we'll go."

I do. I tell him how we attacked Predator, and Brienne took his gun and lured Gray off so I could escape.

"Then he shot her," I say. "I heard the shot and I heard someone fall, and then I heard him calling her . . ." *I can't say it. Won't say it.* "He said something and kept going."

"You're sure she's dead?"

"She must be. When he shot Aimee and she didn't die, he . . ." I stop. "But Aimee was still talking, so he knew she was alive. Oh my God, what if Brienne—"

I run for the door, but he catches me as my bare feet slip in the blood.

"We need to go back," I say. "I never checked. I never even saw her body. I just ran. Oh God, I just ran."

"Which was the right thing to do. We'll go back together. Carefully."

I nod and we start for the door. Then I turn and look back at Aaron. At the gun.

I take a deep breath. I don't want that gun. I really do not. But we don't get to make those choices here. Not if we're going to survive this.

I go back for the gun. I look at Aaron's penlight, still shining on him, but perversely, I can't take that—it feels like stealing. So I take the gun and then I reach down and brush a piece of hair off his forehead, and close his eyes and whisper, "I'm sorry," and then we leave.

## MAX: LUCIDITY

*Lucidity: the ability to think clearly, especially in the intervals between periods of confusion or insanity.*

Max's doctor says that he's almost always lucid. Which Max supposes is true, if you consider a lack of lucidity the true descent into madness. He doesn't spend much time in that realm, but it seems he circles the edges far too often, peeking over the border and judging the distance between it and himself, waiting for a burst of insanity to knock him clear over the line.

He has to think hard to recall the last time he'd trodden as close to the edge as he did a few minutes ago, when Riley came in the room. He didn't even hear her enter. What he'd heard was his name in her voice, the horrified way she whispered, "Max?" and he looked up to see her crouched beside Aaron's body, and it was like before, when Ilsa walked in on him with his hands around Justin's neck.

No, it was not like before. Not exactly. As much as he'd fancied Ilsa, it had been one of his usual fancies, rather like spotting a new pair of boots in the vintage shop and saying, "I wouldn't mind a pair of those." He was a young man who had little trouble winning young women, and that was like being a young man with a full wallet. He spent his charm freely, on this girl or that, never promising more than a bit of fun.

And no, not *that* bit of fun, not yet. He'd seen too many blokes fall down that particular rabbit hole, convinced they were just having that fun, until they had it with a girl who expected more and they felt like rubbish. Then there was his friend Harrison, whose bit of fun resulted in a pregnant girlfriend and an early exit from sixth form, because he was a decent bloke and had a sprog to pay for. No, Max spent his charm freely and widely—take in a film or a row down the river, maybe a romantic picnic, because girls seemed to prefer that to an evening in a noisy pub, and it'd win him easy kisses and often more, but before it went far, he'd lose interest and wander off. Next girl, please.

That was Ilsa. A girl he'd had his eye on and planned to invite to a film and perhaps a picnic if the film worked out.

That was not Riley. When he'd seen the horror in her eyes as she crouched beside Aaron's body, it was worse. So much worse. Because he cared about her. Really cared. And in that moment, he was certain he'd done it. That he'd hallucinated Aaron tinkering with the gun, as he'd hallucinated Justin's demons, and he'd shot Aaron. Somehow he shot Aaron, and Riley knew it and—

And then she'd hugged him, and he'd realized her horror was for Aaron's death. *Of course it was, you self-centered prat.* But that hadn't made him feel any better, because once he got the idea that he might have shot Aaron, he couldn't shake it, not until she convinced him—with logic and reasoning and proof—that he had not. Which was exactly what he needed, and she'd known it, and that makes him feel . . .

He waits for his inner voice to mock him for how he feels about Riley. It doesn't. The shock of Aaron's death has silenced it. Which was, these days, his version of lucidity. When he steps back from gazing into the realm of madness. When he stops doubting which side he truly stands on. Those rare moments when he says, "Stuff it," to the monster that has taken over his life.

*Sod off, schizophrenia. We're taking a little break here, you and me. Ta-ta, old chap. I need to focus. You can come visit later. I'm sure you will. You're not going anywhere. I know that, and right now I don't give a toss.*

While he goes to check on Brienne, he leaves Riley safe in a room with the gun. He suspects she'll be checking the weapon, making sure it won't jam when they need it most, but she doesn't say so—she won't mention it after what happened to Aaron. She doesn't stay behind willingly, either. But he insists, because he finally realized she was injured.

Injured? No, Riley has been shot.

He takes a deep breath and tries not to think about that. "Injured" is, in this case, if not the technically perfect word, the safest one, the one that won't get his heart pounding, thinking of how close she came to taking a bullet through the femoral artery.

But she hadn't. The injury is . . . he hesitates to say minor, because no gunshot wound is minor. She calls it a scrape. It is not a scrape. It is small enough to be manageable, for now, and also large enough to give him cause to leave her in that room.

"Gray might come back," he says. "To check on Brienne if he didn't before, and if he does and we have to run, and your leg gives way . . ."

"Then you'll keep running."

"No, I will not."

"You have to. That's the pact I had with Brienne."

"Too bad. The one you have with me says I'll stop if you fall, and if I fall, you will not stop."

"How is *that* fair?"

"It's not. That's life. Blatantly unfair. And that's our pact."

"No, if you fall, I'll stop."

"Then I'd better not fall. I, however, am not injured. You are. Now stop arguing and get in that room, because I'm not taking another step until I know you're safe, and if you come out . . ."

She waits, and then says, "What'll you do if I come out?"

"An undetermined threat. Always the worst sort. Rather like signing a blank check. Terribly dangerous. Now, stay, Riley."

"Woof."

"Good girl."

Her leg is only the excuse for putting her in that room. The real reason? If she hasn't seen Brienne dead already, then she doesn't need to.

Brienne is just around the next corner. She ran down it, and Gray came around the corner and . . .

No need to think of that. It won't do any good. Max jogs around the corner and sees her, lying sprawled, arms and legs akimbo.

*Akimbo: limbs flung out widely or haphazardly.*

He's heard the word before. Understands the meaning in theory. Now he sees exactly what it means, because it is the first word that comes to mind. Brienne looks like a rag doll dropped from the ceiling, her limbs every which way, her head turned to the side, her eyes shut.

Gray shot her in the back.

Coward.

Max snorts to himself. What does he expect? They *are* cowards. Which makes them no less dangerous. Perhaps more. Contempt is no defense against pistols at ten paces, a shot through the back of a running girl.

Coward or not, Gray won. An innocent girl lost.

Max looks for Predator's gun, but Gray obviously took it. He moves carefully past the blood. Yes, there is blood.

Less than with Aaron, but it soaks her shirt and seeps from under her. He crouches beside Brienne. Her eyes seemed shut, but he sees they're half open. He reaches to close them, as Riley did for Aaron. Her eyelids flicker, and he falls back.

"Max?" Brienne whispers.

"You're— you're—"

"Not a ghost," she says, her voice so faint he has to bend to hear it. "Not yet."

"All right. Just hold on. We'll—"

He starts to rise, but she whispers, "No." Then she licks her lips, her tongue rasping over dry skin. "Nothing you can do."

"No, we can—"

"Max. No. I . . ." Her eyes close as if it's a struggle to talk. "I can't feel anything. Can't get up. Just find Riley."

"I did. She's safe. I—"

"Good. Get her out. Get both of you out. That's your job."

"But—"

"Don't tell her I'm alive. If you do, she'll come back for me."

"I can't—"

"Someone has to get out. That's what she said. She's right. That's the goal. The only goal. Make something up. Tell her a story. You're smart. You'll figure it out."

"But you—"

"I'll keep playing dead. I fooled *you*, right?"

He says nothing. He can't. He's looking at her, arms and legs every which way, and that's how she fell, and maybe she's just staying like that in case Gray comes back, so he doesn't realize she's moved, but Max suspects that's not the answer.

*I can't feel anything. Can't get up.*

He looks at the blood on her back. At the hole in the middle of her shirt.

Shot through the back. Barely holding on. Will she make it? She hasn't said she will, hasn't given any reassurances, because she can't, because chances are . . .

*Don't think of that. Just don't.*

How can he leave her here? How can he tell Riley she's dead when she isn't?

*Make something up. Tell her a story. You're smart. You'll figure it out.*

He doesn't want to figure it out. He wants to fix this. Help her. Leaving is wrong. So bloody wrong.

Except it's not. It's the right thing to do, for him and for Riley, like they did with Lorenzo, and it shouldn't come to that—

*How the hell has it come to that? Can he still be human if he does it?*

And what is the alternative? No, *really.* What is the alternative? Brienne can't move. He could drag her into a nearby room . . . probably hurt her worse and leave a blood trail that will tell Gray not only where she is but that she's alive. That he needs to shoot her in the head. Like Aimee.

Max sucks in breath.

"Max," she whispers. "Please. The longer you wait . . ."

"I know. I'm sorry." *I'm so sorry.* "I'm going. We'll get out. I have a plan. We'll get you help."

"Good lad," she says, in an accent that's probably supposed to be English.

She manages a quarter smile, and he returns it. He starts to get to his feet, then he bends over and says, "Riley said you wanted to be brave. You are."

A real smile now. "I know."

**CHAPTER 20** Max comes back, and he doesn't say a word. He just shakes his head. I hug him, and when he hugs me back, it's fierce and so tight it steals my breath, as if he's holding on before I slip away like the others.

He whispers, "I'm sorry, Riley," and his breath hitches, and I hug him again. Then we separate and I say, "I have an idea," and he nods, a little distracted, still thinking about Brienne, and I'm glad I didn't see her like that, because I'm not sure I could have gone on if I did.

*See, Brienne. Not so brave after all. Just really good at faking it.*

"Predator is right over there," I say, pointing. "Just around the corner."

"What?" He spins to the door. "I wouldn't have put you in here if I'd known—"

"Which is why I didn't tell you. I'm fine. I have this." I lift the gun. "And I haven't heard a peep. Either he's dead or he's close to it. Did you see blood in the hall?"

His fair skin pales.

I hurry on. "Sorry. I know. Brienne. But—"

"No, just hers. He's still in there, then."

"With a cell phone."

"Right." He snaps his fingers. "Yes, yes, yes. Brilliant. Let's go get that, shall we?"

To get to Predator's resting place, we have to pass the hall where Brienne lies. Max gets up beside me then, and when my head turns that way, he prods me forward and blocks my view with "Don't, Riley," and he's right, of course. It feels cowardly not to look, but I don't. I keep going to Predator's room. The door is open, and when we draw close enough, I can see Predator's foot. He's exactly how we left him when we ran.

Did Gray not even come back to check him? Just called or radioed and, when he got no response, carried on? Hurt or dead, either way his partner was useless. No need to check.

I don't search for the phone right away, as tempting as that is. Max doesn't let me. He waves for me to wait and aim the gun. Then he prods Predator with his foot. A light kick. A harder one. A grunt of satisfaction when the bastard doesn't move. He searches for the cell phone while I cover him.

"Bloody hell," Max whispers as his pocket pat-down comes up empty.

Yes, Gray did come back. To get the damned cell phone. We do a more thorough search; but still find nothing.

I remember Predator's gun and ask Max, but he says Gray took it from Brienne. I remember everyone who's been shot with that gun. Murdered with that gun. Everyone dead. Everyone gone. No survivors except us. Well, and Sandy, who got out before—

"Sandy," I whisper.

"Hmm?"

"He's the one who let Sandy go. That means he had the keys."

"Yes!"

Max drops beside me, and we start patting Predator's pockets. He pulls out the keys, grinning, and I give him a thumbs-up and a return grin and—

Predator rolls over. The sudden move knocks Max back, and I'm swinging the gun up, but Predator's too fast. He's been playing dead and waiting for exactly the right moment, and when his hand comes up, I see the flash of metal. A knife. It's coming straight for me, and I try to scramble back, but he stabs me.

The blade goes in. I gasp. Max is on him. He grabs Predator by the hair and yanks him back. Predator slashes at Max. I swing the gun again, and it hits Predator on the side of the head, harder than I would have imagined. There's a crack, and I don't care what that crack means, only that it stops him mid-slash, and he crumples.

I hold the gun on Predator as Max makes sure he's unconscious. Then he sees the blood on my shirt. His eyes widen, and he fumbles to get over Predator's body, but I pull away, saying, "It's just a nick."

"Let me—"

"I'm fine. Just the tip went in." I point at the blade on the floor, and it is indeed only the tip bloodied, but more than that went in—it just wiped clean coming out. Max nods, chin bobbing as he stares at that blade as if reassuring himself.

"I'm fine," I say again. Which is not true. Not true at all. "We have the key."

"Yes. Right."

"Max?"

His head shoots up.

"Can you focus?"

A sharp shake of his head as he rubs his face. "Sorry, sorry."

"Don't be sorry. We have a gun and a knife and the key. We just need to get to the front door."

He blinks and turns to the door. "Yes." He looks at me again. "But you—"

"Right as rain."

He makes a face, but it's a Max-face, a little bit eye-rolling, sliding back to himself as the shock passes.

"Can we get out of here now?" I say. "It's after eleven, and I have a midnight curfew."

He smiles, shaking his head, and then says, "Then let's get you home, Cinderella."

I'm hurt. Really hurt. I try to figure out where the blade went, recall my basic anatomy lessons, but you know the problem with being a high school senior? All my biology labs have been on frogs and fetal pigs, and that's not nearly as helpful as one might imagine.

The pain comes with every breath. It's not a ripping, tearing, oh-God-I'm-dying pain, but it tells me that the blade nicked my lung and maybe more, because it's definitely not a tickling pain either.

I follow Max so he won't see me wincing with every breath. When he does glance back and catch me, I make a face and give an annoyed wave at my leg instead. That works. My leg is going to hurt, but there's no way it's a life-threatening injury.

Is the stab wound life-threatening? I have no idea, but it doesn't matter, because we're fifty paces from the front door, and as soon as we throw it open, there will be an ambulance waiting. An ambulance and Mom and maybe even Sloane, if she's decided this is worth giving up her Friday night plans for.

I chuckle at that, and Max glances back, but my smile reassures him and he returns it and shoots me a thumbs-up, and I mouth, "Right as rain," and he smiles and as soon as he turns away I exhale and let myself wince.

I have one of Brienne's socks under my shirt, and I'm holding it pressed to the spot. It stanches the bleeding. It helps that I'm wearing a navy blue shirt—in the dimly lit hall, it's easy to miss the fact that my shirt is now blood-soaked.

We're almost there. We've slowed, because we don't know where Gray is. Either we're too far away to hear his footfalls or he's finally wised up and taken off his boots.

The front hall is just ahead. Max shoots me back a reassuring grin, catching me off guard, and I fake a stumble, as if that explains my grimace. He still pulls up short, alarmed, but I whisper, "Stubbed my toe. Just what we need, huh?" and he nods, not quite looking convinced, before glancing forward to reassure himself we're close. We are. So damned close that when he peers around the final corner I expect Gray to leap out. I expect him to leap from every door we pass. He doesn't.

We reach the front, and Max takes the keys, holding them tight and silent with one hand while plucking out key after key to try in the lock.

First one? No. Second? No. The third goes in and Max exhales a sigh of relief. Then he turns it and—

Nothing. He keeps turning, faster now, and yanking, and I lean in and whisper, "Back door," and he shakes his head and says, "We need to get you out this one. It'll work. I can—"

"No," I say. "I mean that the key is for the back door. That's why it fits but won't turn."

"Right. Right."

He inhales, calming himself. Then he tries the next key. It doesn't fit. The fifth one does, and the knob turns, and Max shudders then as he exhales. I reach over and squeeze his arm, and whisper, "We did it," and he turns to me, and his smile—that smile—his whole face lights up and he reaches out, hands to my face. Then his gaze drops to my shirt, though, because at that distance he can't fail to see the blood. I can *smell* the blood.

"That's not a scratch, Riley. What the—?"

"Max?" I point at the door. "Paramedics."

"Right. Yes. Of course."

He turns to open the door, but I touch his arm again and say, "Once that door opens . . . I don't want us to go our own ways. I'd like to talk."

He looks over sharply, and my cheeks heat because I know that sounds lame, so I wave for him to open the door. He shakes his head and steps back with a little bow, motioning for me to do the honors. My heart is hammering and it feels like Christmas morning, me bouncing at the top of the steps with Sloane, her acting so calm and "whatever," like Max is now, but when I look into her eyes I can see the excited kid there, and I see that now in Max's.

When I reach for the knob, he leans over and whispers, "I'll be here, Riley. To talk. Whenever you need it."

I smile and pull open the door and then throw up my hands, braced for the light and the shouts and—

Darkness and silence.

I've opened the door into an empty front parking lot.

Which isn't possible. Not possible at all.

I walk out. Behind me, Max whispers, "No. No, no, no." I keep walking, because there must be people out here. A whole SWAT unit and a hostage negotiator and probably half the cops in town. Plus our families. Our families and the media and gawking strangers, lured in by the siren's call of the chaos.

But there are no flashing lights. No police officers. No family members. No reporters. No onlookers. An empty, dark and silent parking lot.

Then Max whispers, "Riley!" and he runs for me. He

grabs my arm just as I see a figure walking around the corner of the building. A figure with a lowered gun.

Max yanks me back inside.

Go back in? *No.* I want to wrench the door open and run outside. I don't. I let Max tug me toward the nearest room. He opens the door and pulls me inside, and when the door closes, it's dark again until he turns on his watch light.

He motions me to the wall behind the door, and we crouch there in silence. Then, after a moment, he says, his voice barely above a whisper, "Tell me it's real, Riley."

"What?"

He shifts, turning to face me, and his pupils are dilated, the fear in his face worse than any I've seen so far, and my heart starts to thump.

"Max?" I say.

"It's not real, is it? It can't be. No one out there? I'm imagining it. I'm hallucinating."

"What?"

"Tell me it's real or tell me it's not." He shakes his head sharply. "Bloody hell, does that even make any sense? How can you tell me it's real or not real if you're part of it? If you never came into that room after Aaron died? If Brienne's not . . ." He sucks in breath. "Or maybe she is. But maybe you didn't get stabbed, which is good. But then we didn't find the keys, either. Of course we didn't find the keys. Bugger it, that was too easy. Much too easy, and I knew that, which is why I imagined you got stabbed, because it can't be too easy. The good with the bad. That's how a proper story goes. We found the keys, which is good. But you got stabbed, which is bad. It wasn't too deep, which is good. But then there was no one outside—"

"Max? You're scaring me."

"I know, I know." He rubs his fingers over his closed eyelids. "I don't want to. Can't. Need to keep it together.

Don't want you to think I'm . . . But I am, right? I am, and there's no denying it. No pretending I'm not. Just another boy, for a while. A boy with a girl. Lovely fantasy, but it doesn't last. Can't last. Isn't real."

"Max?" My pulse races, and I'm trying not to freak out. That's what he's doing. Freaking out. I need to pull him back.

He goes still, his fingers against his eyelids. I open my mouth to tell him to relax, just relax, we're almost out, but his eyes fly open and he says, "Tell me a secret."

"What?"

"Tell me a secret I wouldn't guess. If I could guess it, then that means I'm only imagining you saying it and—"

"I'm glad Darla Porter moved away," I blurt.

He goes still and his brow furrows.

"The little girl whose parents died," I say. "She went to live with her grandparents in Arizona, and I was glad, because it means I don't have to ever see her again. I'm certain she hates me, blames me for what happened, for not saving her parents, so I'm glad she's gone, and I know that's cowardly—"

I'm babbling, barely hearing what I'm saying, and then he's got my face between his hands and he's kissing me. Just a press of his lips to mine, stopping me mid-sentence, and then he backs up, but barely, still close enough for me to see nothing except his eyes. His thumbs rub against my cheeks, wiping away tears I didn't know were there.

"I won't say she *doesn't* blame you," he says. "Everyone must tell you that, and it doesn't help, does it?"

I shake my head.

"It doesn't help, because they don't know if she does or doesn't, and neither do I and neither can you. But I do know you aren't to blame. And I do know *that* doesn't really help either, despite everyone saying it. I wish you didn't feel that way, Riley, but I understand why you do." He gives me a quick embrace, arm's-length so he doesn't hurt me. Then he moves back. "Thank you. I'm sorry that I . . . I stumbled a bit there."

"We all do sometimes."

He nods. "Some of us more than others. But thank you for pulling me back. And thank you for being so good to me."

"You deserve it. Most of the time, anyway."

He chuckles as we part, and I try to cover another grimace of pain as I say, "But you owe me a secret after this."

I'm teasing, but when I say it, his expression falters, eyes clouding, and I start to make light of it, ensure he knows I was kidding, but then he says, "I do."

"You don't have to. I was just—"

"No, fair's fair. And I should, anyway. After all this. Best to get it out in the open, though it might be a little more than you expect."

I think of his father, of what I suspect. "I might already know . . ."

I trail off and wish I hadn't said that, because I don't think he'd want me speculating, but instead of withdrawing, he smiles, and this is a new smile, even better than the last. This one stops me in my tracks. It's a little bit uncertain, but mostly it's pleased with an undercurrent of something like hope, cautious hope, and it's like ripping off a mask and seeing what's under it, that bottom layer, and I stare at him for a moment, and when I pull my gaze away, I can feel my cheeks heating, because I see that smile, and there's a little bit of me that doesn't *want* to walk out the door now, that knows everything will change once we do, and it's not just that I want to stay in touch, that I want to talk. It's more. And I'm afraid that after we walk out that door, I'll never see that smile again.

I turn away, but I move too fast, and I gasp and stumble, and when I go down, I cry out. I can't help it. *The pain. Oh God, the pain.*

Max drops beside me, helping me up as he's cursing and saying, "What the hell am I doing? Not the time for me to lose it. You don't need that; you need a bloody paramedic."

"There isn't one out there."

He shakes his head. "There must be. I saw someone coming around that corner, and I panicked. My fault. Being daft. The police are out there. They have to be. They've just withdrawn. Now let's get you . . ."

He's opening the door, and he trails off, and I think he hears Gray. But he's looking to the side, and I follow his gaze, and I let out a yelp, my hand flying to my mouth as I do.

I see what he does and there is a moment when I feel what he must have, earlier. That this is not real. Cannot be real. And here is the proof. Here is . . .

It's Sandy.

Sandy's body. Slumped over a box. A hole in her forehead. A perfect hole in her forehead.

**CHAPTER 21** "Th-they killed . . ." I can't finish. "Predator. He took her to the front door. And then he . . . But that's not . . ." I turn. "Max?"

Now I'm the one pleading, wordlessly, for reassurance. *Tell me I'm seeing things. That it's all too much, and I've snapped.* But the look on his face says otherwise.

Before he can say a word, I catch the clomp of footfalls. Max grabs my hand. Not my arm now. He takes my hand, and we race out of the room, and he yanks open the front door, and when he sticks his head out, he curses. Then he pulls me through, and I see the figure from earlier. It's not a guy holding a gun. It's a homeless man with a bottle.

Max drops my hand and runs to the man and says, "Is there anyone else here?"

The man backs away.

"Please," Max says. "I'm not going to hurt you. Just tell me, is there anyone here?"

The man continues retreating, his hands raised now, his gaze fixed on Max, who's barefoot, his shirt smeared with blood.

"*Was* there anyone?" Max says. "Please—"

That's when the man sees the gun dangling from my hand. He runs, and Max starts after him. Then we hear a

"Hey!" and I see that the door didn't shut completely behind us. Gray's footfalls pound down the hall. I slam the door, and that only makes it worse, the sound reverberating. Max is back at my side now, yanking me away.

We run. That's all we can do. There's no one out here. No one except a homeless guy with a bottle, and he wouldn't be here if there was a SWAT team positioned around the corner.

No, be honest, Riley. There can't be a SWAT team poised around the corner, because you'd hear them. You'd see the lights. There's no reason for them to hide.

There's no way they packed up and left. No way Gray promised them Sandy, and then Predator decided to shoot her instead, and the negotiation team just let that go.

There is no SWAT team. There never was any SWAT team. Never any hostage negotiator.

How is that possible? How? We—

I fall.

I don't stumble over anything. I'm running and I just drop because the pain is unbelievable. I try to ignore it. We need to get farther, to get away, and I can't slow Max down, can't let him know how much I'm hurting. Can't let him see that every running step is like a knife through me, every breath burns, and fresh blood is gushing from the stab wound. I'm pushing and I'm pushing and . . . and then I'm not. Then I collapse.

"I've got you," Max whispers as he crouches beside me. "I've got you."

*I know.*

"Just a little farther," he says as he looks around.

I struggle to focus over the haze of pain. I was letting him lead and hadn't even seen where we were going. He'd cut left, past the warehouse and into the ruins of a demolished building. That was the only nearby "shelter" in any direction. The nearest buildings are a cluster at least a hundred feet away.

"I-I can't," I say, and it physically hurts to admit that, but I have to. I can't lie. I can't pretend. For his sake, I can't or we'll be halfway between this bit of sheltered ground and those buildings and I'll collapse for good.

"Is it your leg?" he says. "You can lean on me."

He's moving to check my leg and the moonlight catches the front of my shirt. It shines wet. Soaking wet. He touches it and lets out a string of profanity edged with panic as he tugs up my shirt.

"No," he whispers. "No, no, no."

"Just find me a place and go for help."

"I knew it was bad. I saw that. Bugger it, I *saw* that."

"Max?"

My breath comes hard and ragged now, and there's no way to disguise it. I start to tell him again just to help me get to a better spot. That's when we hear the tramp of Gray's boots.

Max picks up the gun. He aims it in Gray's direction, but I smack my hand against the barrel.

"Don't," I say.

"I'm not going to let him find you, Riley," he says. "And after everything he's done, I don't care if I kill him. In fact, I'd be quite happy—"

"No," I say. "It's too far away, and if you miss, he'll know exactly where we are."

Max gives a strained laugh. "The logical answer. All right, then. But if he comes closer, I *will* shoot him."

We peer over the long grass and rubble. Gray stands in the parking lot. He's swearing loudly enough for us to hear every word. Then he turns toward the closest of shelter: this demolished building.

I reach for the gun. "I'll do it."

"No. And we're not fighting over the gun, either. If someone's shooting him, it's me. I can— I have— It'll be better if I do. They can claim . . ." He swallows. "Never mind. I'll do this."

"I can aim. I can shoot."

"Too bad. You're not."

He waves me to silence. I don't want him doing this, but I don't know how to get the gun from him without doing something stupid and dangerous, and he's lining up the shot, and I'm thinking madly, and . . .

A bottle drops. It clinks to the pavement and rolls, and I know it's the homeless guy, maybe peeking around the corner to see what's going on. All Gray hears, though, is a noise, and he turns, his gun rising, and the homeless man lets out a yelp, and his footsteps thunder as he runs. Gray follows.

"We need to get over there." I point at the nearest buildings. "Quickly."

Max nods, and he puts his arms under me, as if to carry me, but I manage a choked laugh, one that I swear is going to make me pass out from pain.

"Nice try, but no," I whisper. "Just help me up."

We rise as soon as Gray turns the corner of the building, vanishing from sight.

I took acting lessons a few years ago, knowing my mother dreamed of me on the runway, and remembering her commenting once that acting lessons helped. I will not say I was good at it—I barely landed a third-string place in the school play. But tonight, as we make our way from the ruins to that building, I call on every iota of acting ability I have.

Each step rips through me. My brain screamed for me to stop, just stop, that I'm making it worse, but I have to keep moving, as fast as I can. As fast as Max will let me. My arm is over his shoulders and his is around my waist, supporting me and trying to slow me down, but I won't let him. Any second now, Gray will realize he's chasing the wrong person. Any second now.

*Oh God, I can't do this. Can't, can't, can't.*

Will, will, will.

Fifty more steps. My shirt is soaked with blood and I feel more running down my stomach.

Twice in those fifty steps, the world fades and I almost lose consciousness. Then, as soon as we reach the first building, whatever willpower I had collapses in on itself. I stumble and then . . . and then nothing. I black out.

I come to with Max over me, frantically trying to wake me. *Please, please, please just wake up, Riley, don't do this, not now, we're there, we're finally there, just come back, come back to me.*

That's why I do it. I come back to him, for him, because I owe him, and maybe that makes no sense, but in that moment it's what counts, that he's in a panic and I need to be okay for him.

Except I'm not okay. I'm really, *really* not. But I manage to surface to consciousness and my eyelids flutter open, and I get my reward then, the biggest sigh of relief, his blue eyes flooding with it as he leans over me, his skin so pale that his freckles seem like connect-the-dots across his nose, and I focus on them, my brain loopy, like the time I had nitrous oxide, and I lie there, imagining tracing constellations from those freckles.

I reach up and brush back a piece of his hair and realize he's lost the band I gave him, it's fallen out or mostly out, and I tug off another and hold it for him, and he takes it and he just shoves it over his own wrist, then he hovers there, over me. He bends and his lips press against mine, not a kiss, not really, just that quick press that tastes of sweat and fear and relief and yet still fear, and my mind keeps looping around, not quite able to take hold.

Then he's fussing, making me comfortable as he says he'll be right back, just going for help, be right back and here's the gun, and try not to move, there's no sign of Gray, just wait and . . .

Except I can't wait. Can't. I wish I could, but I can't. I keep going around and around, and each time I'm a little closer to the abyss, only it's not the same one as before, not a temporary resting spot for my overburdened brain. I know what it is. I know what's happening.

Dying. I'm dying.

I should fight. I want to fight. But I already did, and there's nothing left, and Max is rising now, and then I realize what's about to happen, that he's going, leaving me alone, and that's when the fear hits, the animal panic, as I think of my dad.

I grab Max's hand. "No."

He squeezes mine. "I won't be gone long."

"No. Please, no."

He tries to tug again, but now I do hold on, with everything I have, and the tears come, and he sees them and kneels beside me and whispers, "I won't be gone long."

"Don't leave me. Please. I-I-I'm not going to . . . I can't . . ."

I don't say it, but he knows and fresh panic sparks in his eyes. "No, you're fine. You'll be fine."

"I'm not. I won't be. Don't leave. Please, please, please. I don't want to be alone."

He looks around frantically, as if a car will suddenly appear. An ambulance stocked with paramedics.

"Max? Please. Just stay with me. It'll only be a minute."

That ignites the panic into full-blown fire, and he turns to me, saying, "No. Don't say that. You're fine. You'll be fine. We can do this. Just hold on. You'll be all right." He squeezes my hand and leans over me. "I swear it, Riley. You'll be all right."

"Right as rain," I whisper.

And everything goes black.

# MAX

Max runs headlong down the empty street.

Empty. Why is it empty? How the bloody hell can it be empty?

Because it's almost midnight in an industrial area, and everyone is carrying on as if nothing happened, because for all anyone knows, there's a lovely little group therapy weekend happening at the former warehouse up the road, and really, that's none of our concern, so let's just carry on, shall we? Nothing to see here. Just a group of barmy teens quietly enjoying some much-needed therapy. Basket weaving, perhaps.

He wants to scream. Scream as loud as he can for someone, anyone, to get off their arse and help him.

Please, please, please help me. Help her. She's dying.

No, she's not. She's just unconscious.

*She's dying and you bloody well know it, and if you pretend otherwise, well, then you've got no reason to light a fire under your own arse and get her help.*

That's what he's doing. Running faster than he's ever run in his life as he searches for a light, a car, anything.

How can there be nothing?

*There is, so just keep going.*

He *would* scream if he thought it would help, if he thought anyone would hear except Gray.

Then there's a light. Is that really a—?

Yes!

He veers so sharply he stumbles, but he rights himself

fast and tears down the side street, and the car—the lovely and wonderful car—turns his way. Comes right for him. He runs into the road, waving his arms and saying, "Stop! Please stop! She's hurt!"

And the car swerves . . . to go around him. To steer past the crazy barefoot boy covered in blood.

He throws himself at it. Doesn't think. Just throws himself onto the bonnet as it slows to get around him. The car screeches to a stop, and he slides off, and there's pain.

Don't care about the pain. Really, really don't.

He lies there, motionless in the street, his eyes cracked open just enough to watch a man get out of the driver's seat—a chubby middle-aged man. He walks to Max and looks down. He gets out his mobile and then he stops. Pauses and looks around, as if considering whether he should call for help or drive away as fast as he can.

*Here, old chap, let me help make up your mind.*

Max lunges, grabs the guy by the legs and wrenches. The man goes down, flailing. Max hits him. Doesn't care where. Doesn't care how hard. Just cares that he goes back down. Then Max grabs the mobile and limps off as he dials 911.

## MAX: PERSPICUITY

*Perspicuity: ability to give an account or express an idea clearly.*

That's not something Max had trouble with before the diagnosis. Whatever the jumble in his brain, when he opened his mouth, he was able to formulate his thoughts coherently. It was like standing in the eye of the storm, chaos all around but calm within, when he chose to find it.

Even during the shambolic year post-diagnosis, perspicuity was not a problem, not unless he was attempting to put into words how he felt about his new life, but that was emotion rather than thought or logic, and so it was a very different thing. A messy thing: emotion. Rather like a corner of his room that he allowed to get a little jumbled and soon the disorder was creeping outward, devouring everything, disrupting everything. Like schizophrenia itself. Terribly disorderly, rendering him susceptible to emotion in a way he'd never been before.

And so it is here, as the paramedics tend to Riley—one rushing back and forth to the lorry, the situation clearly critical—and this gormless police officer keeps hammering him with questions, and the words coming from Max's mouth are not indicative of his usual perspicuity, not at all.

Kidnapping and masks and deaths and injuries, and bloody hell, just go there, help Brienne and whoever can be helped and leave him with Riley. He needs to stay with her.

"Your friend is getting the best medical care," the constable says, in his laconic way, as if Riley has twisted her ankle and, really, Max is making far too big a deal out of it.

"No, she's getting *paramedic* care. The care of those with a fraction as much training as a medical doctor. However, I would still like their opinion on her condition. Just let me—"

"I need the whole story first. Start from the beginning, son."

"I am not your son." Max clips his words, allowing his proper accent to slip out. The upper-class toff accent. His mother's accent, and one he'd learned from the cradle and then worked very hard to lose, because so many others worked hard to learn it.

*Contrary as always, Max, old boy.*

But now it comes out, that better-than-thou tone.

"Here is what you need to know," he says. "We were part of a supervised overnight gathering. There was a kidnapping, with no apparent attempt to contact our parents or to extort cash or influence. In the aftermath, eight people were shot, including Riley. Five are dead. Two were still alive when we last saw them. However, given that you seem in no rush to check on them, they may no longer be, and if that costs you your badge, I sincerely hope it is only the beginning of the price you'll pay for your negligence."

"We've sent a car and called for a second ambulance."

"Excellent. Then we are done here. I am going to accompany my companion—"

"You're going to accompany *me*, back to the police station, where we can settle this."

"Settle what? I was the victim—"

"You seem very calm for a victim."

"Two minutes ago you were telling me to calm down, because I was clearly distraught. Now I've done as you asked, and you're faulting me for it?"

"People don't switch that fast."

Max glances at Riley being loaded into the ambulance. They have her on an IV. That's good. But the looks on their faces are not nearly as reassuring.

He starts toward her, completely forgetting the constable.

The officer grabs his arm. "I said people don't do that, boy. You can't go from flipping out one second to acting like you're the freaking king of England the next."

"That would be the king of the United Kingdom," Max says. "There hasn't been a king of England since 1700."

The man screws up his face. "What?"

"Correcting your ignorance, which, yes, I can do, only minutes after being nearly incoherent with worry. It's a special talent. It does not mean I'm any less worried, but simply that I can rein it in to tell you what you need to know. Which I have done. If you require more, you may follow me to the hospital."

"May I, your lordship? No, you'll follow *me*, into the back of my cruiser, and you'll—"

Max collapses. He times it so one of the paramedics just happens to be glancing his way. The woman races over as he sits up with one hand to the side of his head.

"Wh-what just happened?" he says.

"That's what I was going to ask," she says, shining a light in his eyes.

"I-I don't know. I've been feeling woozy, but I didn't want to take you away from Riley." He starts pushing to his feet. "I hit my head when we were inside. I should probably see a doctor. But you go on with Riley. She's the . . ." He staggers and the paramedic catches him. "She's the important one. I'll be fine."

The constable snorts. "Of course you will be. Once you recover from that pratfall."

*Not so gormless after all. Good show, old chap.*

It doesn't change anything, though. Max fakes disorientation well enough that the paramedic insists he ride along so she can check him out. The constable protests. She snaps at him that he can follow if he wants, but she's taking Max. She helps him to the ambulance. He resists all urges to smirk back at the constable.

*Big of you, Maximus.*

It is, isn't it?

As they reach the ambulance, though, any surge of self-satisfaction ebbs fast, because that's when he sees Riley. She's pale and still, hooked up to the IV, with an oxygen mask over her mouth and nose. He scrambles into the back to get beside her, ignoring the male paramedic's "Whoa, slow down there." He sits beside her and takes her hand. It's cool to the touch, and his gaze flies to the monitors, and he reassures himself with their steady blips.

"How is she?" he says. "How deep did the knife go? Did it hit anything? It didn't seem that bad and then—"

"Slow down," the male paramedic says again.

"Just . . . is she all right? Will she *be* all right?"

"She's stable," the woman says. "That's all we can say. Now let's take a look at you."

He shakes his head. "I'm fine."

She eyes him. "So you *were* faking it to catch a ride?"

He glances at the window, judging how far they are from the scene. Not far enough.

"I did feel woozy, and I did hit my head. It's just not critical. *She* is."

He waits for them to say Riley isn't critical. When they don't, his heart hammers louder than her bleeping monitor. He adjusts his grip on her hand so his thumb is on her pulse.

It's strong enough. He keeps it there, for added reassurance.

"The oxygen mask," he says. "Is that just a precaution or did it nick her lung? Is she breathing all right?"

"She is for now."

Max shifts. Not the answer he wants.

*Tell me she's fine. Just fine. I'm overreacting.*

They say nothing more.

He leans forward and frees strands of her hair caught under the mask.

"She's stable," the woman says finally. "We really can't say more, but so far she's fighting and holding on. That's what counts. You've got a tough girlfriend."

"She's just a friend."

*You're holding that hand pretty tight, Max.*

For support.

*And you kissed her, didn't you?*

Her eyelids flutter. He holds his breath, certain he's imagining it, but the paramedics both move, the woman saying, "Riley? Can you hear me?"

Riley's eyes half open. Her gaze swings around, passing the woman bending over her and coming to rest on Max. She smiles and squeezes his hand, and that smile is for him, only for him, as if there's no one else there. She looks for him, and she smiles for him, and it's as if he's been wound tight enough to snap, and now that cord is cut and he wants to just collapse there, with her.

Her eyes close again. The paramedic tries to rouse her, to ask questions, but she's faded back to sleep. Max checks the monitor. Her pulse and her heartbeat continue as before. Still strong. Or strong enough.

"Let's check you out," the woman says to Max.

He nods and lets her shine her light in his eyes as he points out the spot where he supposedly bumped his head. She asks about any medication he's on. He almost says,

"None," because he's spent his life answering that question with "None."

No health issues. No medication save the occasional round of antibiotics, and even that was rare, he being an only child, not subject to those round-robin infections and viruses that plagued his sibling-cursed friends.

No issues. No medication.

But that isn't true anymore. Never will be again, and this is, perhaps, the longest he's gone in the past year without thinking of his condition. An entire hour that he's forgotten he has schizophrenia, forgotten he's in rather desperate need of his meds.

He tells the woman what he's taking. She frowns.

"Are you sure?" she asks. "That's usually prescribed for . . ." She glances at her partner, as if she might be mistaken.

"Schizophrenia," Max says. "Yes." And that's another first. The first time he's been forced to admit to his condition and hasn't cringed as he said it. Hasn't wanted to throw it like a bomb and run before he sees their reaction. He says it matter-of-factly. *Yes, I have schizophrenia. Deal with it. I certainly need to.*

"I'll need my medication once we reach the hospital," he says, rhyming off the dosage. "I was due to take it at ten, but obviously circumstances prevented that."

"You're overdue for your meds?" the man asks.

"Yes," Max says. "Roughly three hours overdue, which only means I should take them as soon as possible, not that I'm in imminent danger of a full-blown psychotic break, so you can stop looking at me like that."

*Hmm, can you blame him, Max? Isn't that what you yourself were worried about a few hours ago? That the clock would slip past ten and you'd be like Dr. Jekyll down-ing his potion?*

No, he was understandably stressed, and he overreacted.

*Good. I'm glad you see that.*

Unfortunately, the paramedics—who one really thought would have known better—did not seem to agree. The woman looked concerned. The man seemed ready to reach for the nearest hypodermic to put Max down if he made any sudden moves.

"I'm fine," Max says. "I escaped murderous kidnappers, got Riley to safety and called 911. I believe those are not the actions of someone experiencing a schizophrenic episode. Call ahead, have my meds ready, and we'll all rest easier when I've taken them. But until then, like Riley, I can hold on."

"You said you were held captive, but no ransom demands were made?" the man says, carefully.

It takes Max a second to get his meaning, but only a second, before he rolls his eyes and says, "Yes, I'm sorry. I was mistaken. I actually stabbed Riley. We were making out behind the building, having snuck out of therapy because, well, therapy is boring and making out is not. But then the next thing I know, I'm holding a knife and covered in blood, and she's dying, but no worries, mate, I'll just make up a story about kidnappers. I'm sure everyone will believe that."

"There's no need to be sarcastic," the woman says.

"Yes, actually, there is."

"You knew what I was implying, though," the man says, his hand sliding to the side as if he's wondering where the closest weapon might be.

"Yes, because I have schizophrenia and am well aware of exactly what the average person expects of me, and while I'd hope for better from medical professionals, you are merely paramedics. Couldn't quite get the grades for med school, I presume?"

The man's eyes narrow.

"You don't appreciate the insult? After you suspected me

of stabbing Riley? I'm not sure which is more egregious—the presumption that by dint of having schizophrenia, I clearly did this, or the presumption that I'm not bright enough to come up with a better story if I did. You did notice Riley open her eyes, right? She saw me and screamed in terror as she woke looking into the face of her would-be killer."

"You can cut the sarcasm, kid."

"Can I? Excellent. You stop looking at me as if I'm about to lop off your head, and I'll stop being cheeky about it." Max lifts his other hand to take Riley's. "There. You can now see both my hands. If I make any sudden move, you have my permission to use that hypodermic you keep eyeing."

"I'm not—"

"Enough," the woman says. "I'm going to call ahead for your medication. We'll be there in a couple of minutes, and the priority is Riley."

"Yes," Max says. "It is." And he turns his back on the man and watches Riley for the rest of the trip.

## MAX: SERENITY

Serenity: *the state of being calm, peaceful and untroubled.*

That's what Max feels now. Serenity.

Riley is fine. All right, perhaps "fine" is an exaggeration—no one stabbed in the chest can truly be considered to be doing "fine." But she is stable and listed in serious—not critical—condition, and the doctor felt confident enough to assure Max she would *be* fine. That is what counts, and so serenity is what Max feels, sitting in the waiting room, waiting for his mother or for permission to see Riley, whichever comes first.

He gave a brief statement when he arrived, and he'll need to give a complete interview to the assigned detectives, but they are at the scene and will get to him soon.

Any earlier worry over how he might be treated has also passed. When the nurse from the psychiatric ward came to see him, he could tell by her expression that—given what she'd likely heard from the medics—she expected a raving lunatic ready for padded-room commitment. When she'd found him coherent and polite and calm, that wariness disappeared and she'd treated him as if he was any other patient. He'd got his meds. She'd brought clean clothing, and he'd answered her questions. She was kind and helpful, and when she left, she'd gone to get Riley's doctor, who'd treated him with the same respect, giving him as much of an update on her condition as she could to a non-family member.

The nurse had then ascertained that Max was comfortable being left alone in the waiting room, and she'd returned to her duties, simply telling him to page her if he needed anything. Treating him like a normal person, despite knowing his condition. He appreciated that more than he'd have imagined possible.

Yet another reason for serenity . . . A few minutes ago, he overheard someone talking about "another girl" brought in from "that kidnapping." He'd inquired—politely—and been told it was Brienne. She's alive. That's all the nurses know, but it's enough for Max.

Riley will be fine. No one has locked him up in the psych ward. Brienne has survived. And so, yes, a few moments of serenity.

"Do you know when I might be able to see Riley Vasquez?" he asks, oh so politely, when a nurse pops his head into the room.

"That will be up to her family. They're with her now."

"Good. Thank you."

As the nurse withdraws, he catches sight of a young woman, and he jumps up with Riley's name on his lips. It isn't her, of course, but the young woman has stopped, as if overhearing his exchange with the nurse. She sees him. She tilts her head and then turns away, and he hurries out the door and says, "Sloane!"

She stops. She turns. She doesn't smile or acknowledge him or even step his way. She simply gives him a look, as if considering whether this is really worth her time.

Her resemblance to Riley is not as strong as he thought at first. She's smaller, a bit older. Prettier too, in a way he fully admits while feeling no disloyalty to Riley, because it is merely a factual assessment. Sloane is, as Americans would say, a knockout, and she knows it, her chin rising as if to say, *I am beautiful and you will admire me.* He tries not to laugh, because that look erases any resemblance to her sister, and makes him decide that even wan and pale on her deathbed, Riley is the more attractive one.

He jogs to Sloane, and she gives him a once-over. Assessing, considering, and then dismissing. Worth two seconds of contemplation and no more—which is, he guesses, more than most blokes get from Sloane Vasquez.

"Max," he says, extending a hand, which she gives even less contemplation and certainly doesn't shake. Nor does she give any sign that the name means anything. In other words, Riley has never mentioned him from group therapy. Shocking, really.

"You're the guy who rescued my sister," she says.

"We rescued each other."

"The Brit," she says as he speaks a full sentence. "From her group."

"She mentioned me?"

"She said you were a jerk."

He laughs. Sloane does not. She isn't teasing—she's just telling him what her sister said. Blunt honesty.

"Perhaps," he says. "Or perhaps she just needed to get to know me better."

She rolls her eyes and turns away. Dismissed, old chap. Don't joke with this one. She's not Riley. She'll think you're an idiot, or worse, flirting with her.

Max jogs in front of Sloane. "How is Riley? Is she awake yet? You've been to see her, haven't you?"

Sloane stops. Another cool assessment, this one for her sister. Are you worth *her* time? *Her* attention? When she finishes considering, she seems to decide that the answer is probably no but given that he helped Riley, he might deserve a little of *Sloane's* time. Just a little.

"She's still out cold. They have her on a lot of pain-killers. The doctor says she'll be fine. Mom's freaking out, of course, but . . ." She trails off and shrugs. "That's what moms do. I don't think the doctor would say she will be fine if she won't."

"They wouldn't. It's a liability issue."

He smiles again—can't help it. This is Riley's sister, and he wants to coax some positive reaction from her, get her on his side, as ridiculous as that might be. Of course she doesn't smile. She nods, as if accepting what he says at face value. Then she looks up at him.

"It's true what they say happened?" she asks. "Kid-nappers? And the others? Dead?"

Max's smile evaporates as he nods.

Sloane closes her eyes, and she goes still for a moment before she shakes her head, and when her voice comes, it cracks a little. "Poor kid. She just can't catch a break, can she?"

Max says nothing to that. What can he say? He knows that when the doctor insists Riley will be all right, she means physically. The rest . . . ? He's trying not to think about the rest.

"How was she?" Sloane asks, her voice lowered. "In there? I can't imagine . . ." She swallows.

"Riley held up fine." Max pauses and then he shakes his head. "No, she didn't just *hold up*. She held us together. She kept us going. As horrible as it got, she never stopped trying, never stopped thinking and planning and pushing us."

Sloane's poise falters then as her eyes tear up. "Of course she did. Of course she would. She saved that little girl, you know. No matter what she might say during that therapy crap—no matter what she might think or feel—she saved her."

"She saved me too."

Sloane nods and turns to go, but only stands there, gaz-ing around as if forgetting what she's supposed to be doing. Then she looks back at Max.

"I'll make sure they let you see her when she wakes up. It might be a while. The doctor said she could be out all day, but if you give me your number, I'll text."

"I don't have my mobile," he says. Which is technically true.

"Mobile? Oh, right. Cell phone. No, of course you don't. It's still back . . ." She goes quiet, as if thinking about what happened, and then sharply shakes her head. "Okay, e-mail then?"

*Haven't checked it in months, but sure.* He gives her the address, and she puts it on her phone and promises to let him know when Riley wakes up. She's about to go, and then she stops and asks, "How about you? Are you okay?" as if belatedly realizing perhaps she ought to inquire.

"I'm fine," he says. "But if Riley asks about me when she wakes up, tell her I said I'm right as rain."

"Right as . . ." She shakes her head, a little of herself seeping back with a faint eye roll, as if to say she won't ask what that means because, really, she doesn't care. "I'll tell her. Anything else?"

"No, that's—" He stops and takes a deep breath. "Tell her I still owe her a secret, which I'll give her as soon as I see her."

Sloane gives him a *whatever* shrug, her attention already moved on, oblivious to the expression on his face, which he suspects is similar to the look of a hiker facing down a grizzly bear. A terrifying prospect, but it has to be done. Can't turn and run. That would only make it worse. Riley deserves to know he has schizophrenia. If he's hoping this is the start of a friendship, then she has to know.

"Right as rain. Owe her a secret. Got it." Sloane starts to leave. Then she stops and says, "The answer is no, by the way. So if that's your motivation, don't bother."

"The answer to what?"

"If you're hanging around because my sister is hot. Hoping that rescuing her wins you a fast-pass ticket to her bedroom."

"What? No," he says quickly. "I wouldn't— She isn't— I mean, of course she is, but no. I would never take advantage."

"Good. Because the answer is no, and if you even try, I'll cut you off at the knees." She meets his gaze.

"Er, right. Yes. I understand. Just tell her—"

"You're right as rain and you owe her a secret," Sloane says as she walks away. "Got it."

*That went . . . well. Possibly. Better than horrible. Less than wonderful.*

When he turns back to the waiting room, there's a bounce in his step that insists it did indeed go well, that he got as much approbation from Riley's sister as he was ever likely to get. Better yet, she's promised to let him know when he can see Riley. So it was good. Very, very good.

He's still smiling as he notices a woman at the nurses' station. She has her back to him. Tall, blond, angular and speaking very precisely in her very precise upper-class accent, dressing down the poor nurses for some slight or other.

Max walks over as she's telling the nurses that they really ought to keep a better eye on her son and don't they understand the situation and do they let patients simply wander about.

"No, Mum," he says as he stands behind her. "They had me chained to the wall, but I managed to escape. Entirely not their fault."

She turns so fast she bumps into him. Then she gives him a hug, which surprises him. Public displays of affection are *not done* in his family. Yet she hugs him, briefly but tightly, and then she puts her hands on his shoulders, her gaze assessing him as sharply as Sloane's. She turns to the nurses.

"Has he been seen? I certainly hope he's been seen. He might not claim any injury, but you cannot take his word for it—"

"Mum?" he cuts in. "I've been seen. Thoroughly examined. I'm fine."

"Did you get your medication?"

He tries to stifle the twinge of annoyance at the way her voice drops when she says this, rather the same way she talks about her alcoholic brother "having a tipple" in that whispered and embarrassed tone.

"Yes, Mum. I really am fine. Let's leave the nurses alone. They have quite enough to do."

He's leading her away when Sloane comes sweeping down the hall. She gives his mother only the briefest of glances, barely long enough for him to say, "This is my mum," and not waiting for a proper introduction before saying, "Mom says you can come see Riley anytime. Well, not right now because the doctor's in there. But if you want, you can come in before you leave. I'll warn you, Riley isn't conscious, so I don't really see the point."

"I'd still like to see her. Thank you."

A "suit yourself" eye roll, and she starts to walk away and then glances back, and he says, "Yes, I've been warned. Haven't forgotten," and she says, "Good," before swanning off, leaving him smiling after her.

"Pretty girl," his mother says.

He shrugs and looks over to see her giving him a very different sort of assessment as her eyes narrow.

"No, Mum, I'm not flirting with pretty girls in the hospital. That's just Sloane. Her sister is the one I—" He stops. "The one I rescued. Well, no, I didn't actually rescue her. More of a mutual-rescue situation."

He grins at her. She does not smile back. Instead, she says, "I suppose this sister is also very pretty."

"Yes, she's, like, totally hot. Which is the only reason I helped her escape. If she'd been a complete cow, I'd have left her behind."

"There's no need to be shirty, Max."

"Yes, there is, because your implication is that I only helped her because she's pretty. Or that I'm only eagerly waiting to see her because she's pretty. She *is* pretty. She's also smart, funny and sweet, and was, a mere hour ago, fighting for her life after being both shot and stabbed. I'm going to see her now, because even if she's unconscious, she's still very pretty." He leans over and whispers, "In fact, to be honest, pretty girls are better that way. No talking required."

She gives him a sour look. He grins and, in return, gives her a one-armed squeeze.

"I'm going to pop in and see her," he says. "I'll be back in a minute."

"Max?" she says as he starts to bounce off, and he considers pretending he didn't hear her, but he wasn't raised that way. Nor does she deserve rudeness.

He turns, and she says, "Are you all right?"

He resists the urge to say "Right as rain." He'll save that for Riley. Instead, he smiles and says, "Very all right, *Maman*. More all right than I have been in a long time. Don't I seem it?"

"You do seem very happy."

"There you are, then."

She hesitates and then says, "You've just escaped dangerous killers, Maximus. Perhaps *happy* isn't the proper emotion?"

She lowers her voice as she says it, just as she did when she asked if he'd had his meds, and again he resists the urge to tense.

*See, Max, you don't need to watch so carefully for signs. She's there to do it for you.*

"It's actual happiness, Mum, not inappropriate affect."

"I wasn't suggesting—"

"I'm happy because I survived and Riley survived and we'll both be fine, and we did it. *I* did it. I faced hell tonight and I got through it just as I would have before this mess started."

"I know, and that's admirable, but it doesn't mean—"

"Yes, I know. It doesn't mean I'm better. I'll never *be* better. But I accomplished this, and I'm going to ask you to let me have my victory. Just a taste of normal, all right? Don't worry. I won't let it go to my head."

Her gaze drops. "Yes, of course. I'm sorry, Max. I didn't mean—"

"You're just watching out for me. I know." Another one-armed hug, and this time she accepts it. He even smacks a kiss on her cheek before saying, "I'll only be a moment." Then he starts loping off.

He gets exactly three steps before a voice says, "Maximus Cross?" and he turns to see two plainclothes police officers bearing down on him.

"We need to speak to you."

**CHAPTER 22** I'm not dead. That's my second thought on waking. Yes, it should probably be my first, but there was that groggy moment when I opened my eyes and saw white and heard murmuring voices and the exact state of my existence wasn't obvious. Then one of the voices came clear—Sloane's—and that answered the question.

Did I really think I died in that alley? Yes. I don't know how close I actually came to it, but in that moment, lying there, I'd been certain that's what was happening, and equally certain there was nothing I could do to stop it.

I always expected that when the end came, I'd fight like hell. I had, up to that point, but then I'd crossed over it and the inevitable seemed, well, inevitable. Like seeing a meteor falling and you're running as fast as you can until the shadow covers you and you look up and realize it's too big to outrun. In that moment—that final moment—all I'd cared about was that I wasn't alone. That someone *else* cared enough to stay at my side. And so, when I wake, there's one name on my lips.

"Max?" I whisper, lifting my head.

He's not there. Nor does anyone immediately rush to my bedside, as they do in the movies. That's because no one happens to be looking my way. Mom's talking to the doctor

— 217

with her back to me. Sloane is at the window, looking out. They don't hear my scratchy whisper.

I slump back onto the bed, and that's when Mom turns, and she sees my eyes open and gives a little chirp of an "Oh!" as she rushes over, and that's when I get my cinematic moment, family clustered at my bedside, telling me how glad they are that I'm awake, how I've been through so much but I'm fine now, crying happy tears.

Okay, Mom does all that. Sloane stands at my bedside and says, "Thank God you're awake. You were starting to smell." And Mom says, "Sloane!" and I wait for my sister's usual "What?" but instead she smiles at me and leans over to kiss my forehead and whispers, "Good to see you back. But you *do* smell."

"Thanks." I shift and I brace for pain, but nothing comes. Good meds, I guess. "How long have I been out?"

"It's Sunday," Sloane says. "Which means you're twenty-four hours overdue for a shower."

"I'll get right on that," I say. "How much longer do I need to be here?"

The doctor starts explaining my injuries. After the first line I lift my hand. "Not to be rude, but can I just get an estimated time of departure?"

"We'd like to keep you for a few days," she says. "There's always the risk of infection, and you've been through a trauma—"

"Got it," I say, and I really *don't* mean to be rude, but there are more important things on my mind. "How's Max?"

When silence answers, I boost myself up. "Max? The guy I came in with? He was with me, right?"

"He was," Mom says in a very careful tone, one that starts my heart pounding.

"Is he okay? Did something happen? He was fine when I passed out."

"He said to tell you he's right as rain," Sloane says.

I have to smile at that. I exhale and lean back into the pillow. "Okay, good." One second of rest, and then I'm up again. "What about Lorenzo? He was one of the counselors."

"He didn't make it, baby," Mom says. "But the girl did."

"Girl?"

"Brienne, I think her name is?"

"Brienne?" I shoot up fast enough that I *do* feel pain stabbing through me. "She's alive?"

"In critical condition and unconscious, but stable." Mom looks at the doctor. "Is that right? She's stable?"

The doctor nods and then says, "I should alert Detective Buchanan that Riley is awake."

"Right," I say. "The whole kidnapping thing probably needs a statement, huh?" I smile. No one else does. Not a laughing matter, and they're right. I think of Aaron and Aimee and Lorenzo, of Maria and Gideon and Sandy, and my smile disappears as I slide back down in the bed. The doctor leaves.

Mom comes over and holds my hand. "It's all right, baby. We'll get this sorted out."

*Sorted out.* An odd way to put it. I'm quiet for a minute. Then I look over at her. "I'd like to see Max."

When she doesn't answer, I say, "Duh, right. If I've been unconscious since Friday, he's long since gone home."

"Actually—" Sloane begins, but Mom cuts her off with a look.

I continue, "I know the police will want to get my statement before I see him, but I'd like to speak to him after, if that's possible. I don't know if he left a number or some way to get in touch—"

"We need to talk about him," Mom says, and her grip on my hand tightens.

"About Max?" I catch her expression, the wariness there. "Did he say something? He can be a bit of a smart-ass. If he made some comment—"

"It's not that."

"He's okay, though, right?" I push up again.

"Depends on your definition of okay," Sloane mutters.

"Wh-what?"

"You do know he's crazy, right?"

"Sloane!" Mom says.

"What? It's true."

"Sloane? Could you please step outside?"

My sister slouches into a chair instead.

"Mom?" I say. "What's going on?"

"I'm not sure how much you know about this Max boy, Riley. About why he was in therapy."

"He never said. There seemed to be, well, maybe some kind of abuse? I could be wrong."

"Yep, you are," Sloane murmurs, too low for Mom to call her on it.

"I know he's on medication," I say. "For a heart condition."

"Not a heart condition," Sloane says, and when Mom turns on her, she says, "Just spit it out, Mom. Before she totally freaks."

"He has schizophrenia," Mom says.

"Now you can freak," Sloane says to me.

I barely hear her. I'm thinking of what Mom just said.

"Schizo . . ." I'm trying to remember everything I know about that. It's not much. "That isn't multiple personality, is it? I know 'schism' means split. But that's not it."

"It means he's crazy," my sister says.

"Sloane!" Mom says.

"What? The doctor said it means he hallucinates, hears voices, can't think straight, is prone to violence, and can't tell what's real and what's not. Classic definition of crazy."

"Sloane?" Now it's me saying it. "Can you step outside? Please?"

She looks honestly taken aback at that. Maybe even hurt.

"I'd like to speak to Mom," I say. "Max saved my life, and I need to have a serious conversation about this without listening to you insult him."

"I'm not trying to insult him," she says. "I'm just telling you what the doctor says. Maybe 'crazy' isn't the right word to use—"

"Would you use it for me?"

"Of course not. But you're just having problems. He's been diagnosed with a serious mental disorder."

"Then call it that. Please. Because PTSD *is* a mental disorder, not a 'problem,' and I'd rather not worry about my sister calling me crazy."

"I'm sorry," she says, and looks as if she means it. "I'd never call you that. But what they're saying about him . . ."

I brace myself. "What are they saying?"

"There's some confusion, baby," Mom says. "About exactly what happened."

"They say he did it," Sloane blurts.

"What?" I say.

Mom tries to hush her, to take some gentle and round-about path to the answer, but I don't want gentle or roundabout.

"They're saying he did what?" I ask Sloane.

"All of it," she says. "Killed those kids. Shot you. Stabbed you."

I bolt upright so fast the pain leaves me gasping. "What? No. Just *no*. That's—" I take a deep breath.

Speaking of crazy.

No, really, this *is* crazy.

Am I awake? I can't be. Because this is absolutely nuts. How could they even think—

I can't panic. I need to focus on facts. It's just some confusion, and I can clear it up if I calm down.

"At least one of the kidnappers was killed," I say. "Maybe two. There's a body. Proof."

Mom shakes her head. "No, there's isn't, baby."

"What?"

"All they found were those poor kids and the two counselors."

"And the gun," Sloane murmurs. "They found Max with the gun."

"A kidnapper's gun. Which we took. If it was his, how the hell would he have gotten it in? There was a metal detector—" I shake my head sharply. "No, I'm not even dignifying this with discussion. I was *there*, Mom. What are they saying, that I had a breakdown? Hallucinated three kidnappers and a night of hell?"

"They say you're confused," she says softly.

"What? *Confused*? They honestly *are* claiming I imagined the whole thing? That's . . . That's . . ." I can't even finish.

"They say he's very persuasive. Schizophrenia often results in social issues—withdrawal and isolation—but every case is different, and this boy is very intelligent, very charming. He had a psychotic break and convinced you there were kidnappers in the building."

"And I then had my own hallucinations? Because I *saw* them, Mom. *Talked* to them. Watched them kill . . ." I swallow and she reaches for me, but I pull back. "I was *there*. Max didn't need to convince me of anything."

"They say the repeated trauma may have resulted in a derealization. That means—"

"I know what 'derealization' means," I snap, and maybe she doesn't deserve that, but there have been times I felt as if my mom doesn't quite get me. Never like this, though. Never like this.

"Derealization is an extreme symptom of PTSD," I say. "Where reality seems unreal. Last night certainly did seem unreal, but derealization would not cause me to completely misremember what happened."

"The doctor also suggested a possible fugue state."

"Which is basically amnesia. In other words, they're suggesting I experienced a fugue state due to the trauma and then allowed Max to fill in the blanks. That would mean I'm lying right now. That I don't actually remember what happened—only what Max told me—and now I'm pretending I do remember it."

"Of course not, baby. You're just confused."

"The word is 'lying,' Mom. Outright lying to protect Max. Why? Oh, wait. Let me guess. Because he's cute."

"Mmm," Sloane murmurs, her first interjection since Mom started. "He's a seven. That's not cute enough to lie for."

I glare at her. "No boy is cute enough to lie for."

"Depends on the lie, but yeah, not for something like that. And definitely not for a seven." When my glare sharpens, she says, "What? I'm agreeing with you."

"No one is saying you'd lie for him because he's cute, Riley," Mom says. "If they did, I'd set them straight. I think they're implying that you're honestly confused, and you believe that you saw—"

"What I *saw*," I say. "There's no *believe*. A man shot me as I was running away with Brienne. Max wasn't even there. He *was* there when the *other* guy stabbed me—Max was pulling him off before he *killed* me. That is the only violent thing Max did, and it was to protect me. It was hell in there, and whatever is wrong with Max, he kept it under control. He *avoided* violence, and that's why I thought maybe there was abuse in his past. Now I realize he was avoiding it because he knows he might be prone to it, as part of his diagnosis. He kept it under control in every way, and I owe him my life."

It's a good speech. An impassioned defense. When I finish, I expect Mom to hug me and tell me that she believes me and we'll sort this out. That it's a mistake, and it'll be fixed, and we'll do it together. But she only stands there, shredding a tissue between her fingers.

"It may have *seemed* as if he saved you, baby—" she begins.

"Go."

"Riley, I know this is tough—"

"Go!" I snarl the word and she falls back. "Get out of here. Now. Or I'm going to scream, and then we'll see who they think is the crazy one. Maybe *that's* the answer. Maybe I did it. Huh? Have they considered that? Makes more sense, doesn't it? That can happen with PTSD. You lose it and go nuts, and poor Max, well, he hallucinates, so it was easy for me to convince him there were kidnappers."

"Riley, don't. You're—"

"Count of ten, Mom. If you're still in here, I'm screaming until someone comes and then I'm confessing. Ten . . . nine . . ."

She leaves when I get to six.

**CHAPTER 23** I'm so furious I can barely form words when the nurse stops by. I manage to tell her that I want to speak to the police—now. When she returns a few minutes later to say they're on the way, I'm already on my laptop, researching schizophrenia so they can't bullshit me.

Max has schizophrenia.

My initial reaction had been confusion, as I struggled to remember what it was. Once I did, I thought only, *That fits.* Overly worried about getting his meds, avoiding violent confrontations and, of course, the part where he'd warned me he sometimes got confused, imagined things that weren't there.

Yet after I look it up and it really hits . . . I'm kind of angry and a little bit hurt. No, I *am* angry and I *am* hurt, and I cannot deny it.

I sit on my bed and stare at the wall, and I want to pull up the covers and roll over and shut the world out, because after four months of sleepwalking through my life, the one guy who made me feel something—really made me feel something, brought me back to myself and made me care—he lied to me. Told me he needed meds for a heart condition. Went through hell with me and never mentioned that he was suffering from a serious—yes, a *very* serious—mental ill-ness. And it wasn't like hiding an eating disorder, where it was none of my business under the circumstances. This one mattered.

I keep thinking about what we went through. No, that's not exactly true. I keep *feeling* what we went through. Reliving not the horror of that warehouse but the parts that weren't horrible. The parts with Max, the ones where he went from being the jerk at the back of the room to the guy who'd held my hand when I thought I was dying, who'd sworn I wasn't dying—not just gentle and empty words but words he'd meant, passionately meant, as if he could stave off my death with them. I remember the boy who kissed me, tasting of fear and panic. I remember all that, and I remem-ber how I felt about him. How I *feel* about him. And now finding out this? It hurts. It hurts so much.

But this isn't the time for recriminations. As angry as I am, I acknowledge that he did warn me, in his way, and even if his explanation had been a lie, the warnings had not. He had made sure that if anything went wrong—if he started seeing or hearing things—I wouldn't be caught off guard. So I'll give him that, and while it does take the edge off my anger, it doesn't ease the hurt. The only way I'll deal with that is to face him and get his side of the story. First, though, I need to be prepared. To fully understand his condition.

So I continue my research.

On a scale of grave mental illnesses, schizophrenia is near the top. It isn't a temporary bout of depression. It's seri-ous, and it's life-altering, and it's permanent. While I hate to give Sloane's snark any credence, schizophrenia really is what most people think of when they say someone's crazy. It's the homeless guy arguing with himself. It's that story in the news, the one where someone was murdered horribly and all you can think is "How can someone do that?" and the answer is "Schizophrenia." But it's not always like that. It's not *often* that, the same way the average person with PTSD isn't likely to snap and start shooting from a balcony. The extreme cases are the scary ones, though, and those are the ones that make the news.

Schizophrenia, like many mental illnesses, isn't easily treated. In fact, it's one of the toughest, because not everyone suffers the same symptoms. Max clearly doesn't have a problem with personal hygiene. Nor does he seem to have any trouble with social interaction. Most schizophrenia symptoms can be controlled with medication, which must be tailored to the individual and the symptoms. The side effects are not negligible. They can include drowsiness or restlessness, tremors, muscle spasms, blurred vision . . . the list goes on.

There is no question of anything—and I mean *anything*—we experienced in that warehouse being Max's fault. The only event I hadn't witnessed myself was Aaron's death. I remember how freaked out Max was, and now I know why. He must have been questioning the sequence of events himself, because the thing about a mental illness like schizophrenia is that you don't know when a situation isn't what it seems. You might know it's possible you're imagining it, but when it's actually happening, there must be no way to tell reality from fantasy.

Everything I read says most people with schizophrenia can't tell the difference while they're experiencing an episode. That's why Max had panicked. He knew his meds had run out, and he was terrified he had somehow played a role in Aaron's death. *That's* what I remember—his terror—and that's when I truly forgive him for not telling me the truth.

He warned me, as best he could, in case something went wrong. What he has, though, isn't something to be taken lightly, to be shared in casual conversation. I hate to talk about my anxiety and my depression. I've seen how people react to it. Now—through Sloane—I've seen how they react to schizophrenia, and I suspect her response is actually relatively benign, if inconsiderate and infuriating. Say "schizophrenia" and people remember those horrible news stories, and having seen that terror on Max's face, I think that's what he recalls too. But he did nothing wrong Friday night. The evidence in Aaron's death supports Max's story completely. Now I just need to make sure the police know it.

Two detectives arrive about thirty minutes later. I'm still online, watching videos of people talking about their experiences with schizophrenia, because I want to understand. After everything Max did for me, I owe it to him to try—as best as an outsider can—to understand.

The detectives are two guys named Buchanan and Wheeler. I don't know either, and I'm disappointed by that. I'd hoped they'd be familiar faces, detectives who knew me from Christmas parties or summer picnics. Detectives who had some idea what kind of girl I am—not the sort to get "confused" or lie for a boy. But it's a big-enough city that I don't know every cop and detective. Far from it.

As Buchanan grills me, I realize they honestly believe Max did it. There's absolutely no doubt in their minds, and all they're doing now is gathering evidence to prove it so they can charge him. Meanwhile, he's being "held" in the psychiatric ward downstairs, apparently because his mother was such a pain in the ass that they agreed to let the hospital hold him rather than put him in a cell.

Kudos to his mother, then. But her fight isn't helping change their minds about him, because these two seem as ignorant as my sister when it comes to schizophrenia. I hate saying that. I really do, because I realize there's a stereotype of cops as dumb bullies, and most are the polar opposite of that.

Maybe these two have just seen too many violent schizophrenics. Maybe they had a really bad case where one committed some terrible crime. Maybe they don't know anyone with schizophrenia beyond the scope of policing. Whatever the excuse . . . well, there is no excuse, but whatever the cause, they have made up their minds. There is a schizophrenic teen and six bodies, and the link is obvious.

After they leave, I calm down enough to sort through the "facts." I make notes so I can help Max, and as I do, as much as I hate it, I can see why the detectives have concluded Max is guilty.

Because there is no proof that we were kidnapped.

Predator must have survived his injuries. They'd removed Cantina and cleaned up all evidence that they'd ever been there.

As we'd guessed when we escaped, they faked their contact with the hostage negotiator—it must have been another partner playing Agent Salas. They'd never contacted anyone. At all. While we were running for our lives, our families had carried on with their Friday night, believing their kids were safely at a therapy sleepover.

That made no sense. The purpose of kidnapping is to make demands. So I can't blame the detectives for thinking something is seriously wrong with this scenario. When they learned one of our group had schizophrenia, they must have thought, "Aha!"

At that point, the fact they had a living witness who said that wasn't how it happened should have made them take a harder look. Maybe it did. But in talking to them, I got the feeling they didn't consider me a real witness. I had "problems," as they described it. I'd "been through a lot," they said.

*There's only so much one person can take, Riley. Eventually something has to give, and you're so young and you've had so much happen. First your dad, and then the people you babysat for, and I know how terrible that must have been.*

Do you, Detective Buchanan? Do you really? You can't. Sorry.

Part of it was my youth, but I got the feeling they might not have been so quick to decide I'd been unduly influenced if I had a Y chromosome. I'd lashed out earlier with Mom, wondering if they thought I was susceptible because I'm a girl and Max is a cute guy. That actually did seem to play a role in the detectives deciding I'd fallen under his spell. He's cute and charming and a year older than me and has a British accent. No, seriously, Buchanan actually said that.

*I know my daughter loves boys with accents. Especially British. She goes nuts for those One Direction kids. It's the accent. It makes them sound like something out of romance books, with lords and earls and whatever. Girls love that stuff.*

*Actually, no, detectives, I have issues with the class system and its lingering effects on British society.*

Buchanan just thought I was being a smart-ass then, and commented that I must have gotten along really well with Max.

So there it is. I'm not a valid witness because I have mental health issues, I'm under eighteen and I'm a girl. And Max is a cute boy. With an accent.

There's more. I wish I could say there isn't, because by that point I just wanted to paint them as incompetent morons, not merely jumping to conclusions but skydiving onto them.

The lack of evidence to support our story is one strike against Max. Me as the only witness is another. There's Brienne too, of course, but she hasn't woken up. I pray she'll recover, and that has nothing to do with helping Max's case, because I get the feeling nothing she says will help him. I need hard evidence.

They have that evidence. Or so they think.

Max was found with the gun that killed Aaron and Gideon. Aimee, Maria and Brienne were shot with Gray's weapon and Lorenzo and Sandy with Predator's, which ballistics should prove, but the detectives will only argue Max had backup weapons.

They have the knife used to stab me too. Like the gun, it has Max's prints on it because he disarmed Predator. There aren't any other prints. Our captors wore gloves.

So what do the police have as evidence? One messed-up witness. One comatose witness. Two weapons with Max's prints all over them. They found preliminary gunshot residue on his clothing too. It also has bloodstains: Lorenzo's, Aaron's, Brienne's and mine.

It's damning evidence. I need to do more than protest his innocence, I need to prove it. Which means I have to figure out what the hell happened in that warehouse, where a teen therapy group was massacred for apparently no reason at all.

There *is* a reason. There's always a reason. Now I have to find it.

**CHAPTER 24** I need to talk to Max. The possibility he can add more to my understanding of the situation is a good excuse. So is "offering support when he needs it." I'm not sure he'll want that support. The guy who sat in the back of the therapy room doesn't strike me as someone who particularly wants to talk about his problems. Really, though, I just need to see him, to speak to him.

I've now been in the hospital nearly thirty-six hours. Awake for the past eight. That doesn't mean I'm ready to start doing flying lunges and *passata sotto*s, but I'm on my feet and ready to do battle in a very different way. Which is good, because in my current state of mind it's probably best not to hand me a saber.

I don't ask permission to leave my room. I pull on jeans and a shirt that Mom brought for "when I feel better." Then I sneak from my room and down the hall.

I need to find the psychiatric ward. My plan is to take the stairs down a level—where no one will recognize me—and check out the hospital map by the elevator. I get into the stairwell, and I'm quietly closing the door when a voice says, "Going somewhere?"

I turn to see Sloane with her arms crossed.

"Wh-what are you—?"

"I saw you putting on your clothing and figured you were about to take an unauthorized stroll. Being unauthorized, I knew you'd leave this way. Dad's not the only detective in the family. I learned a few tricks. Apparently you did too, sneaking down to hear Max's side of the story so you can defend him."

"What? No. Yes, I'm sneaking from my room, but only because I want . . ."

"A cigarette?"

I give her a look. "A candy bar. I'm hungry."

"Great. Reese's cups, right?" She reaches for the door. "There's a vending machine in the waiting room. I'll walk with you. I might even pay."

"Aren't visiting hours over?"

"Nice try, but no. As the immediate family of the poor kid who just went through hell—again—we're allowed to stay as long as we want. Mom knows you don't want to see her right now, so I promised to stay. All night. They're bringing me a cot so I can sleep *right beside* you."

"You don't need to do that."

"But I am. So two choices, kid. Either we hit the vending machine on the way back to your room or we hit it on the way back from Maximus's room. Is that really his name? I looked it up, and it's not even a real name. It's Latin for 'greatest,' which is pretty damn optimistic. It also means 'largest.'" She pauses. "Now that one's more interesting."

"Don't."

"Don't what?"

"Say what you're going to say."

She grins. "And how would you know what I was going to say unless your mind went in the same direction?"

"Yes, his name is Maximus, but he really prefers Max, so let's stick with that."

"Not crazy-British-dude?"

"Sloane . . ."

"What's Brit-talk for 'crazy'? Barmy, isn't it? Can I call him that?"

"No, you cannot—" I take a deep breath. "You don't understand."

A moment of silence. Then, "No, I guess I don't."

"Can we talk about it later?"

She nods. I start to leave. She moves into my path. "We *are* going to see Max, Riley. I'm not stopping you. I'm just giving you a hard time."

When I turn with a wary look, her lips press together before she says, "Seriously? What do you think I'm doing? Setting you up so I can tattle? Have I *ever* done that?"

"The tree house."

"I was eleven, and I only did it because you're Little Miss Perfect, and I was tired of being the one getting in trouble all the time. I wouldn't do anything like that now, Riley." Her voice drops, gaze meeting mine. "Not after everything that's happened. I hope you know that."

I nod. "Okay."

"As for talking to Max, I agree you should, because this whole thing stinks of bullshit."

I must look surprised, because I get another of those annoyed looks. "I might not get your grades, but I'm not stupid. I met Max while you were out cold. He seemed fine. Mom says it's because he was back on his meds, but he couldn't have gotten them more than an hour before I saw him, and they aren't going to turn a raving lunatic into a normal guy that fast. Hell, if he was anything *close* to raving when he came in, they'd have put him straight in the psych ward. So I don't know what's going on, but if you tell me you were kidnapped, then I believe you. Mom would too, if she wasn't so freaked out."

I say nothing and she continues, "They had to give her stuff to calm her down, Riley. Valium or whatever. While you were being treated. She didn't want to take it, but the doctor said she needed to be calm for you when you woke up. So she took the pills and obviously it wasn't a good idea, because she's out of it. *She's* the one who's confused. Not thinking straight. So now I need to step up. Play the adult. Yadda, yadda."

"Which means helping me sneak in to see Max?"

"I'm only eighteen. I'm still working on the responsible-adult thing."

I shake my head, and we go down the stairs two flights. The next hurdle: finding Max's room. As we start down the hall, I see I've made another mistake. This isn't like the other wards, where you can walk along rows of open doors and peek inside. The doors here are all closed. Luckily, Sloane came prepared with a room number. But the location means there's no getting past the nurses' station without being spotted.

As we're considering our next move—Sloane suggests rappelling down to the window from the floor above—the nurse on duty heads off on her rounds. Which leaves a med intern sitting behind the counter, hard at work and seemingly unlikely to leave.

"I've got this," Sloane says.

She motions for me to stay hidden around the corner. Then she walks to the counter. When she speaks, it's in a tone I know well: a little breathier and higher-pitched than her usual voice, and a whole lot less confident. I once called it her helpless-kitten voice. "Um, no," she said. "My helpless-kitten voice is much softer. This is my helpless-*sex*-kitten voice."

She uses that voice to explain her dilemma to the hapless young intern. Her sister—her poor little sister, Riley Vasquez . . . perhaps he's heard of her, the one who'd saved a little girl when her parents were horribly murdered and now barely survived another attack? Yes, *that* Riley. Poor baby. She's having *such* a hard time of it and now people are saying all these things about the guy who'd saved *her*, and she's so confused and upset and sinking fast into depression, and given her injuries, she needs to stay strong, doesn't she? Yes, the intern agrees, she does.

Which is why, Sloane says, her poor baby sister just needs a few minutes—*a few minutes*—to speak to Max Cross. She needs resolution. She needs closure. And this young intern can give her that just by going to the restroom. Decide he really should scrub his hands or something. And Sloane would be grateful—so very grateful—and maybe, if he has time later, they can grab a coffee together in the cafeteria? Yes? Really? OMG, he has no idea how happy he's made her. Squee! She could kiss him. But for now, she totally owes him a coffee. So if he can just take off before the nurse gets back . . .

**CHAPTER 25** My hands tremble as I walk up to Max's door. I need to find exactly the right expression before I walk in. No apprehension. No uncertainty. No sign that I believe he did anything wrong. Also no sign that his condition changes my opinion of him.

But I also can't rush in with smiles and hugs. I can't seem too eager to reassure him, because that's just as bad. It says I *do* have doubts but I'm trying very hard to pretend otherwise. I also can't act as if what he has is no more serious than a common cold, because that's as ignorant as giving him a wide berth.

Eventually, I just take a deep breath and push open the door, because it's all I can do. I *feel* the right things. I know he didn't do anything wrong. I know his condition is something neither to run from nor to brush under the rug. Most of all, though, I know *him*, and maybe that seems naive after only one evening together, but those hours felt like a lifetime, because they were, in a way—a brief period of time in which our lives could have ended at any moment and we completely relied on each other to make sure that didn't happen. For those few hours, we were as unguarded as it got— no masks to hide behind.

Sloane stays in the hall while I tap on his door and then walk in. Max sits by the window, writing in a notebook.

Without turning, he says, "Yes, I had a shower. Two today, in fact, just so you'll stop asking. I do not need a bath."

"Good," I say, "because I wasn't going to give you one."

He turns, and he smiles. No, not a smile—a grin, wide as can be.

"Riley," he says as he rises. "I didn't think they were allowing me visitors."

"They aren't."

"You snuck in? Excellent. I am both impressed and flattered. But should you be up and around already?"

"I'm encouraged to make short forays from my bed. This was short. Relatively speaking."

For a moment, he keeps grinning. Then he reaches up and rubs his hand over his mouth, wiping away the smile.

"So you heard," he says.

I nod.

"I'm . . ." Another rub of his mouth. "I'm sorry, Riley. For not telling you. I just . . ."

"You don't tell anyone unless you absolutely have to?"

"I considered getting it on a T-shirt, but the man at the shop couldn't spell 'schizophrenia.'" He makes a face. "See? Even joking doesn't work. It just sounds rather desperate."

"You did warn me—about the confusion, seeing things and such. So while I still think you should have told me, I won't mention it again."

"I'll still apologize again."

I walk over and I hug him. He tenses at first, but it seems to be surprise rather than resistance, and he pulls me into a quick, fierce hug as he says, "Thank you. For coming."

"How are you doing?"

"Well enough. You've heard what happened? Why I'm still here?"

238 —

"Because they blame you. That's bullshit."

He blinks. Then he chokes a laugh.

"What?" I say.

"I've just never heard you curse."

"Oh, I do. Just not out loud most of the time. This deserves cursing. It's poor detective work and prejudice and—"

He presses a finger to my lips. "I know. Even worse is the way they're dismissing anything you say. I can understand the conclusions about me. Not believing you is unforgivable. Still, I'm not worried. It really is just prejudice, and with a little detective work, they'll sort it out. I don't appreciate being stuck in here until they do, but . . ." He shrugs. "Mum has retained a barrister. He says it'll be sorted in a day or two. Until then, I'm considering this a well-earned vacation. Even if the food is not quite up to snuff."

"You're doing okay, then?"

"Right as rain."

I roll my eyes.

"Right as somewhat-inclement weather, then," he says. "This too shall pass. I'm not concerned. Can't be. This is my life now. The new normal for Max Cross."

"I'm sorry."

He makes a face again. "That sounded bitter, didn't it?"

"No, it's—"

"Honesty, Riley. These days, I really appreciate honesty."

"It sounded frustrated."

He nods. "Well, that too shall pass, I hope." He shoves his hands into his pockets. "On that note, as long as we're delving into the dark pit of honesty, is there anything you want to ask? These days, I'm something of an expert on the spectrum of disorders commonly known as schizophrenia."

"I think I'm okay. I looked it up. By that I mean I researched it, not just that I read the Wikipedia page."

He smiles. "Of course you did. Well, here's the short version. Thankfully, I don't experience hygiene issues. I do hit the markers for delusions. Not truly paranoid, but rather a run-of-the-mill inability to tell reality from the wild imaginings of my overactive brain. I've been on various medications, as they try to find the right mixture. They seem to have done it, which doesn't mean I'm *cured*—I can't be cured, and that's not bitterness or frustration. It's reality. Must face it."

"You seem to be."

He laughs. "I thought we were in the honesty circle here, Riley. I go to therapy and sit in the back and offer only mildly witty commentary. That's not facing it. It's not even coping, really."

"But you're taking your meds. I read that can be a problem. That people think they don't need them."

"Oh, believe me, I know I need them. But, yes, it's . . ." He shrugs. "There's always the worry that the meds will lose their effectiveness, and since I don't notice when I'm off my trolley, I won't see problems until it's too late."

"Off your trolley?"

He smiles. "Off my trolley, lost the plot, away with the fairies . . . I've got a drawerful of them. Feel free to add any to my collection."

"Plumb loco?" I say. "Combining the English word 'plumb,' meaning depths, and 'loco,' which is Spanish for crazy."

The smile grows to a grin. "I will add that one. If you have any Spanish idioms, I'll take them too, though I won't presume you know more Spanish than the average American, because that would be stereotyping."

I laugh. "It would be, thank you. But my Spanish is better than average, as is my Latin."

"Latin?"

"I'm Catholic. I also know some French, but only enough to get me through a freshman trip to Paris. I'm completely illiterate in British, though."

"I can teach you."

"Perfect."

He's about to say something when the door opens. Sloane walks in. "Time's up, kids. You have five seconds to spit out your goodbyes."

"I'll be all right," Max says to me.

I nod.

"You just take care of yourself," he says. "Rest up. I'll see you on the outside."

I smile, and he leans over to kiss my forehead. Then he says to Sloane, "Note: the forehead. No liberties taken."

"Shaking hands is highly underrated."

He rolls his eyes.

"You think I'm kidding?" she says.

He puts out his hand for her.

"Not what I meant," she says.

"Ignore her," I say. "Take care, and if I can get down again, I will. Otherwise, I'll see you on the other side."

He smiles and shakes my hand, and I pull him into a quick hug, which earns something suspiciously like a growl from my sister. We say our goodbyes and part.

We're back in the stairwell when Sloane says, "I wasn't joking back there. You need to be careful with him."

"We're friends."

"Good. Keep it that way."

I sigh.

"I mean it, Riley. He's got a thing for you."

"I think he's a little too preoccupied for that."

"Guys are never too preoccupied for that. Or girls, for that matter. He likes you. He wants to be more than friends. The answer is no. I've already told him so."

"Please tell me you're joking." I remember their little back-and-forth in the room. "You did, didn't you?"

"He's not boyfriend material, Riley. And before you give me shit, it's not because he could flip out. That is a factor, obviously. It has to be. But he's dealing with a lot, and you're dealing with a lot, and those two things do not go well together. You don't need romantic complications in your life right now. If he thinks he does, tough shit. I don't care about him. I care about you."

"I would say that's very sweet, if it wasn't also incredibly presumptuous and a bit condescending."

"Good. I'd be more insulted by 'sweet.' Now that you know Max is fine—"

"I need to see Brienne."

"She's in a coma."

"Which means it'll be a short visit. And that you don't need to accompany me."

"Fifth floor," she says. "Move it."

# CHAPTER 26

Brienne is still comatose. The bullet grazed her spine and there's swelling and the possibility of lifelong damage. Hence the coma, to give her body time to rest.

There's no sneaking into her room, not in the ICU unit, but I'm glad of that. She's the only "real" witness—the only one whose account the police might respect. If the killers realize that, they could come back to finish the job.

I worry that I might not be allowed to visit, but when I tell the nurses who I am, they let me go in with Sloane. We stand by Brienne's bed. She looks as pale as the sheet pulled up around her. Machines hum and beep, but it's a steady and reassuring sound as I hold her cool hand. Then I hear a voice in the hall.

"Brienne's my sister," a guy says.

I go still. The news said Brienne only has one brother, which means the guy out there is the one who sent her into that therapy sleepover. The guy who played lookout for the Porters' killers.

I can't move. I'm still holding Brienne's hand, but I can't even feel that. Sloane doesn't notice. She's busy listening as the nurse explains that Brienne already has visitors.

"Who?" her brother asks.

I grip the bedside with my free hand, fingers digging in, gaze tripping around the room for an escape.

*How about hiding under the bed, Riley?*

That snaps me back to myself. I can't hide. I have to face him. I *should* face him, because now I know the truth, and as much as I might want to help Brienne, if this guy can lead me to the Porters' killers, then I'm going to turn him in. Which means, eventually, I will need to face him. Might as well do it now.

"What the hell?" he says when the nurse tells him who's in the room. "The girl who almost got my sister killed? You know what that crazy freak did, right? Her and her psycho boyfriend?"

Too late, I realize Sloane is on the move. She's stalking out of the room, and I jump to pull her back, but she's already in the hall, her heels clicking across the linoleum.

"Hello," Sloane says. "Let me introduce myself. I'm the big sister of the *freak* you were just talking about." A moment's pause, then, "Hey, asshole, my eyes are up here. You can stop checking me out. You didn't have a snowball's chance in hell even before you insulted my sister."

"You little border-bunny—"

"Do I sound like I crossed a border recently? Do I look like a gangbanger? Damn, you are one dumbass, white-trash trailer-park cracker. Okay, your turn."

"My turn for what?"

"Insulting me. That's what we're doing, right? Exchanging slurs? Or maybe you're just dumbass enough to think I was complimenting you."

*Stop, Sloane. Please stop.*

Of course, she doesn't. She's just building up steam.

"You want to call my sister a freak? I can damned well guarantee that when *your* sister wakes up, she'll tell you that *mine* did everything she could to save her ass. And that's not because Riley claims she did. She hasn't said a single word about what happened to Brienne. It's because I know my sister. She did her best, and they both got shot, and maybe my sister was the one Max got out of there, but it's not because he's her *boyfriend*, you moron. It's because your sister had been shot in the spine and couldn't move or be moved. I don't know what my sister did for yours, but I do know what Max did—he made sure the police got paramedics in there for Brienne. How does that make sense if he's the one who shot her?"

"Because he's crazy. He doesn't have to make sense. All I know is my sister is in that hospital bed while yours is up and walking around."

"*Barely* up and walking around, and only because she's worried about Brienne."

"Or maybe she was trying to finish what her boyfriend started."

One of the nurses protests.

Sloane says, "I'd smack you for that, if you wouldn't claim it as proof that Riley comes from a violent family. So I'll settle for saying that the opinion of anyone who wears a wife-beater is universally considered invalid. Next time you want to be taken seriously, dress like a grown-up."

"You stuck-up little bitch."

"Oh, so I've gone from a *chola* to a *fresa*? Excellent. Not entirely accurate, but much closer."

I step from the room. "Sloane? Can we go, please?"

I try not to look at Brienne's brother. Of course, that's impossible, given that he's standing two feet from my sister. He's average height, his blond hair cut short, dressed in jeans and a tank top—the wife-beater Sloane mentioned. Even without looking his way, I can feel his gaze on me. *He was there.* When the Porters died, he was there, and I have to stop thinking that before my knees give away and I fall into a whimpering puddle.

"Sure, let's do that." Sloane quick-steps over and takes my arm. "We're done here. Time for you to get some rest."

She starts leading me away. Brienne's brother steps into our path, and I do a scared-cat jump. I recover fast, but he's seen it, and he doesn't say a word, he just stands there, his eyes narrowing as he studies me. I try to erase any expression. I try so damned hard, but reactions whip through my head at break-neck speed—*He was there. He knows the people who killed the Porters.* And—*Oh God, I can't let him see that I'm scared of him. I can't let him suspect Brienne told me anything.*

Stop thinking about the Porters. Stop, stop, stop.

As Sloane pulls me away, I say, "I didn't do anything. Whatever you think of me—of Max—it wasn't like that. It really wasn't."

Does he buy the excuse? Come to the conclusion that I'm cowering because of his insults and insinuations? I don't know. And the longer I look at him, the more suspicious he'll become, so I let Sloane lead me away.

When we get to my room, she says, "What was that all about, Riley? And don't tell me his bullshit freaked you out. I hear you nearly bit the detectives' heads off for suggesting Max did it. You're not going to let a swaggering wannabe like that spook you."

"I . . ." I look over at her before I climb back into bed. "Can I talk to you about it tomorrow?"

"Why not now?"

"Because I need to work through a few things first."

She sits in silence for a minute. Then she says, her voice uncharacteristically quiet, "Maybe it would help if you worked through them with me."

"No, that's okay."

She settles into the chair, pulling her knees up, then says, as nonchalantly as possible, "It's because I'm not as smart as you, right?"

"No, I—"

"I'm not. Hardly a big secret. Everyone worries about your grades sliding to B's and C's, and that's what I got on a good day. You're hardly going to brainstorm with the sister who couldn't get into college."

"You didn't apply to college. You're taking a year off to consider your options."

"Which is shorthand for 'I knew I wouldn't get in, so I didn't try,' and the options I'm considering aren't Yale versus Harvard. It's whether I go to the local college or take more high school classes to boost my average. But this isn't a pity party. You work hard in school. I didn't. So I don't blame you for not wanting my help on the thinking part."

I turn to face her. "I honestly need to work it through first, Sloane. Brienne told me some things, and I need to figure out what I can say, and whether her secrets can get anyone in trouble—including you."

"You don't need to worry about me. I'm the *big* sister, remember?"

"By fourteen months."

"And a whole lotta extra life experience, kiddo. Fine. You think it through. Just . . . don't think too hard."

I give her a look.

"I mean it," she says. "You think too much, Riley. Something gets in your head and you just can't get it out, and you go around and around with it. Maybe you think you're working it through. But you're just worrying more and feeling worse. What you need most right now is a good night's sleep. I can ask the nurses to give you something if that will help shut your brain off."

I shake my head. "I need to look up a few things."

She sighs. "Of course you do."

I hesitate. "We were going to talk about Max. About schizophrenia. Do you still want to hear it?"

She looks up and meets my gaze. "I do."

So I explain, and I can see her taking it in, considering, assessing. She might say she's not as smart as me, but she isn't stupid. I tell her about Max and try to explain what he's going through, and she listens, and then she says, "Okay, I won't call him crazy anymore. Even if I suspect he'd still be a little nuts *without* the mental illness."

I smile and shake my head. Then I take out my laptop to do some research.

**CHAPTER 27** I find Brienne's brother online. Not on Facebook or any other social media site. River Ruskin really doesn't strike me as the type to tweet selfies.

Yes, as Brienne said, his name is River. Since I doubt his parents are hippies, I'm guessing he's named after the actor. I'm not one to talk, though. My dad wanted to name me Ripley, after Sigourney Weaver's character in *Alien*. Mom insisted on dropping the *p* to make it more mainstream. We are all victims of our parents' tastes.

With that name, though, it's easy to search for him online, and I find several references to an incident the year before, when he was arrested on drug charges. The case wasn't big enough to make the paper, but in the age where most of us *are* on social media, that doesn't matter. A handful of his former school peers heard the rumor and commented on it, and I put together enough of those comments to get a snapshot of River Ruskin.

He dropped out of high school three years ago, after having spent more time smoking up than attending classes. No known occupation these days, though his peers suspected he was doing the same thing he had been in school: selling dope. Last year's charges had been dropped. After that, River apparently moved on to bigger and badder things, working with the guy who murdered the Porters.

So River plays lookout for the Porters' killers. Brienne overhears. Brienne promises to join the weekend therapy session to find out what I know. Brienne and I are both taken hostage at that session. We're both shot and almost killed. I'd be crazy not to look for my link here. The problem? I can't see it. The obvious answer is crazy. That the guys who killed the Porters wanted to finish the job. Eliminate the witness. But it's been four months, and I haven't exactly been in hiding. The hostage plan was far too elaborate for a simple assassination. And why the hell would River let his sister go in to talk to me if I was about to be killed?

Also, presuming everything that happened that night was about eliminating me seems . . . well, weirdly egotistical. Also paranoid. I'd also like to say it's preposterous—that kind of thing doesn't happen, right? But I'm a cop's daughter, and the night I overheard my dad and his coworkers talking at their poker game was far from the first—or last—time. I was a curious girl who, admittedly, had a macabre turn of mind. I'd listened in often enough to know that people committed murder for the slimmest of motives and rarely had an excuse like schizophrenia.

Murdering potential witnesses is actually common in certain circles. Which is why, for the first month, Mom wouldn't let me leave the house alone. Oh, sure, she'd find an excuse—*Sloane has to drive past the school anyway*; *I want to go to the bookstore too*—but I knew the reason. She'd been worried.

I don't want to think this could have been about me, and it's not just because that sounds self-centered. If it is about me, that means I'm responsible for six deaths. They all died because of me. Yet that's crazy, isn't it? To think these guys would murder six people to get to me? But what if they'd planned to kill only me, and then everything went wrong, and they panicked and . . .

I'll stop there. As Sloane says, you can overthink things—get trapped on the hamster wheel of your own thoughts and fears. I'll stick this in my mental back pocket: River could have been involved.

I dig deeper on Brienne. From what I see on social media, she's an average teen. Sixteen years old. A former cheerleader, having quit the squad in the past year to focus on her grades, much to her friends' dismay and befuddlement. She's stayed on the track team, though, and has an active social life. A normal kid. Someone I could be friends with. No, strike that—someone I *will* be friends with, if she'll have me, when she recovers.

When I dig into Brienne, though, I discover something I should have thought of, and I'll blame the oversight on the fact that I have way too much on my mind. It's been thirty-six hours since we escaped that warehouse, meaning our case is all over the news. Brienne isn't named in most articles—she's an "unnamed sixteen-year-old in critical condition." A few of the online sources identify her, though. And they all identify me, because I guess I lost my right to underage anonymity when I was outed in the Porter case.

Our story is everywhere. It's the perfect news for a slow week: teenage girl survives babysitting slaughter to be hunted by psycho killer during therapy weekend. Except the "psycho killer" isn't Gray. It's Max.

He's eighteen, which means there's no issue with identifying him. Which they do. With particular glee, a few point out he made the news in Britain a year ago, in "another violent incident." They don't elaborate, and when I search on his name, I get nothing, likely because he'd been a minor at the time. But this too makes a great story: the crazy British teen who flees his country only to murder six people here and, really, what has our immigration system come to that they can't keep out guys like this?

Three of the articles hint at a stronger link between Max and the tragedy in the warehouse. More than the fact he has schizophrenia and there is "forensic evidence linking him to the crimes." They mention something found on his computer. A manifesto. That's all they say. I think I know what the word means. I've heard it before, in cases like school shootings. The killer writes a blog or records a video in which he explains his motive. But there is no way in hell Max wrote such a thing, so I think maybe I'm misunderstanding the word. My dictionary app insists I'm not, though.

"Do you know anything about a manifesto found on Max's computer?" I ask Sloane.

She looks up from the magazine she's been reading. "What?"

"A manifesto. It's—"

"It's a declaration. Why someone plans to do something."

"Right. Sorry. I found references to one on Max's computer."

She sets down the magazine. "I didn't hear anything about that. Must be a mistake. You know how journalists are. Dad always said if they can't break a story, they make a story."

"I guess so."

"Time to shut off that laptop yet?"

"I want to make notes while they're fresh in my mind."

She sighs. "I don't know how they *won't* be fresh in your mind tomorrow, when you won't stop thinking about them all night. Thirty minutes. Then lights out."

"Yes, Mom."

**CHAPTER 28** The next morning, I find the hospital bag of my belongings from "that night." The clothing I'd been wearing has been confiscated. But there are the things I had on me, including the map I'd taken from Lorenzo's backpack.

"What's that?" Sloane asks as I set it aside with my stuff.

I tell her, and she picks it up. "One of the counselors had this? In his bag?"

"That's what I said."

"It's not a question, Riley. It's a WTF? Or in terms you may better understand, why on earth would a counselor have a detailed blueprint of the building? Was he planning a scavenger hunt?"

When I don't answer, she says, "Hint, baby sister. I don't really think he was planning a scavenger hunt. But he might have been part of a whole lot deadlier game."

"You think he . . . ? But they shot him."

"Well, duh. I remember once I was talking to Dad about jobs with the highest mortality rate. The answer, by the way, is logging. He said that was wrong. By far the highest mortality rate is in the jobs criminals sign on to do with guys they don't know. The minute things go wrong, they're dead.

— 253

Hell, even if nothing goes wrong, they're probably dead. They were a means to an end."

I remember what Gray said when Predator shot Cantina. *One less share of the pie.*

"It would make sense that they'd need an inside guy," I say.

"Uh-huh."

"Lorenzo was a last-minute replacement. I remember Aimee saying that. Maybe he came on so he could feed them exactly what they needed to know about the group and the building and the timing. He could help keep us calm. Which he didn't do overtly, but he didn't fight, either. He told me to explain hostage situations to the others, probably to reassure them that everything would go fine. Then, after he was shot, he said Aimee—the other counselor—had the cell phone and meds, but they weren't where she said they'd be."

"He moved them."

"And Gideon is the one who actually shot him—by accident."

The door opens. Mom walks in, and I forget what I was saying. Another question surges to the forefront.

"I read online articles covering Friday night," I say. "What's this about a manifesto on Max's computer?"

She stops mid-step and blinks.

Sloane moves forward. "What she really means is, 'Hey, Mom, I'm doing much better, and I'm up and around and busy figuring this mess all out, so when you get a second, could you tell me about this manifesto thing?'"

I remember what Sloane said about the doctor giving Mom something to calm down, and I should excuse her for that, and I do, a little, but there's still that part of me that needed my mother to believe me yesterday.

"Tell me about the manifesto," I say.

"I . . . I don't know what—"

"I saw it mentioned online. If you don't know, then I'd like to speak to the detectives again."

She's quiet. Thinking it through. I can tell she'd rather feign ignorance, talk about something more cheerful, more reassuring, but after a minute she says, "He wrote something on his computer, Riley. Explaining what he planned to do and why. I know you're convinced he isn't responsible, but this proves he is. It was . . . ugly."

"What did it say?"

She fidgets.

"If you want to persuade me he's guilty, you're going to need to tell me."

"It said he was angry. Fed up with his diagnosis and how he's treated because of it. It said he doesn't think he has schizophrenia, and that's just a label they're using to oppress him. He ranted on about conspiracies and persecution. He said he was going to take revenge Friday night, that you were all spies out to get him and he'd kill you all. Especially you."

"What?"

"The letter singled you out. It said you wouldn't pay attention to him, which proved you were a spy. He called you . . ."

When she trails off, I prod with "What'd he call me?"

Her mouth tightens. "'That Mexican bitch.'"

I snort a laugh, and she straightens fast. "This isn't funny, Riley."

"Actually, it is. *They* called me Mexican. Our captors. So did one of the victims. Max asked why everyone presumes I'm Mexican when the only Vasquez he knew was a Spaniard. He would never have called me that. He's being set up."

"No, baby, he's covering his tracks. He asked you about that so he could later *claim* the letter was fake."

"The point of writing the letter, Mom, is to take responsibility. If he's going to deny that, why write it?"

"He has mental problems, Riley. Serious mental problems."

"And because he has schizophrenia, that's your answer for everything, is it? That he's crazy, so who knows why he does anything?"

"I never said crazy—"

"As for Max not believing his diagnosis, he told me he needed medication—the sooner the better—and that I needed to be careful because he sometimes saw or heard things that weren't really there. That isn't a guy rejecting his diagnosis."

She goes quiet again.

"I know that silence doesn't mean you believe me. It means you don't want me to be disappointed when I find out I'm wrong. I'm not going to do anything stupid, Mom. The evidence will exonerate him. I'm certain of that."

"I hope you're right, baby."


I don't even have time to process the implications of that manifesto before Detectives Buchanan and Wheeler return. They don't talk to me. They want my mother, because clearly, despite being only six months from the age of majority, I'm still a child who cannot be told "important stuff." I am, however, old enough to know when important stuff is being discussed and get my ass someplace I can eavesdrop.

Max is about to be charged with six counts of murder.

It's not just the manifesto or the fact that his prints were found on a gun. Two more weapons have been recovered: Predator's and Gray's guns. Both have Max's prints on them.

That is, of course, impossible. That is to say, it's impossible that he actually touched those weapons. Yet his prints are on them, which, combined with the manifesto, means he was thoroughly and completely framed . . . before we ever set foot in that building Friday night.

I'm no computer whiz, but I presume it would be possible to get the manifesto into Max's computer, dated to look as if it had been there before Friday. They could then have gotten his prints from Friday, put them on the other weapons and then dumped both in the warehouse. But I don't think that's what happened at all. It's too haphazard. Gray was not haphazard. He didn't take us captive and then, when things went wrong, kill us all and later say, "Shit, we left witnesses. Wait! One's a schizophrenic. Let's pin it all on him!"

Even as I'm thinking that, I stop. Mentally rewind.

*When things went wrong, kill us all.*

That's not what happened, is it? I remember Sandy dumped in that room. That was always the plan.

*Kill us all.*

I should be dead. I wasn't supposed to be marched down that hall by Predator and released—I was supposed to be marched down that hall, shoved into that room and shot.

If Gideon hadn't protested, that's exactly what would have happened to me. Gideon blew everything to hell. And Gideon saved my life.

We were all supposed to die. And Max would take the fall.

The hostage scenario was to keep us calm. Convince us we'd all be free soon, and then kill us, one by one. Instead of fighting back, we'd happily walk down that hall to our deaths, thinking only of freedom, a few steps away.

Once we were dead, all they had to do was frame Max. They'd have killed him last to make it look like a suicide. One gun—Predator's—would have been responsible for all deaths. They only had to put Max's prints on it, which would have been easy enough to do while he was lying there, dead. The manifesto was already on his computer, ready to be found in the wake of the tragedy.

Why?

Why would anyone want seven therapy kids dead? How could we have any possible connection beyond that weekend?

I don't know. Right now, I don't care. Because Max is about to be arrested and charged with six counts of murder.

## MAX: REALITY

*Reality: the world or the state of things as they actually exist, as opposed to an idealistic or notional idea of them.*

Max has been clinging to the certainty of exoneration. The reality, however . . . yes, the reality is much different, and while his mother might insist no charges will be laid, she has not helped allay his fears. They sit by the window. He's writing. She's staring out, searching for words that don't come, until finally she says, "Is there any chance . . . ?"

"That your son gunned down six people?" he says, not looking up from writing.

"Certainly not. But Mr. Robb . . . your lawyer . . ."

"I know who Mr. Robb is, Mum." He puts down his pen. "The drugs *alleviate* the mental confusion. They don't add to it."

"Yes, well, Mr. Robb needs to know if there is a possibility, however remote, that you did *anything* Friday night. Perhaps involving the boy who accidentally shot himself. You said you tried to stop him. If you grappled for the gun, or if you even grabbed it . . ."

"I didn't touch Aaron or the gun. Not while he was holding it. Riley says—"

Her lips tighten. "I don't care what this Riley says. You are putting far too much stock in the words of a sixteen-year-old girl."

"*Seventeen*-year-old girl, who is also my sole witness until Brienne recovers. Riley's dad was a police detective, which means she knows far more about crime scenes than I do. With Aaron, she demonstrated from the physical evidence that I was not within contact distance at the time of the shooting."

"This girl's father was shot, wasn't he? Killed in the line of duty?"

"Yes."

"And she herself witnessed the death of the couple she babysat for?"

"Yes . . ."

"There aren't any suspects yet in that case, are there?"

He blinks at her, wondering for a moment if his meds *are* working, because she can't possibly be insinuating what she seems to be.

She continues, "It seems terribly coincidental that she'd be caught up in this only a few months after that tragedy."

"Yes, it is terribly coincidental, which is why I won't be at all surprised if the police find a link between those two murders and the ones on Friday night."

His mother says nothing.

"That link is *not* Riley," he says. "Really, Mum? What are you suggesting? That she just happens to have undiagnosed schizophrenia and experienced a psychotic break while I was with her . . . and then used my schizophrenia to make me doubt what I saw? So when Brienne wakes up and gives the *same* story, does that mean she has schizophrenia too? Or no, wait, it means we've both been seduced by Riley's charms. Fallen under her sway."

"I'm not accusing anyone—"

"No, you just suspect I'm lying. Maybe I really did do something. Or maybe I'm covering for Riley. Your son isn't merely schizophrenic, he's a pathological liar."

"That is not what I said at all, Maximus. I do not believe for one moment that you are responsible for this. I was merely saying that if you did *anything*—at all—you need to tell us, because otherwise, if these detectives find out, it's a slippery slope."

"Slippery slope. Huh. How about this: if my lawyer wants to speak to me, please have him speak to me directly. I am legally an adult. Sending my mother to relay his concerns is insulting. I expected better of you."

She doesn't like that. She argues, of course, but the accusation has the desired effect, sidetracking her until she has to leave.

Then he's alone in his room. Writing again, for the first time in a year. It's not his usual fare—the wild and blood-soaked fantasies that everyone thought were so clever and so original . . . before the writer was diagnosed with the crazy bug.

No, Max is writing the story of a girl, one who may bear a marked resemblance to Riley Vasquez. It's a fantasy story, of course, set in some make-believe land where his heroine's father has been murdered by bandits and then she goes into service, only to see her employers brutally murdered. All right, perhaps it is not quite a bloodless tale . . . He's leaving the actual killings out for now, in case the journal is found. In the current scene, the girl has just been accused of her employers' deaths and has set out on a quest to prove—

The door behind him creaks open. He keeps writing. Footsteps tap behind him. Then a voice at his ear, whispering, "You need to get out of here."

He slaps the book shut and gets to his feet, turning to face Riley. "What?"

She talks fast. Almost too fast. He should be accustomed to the American accent after a year stateside, but let's face it, he hasn't exactly led an active social life in the past year.

*Really? And whose fault is that?*

*Mum, I think I need to get out for a while.*

*Splendid! Let's go to a show.*

*That's not what I mean. I was thinking I could take a class. Just one. To keep me in the swing of things. For when I start uni.*

*Silence.*

*I am going to go to uni, Mum. As soon as the meds are sorted. I'll take a half load the first year and see how it goes. The best way to prepare, though, would be to start now with one course.*

*Not yet, Max.*

*Then when?*

*Soon.*

*I am eighteen. I can bloody well—*

*Don't use that language with me. You may be an adult, but if you need to throw that in my face, you're not acting like one, are you? You are temporarily under my care, despite your age, and—*

"Max?" Riley says.

"Yes, I'm listening."

Which he is, even if he's struggling to keep up, and it's not just the accent and how fast she's talking—it's what she's saying. He cannot believe what she's saying.

*Really, Max? Really? No, you believe it just fine. It's exactly what you feared.*

*Reality: the world or the state of things as they actually exist, as opposed to an idealistic or notional idea of them.*

This was his new reality. A world where, when anything went wrong, the blame would land squarely on his shoulders because he was, certifiably, crazy. Any act of violence that involved him could be laid directly at his feet—the perfect walking-and-talking scapegoat. He could whine and moan about that, but he'd already proven it wasn't a baseless accusation, hadn't he? After what he'd done to Justin?

This was what he has to look forward to: a life spent waiting to be accused of exactly this. A life spent knowing that when the accusation comes, it might very well be valid. That he might very well have done it.

Which was no life. No life at all, and furthermore, not one he cared to live. And that—*that*—was his choice, wasn't it?

*Max?*

Nothing. Never mind. Go away.

"What?"

He jumps, sees the look on Riley's face and realizes it was her saying his name, not his inner voice, and worse, he'd replied aloud.

Bloody hell, bloody hell, bloody hell.

"Sorry," he mumbles. "I didn't mean— That wasn't for you. It's . . ."

He realizes what he's saying and sees the look on her face. *Oh, yes, that's better, Max. So much better.*

"Voices," she murmurs, and she nods abruptly, as if processing this as fact and moving on. "I know that's a symptom, so okay."

"It's not . . . I don't . . ." He takes a deep breath. "It's not really like that. It's . . ." He trails off and shrugs. "Never mind."

"No, go on. Please."

He squeezes the bridge of his nose. "I don't like to make excuses. To minimize my condition. I was going to say it's not that kind of a voice, but how do I know? It might very well be. Or perhaps it's evolving into that. All I know is there's a voice. It's mine. It's always been there. It doesn't tell me what to do. It just . . ." He shrugs. "It's like me arguing with myself."

"Doesn't everyone do that?"

"Maybe. Perhaps mine is different. I just . . . I don't want to deny that I have a symptom if I do. For now, I'll just say that it's never told me to do anything stupid. It's usually telling me *not* to."

"What was it telling you *not* to do this time?"

He tenses. She pulls back.

"Sorry," she says. "I'm prying. We shouldn't be talking about this anyway. We really do need to go, Max. If you do it now, you've only left a hospital against doctor's orders. That's not a crime. But as soon as they tell you you're being charged . . ."

"It's entirely another matter."

"Yes. Will you come with me?"

He manages a quirk of a smile. "Are you offering to take me away from all this, Riley Vasquez?"

She returns the smile, a little too bright, relieved he's back to himself. "I am. We're breaking out of here. Sloane is all set with a distraction. As soon as you're ready to go . . ."

He shoves his journal and pen into his jacket and pulls it on. "Ready."

**CHAPTER 29** As I told Max, getting us out of the hospital isn't illegal. Of course, we can't just stroll out, either, or I'm sure someone would summon the police to get those charges laid ASAP. So Sloane distracts the floor staff while we sneak out. Yes, Sloane is letting her little sister leave with a guy accused of mass murder. That took some work. While she calls bullshit on the charges, she wasn't keen on me leaving the hospital with anyone, given my condition. I convinced her, though, and she was the one who'd offered to help with the staff and then keep an eye on Brienne, in case the killers came back.

Max's boots and jacket are evidence now, but his mother had brought him replacements from home—another pair of Doc Martens and a vintage leather motorcycle jacket. Not that he'd had much use for either in the hospital, but I think she was trying to make him more comfortable, like my mother bringing the tattered stuffed marmoset my dad brought home from a training trip when I was little.

Max and I assume that once the detectives realize he and I are gone, they'll put out a BOLO for a Hispanic teen girl walking with a blond guy. We split up and take side roads until we're far enough away that it seems safe to regroup and talk.

I tell Max everything—from Lorenzo to Brienne's brother. Then I tell him all of my research and my plans. He says nothing until I finish, and then, "That's . . . brilliant."

I look over sharply, thinking he might be, if not exactly mocking me, maybe a little amused. But he seems stunned. After a moment he says, "I don't know what I've done to deserve this, Riley."

"You saved my life."

He goes quiet, his boots clomping on the sidewalk. Then he says, "I could have got you killed."

When I look over, he's facing straight ahead.

"You need to know that," he says. "To understand. What I'm capable of."

"I know you can have delusions. There was something in the articles about a violent incident back in England."

He stiffens. I hurry on, "I'm guessing there's some truth to that. From the way you tried to avoid fights in the warehouse, I thought maybe your father abused you . . ."

His head whips my way. Then he lets out a sharp laugh. "Excellent deduction, but no. My father can be a bit of a bastard, but he's never raised a hand to me. Neither of my parents has. They say that's one possible precipitating factor for schizophrenia—an abusive family life—but it isn't the case with me. We have our issues, but they're more issues of expectation. Only child. High-achieving parents. Formerly high-achieving son."

"I'm sorry."

A pained chuckle. "That sounded bitter, didn't it?"

"Frustrated."

He shrugs it off with a roll of his shoulders. *Rather not talk about it, Riley. Let's skip the therapy and stick to the plan, shall we?*

But after a few more steps, he says, "The incident . . . what you read in the papers. I should explain."

"Only if you want to."

"No, but I ought to. It's only right. So you understand what could happen."

We round two corners before he continues. "I thought my best friend was possessed by demons. The twelve Malebranche from Dante's *Inferno*, though the only one who'd talk to me was the leader, Malacoda."

"That's very . . . specific."

"I'm very particular in my special brand of crazy."

He glances over, seeming to expect a smile for that. Instead, I say, "You shouldn't say that."

"That I'm crazy?"

"You have schizophrenia. It's not crazy."

"No? Then what is?" He looks at me, and any trace of good humor vanishes. "If schizophrenia isn't crazy, then what exactly *is* crazy, Riley? I see things that aren't there. Hear sounds that aren't real. I thought my best friend was possessed, and I throttled him for it. Strangled him, trying to free him from the demon. If someone hadn't caught me, I might have killed him, and please do not tell me I wouldn't have done that, that I don't have it in me, because *I* don't know what I'm capable of anymore. I no longer have the luxury of saying I know what I am and what I will and will not do, and I never will again."

He sees my expression and says, "Bloody *hell*," and rubs his hands over his face. "I'm sorry, Riley. You didn't deserve that little rant."

"You're frustrated. Understandably and—"

"Can we not talk about it?"

I'm silent for three heartbeats. Then I say, slowly but firmly, "You started this discussion, Max. I didn't bring it up. I don't know how you want me to respond, but clearly I'm not doing this right, and I'm sorry for that. But I'm not the one who raised the topic or is prolonging it."

"Right." He shoves his hands in his pockets. "Yes, of course."

"You felt you had to explain, but you don't want to talk about it."

"Talk . . ." He yanks his hands out and runs them through his hair, and the band I gave him shoots free and bounces to the sidewalk as he mutters, "Talk, talk, talk."

"Too much talk. I know."

"No, Riley. That's the thing. I do want to . . . I want to . . ." Hands back in his pockets as he mumbles a curse I don't catch, and then, "Focus, focus."

I look up at him. "I know I'm not doing what you want, Max, and I'm trying to figure out what that is, but I can't. So you're going to have to tell me. What do you want right now?"

He kisses me. I don't see it coming. Well, yes, I see him moving forward, but we're standing so close that by the time I see him move, he has my face between his hands and he's lifting it into a kiss. A deep kiss, nothing that can be mistaken for the equivalent of a friendly hug or squeeze. This says more. So much more, and it's everything I didn't realize I wanted him to say until he's kissing me and all I can think is, *Yes. I like this. I really, really like this.*

He backs up fast, his hands dropping. "No, not that. Sorry. Not that."

"Um, I didn't start . . ."

"Yes, I know. It was me. But you can't let me do that."

"Okay . . ."

"Stop me if I do that. Or if I do anything else. If it seems I might hurt you."

"So . . . stop you if you try to kiss me or kill me?"

"Yes."

I bite the inside of my cheek then. I have to, because I

want to laugh at that, at the absurdity of it, but his expression is perfectly serious.

"What I'm trying to say, Riley, is that you can't trust me. Yes, I'm on my meds." He reaches into his pocket and there's a small collection of pills in his palm. "My mum gave me extras, as a security blanket. She knows I worry. That may seem as if it's enough. I'm on the meds, and I'm as level as it gets for me, and I've never done anything while I've been on this dose, but that doesn't mean I *couldn't*. I'm eighteen. I've only been diagnosed a year. My condition is still changing. *I'm* still changing. I need you to be aware of that and to tell me if I start acting odd."

When I don't reply, his lips twitch in the barest smile. "Yes, odder than telling you to stop me if I try to kiss or kill you. For me, that's a normal level of odd."

"Okay."

He eases back and studies my expression. "Do I scare you, Riley?"

"No."

He nibbles his lip as he keeps studying me. "I don't want to, but I think I should. I think it's safer for you if I do."

"You don't scare me, Max. I understand that I need to be careful around you. I understand that I need to be watchful. I understand that if you do something that worries me, I need to get the hell out of your way and not tell myself I'm overreacting, even if I am."

"Exactly!" He throws his arms around me in a hug. "That's exactly it."

I look up at him as he embraces me. "Should you be doing this?"

He sighs. "Probably not."

He backs away, and we both break into a laugh. He runs a hand through his hair and then stops short and looks about the ground for the band.

"Here," I say, peeling another from my wrist.

"No, got it." He retrieves the fallen band, and then pauses and takes the one I'm offering, putting it onto his own wrist with "Backup." His cheeks flush, and I'm not sure why, but it's gone in a blink, as he fastens his hair again and waves at the sidewalk, saying, "Shall we?" and we continue on.

I have a plan. It is not a great one. I'm sure it could be, if I were a detective. Or a criminal. The truth is that I'm not equipped to solve this mystery. Sure, I can pull the "I'm a cop's daughter" routine, but that only gets me one step down a very long path. I have no experience interrogating witnesses. No right to interrogate them. Certainly no skills for either convincing or forcing them to answer my questions. I don't know how to pick a door lock or search an apartment or break through laptop security.

Max knows none of the above either, because we're a couple of middle-class teenagers whose idea of rebellion is blowing off a first-aid course to sneak into a summer concert. When I admit that, Max tops my badassery by confessing that he once stole a punt from Oxford to take a girl for a river ride. Or that's what he told her, when the truth was that he'd gotten permission to take it, because his mother was a prof there, and he certainly wasn't going to risk his own future admission by doing something "daft" just to impress a girl.

On top of our complete lack of experience, we also have situational factors to contend with. Namely, that I've been knifed and shot, meaning I can't exactly run, jump or fight. And Max is wanted by the police for six murders, and soon every cop in the city will be looking for him.

Still, I have a plan, even if it's not quite as impressive as I might like. There are people I want to speak to. With any luck, those conversations will lead to links and clues we can pursue.

I'm convinced now that Lorenzo was in on the scheme. Max agrees with my reasoning. If Lorenzo was part of it, then the most likely motivation would be money. Through his wife, I might be able to confirm that, maybe get a sense of his plan for the money—*we were just about to move into a new house*—or proof they were in serious financial straits—*he was having such a hard time, struggling to pay his mother's cancer bills.*

The first stop on my list is Lorenzo's apartment, where Max waits outside. At this point, I'm not a suspect in anything, and while Lorenzo's wife might be surprised to see me on her doorstep, she'll almost certainly be too deep in grief to have paid much attention to reports on my condition. I'll tell her I was just released from the hospital and came by to offer my condolences.

It's a pretty good plan. And it goes wrong the moment Lorenzo's apartment door opens and the woman standing there is older than my grandmother.

"Is Mrs. Silva in?" I ask.

She shakes her head and starts to close the door. When my hand shoots out to stop her, I think I startle both of us. She falls back with a squeak and I do too, and she nearly slams the door before I can grab the knob.

"I'm sorry," I say quickly. "I know this is a bad time, but—"

She cuts me off with a stream of Spanish so fast that I have to struggle to catch the gist of it. I claim I'm fluent in the language, and I am . . . compared with most kids in my school, who know only enough to successfully order beer and margaritas on a trip over the border.

This woman thinks I'm selling something and says that her grandson has died and if I don't let go of this door she's calling the police.

"*Soy Riley Vasquez*," I say quickly, introducing myself. Then I slow my Spanish, picking my words with care, knowing how bad my accent is. "I was with your grandson. I'm one of the survivors."

Her eyes round when I give my name. When I say the rest, she reaches out and pulls me into a hug, and I get another string of rapid-fire Spanish in a very different tone as she pats my back and then tugs me inside.

"You were with him," she says, still in Spanish. "You were the last to see him."

"I-I—" I'm not ready for this. Damn it, I should have been ready. Of course his family would want to know about the end. Did he say anything? Exactly what happened? Because the police never tell you everything, and you so desperately want to know.

*Was someone with you when you died, Dad? Did they hold your hand? Did you have any last words?*

These are the important things. These are the things no one tells you, because everyone is focused on the crime, on solving it, on fixing the damage. Only it isn't justice you want right then. It's not even justice you want eighteen months later. It's comfort. It's knowing that he didn't die alone. That he didn't linger in pain. And I can say neither of those things about Lorenzo.

But I have to say something, and it doesn't matter if I think he was an accomplice to six murders, because that has nothing to do with this woman. She deserves better.

I want to lie. I want to say that I was there when he died and he went quickly. But if she's heard anything different, then I'll only make it worse.

So I tell her that he managed to escape after he was shot, and I found him and talked to him, and his concern was not for himself but for getting us kids out. That I held his hand and I talked to him but he wanted us to go, to escape, and that we tried as hard as we could to find a phone so we could get him help.

She nods as I talk, and then she hugs me, and I know I've said the right thing and I will not feel guilty that it's not entirely the correct thing. It's true. Every word. That's enough.

"You tried to save him," she says.

"Yes."

"And he tried to save you."

"He did. Me and Max."

She stiffens, and I realize I should have left Max out of it.

"I-I should go," I say. "I just wanted to give my condolences—"

"Have they arrested the boy?"

"Max? I don't know."

"It is not your fault. I hope you understand that."

Now I'm the one tensing. Before I can speak, she says, "The boy is sick. They say it is a mental illness. So I cannot blame him. I will pray for his soul and pray that I am able to forgive him."

I nod and try to back away again, but she catches my arm. "Some people may blame you. Because of what he said. But you must remember he is sick. Not in his right mind."

I realize now what she means. "Because of what he wrote in his manifesto. That he wanted to kill me."

"Yes, it was the ravings of a sick child, and if anyone is to blame, it is that therapist of his." She crosses herself. "I should not speak ill of the dead."

"Aimee, you mean?"

"It was in her notes. She knew about him, how he felt about you, and she did nothing."

"She wrote about me in Max's therapy notes?"

"That is what the detectives told my Lorenzo's wife. She told me afterward, poor girl. It was in this Aimee girl's notes from their private sessions. The boy was in love with you, and he was angry because you did not return his affections. The girl worried he might become violent, and then she let him come to an overnight camp with you?" Grief and anger cloud the old woman's face. "What was she thinking?"

I should be asking myself the same thing. But I'm not. Because I think I know the answer.

**CHAPTER 30** Max waits around the side of the building. We perch on an empty bike rack.

"I'm going to ask you a question," I say, "and no matter how much it may seem absolutely none of my business, there is a point to it. An important one."

"All right."

"It's about your sessions with Aimee. I know you didn't talk in the group sessions. I'm guessing you had private ones?"

"Once a week."

"What did you talk about?"

He shifts his weight. "The usual."

"Max . . . I'm not prying. There's a reason, and I need to hear your answer so I can form an unbiased opinion on something."

"The usual means exactly what one might expect from therapy with an eighteen-year-old schizophrenic. They start by pussyfooting around the 'so, any violent and paranoid impulses lately' question. I've learned to get that out of the way in the first five minutes. It's rather like confession. Listing all those impulses you might have over the course of daily life, like cursing at someone who cuts you off in traffic. That's as far as it goes with me since the meds got straightened around, and there's precious little of that. I'd need to actually be allowed to drive a motor vehicle to curse someone out for cutting me off. Or be permitted to leave the house on my own."

"You aren't allowed to leave the house?"

He makes a face. "Sorry. Flash of petulance there. It happens. Just ignore it. So I would make my tiny confessions and then we'd discuss my *feelings*. Because, really, there is so much variety to discuss. One day I'm bitter and angry, and the next I'm thanking the good Lord for allowing me such a marvelous opportunity to test my resilience." He pauses. "And *that* was bitter and angry sarcasm. Now you see why I don't like to discuss my life these days. Because it hardly shows my best side."

"I don't blame you." I pause. "Sorry. I know you don't want me saying that."

He passes me a wry smile. "To be perfectly honest, I rather like hearing it. Much better than what I hear in here"—he taps his head—"which tells me to stop whining about my lot in life and deal with it. Which would be lovely, except . . . I *want* to deal with it. Stiff upper lip and all that. But it's not exactly working out so far. Now, back on task. Aimee. Lovely girl. Rubbish therapist. She'd tell me that I have the right to be bitter and angry, but the difference when you say it is that I feel you mean it. She's just reciting what she's been taught. So that was it, really. *How do you feel about that, Maximus?* I feel shitty. Absolutely shitty. *As you should, Maximus. Now, let's explore those feelings of shittiness some more*." He rolls his eyes. "That was the extent of it. Feelings, feelings and more feelings with absolutely no attempt to solve the core issues causing those feelings."

I nod. "Okay. Another question, then. This one is going to sound weird and random—"

"You don't need to keep explaining, Riley. I know there's a point to everything you're asking."

"Did you ever talk to Aimee about me?"

That startles him, and he rocks forward. "What?"

"Did you ever, in any context, talk to Aimee about me?"

He seems ready to duck the question, even more uncomfortable than when I asked about therapy. Then he says, "She brought you up. A few times, actually. The first . . . She said I was 'watching' you." He air-quotes "watching." "I didn't like the way she said it, as if I were stalking you, and I let her know that."

"What did you say?"

He shifts and looks off into the distance.

"You don't have to answer, obviously," I say. "I can tell you what she said, and you can tell me what happened—"

"And then it will sound as if I'm tailoring my answer to hers, which doesn't help you at all. She said I was watching you. I said if I seemed to be, then it was simply that's where my gaze landed when I was daydreaming, and yes, I may look your way now and then, but you're a pretty girl and it'd be odder if I *didn't*."

Before I can respond, he continues, "She didn't drop it there. Later, she said she caught me 'following' you after a session. You went to use the toilet, and I headed the same way. Then I turned back. I could have said I changed my mind, but I was honest. I told Aimee that you'd said something in therapy, and I wanted to comment on it in private, but I chickened out. An impulse quickly stifled. Following you down a hall *once*—and then turning back—hardly constitutes stalking. But that's what she suggested. I was not pleased. So she changed tactics. Rather than intimating I might have an unhealthy interest in you, she began suggesting I had a perfectly healthy one. That perhaps she could have the two of us in for joint counseling, because I might be more comfortable talking if it was only you. She made it seem like it was just therapy, but . . ."

He adjusts his stance, leaning on the bike rack. "It felt as if she thought I fancied you and was trying to match us up. I called her out on it. I said dating was the last thing on my mind right now, and as my therapist, she should be arguing *against* it, not trying to set me up. She got defensive, said that wasn't what she was doing, accused me of transference, that I did fancy you and was putting that on her." He purses his lips. "It may have been the only time we had an honest conversation. Certainly the first time I got a reaction out of her."

"And then?"

"That was it. We had one more session after that, but when she brought you up, I pulled my high-and-mighty routine and told her to stick to her job and suggested your family would not be pleased to know she'd been trying to match you up with a diagnosed schizophrenic."

There's at least a minute of silence before he says, "Dare I ask what she said? I'm guessing you heard something up there from Lorenzo's wife? That Aimee made some comment about me and you, presumably one that supports that manifesto rubbish?"

I tell him what Aimee's therapy notes say. There wasn't a moment when I thought they could be true, but if there had been, the horror on his face would have eradicated that.

"She said—? No. Just . . ." A violent shake of his head. "*No.* Absolutely not, Riley. That's . . . I can't . . ."

"I didn't think it was true."

"Thank you, because . . . No. Just . . ." He points at his mouth. "Loss for words here, which, as you might have noticed, does not happen often. I understood the manifesto rubbish—that was someone framing me, and if you're going to explain why an eighteen-year-old boy does something daft, the obvious answer is a girl. But for Aimee to say I . . . Yes, I admitted I might . . . if the circumstances were different . . .

But no, just *no*. Even if I did fancy you and even if you rejected me—which obviously did *not* happen—I've never kept after a girl who wasn't interested. I don't have to . . ."

"You don't have to force girls to go out with you."

"That sounds cheeky. But I've never needed to, and I wouldn't, and . . . I don't even know where to go with this. I have no idea why Aimee would say that. Why she'd say any of it. Including that she was concerned I'd turn violent. The worst thing I confessed to was that I occasionally want to tell my mother to clear off and leave me alone."

"That applies to all mothers at some point."

He manages a half smile, but it's strained. This has spooked him, in a way the manifesto didn't. "I don't know what to tell you, Riley. I don't know if it's possible that I said something I don't remember, that I lost the plot for a few moments and said things I can't *imagine* I'd ever say, but if I did, why wouldn't she tell me? Tell my mother? Why would she *ever* let me go to that overnight with you?"

"How did you end up at the weekend session?"

"Hmm?" He looks up and his eyes are unfocused, questions still swirling too fast for him to rise far from his thoughts. "How . . . ? Right. That's the thing. It was her idea."

"Tell me about that," I say. "How it came about."

He shrugs, as if wanting to throw off the question and pursue more important ones. "Aimee suggested it. I said no. Bloody hell, no. Sleepover group therapy? Absolutely not. She went to my mother and convinced her it was what I needed—the social interaction and all that. I still argued, but then I found out you were going and—" He stops, eyes widening as he realizes what he's said. He runs a hand through his hair, partly dislodging the band again. "Bugger it. That doesn't help my case at all, does it? Yes, all right, I thought if you were going, perhaps I could speak to you."

"About what?"

Another shrug, his cheeks coloring. "Just speak to you. I knew I should be making more of an effort, and you seemed like someone I could talk to. *Not* in the way Aimee thought. And I never mentioned to her that I wanted to speak to you, because that would have only exacerbated the situation, so . . ." He clears his throat and eases back. "That was it, then. My mum wanted me to go, and I decided I was not utterly opposed to the plan."

"It wasn't Lorenzo," I say.

"Hmm?"

"We know they needed to have someone on the inside. That map made me think it was Lorenzo. But there was no proof it was his map and that it wasn't planted, like that manifesto and your fingerprints. The fact he was added at the last moment seemed suspicious, but it was just bad luck. Aimee needed a co-therapist for the weekend, to make it legit."

"And when the first one backed out, she got Lorenzo to fill in."

I nodded. "But he didn't play any role. He couldn't—we weren't *his* patients. Whoever arranged this had to make sure you and I were there. If Aimee wrote those notes before she went to the sleepover Friday, it was preplanned. We had to be there. You are the scapegoat and I'm the reason you went off. Like you, I resisted going—not my idea of a fun weekend. She also did an end run around me to my mother. It was Aimee who sent us after the cell phone that wasn't there, along with the meds that also weren't there. Did you hear what she said to Gray before he shot her?"

"*Oh, it's you.*" Max nods. "I thought she mistook him for Aaron, that the lighting was poor and they're of a similar size."

"I thought the same. Then, after he shot her the first time, she said, 'Why me?' and he said that her job was done, we didn't need more therapy, and he didn't need any loose ends."

"Which made sense in context, but makes even more sense if she was in on the scheme. You, Riley Vasquez, are absolutely brilliant."

He gives me a smack on the lips, like a high-five. Then he pauses and gives me a real kiss, his arms around me, pulling me against him, and *damn*, it's a kiss, and it's far from my first, but at that moment, it feels like it. Then he stops short and backs up sharply with, "Right. Sorry. No. You need to stop letting me do that."

"No, *you* need to stop that. Because it's kinda not my responsibility."

"Yes. Of course." His gaze drops lower as he fidgets. Then he stops. "Does that mean you don't mind it?" Before I can answer, he straightens. "No, sorry. Not the point. Not the point at all. If you don't, that's . . . well, that's good. Or it would be. Except that the larger problem is that I can't be kissing . . . That is to say, I shouldn't . . . No, I *cannot*."

"Then *stop* kissing me, Max, because you're setting up an expectation you have no intention of following through on."

"Yes. Of course. I didn't mean . . . It was an impulse, and I apologize for indulging it."

"Once is an impulse. You've kissed me more than once."

"A repetitive impulse?"

I give him a hard look.

"A new symptom?" he tries.

A harder look.

He sighs. "All right. Not a symptom. It's just me. I . . . You're . . . Aimee may have been a poor therapist—and an accomplice to mass murder—but she was not entirely mistaken in thinking I fancied you. I just . . . It wasn't the way . . . That is . . ."

"Let me cut through this, because as much fun as it is to watch you squirm, getting your name cleared is a little more important right now. You're kissing me on impulse when you know you shouldn't. Now, it could be that you're pulling that bad-romance-novel crap." I put on my best romantic-hero voice, complete with extravagant hand gestures. "'No, we shouldn't be together, really we shouldn't . . . unless you want to and can convince me all my fears are for naught.'"

He sputters a laugh. "No. That's rather brilliant, but no."

"I didn't think so. You're not the type."

"Not a romantic hero?"

"Not a *bad* romantic hero."

That gets a grin. "So I'm a good—"

"Enough. Your ego may have taken a blow with your diagnosis, but in some areas I suspect it doesn't need bolstering."

"It can *always* use—"

"No. So cut the bullshit, Max. If you want to kiss me, kiss me. You're good at it, though I probably shouldn't admit that. But I'm not complaining, and I'm not expecting anything more out of it, because you aren't the only one dealing with a lot these days."

His smile fades. "Of course. Sorry. That was rather self-centered of me."

"Forgiven. Point is, kiss me or don't. Just stop apologizing if you do, and don't you dare tell me *I* should be the one to stop you."

"Yes, ma'am."

"Now, back to the important stuff."

"Kissing isn't important?"

"Focus, Max."

"I can't. It's a symptom."

"It's an excuse. Focus. Or I'll leave you behind."

"Mmm, no, you can't," he says "I have a condition that makes it unwise to abandon me in public places."

"Bullshit. But if you feel that way, I can make sure you're well taken care of . . . with one call to 911."

"You don't have your mobile."

"Pay phone."

"They still have those?" he says. "All right. I'll focus. Lorenzo was an innocent victim. Aimee was the inside connection. Or that is our working theory, and to substantiate it, we ought to pay a visit to her residence. We'll need to locate the address."

"I have it."

He smiles. "Of course you do. Tallyho, then."

I slide off the bike rack. "By the way, that's a fox-hunting term, possibly derived from a French word used to work up hounds on a hunt. In fox hunting, it means that the target is in sight. NASA astronauts use it when they spot something in space." I glance over. "I looked it up."

"Of course you did." He twists for a quick kiss on my cheek. "Because you're brilliant."

I sigh. "Less kissing, more keeping-your-ass-out-of-jail, okay?"

"Yes, ma'am."

# CHAPTER 31

Lorenzo and his wife lived in a decent apartment in a decent part of town. That is, I suppose, what one would expect for a thirty-year-old counselor and his schoolteacher wife. Aimee was younger than Lorenzo, and she can't have been making significantly more money, but she has a nice Victorian house in the kind of neighborhood young professionals aspire to. It's possible that Aimee came from money, but when I look at this neighborhood, it only supports my conclusions.

I'd hoped there was more to it. Yes, there is no excuse for helping to murder any innocent person. Yet I wanted, if not to exonerate Aimee, at least to understand how this person I trusted—this person I liked—could do such a thing. I wanted to learn that she had a child I didn't know about and these ruthless killers kidnapped him and forced her to help them, and all along she'd been planning ways to save us, but then everything went to hell and she couldn't.

Which is bullshit. She led us on a wild goose chase for the cell phone and meds. Even after everything went wrong, she stuck to her role. I cannot understand that. I can't even begin to try.

As we walk down her street, no one suspiciously peers out of a window or slows to eye us from their car. We're just a clean-cut teenage couple, cutting through their peaceful neighborhood. Even with the tied-back hair, Doc Martens and motorcycle jacket, if Max reached into his pocket, you'd expect him to whip out a sketch pad, not a semi-automatic.

Aimee's house is the second from the corner. We scout the landscape and decide the yards are wooded enough to attempt a back-way entry through the neighboring one.

Yes, we plan to break in, despite the fact that neither of us has any experience with it. I'm relying on my extensive knowledge of fictional representations of breaking and entering. Max is relying on . . . me. This should go well. Climbing the first fence reminds me how much more recovery time I require. I manage it, though, with Max's help.

While Max stands guard, I creep to the back door. I send up a Hail Mary, on the very slim chance of divine intervention, because I'm going to need it. I hope that Aimee left her back door open or a window ajar. If necessary, though, I will break one of those windows. I'm already mentally planning how to do it—seeing one on the basement level, sizing up whether I can fit through, spotting a rock in the garden that will work, wondering if I dare ask Max if I can borrow what is likely an expensive and rare jacket to wrap the rock in so it'll make less noise when I break the glass.

I'm turning the knob, my sweater sleeve pulled over my hand to keep it fingerprint-free. My mind has already moved on to the window-smashing plan, because there's no way this door will be open. But it's not only open—it *opens*. It jerks wide, someone on the other side pulling as I'm pushing, and I leap back thinking, *You idiot! Just because she lives alone doesn't mean her house will be empty!* And then I see River Ruskin. Standing there, holding the knob in his gloved hand as he stares at me.

His other hand slams out, and I think I'm a goner. There will be a knife in that hand, maybe even a gun, and I was stupid, so damned stupid, thinking I could investigate murder—*mass* murder. Me. A seventeen-year-old high school kid whose only claims to any expertise are a detective father and a penchant for crime novels. Stupid, stupid, stupid. And now dead.

Only there isn't a weapon in his hand. All he does is shove me aside and run past, and that's when he sees Max—a bigger guy, in combat boots and a leather jacket, charging straight at him. River reaches for whatever weapon he has in his pocket. I grab the first thing—the only thing—I see, and I swing it at his head. And damn, that hurts. Hurts so much that it feels as if he stabbed me. He didn't—it's just the fact that I'm swinging a garden shovel as hard as I can, forty-eight hours after I *was* stabbed. The pain is bad enough that I don't even see the shovel connect. Everything goes black, and I start to fall.

My arms shoot out wildly in the dark. I hit something. It's soft. It gives a not-so-soft *oomph*. The darkness clears, and I see Max grabbing me. I ward him off with, "River!" and he pauses, frowning, as he wonders why the hell I'm talking about bodies of water at a moment like this. Then there's a flash of dismay, as he thinks this incongruity proves he's having trouble with his reality settings. Before I can open my mouth again, his lips form an "Oh!" of comprehension and he turns sharply . . . and looks down.

River lies motionless on the ground.

"Huh," Max says. "You really hit him."

I scramble over, and Max says, "You didn't kill him, Riley. It was a garden spade."

We both kneel beside River, checking vitals. He's fine. Just unconscious.

"We should get him into the house and question him," I say.

Max's lips twitch.

"What? Do you have a better idea?"

"I do not. I'm simply reflecting on the fact that you are a very remarkable girl, Riley Vasquez."

"You're not going to kiss me again, are you?"

"Do you want me to? You can ask, if you do. No need to be shy."

"If I wanted it, I'm quite capable of initiating it."

He smiles. "Even better."

"Focus . . ."

"Completely focused."

"On him." I point at River.

"I don't want to kiss him. I'm sure he's a nice bloke—"

"We need to get him in the house."

"Right." He shucks his jacket. "I'll do that."

"Can you lift him?"

"I'm not thin; I'm wiry. It's all muscle. Go on inside, prepare the way and ignore any humiliating grunts of exertion you hear from the yard."

Despite his self-deprecating commentary, Max doesn't seem to have much trouble hauling River in. I pull butcher's twine off a shelf, bind River and then gag him with a dishcloth. Max is impressed, which of course he lets me know, with a steady stream of banter and flattery and flirting.

I'm trying to save his ass from jail, and he's flirting. I could give him shit for that, but he knows how much trouble he's in. He's helping me, and he's watching out for me, and he's doing everything he should. It's just . . . I don't know how to describe it. There's almost a giddiness to his goofing around, a relief. It's not gallows humor. He seems, in a weird way, genuinely happy.

We're not running for our lives anymore. We're just solving a crime, and yes, his freedom may be at stake, but there's a sense—a profoundly unsettling sense—that this is what he expects. That naturally he'll be blamed for the murders. So he'll leave the outrage to me, in an almost amused way, pleased that I care enough to be outraged on his behalf.

He certainly *hopes* we'll find the answers he needs. Yet the overall situation is what he expects, as a guy with schizophrenia, so he might as well relax and enjoy himself.

While Max is prepared to do whatever I need, the one thing I won't ask of him is violence. Rather than shake or slap River awake, I get ice water from the fridge and dump it on his head. He wakes with a start, realizes he's bound and gagged, and fights madly . . . until he sees who captured him. Then he stops, his eyes narrowing.

"I'm going to remove the gag," I say. "But if you scream, I'll put it back in."

His eyes narrow more, offended at the suggestion he'd scream.

"You broke into Aimee Carr's house," I begin. "You aren't carrying anything, so you didn't find what you were looking for. What was it?"

I pull out the dishcloth so he can speak, and he says, "I didn't break in. I came to see her family. To say I was sorry about what happened."

"Great. Where are they, then?" I wave around the empty house. "No, let me guess . . . You offered your condolences, and then you got tired, so they let you sleep on the couch while they left to make funeral arrangements."

It's only when Max snorts that River realizes I'm being sarcastic. Up to then he seemed relieved, as if I'd given him an excuse he could use.

"I could ask you the same," he says after a moment's thought. "You were breaking in when I was leaving."

"No, I was coming to do exactly what you claim you were: offer condolences."

"By just walking in?"

"I was about to knock when you pulled open the door."

He hesitates, and he's trying to reimagine the scene, to prove I'm lying, but I suspect in the shock of seeing me there he didn't notice my hand was on the knob.

I continue, "You broke in. I want to know—"

"The door was open," he says. "I walked in, and I called to see if someone was here."

"He's not going to give you a proper answer, Riley," Max says.

When Max speaks, River jumps. He twists to stare at him. "You're . . . You're . . ."

"A random mate who just came along for the ride?" Max says. "I'm quite certain my photograph is in the paper, but that would require *reading* the news. A little beyond you, perhaps?"

"I know who you are," River says.

Max sighs. "That was, I believe, the gist of what I was saying. You figured out who I was when I opened my mouth. What gave it away? The sudden stream of crazed ranting?"

"It was the accent," River says, the sarcasm soaring over his head again.

Max rolls his eyes. "Yes, I'm the bloke who allegedly attempted to murder your sister. I could defend myself against the charge, but perhaps if you believe I'm guilty, you'll answer Riley's questions a tad more readily."

River stares like he's talking in a foreign language.

Max speaks slower. "Answer Riley or she'll walk out and leave you with the schizophrenic and a kitchen full of sharp implements."

River studies him as if he suspects this is not quite the terrifying prospect it should be. Then he squares his shoulders. "I was coming to speak to the family—"

"I know you were there when the Porters were killed," I cut in.

Max's chin shoots up, and he shakes his head hard, telling me I don't want to go there. I focus on River, who has gone very, very still.

"I saw you that afternoon," I say. "Just before the murders. I was in the front room upstairs and I looked down and saw you. I didn't think anything of it. You were just some kid hanging around. Then I met you at the hospital with Brienne, and I knew there's no way I just happened to be in a hostage situation with the sister of the guy who was randomly hanging out at the site of the *last* shooting I witnessed. You were the lookout."

At this point, he should quiz me to be sure I'm telling the truth. Where was he standing that day? What was he doing? But he's not bright enough for that, and only says, "You're wrong. Maybe you saw some guy who looked like me, but—"

"Fine. Play it that way. You don't want to talk to me, you can give your alibi to the police."

He goes even more still than before, if that's possible. He's breathing hard, struggling against a surge of panic.

"She found out, didn't she?" I say. "Brienne. Somehow she learned you were involved, and she threatened to tell someone, and you somehow got her to that therapy session. She was supposed to die there with me."

"What? No. I'd never— My *sister*? *No.* All she was supposed to do—" He stops short as he realizes what he's saying.

"Cat's out of the bag," Max says. "Can't stuff it back in now. If you try, we'll be making that call to the police. What was Brienne supposed to do for you?"

"Talk to you," he blurts to me. "Find out what you know. Yes, Brienne overheard something, and worse, *they* found out, because I was on the phone and she said something, and they heard her. They made me send her. Either she went to that therapy thing or I was in deep shit."

"Sounds like you were in it already," I say.

"It was a stupid, *stupid* thing. I promised some guys I'd get their product from the supplier. I was the delivery boy, that's it. But I got caught, and it was enough dope that I was looking at twenty years. These guys promised to get me out of that. In return, I owed them this favor—standing guard while they pulled a hit. That's all I did: stand guard. Just like I only carried the damned dope. But it just keeps getting worse, one thing leads to another, and now my sister's in the hospital and—"

"Pulled a *hit*?" Max says.

River seems annoyed by the interruption. "It means they were hired to kill those people."

"I watch enough American television to know what a hit is, thank you," Max says. "But you're saying that the murder of the Porters—the people Riley babysat for—was a professional assassination?"

"That's what these guys do. The ones who got me off the drug charges. They kill people for money. The job was to off that guy and his wife. The guy's business partner wanted him out of the way and didn't want the wife getting his share."

**CHAPTER 32** I know why River is talking. Well, besides the fact that we've threatened to call the cops. Dad always said that was the difference between the hardened criminals and the people who just screw up really bad: the screwups feel guilt. They want to confess. They want to be told that it's not so bad, and that you understand how it happened and they aren't really terrible people.

"You didn't have a choice," I say. "You were looking at twenty years for the drugs, and if these men didn't hire you to stand watch, they'd have hired someone else. You couldn't have stopped them from killing the Porters." *Except, you know, by turning them in before they did it.* "And the little girl wasn't a target, right?"

"No, not at *all*," he says emphatically. "It was the client's fault she was there. He told the guys that she'd be with her aunt, and it'd just be the couple at home, and they weren't supposed to be leaving for another hour. Then we get there, and the couple are already getting ready to leave, so they had to move fast. It wasn't until the news hit that they realized the kid had been there all along."

"Which is when they started worrying that I saw something."

He nods. "One of the guys says you *did* see him. Out front."

"I saw a gun. That's all. If I got a look at the guy's face, there would have been sketches released."

"That's not what they heard. They have contacts on the force who say the cops running the case claim you did get a better look. That you just don't remember everything yet, but when you do, they'll have enough to make a case."

"Meaning if I die, your friends are free and clear."

"They *aren't* my friends." He shifts, meeting my gaze, struggling for sincerity. "And if they planned to kill you, why would they want Brienne to talk to you?"

I know the answer. I'm not telling him, though, because once I do, I have a feeling I'll get nothing more from him. Instead, I say, "Tell me about Aimee."

His face screws up.

I resist the urge to sigh. "The woman who lived here? She was my therapist. She got me to enroll in that weekend, and I'm guessing she helped Brienne get in."

"She's with one of the guys. His girlfriend. That was how it started. She's a therapist, and she works with kids sometimes, so they had her go after you to find out what you knew."

Yes, Aimee had indeed "gone after me." She'd contacted my mother directly, saying she'd read my story in the paper and she had experience with similar cases, and while she heard I was in therapy already, she'd like to offer her services if I needed extra help. It'd been perfect timing, because Mom had just fired my therapist, which Aimee might have heard through the grapevine.

River is still talking, faster now, eager to convince me. "Only you wouldn't tell Aimee anything about what you saw, so they figured maybe you'd talk to another girl *in* therapy: Brienne."

Which makes sense, and I don't blame him for buying it. I prod him for more on Aimee. He says he broke into her house hoping to learn more about her, and maybe that suggests he's not as stupid as he seems. That he suspects there's more to this than he thought. He's just hoping he's wrong. I'm about to shatter that hope.

"You said there was no reason why they'd send in Brienne to question me if they planned to kill me, right?"

He nods.

"So it's just a coincidence, then? You work for hit men. I witnessed a hit. Your sister overheard it. Now she joins up with me at therapy for one weekend, and it's the same weekend that someone chooses to randomly murder a group of kids?"

Sweat trickles down his cheek and his gaze shoots to Max. "He doesn't need a reason. He's nuts. A psychopath."

"Does he look like a psychopath?"

River gives an abrupt laugh at that. "You think killers *look* like killers? You really are a sheltered rich kid, aren't you? In your world, the bad guys walk around with sneers and scruffy beards. It's not like that, little girl. Not at all. If you saw the guys I work for . . ." He shakes his head. "Believe me, there's a reason you passed one of them on the street and never took another look. The face of a psycho looks like everyone else." He peers at Max. "Like you. You look normal, but you're crazy."

"Could I kill someone if I'm not on my meds?" Max says. "Yes. Could I slaughter six people? I'd certainly like to think not, but I suspect, once it snaps, there's no difference between one and six. If I could tell the difference, I wouldn't even kill one, would I?"

River just stares like he's speaking Greek.

"I could kill someone if I was in a psychotic state," Max says. "Maybe even six people. But do you know what I can't do? Switch it off and act normal again a few minutes later. I almost strangled my best friend because I thought he was possessed. When they caught me, I kept trying to strangle him until they pulled me off. I didn't deny that I did it. I didn't make excuses. I just kept on acting crazy, because that's what crazy is. It's your reality *at that moment*. I didn't go into a fugue state where I had no idea what I was doing. I remember every last detail as if it happened two hours ago, because for me, it did. It happens over and over, and I cannot get it out of my head, because I can't pretend it was someone else—it was me, and I remember what it felt like to have my hands around his neck. I remember the girl screaming when she found us. I remember the look in my best friend's eyes. I remember the smell of him when he shat himself, because he was so sure he was going to die."

Max has to stop for breath, and I . . . I want to cry. I see the look in *his* eyes, hear the pain and the guilt and the self-loathing in his voice, and I want to do something, any-thing, and I can't, because this isn't therapy. It's everything he should have said there. Everything he couldn't say, and now I know why, because if I can't talk about the Porters—what it was like to see their bodies, what exactly I feel—then I sure as hell can't expect him to share, because his private hell is ten times worse.

He couldn't spew that anguish to strangers in therapy and then watch them awkwardly try to deal with it. He does it here because I can do nothing. No, that's not true—this isn't about me. He does it because he needs to explain this, to make his point to River, and he can say it without fear that I'll make noises of comfort and understanding about something I can't understand, not really.

He pauses only a moment, enough to catch his breath, before he goes on. "What happens to me, it doesn't come with amnesia, temporary or not. I don't pass out and forget what happened. It's not an alternate personality. It doesn't feel like something from a half-remembered nightmare. It's *reality*. And it doesn't switch off like a light bulb. If I shot Brienne and the others, the police wouldn't have found me jumping in front of a car, desperate to get an ambulance for Riley and your sister. I wouldn't have made up some wild story about a hostage-taking. I certainly wouldn't have had the mental wherewithal to persuade Riley that such a story was true. I'd have been running down the street, holding a bloodied knife and a smoking gun, ready to tell the world that I'd rid them of aliens posing as teenagers or some such rubbish. I *would not realize* I had done anything wrong."

He stops again. He's shaking, and I want to reach for him, but I know I can't. Not now. What he needs now—what he needs always—is support and understanding, not sympathy, because he hates the sympathy and the poor-you as much as I do. It feels like putting on the mask of a crying child and convincing the world you deserve their sympathy when it's the last thing you feel you deserve.

"Do you understand that?" I say to River.

He nods dumbly.

"Max didn't do any of it, and I think you already suspected that, regardless of what you said in the hospital yesterday. There is a way this wasn't a coincidence. And a reason why—if it's the guys you worked for—they'd shoot Brienne."

"Because things went wrong," he says. "They set this up to kill you—*and I did not know that, I absolutely did not know that*—and things went wrong, and Brienne was shot accidentally. They mistook her for one of the other girls—"

"They'd already shot both the other girls. And obviously there was no way they mistook her for me."

Sweat streams down his face now. He does not want to think he sent his sister in there for people who would kill her, because then he has to admit how stupid he was, thinking she'd be safe when his employers murder people for money. He needs it to have been an accident. I understand, but I can't let him think that or he's not going to give us what we need.

"They didn't mistake her for anyone. They murdered every last—"

"Yes," he blurts. "Yes, all right. Things went wrong, and they killed everyone. They knew who she was, and they shot her anyway to tie up all the loose ends when it went bad."

"It didn't go bad. Killing everyone was their plan from the start."

"What? No. That's nuts. They planned to cover up your murder with a hostage-taking. They'd get money out of the rich kid's father. I heard them say they had a big score coming, some business guy with a bottomless bank account. That was the plan. I see it now—I just didn't put it together at first."

"They never initiated any negotiations. The only way they were getting money from Aaron's dad . . ." I trail off as I realize what I'm thinking.

"Is if they were hired by him," Max finishes for me.

"No, that really *is* nuts," I say. "No one is going to hire a hit man to kill his own son."

River snorts. "You are such a sheltered rich kid. There are plenty of parents who don't give a shit. Like mine. And I know, from working with these guys, that there are people who'd put a hit on their grandmother if there was profit in it."

"But there *was* no profit. Aaron's dad found out he was gay, but no father is going to kill his kid for that."

"Don't be too sure," River mutters.

"There was profit in it, Riley," Max says quietly. "The divorce settlement. I have no idea what kind of money they could be talking for child support and trust funds and whatever else, and I'm still with you on this—I don't see how a parent could hire someone to murder his son for *anything*—but add up the factors and . . ." He shakes his head. "No, sorry. I still can't fathom it."

"Doesn't mean it's not true," River says.

I remember what Aaron said about why he'd been at the sleepover. His father arranged it. Insisted on it. Threatened him if he didn't go. I feel like I'm going to throw up.

"So that's what happened," River continues. "A hit for money plus one to remove a potential witness. But it went wrong and—"

"The only thing that went wrong is that they had to abandon their plan and turn an organized mass murder into a free-for-all. They pretended it was a hostage-taking. Then they began releasing kids. Do you know how they released them? Took a girl—Sandy—to another room and shot her, letting us think she got out. *No one* was supposed to get out. Including your sister. Part of this *was* about cleaning up loose ends. Brienne was a loose end."

"That's— No— They wouldn't . . ." He swallows, as if realizing how ridiculous that sounds, to say that the hit men he worked for wouldn't murder his sister. "But . . . but I'd find out."

"I don't think they're too worried about you," Max says.

"They'd never have told you they were behind it," I say. "It would have seemed like Max killed everyone, including your sister. But I'm still alive. Max is still alive. Brienne is still alive. And we all know the truth."

"No," he whispers, his eyes widening. "Brienne!" He tries to scramble up. "I need to get to the hospital."

"Sloane is watching her."

He stares at me blankly.

"My sister."

"That girl I met? Seriously? She's probably taken off with the first cute intern who looked her way."

"Sloane is watching your sister, and the nurses' desk is right outside the door. Brienne is safe. No one can get to her."

"Of course they can. You don't understand. They can

get to her *easily*. They—" He stops himself and shakes his head.

"And here's the part where you tell us all about them," Max says.

"After I see my sister."

"No," Max says. "Tell us, and then you see her."

River's jaw sets. Then his legs shoot out, in an awkward kick that still makes contact. Caught off guard, I fall back with an *oomph*. Max jumps in and grabs him by the back of the shirt, but River starts flailing, struggling madly, and I know that twine isn't going to hold, and I know I'm in no shape to take him down if he gets free, and I can't ask Max to do it.

"Okay!" I say. "Okay. We'll take you to Brienne. You'll see she's all right, and then you'll tell us what you know or I'm going straight to the police."

**CHAPTER 33** We untie River. Max uses River's own switchblade to do it. He keeps the knife to use as a threat. I take Max aside.

"Let me have the knife," I say. "If he needs to be threatened, I'll do it. I know you hate—"

"Am I acting odd?" Max whispers. He gives a tired quirk of his lips. "Odder than normal?"

"Of course not. That isn't why—"

"That should always be 'why,' Riley. If I pick up a steak knife at dinner, you need to ask yourself whether I've been acting normal."

"That's—"

"You can argue with me about it later. I know that's not why you don't want me having the switchblade, and I appreciate the thought. But I'm the one he's frightened of. Ergo, I must play bad cop today."

We're heading out. River is in the lead. He drove, and his car is down the block. Max is right behind him. The knife is in Max's pocket, but River seems in no hurry to test how quick he is on the draw. His concern is his sister.

Max makes River help me over the fence. I'm struggling

to stay upright and my only goal now is not to collapse. My side is burning and my legs keep threatening to give out. We scale the fence, and we're walking to the corner when two figures turn it.

I don't react at first. It's a residential neighborhood. Two men in suits have just come around the corner, and I'm focused on moving forward and watching River. It's River who reacts, stopping short and turning fast, about to run, and Max sees that and *he* reacts. He grabs River by the back of the shirt and then someone says, "Thank you, Max," and we all go still.

I turn to the two men, one now taking River as Max grabs my arm, and the second man says, "Uh-uh. If you're going to run, Max, please don't take Riley. I think you've gotten her into enough trouble."

It's Buchanan and Wheeler, the detectives.

"It's over now, Riley," Buchanan says to me. "He can't hurt you."

I protest, saying that Max never hurt me, that it's all a mistake, that we have answers now, and River is telling me to shut up, just shut the hell up, and Wheeler takes him and Buchanan is on his radio, calling for backup. Max is looking left and right, as if trying to figure out what to do.

Should we run? *Can* we run? No. We can't, and I don't see the point. We may not have everything we need, but we have answers, and the police have River. Time to let this play out.

I glance at Max, and it's as if he's read my mind. He's nodding and indicating we should go with them, that it'll be all right. So we let Buchanan lead us to their unmarked car while Wheeler waits for a backup cruiser to take River.

# MAX: ALACRITY

**Alacrity:** *brisk and cheerful readiness.*

To say that Max accepts the current situation with alacrity would be an exaggeration, but not, perhaps, as much as one might think, given that he is in the back of a police car, disarmed, cuffed and about to be charged with mass murder.

Riley argued about the handcuffs. He stopped her and accepted them with something approaching alacrity. The end is near. He's certain of it now. The police have River, and the young man will, as they've discovered, talk without even an application of implied force. He got in over his head, and he desperately wants out, and he wants to protect his sister, particularly since it was his own stupidity that got her into this bloody mess.

When Riley recovers from the shock of Max being arrested, she immediately asks Detective Buchanan to put a security detail on Brienne. That's where her mind goes—to the welfare of others—because that's the sort of person she is. The sort who'd break him from a psychiatric ward and set out— two days after being shot and stabbed—to clear his name.

And she kissed him.

Well, more accurately, she allowed herself to be kissed by him. But she'd made it clear those kisses were not unwelcome, and even if he knew it shouldn't lead anywhere—really shouldn't—what matters is that for those few moments, she let him be something he never thought he could be again. A boy with a girl. A boy flirting with a girl, teasing a girl, kissing a girl and being kissed in return. A boy who fancies a girl being fancied in return.

*Mmm, quite certain it goes beyond mere fancying, Maximus. You are indeed mad about the girl.*

Doesn't matter. Doesn't matter one bit.

*So when this is over, you'll be fine with a handshake and a fare-thee-well?*

No, but I'm hoping we can be friends.

He swears he hears the voice laughing, but he silences it. It doesn't matter if this relationship goes nowhere—*all right, it does, but he'll survive*—what matters is that it happened at all. That Riley knows what he is, understands it as best she can, which is to say that while she can't *fully* comprehend the situation, she's done her best to try, and that means even more than the kisses. She didn't run in the other direction. Nor did she try to make him into some misunderstood and broken hero in need of a damsel to tell him he was perfect and wonderful and to hell with what the world said. Riley got it, eyes wide open, and she still let him kiss her. Still smiled for him. Still looked out for him. Still worried about him.

The detectives had parked in the driveway of a seemingly empty house for sale. They're keeping this arrest low-key, which Max appreciates, as he appreciates the fact that Buchanan waited until they were at the car—out of sight of anyone—before bringing out the handcuffs.

They're in the car now. Buchanan is saying that someone spotted them from the papers and called it in, but Max isn't paying much attention. It doesn't matter how they got there—they have him now and all that's important is that Riley won't get in trouble for leaving the hospital with him. He's saying nothing about that yet, because if he tells the detective this is his fault, she'll jump in with the truth, and he doesn't want that. He'll take the blame when she's not there to seize it for herself.

Buchanan is in the passenger seat, on the radio, calling the hospital about Brienne. He doesn't seem convinced she's in danger, but he's not taking any chances.

Max's hands are cuffed in front of him and he's resting his fingertips against Riley's leg. He would talk to her, reassure her, but she's intent on what Buchanan's saying, so he limits his reassurance to that touch, and when he shifts, she absently reaches over and squeezes his hand, and that feels . . . it feels like the first time he held a girl's hand—when he reached out and braced himself, ready to pretend he'd only accidentally brushed hers, but she'd taken his and it was like winning top place in class and scoring the winning goal all in one. Only this, this is better, because that had been some girl whose name he can't even remember, just a girl he'd somewhat fancied, at an age when the girls began fancying the boys and the boys weren't quite ready but felt as if they ought to. That was just a girl. Riley is not just a girl. She is . . .

*Tell me again how you're going to walk away, Max.*

*We'll still be—*

*Friends. Ah, yes, of course. And that'll be enough.*

It has to be, because he doesn't get the rest. Not anymore. Can't ask for that, can't expect that, might never have that again, because the risk is too great, and if he cares about someone, then he cannot allow that—

He cuts himself off, his breath coming so fast that Riley looks over sharply, alarmed. He forces a smile and squeezes her knee. She doesn't buy it, leaning in to whisper, "Are you okay?"

"Right as rain."

That makes her roll her eyes and makes her smile too.

It isn't just about him. He shouldn't hope for more with

Riley, because she's dealing with her own problems, and what she needs—what they both need—is a friend.

The car moves and they both jump, looking over their shoulders to see the trunk open. It shuts and Wheeler walks to the driver's side and gets in without a word.

"All set?" Buchanan asks.

Wheeler only grunts.

"You're the chatty one, aren't you?" Max says, and he's being perfectly friendly, but Wheeler fixes him with a look, and Riley tenses and he knows she's thinking he shouldn't have said anything, so he smiles and says, "All right, then. Take me to your leader. Or your station, as the case may be."

"You don't seem terribly concerned, Max," Buchanan says as Wheeler backs out the car. "I've heard that's a symptom, though."

"Inappropriate affect," Max says. "It is indeed a symptom. However, it's not an explanation. Not today." He smiles. "Today I'm just relieved. We have our answers, and I'm quite certain this whole mess can be cleared up by teatime."

"Huh. Isn't that another symptom? Delusions?"

Riley's lips tighten, and he knows she wants to tell them to grow up and act like professionals, and when she says, "I don't believe sarcasm is in order, Detective," Max smiles, not only at the comeback but at the way he predicted it.

Because he knows her. And she knows him.

*And oh how happy you will be, fa-la-la-la-la.*

Bugger off.

There's no rancor in the curse. He smiles when he says it, if only in his head, and that silences the voice.

"We know what happened that night," Riley says. "We figured it out."

"Did you now? What did you figure out?"

"It was hit men."

The two detectives look at each other . . . and burst out laughing.

"It *was*," she says. "The Porters were killed by hit men hired by Mr. Porter's business partner. They set up the therapy camp to kill me, because I was the witness."

"That's kind of overcomplicating things, isn't it?"

"There's more to it than that. They planned another hit in the same place: Aaron Highgate. They set it up through Aimee, who was dating one of them. I'll tell you the whole story at the station. River Ruskin can back us up."

"How much did you pay him for that?" Buchanan asks.

Temper sparks behind her eyes. Max squeezes her leg, telling her not to worry, these are just two idiots who don't have the power to put him in jail for more than a day or two. He knows how this works. He'll explain everything to his lawyer, who will talk to the Crown attorney—or whatever it's called in America. It's the Crown that lays charges, not the detectives. This is just a frustrating obstacle.

He leans in and tells her as much, and she nods, knowing he's right.

"What poison is he whispering in your ear now, Riley?" Buchanan says.

"The truth," she says.

"The truth is that your boyfriend is a psychotic killer who was obsessed with you and murdered six people because of it. But hey, now he's got you, so it was all worthwhile, wasn't it, Max?"

"I didn't kill anyone," he says. "Which we will prove, so save your breath—"

"Did you read the manifesto, Riley?"

She says, "I heard enough about it to know it's fake, which computer forensics will confirm."

"And the supporting evidence? The other documents we found?"

"What other documents?" Max asks, but Riley says, "Whatever they are, it's the same thing. Forgeries."

"Oh, really?" Buchanan twists to face Max. "Is that right, Max? Those suicide notes were fake? Because they sure looked real to me."

Max imagines his mouth opening. He imagines words coming out. Words like *I don't know what you're talking about*. Only that doesn't happen. He sits there, trying to unhinge his jaw. Trying to open his mouth. Trying to get words out. And he just sits there, unable to find breath, much less words.

"Suicide notes?" Riley says, and he struggles to decipher her tone. He studies her face, and he picks her words apart, sifting and sorting madly. Is that disbelief? Confusion? Shock and disgust?

*Say something, Max. Open your bloody mouth and say something.*

Lie to her.

"Rough drafts," Buchanan says. "Four of them, locked away under password protection—which, by the way, Max, is only going to keep your mother from seeing them." He turns to Riley. "Your boyfriend started four suicide notes in the past month, saying how he couldn't go on, and all the usual teen-angst bullshit."

"*Teen angst?*" Max says, and that's when the words come, not when he wants them, not the ones he wants, but this—two words on a bubble of rage—and once they're out, the rest come, even as that voice inside screams for him to shut up, just shut the hell up.

"I spent my whole life being told how much promise I had, how much potential, how bloody brilliant I was, how bloody talented I was and how I could make anything of my life. And now? *Now?* Now the most I can hope for is that I don't end up wandering the streets, yelling at strangers and ranting about the end of the world. Forget university. Forget a decent career. Forget a wife and kids and a house in the country and everything else that is the bare *minimum* of what I could have expected from my life before. I get a lifetime of *existing* and being a bloody success if I manage that without buggering it up. So yes, I wrote those letters, because that's my plan B. It's not plan A yet, but that's no one's business except my own."

When he finishes, Buchanan slow-claps, and that's the worst of it, the most humiliating and horrible of it. Max is straining against his seat belt, feeling as if he's spewed the most secret and shameful part of his life . . . and Buchanan slow-claps. Then Wheeler turns from the steering wheel and smirks at him, and that smirk . . . that smirk . . .

For a split second, Max tumbles down the rabbit hole. He sees that smirk and it's not even the smirk—it's Wheeler's eyes. He sees something in his eyes and images flash—other eyes, other smirks, hidden behind a mask, but knowing they're there. The images come fast and hard. A laugh. A chuckle. A sarcastic word. A sneer. Then gunfire and blood and—

"Are you done, Max?"

Max stares at Wheeler, but the man is facing forward again, driving. He looks over at Buchanan.

"Hello," Buchanan says. "Are you stepping off your soapbox, boy?"

Max blinks.

He's losing it. Something's wrong. The meds—

No, *the meds are fine. This is what we call stress, Maximus.*

Which is one of the problems with medication. It's not an impenetrable shield. The madness can still creep through. He can still snap if the pressure is too much. This is what's never going to change, never ever going to change, and—

*Really think you ought to consider the man's advice and get off that soapbox, old chap.*

Sod off and—

*Riley.*

That's all it takes. One word and Max's head snaps up, whiplash-fast. He jolts back in his seat as the air thins.

Riley.

He's just confessed to contemplating suicide, and she's sitting right there. She risked everything to save him from that warehouse, to save him from prison, and he admitted he's thinking of ending his life.

*I appreciate the effort, Riley, really I do, but it was all for naught. Sorry about that. Terribly sorry.*

*Tell her it's not true.*

But it is.

*Tell her you've changed your mind. That you made a mistake, and you see that now, and you won't ever do it.*

But that's not true.

*Who cares? Say it, you idiot. Just say it.*

No.

He can't tell her it isn't an option anymore, because it is. It always will be. He can say he's not going to do it tomorrow. That even before all this, he wasn't going to do it tomorrow. This is why he keeps writing those bloody notes. He's working it through. He gets to the end and realizes he doesn't want to take that step, but he doesn't delete the notes, either, because saying he doesn't want to take the step now does not mean he's sealing off that path forever.

*Then look at her. Stop whining and look at her.*

He can't.

*Coward.*

Yes. He is.

"Max?"

— 309

She whispers his name, and it cuts through him like a blade. Right in the gut. A white-hot blade that keeps him pinned to the seat, unable to move, unable to look over.

*No, Max. Not unable. Unwilling. If you care about her, look over and lie. Tell her what she wants to hear. Tell her you're all right.*

He does care about her. Which is why he's not going to lie. He's not going to make her think everything is fine and he'll never do it, because then, if he ever does, she'll feel as if she failed, as if he was, in this moment, back on track and she failed to keep him there.

*Then don't lie. Tell her you won't do it and mean it.*

"Max?" Her voice is so low now he can barely hear it, and he can sense her leaning toward him, hovering there, her worry palatable.

"Max? Talk to me. Please."

He turns away and hunches down in the seat.

# CHAPTER 34

Max wants to kill himself.

It doesn't matter how many times I've thought those words in the last few minutes, each time they're like a punch in the stomach.

He wants to kill himself, and I had no idea. *No idea.* I thought I understood, and I was so damned proud of myself for that, for doing the research, for trying to understand what he's going through, because I wanted to be the one who got it.

I wanted to be the one who helped him.

No, I wanted to be the one who saved him.

The thought is like grinding a fist on my punched stomach, and it's all I can do not to double over and retch. Save him? Really? How pathetic is that? How arrogant is that? I couldn't save the Porters. I couldn't save Sandy or Gideon or Maria or Aaron or Lorenzo. I didn't do a damned thing for any of them. But by God, I was going to save Max. I'd be the one person who believed in him, and I'd do more than believe in him—I'd storm out of that hospital and I'd clear his name, and I'd set him free.

Free.

To kill himself.

Because that's what he wants, and I never saw it. Never had any idea. Oh, but I understand his situation. Really I do.

No, I don't. I had no idea what he was going through. I saw the despair and the hopelessness. I saw the frustration and the rage. I saw the absolute agony in his face when he talked about strangling his friend, about what it felt like to do that, to live with doing that, to live with knowing he could do that again.

I saw the fear when he kept warning me to be careful around him, and I knew he was thinking he could do the same to me, but I didn't really understand what that means *to him*. To say "I like this girl" and "I want to be with this girl, but I can't, because I don't know if I'll wake up in the night and wrap my hands around her throat and maybe I never will but I can't live with the possibility."

*I can't live with the possibility.*

I still want to save him.

I think that's the worst of it. I still want to take his hand and tell him he can get through this. That I'll help him. We'll come up with a strategy, and he'll see things aren't as bad as he thinks, and it'll all be fine. Right as rain.

Complete and utter bullshit.

It will not be fine, and whatever he decides to do about that is his choice. Not mine. Not his mother's or his father's. Because this isn't about us. Those notes aren't a cry for help. He isn't angry and looking to hurt someone. This is about him. Entirely about him. And I don't want it to be. Because I care about him, and I don't know how to care about someone who's thinking of ending his life, how to take that risk when everything already hurts so much, when I'm barely walking through life myself.

I'm huddled in my corner of the backseat now. He's retreated to his, and that's as clear an answer as any. He doesn't want my help. Doesn't need it. And I feel so alone. I feel like I finally found something—found someone, found what I needed to get through all this, someone to lean on and laugh with and talk to—and . . . no. That's not what I found at all. I'm sinking, and I didn't grab a life preserver, I grabbed an anchor, and either I let go or I sink with it, and I don't want to let go. I don't want to let go.

I feel something touch my fingers, and I see Max's hand, his pinkie hooking mine. I lift my gaze, and he works on something like a smile, he works so damn hard at it, and I . . . I burst into tears.

It's not what I want to do. It's the last thing I want to do. But I see his expression and the tears come, and he moves fast, stretching in the seat belt, his cuffed hands taking mine, and I fall against him and he whispers, "I'm sorry, Riley. I'm so, so sorry. I don't want to hurt you. I never want to—"

"That's enough," Buchanan says. "Get away from her, Max."

"Just a moment," Max says. "Please. I'm still hand-cuffed. Just give me a moment."

"I said get the *hell* away from her, you psycho—"

"Stop that," I snarl, pulling away from Max. "Act like a damned professional."

"Excuse me?" Buchanan twists in his seat. "Don't you tell me—"

"*Enough*," Wheeler says. "You get back from him, Riley. You too, Max."

His voice is oddly rough, like he's lowering it, and that doesn't matter, because as soon as he speaks, I don't hear *Riley* and *Max*. I hear *Miss Riley* and *Maximus*. And I stare at his profile. I stare as hard as I can, my heart thumping.

When Wheeler first got into the car, Max made a smart-ass comment and Wheeler had given him a look, and that look . . . something about that look . . . I'd flinched, because in that flash of a second I'd seen eyes behind a gray mask. It had passed in a blink. Memory playing tricks on an exhausted mind.

"So you can talk," I say, and somehow I manage to make it sound casual, though my heart thuds like it's ready to burst from my chest.

Wheeler grunts and turns his attention to the road.

"How long have you two been on the force?" I ask.

"What? Are you questioning our credentials now?" Buchanan says, and I struggle to hear another voice in his, to hear Predator, but it's not there.

"I'm just making conversation," I say.

"Twelve years," Buchanan says.

"And you, Detective Wheeler? Now that we've established you're not mute."

"Fifteen," Wheeler says.

Damn it, I need to hear him talk . . . in more than one-word answers.

"And before you were on the major crimes squad? Any other units?"

I don't hear the reply, because as soon as I think of other units, I think of the SWAT team, which makes me think of hostage negotiations, and a memory flashes. An audio one. A voice on the phone, a little distorted.

The hostage negotiator.

I look at Buchanan. Even as the theory was forming in my head—the unbelievable theory that Wheeler is Gray—I thought Buchanan played no role in it. He clearly wasn't Predator. But there was another person involved that night. One I was certain survived. The man on the phone. The fake hostage negotiator.

**CHAPTER 35** I look over sharply at Max. I'm trying to figure out how to tell him, but his gaze is fixed on Buchanan with such intensity that I know he's caught something too. He looks over at Wheeler and he's searching, a little hesitant now, and when he notices me watching, he pulls back fast, and I can tell he's second-guessing.

I tap the gray vinyl on my door handle. I point to the gray lettering on my shirt. Then I direct my finger to Wheeler. And Max's eyes close with such relief that he swallows and nods. He's not imagining the connection. And as soon as that first flicker of relief passes, his eyes fly open with such an "Oh, shit!" look that it ignites my own panic.

We're in the car with Gray.

Gray and his accomplice.

They aren't really police detectives. They fooled everyone at the hospital. The real police got Max's story, and they knew it wasn't him, and they lost interest and . . .

The manifesto.

It was in the papers. The papers blamed Max. The papers mentioned the manifesto. There's no way in hell the police *wouldn't* be questioning me and preparing to arrest Max and . . .

And if the police are investigating, and these are the only detectives we've seen . . .

They're not pretending to be cops.

They are cops.

My brain screams no. *No, no, no.* There is no way officers of the law would ever pervert justice in this way, to become hired killers.

*You really are a sheltered rich girl.*

I hear River's words, and I know they're true, because whatever pedestal I might put police on, a profession doesn't cleanse you. There are cops who have committed murder, just like there are schoolteachers and truck drivers and stay-at-home moms who have done the same. I might not want it to be true. But that doesn't mean it isn't.

I still try to tell myself I'm wrong. It fits, though. Who else would be able to frame Max so well? They knew they could catch the case—it must have happened on their turf, and it happened on their turf because they chose the location.

River said the hit men helped him get out of those drug charges. Who better to do that than cops? What better reason for River to keep quiet than knowing that the law— which a guy like him wouldn't trust anyway—is behind the crimes he helped with? He said they had access to the Porters' case file. Of course they did. And what had River done when they arrested us? Freaked out. Absolutely panicked, and I thought it was because they were police and he has committed crimes. No. It was because these were the very men he'd just ratted out.

They hadn't called a backup car for River.

They hadn't called the hospital to protect Brienne.

We weren't going to the police station to be questioned.

I grab the door handle. It's a stupid thing to do, because there's no way that door will open. But I act on instinct—the instinct to throw it open and grab Max and roll out like some kind of action hero.

The door doesn't budge.

"Hey!" Buchanan says. "What the hell are you doing?"

Max's cuffed hands land on my knee, and they squeeze hard enough to hurt, and when I look at him, I see my own panic reflected back, but he's struggling to keep it under control as he madly shakes his head.

*Don't give it away, Riley. Please don't give it away. Play dumb. That's our only chance.*

Which seems like no chance at all. Certainly not a plan. But he's right. The moment we let them know that we've figured it out, they won't take their eyes off us.

I'm straightening in my seat when Max's gaze goes to my stomach. His lips form a curse, and I look down to see blood seeping through my shirt.

"Riley's hurt," Max says. "Her injuries have opened up again, and she's bleeding."

It takes two long seconds for Buchanan to look. Two seconds to remind himself that this should be a cause for concern. He glances over the seat and grunts, "It's a little blood."

"She needs to go back to the hospital," Max says. "You aren't charging her with anything, are you? It was my fault. I tricked her into leaving with me."

Any other time I'd have jumped to his defense. But that wasn't the point here, and instead I mumble, "It wasn't really *tricked*, but I had no idea he was about to be arrested. And he said we'd only be gone"—I inhale sharply, wincing as if in sudden pain—"an hour at most."

"Can we drop her off at the hospital?" Max says. "Or call a backup car to take her?"

Of course, we don't really expect them to agree. Max is confirming our theory while distracting them from my escape attempt.

"Can she at least call her mother?" Max says. "You confiscated River's mobile. Can she use that and let her mom know she's all right?"

"The hospital knows she's with us."

"Can you give her painkillers?" Max asks. "Tylenol, aspirin . . ."

"Can you shut the hell up?" Wheeler growls. "I know it's a strain for you, Maxi—" He stops before saying "Maximus" and retreats into silence as Buchanan shoots him a look.

As Max has been trying distraction techniques, I've been frantically looking for a way out of this car. All I can think about is River and what happened to him, because I have no idea where he is, but I'm sure he's not alive and I'm equally sure we won't be either if we finish this ride.

I might be able to smash out the window with my elbow, but that's on a good day, and even if I managed it, they'd have guns on us before I could squeeze through, and if by some chance I did get out, I'd leave Max behind, and that isn't happening. *Is not happening.*

I could try to catch the attention of a passerby. They'd probably think I was just goofing off, but I would still try . . . if there were anyone around. We're in an industrial area, and I see cars in parking lots, but very few of those, and I swear half the buildings have For Lease or For Sale signs on them and boarded-up windows and . . .

I see rubble. Up the road. The remains of a demolished building. And I remember me and Max huddled in it as I lost consciousness.

*Don't leave. Please, please, please. I don't want to be alone.*

I know where we are. Oh God, I know where we are.

Max takes my hand and squeezes it and forces a smile for me, and I know he didn't see the rubble, doesn't know where they've taken us, and I don't know whether I should tell him or—

The car turns. Darkness yawns ahead. An open warehouse door. The car drives inside.

"Where are we?" Max asks, trying to sound calm.

The men don't answer. I won't call them detectives now or police or even cops. They are men. No, they are killers. Hired killers. That negates anything else they are, anything else they might have been.

Wheeler gets out. We turn to see him head for the big garage door, presumably to shut it behind us, and I think, *We're dead.* This is it. Any chance we had, we've lost. Dad always said that if anyone ever grabs me on the street, I need to get out of that car before they take me to their destination, because once I'm there, they can do whatever they want and . . . *Dad, oh God, Dad, why didn't I listen to you?* Why didn't I kick out that damned window and who cares what happened then, because it's going to happen now. We're dead and—

Max squeezes my hand until he gets my attention, and when I look over, he whispers, "We'll do our best."

Not *We'll be okay.* Not *We'll get through this.*

We'll do our best.

Because that's the truth, the only truth, and he isn't going to lie to me. He lied to me before, about the meds, about his condition, and he won't do it again. Not about the suicide notes. Not about this. I look at his face, fear waging war with conviction. Conviction that we *will* do our best, because that's all he can be sure of, and that's enough. It has to be enough. It is.

He says, "We'll do our best," and I love him for it. I don't care if that's foolish or naive, or if I can hear Sloane saying, "You've known him only a few days." I love him. I lean over to kiss his cheek and whisper, "We will. We absolutely will."

If anyone can get out of this, we can. Not you. Not me. *Us.* Together.

Wheeler closes the garage door and the garage is pitched into darkness, lit only by the car's headlights. Then he walks to the trunk. He opens it. And he pulls out River's body.

He pulls out River's body, bound hand and foot and gagged, and he throws it to the floor. Then River moves. He starts squirming and struggling, and I realize they brought him alive. Thank God he's still alive.

Wheeler cuts the zipties with a knife. He pulls off the gag. River stumbles to his feet, saying, "I didn't tell them anything. Whatever they say, it's a lie. They figured some stuff out, and they tried to get me to say it was true, but—"

"Run," Wheeler says.

"What?"

Wheeler waves at a side door. "Go. Run. Before I change my mind."

River runs, and I exhale. They don't realize what we know. They're setting him free and now they'll carry on pretending to be detectives and—

Wheeler shoots River in the back of the head.

At first, I don't realize what's happened. I hear the suppressed shot, even more muffled by the closed car windows, and I don't recognize it. Then River's head flies back and his arms and legs keep going for a second, kicking out as his body seems, impossibly, suspended in midair. I see the blood spray. I see blood and brain and bone, and I start to scream.

**CHAPTER 36** I scream as I never screamed at the Porters', never screamed at the warehouse. But now I do, and I don't even realize I'm doing it until I hear the high-pitched shriek and feel it ripping from my throat.

Buchanan scrambles over the seat and slaps a hand to my mouth, saying, "Shut up! Shut the hell—"

"Don't touch her!" Max snarls, and knocks Buchanan's hand aside. He pulls me to him, as best he can, his hands still cuffed. He tugs me against his shoulder and whispers, "Shh, shh, shh. I know, Riley. I know. But you need to be quiet. Please."

I squeeze my eyes shut and get myself under control. I keep seeing River, shot in the head. Keep hearing Wheeler saying, "Run," and I didn't think it was possible to hate him more, but I do. Somehow I do. I want to scream and howl at him. I want to . . . I want to . . .

I push the thought aside. Can't go there. Won't think that.

"It's my fault," I whisper. "My fault. I pulled River into this. I made him talk."

"No," Max says fiercely. "He got himself into this. His choices got him into it, and he didn't deserve what just

— 321

happened, but it's no one else's fault—just his and . . ." He shoots a glare at Wheeler, who's strolling around the car.

Yes, strolling. I see that walk and the cocky look in his eyes and that I'm-so-clever smirk on his face.

Gray.

This is Gray, unmasked. Yet not unmasked at all, because this *is* the mask: the face of an ordinary man. He wore his real face in the warehouse. The face of a monster. An inhuman, alien thing.

Wheeler opens Max's door. "Why'd you have to go and do that, Maximus? Shoot the poor kid as he was running away?" He shakes his head and *tsk-tsk*s and I lunge at him, cursing and snarling, scrabbling over Max as I launch myself at Wheeler. But Max grabs me and holds me back.

"That's funny," Wheeler says. "You don't look the least bit surprised. Dare I guess that you'd already figured out who I am? Such clever children. For children, that is. Crazy, messed-up, broken children. Come on, Miss Riley. You can get out of the car now. Just don't bother rushing me again." He waves the gun. "I have a plan, and shooting you doesn't exactly fit, but I can *make* it fit. So don't test me."

"May I get out?" Max asks.

"Oh, listen to that. So polite. Proper grammar, even. Why, yes, Maximus, you may get out."

He does, holding me back until he's standing, and then keeping me behind him as I get out.

"Look at the chivalry," Wheeler says. "Polite and chivalrous and even kind of cute, if you go for the tortured-bad-boy-wannabe look. I can see why you fell for him, Miss Riley. Of course, it helps that in your own way, you're almost as screwed-up as he is. Birds of a feather and all that." He walks to Max and cuts the strap on his wrists. "There. I reward your intelligence by setting you free."

"No," Max says. "You have two guns on me, and the

longer you leave my hands tied, the more likely the bruising will show up in an autopsy. Especially if I panic and struggle."

"Did they teach you that in school? The British school system really does provide a liberal and all-encompassing educational experience, doesn't it?"

"More like too many hours spent watching *CSI*," Buchanan says, coming up beside us.

Wheeler snickers.

"You brought River here to kill, so it will look as if I did it," Max says.

"Mmm, maybe not so clever. Running a few steps behind, are you, Maximus?"

Max opens his mouth, and I suspect he's going to say no, he's just trying to hurry this along and get to the point. But he wisely doesn't.

"Yes," Wheeler says. "That's part one. Part two?" He turns to me. Buchanan has moved closer, gun trained on Max. "On your knees, Miss Riley. You're about to beg for your life, but Max here isn't going to listen. If he can't have you, no one else will." He lowers his voice. "He's kind of crazy that way."

"You don't really expect her to—" Max begins.

"Go along with it? Actually, I do. Because she knows you're both going to die, and her option is one to the head . . . or a much slower and messier death, as you decide not to grant her mercy but to make her pay for being such a stuck-up bitch."

"How about if I actually shoot her?" Max says quickly.

"What?"

"I'll do it. That'll pin the shooting squarely on me. Not just my fingers on the gun, but powder and blood splatter and everything else you need to prove conclusively that I shot her."

Wheeler lets out a belly laugh. "Oh my, it seems chivalry *is* dead. Or it dies very fast in the face of actual death. Not much sense winning brownie points with a girl if she won't survive to let you spend them, huh, Maximus? You'll shoot her and frame yourself and then we can arrest you instead of staging your suicide." He fakes a deep frown. "Unless you're actually just trying to get me to hand over the gun. Oh, you almost got me there, my boy. You really did."

"I'm not trying to do either," Max says, as calmly as he can. "Handing over the gun won't help when your partner still has his pointed at me. And I didn't say I'd kill Riley. I said I'd shoot her. A nonfatal shot. Then I'll kill myself."

"No!" I say, lunging against Buchanan's restraining hand.

"Then I'll kill myself," Max repeats. "Riley survives, and she tells exactly the story you want her to tell, because she knows what you are and that you'll have no compunctions about coming after her family."

"Compunctions," Wheeler muses. "Good word. But we also have no 'compunctions' about killing her right—"

"I know," Max says quickly. "But this will be even better. You'll have the forensic evidence for your case, and you'll have an eyewitness."

"Nice try," Wheeler says. "But no." He waves Buchanan over and they switch weapons. "My friend here will do the honors on Miss Riley. Not because I have any 'compunctions' about doing it myself, but because I know you better than he does, Maximus. So I'll keep an eye on you while he does your work for you, using the proper gun, of course."

He turns to me. "Miss Riley? It has been a pleasure. You may have been a pain in the ass, but I rather enjoyed the challenge. In this job, it's the same old, same old. Walk up and pull the trigger. At most, you get a moment of 'Oh no, please don't kill me!' Almost like factory work. Repetitive and dull.

You livened things up. Worthy adversaries, you and Maximus. Now kneel."

I do. As I lower myself, I'm eyeing Buchanan's knees. One sharp hit in the back and they'll buckle. Do I still have the strength to do it? I have no idea, but I need to try.

I'm lowering myself into position, visualizing my strike, and then—

Max launches himself at Buchanan. I strike the back of the man's knee as hard as I can, and he does crumple, but it's because Max has hit him, and they're going down, and the shot fires.

No, the shot fires *before* they go down. It fires, and then I hit Buchanan, and then Max does, and the shot isn't from Buchanan's gun. It's from Wheeler's, aiming at Max. The gun fires. The bullet hits. Blood sprays.

Buchanan drops his gun. I'm not sure when or why or at what stage in that split-second sequence. What I see first is not blood. It's a falling gun, and then it's in my hand, with me gripping it by the barrel.

That's when I see the blood, and out of the corner of my eye I see Max and Buchanan go down, and before I can look, before I *dare* to look, I see another gun. Wheeler's. Rising.

I scream. I scream as loud as I can, and I run at Wheeler, the gun still in my hand as I fumble to get a proper grip on it. Wheeler swings his weapon at me and . . .

And he slips. I don't know what on. It's not even a slip as much as a tiny stumble and stagger, his foot sliding out from under him. But it throws him off balance, and I'm swinging up the gun, and he's right there, and the gun hits his forearm, hits it in exactly the right place, and his hand opens on reflex and his own gun drops, and I kick it away.

And then I'm holding a gun on him. Miraculously, somehow, I'm holding a gun on him, and I look down to see what he slipped in, and it's River's blood. The irony. Yes, the irony.

I hear a groan, and that snaps me out of my moment of victory as my chest seizes, and I remember the shot, and I spin to see both Max and Buchanan on the ground. And blood. There's blood.

"Riley!" It's Max. He's pushing himself up and waving frantically at me as I catch a blur of motion. Wheeler rushes me. I back up fast, careful to stay out of that snaking stream of blood.

"I'm fine," Max says, and he sounds about seventy percent correct. There's a catch in his voice, a small hiss of pain, but he's on his feet, his hand clamped to his side. "It went through me and hit Buchanan. He's gone."

And there is, in that, a second shot of irony. Wheeler shot Max and killed his partner instead. Then he tries to shoot me and slips in his last victim's blood. Bitter, ironic coincidence. Or perhaps a little more. If I care to see divine intervention, I'll see it here. Like a parent watching a toddler stumble around, insisting she reach her goal on her own, and then finally saying, "All right, you've done enough," and easing a couple of immovable obstacles out of her way.

Max is fine. Or fine enough. Buchanan is down. And Wheeler? Wheeler is at the other end of a gun barrel. *My* gun barrel.

I see him down that barrel, and I think of Sandy, shot and discarded in a supply closet. I think of Gideon and Maria, dead in pools of blood, staring in shock. I think of Lorenzo, fighting for his life and losing. I think of Brienne, saying "I'll be brave," Brienne shot in the back. Of her brother, given the chance to run only to be gunned down. I even think of Aimee, because it doesn't matter if she was part of this, what I'm thinking isn't of the fact of her death but the way he did it, walking up to a former partner, someone he knew, someone who trusted him, shooting her once and, when that failed, shooting her in the head.

That's what I'm remembering, not just the deaths but how he did them. How cruel and how callous and that smirking I'm-such-a-clever-boy look in his eyes. He orchestrated the deaths of seven people and would have added three more if he could—Brienne, me and Max—and what did he have to say about that? Told me that Max and I were worthy opponents. Offered us the highest praise he could. That we were prey worth killing.

"Riley . . ." Max says carefully.

"He murdered seven people," I say.

"Mmm, no," Wheeler says. "Actually, I believe my partners—"

"You were in charge. You planned it. And to you, it meant nothing. Their lives meant nothing."

"Oh ho, is that what you want, Miss Riley? An existential conversation on the value of life? The value of his life?" He points at River. "A thug kid so dumb it's a wonder he survived this long? His equally stupid sister? What kind of lives do you think they had coming? Petty crime and jail time for him. Babies and black eyes for her."

I'm shaking as I hold the gun on him, as I listen to him and I remember them. Really remember them. Sandy, the girl who came to therapy out of love for her parents, to prove she'd made a foolish mistake and she took responsibility for it and they'd never need to worry that she'd repeat it. Maria, the girl who found the letter opener while the rest of us were too terrified to move, the girl whose T-shirt said she thumbed her nose at labels, stood up and said, "Yep, that's me—deal with it." Gideon, the boy who was scared, so damned scared, lashing out in his terror. And Aaron, the boy who could be exactly what you expected . . . and the polar opposite of what you expected, a self-centered jerk who wasn't self-centered at all, who'd tried to convince our kid-nappers to free us and just keep him.

I remember them and I hear Wheeler, and all I can think is that I want him to shut up. I want to shut him up.

I don't want to put a bullet in his brain. I want to shoot him, over and over, until he's on the ground, howling in agony, and then, maybe then, he'll understand what he's done, when he's dying slowly—

"Riley?" Max is right behind me, leaning down, his breath whispering against my ear. "It's all right. It's over. I've got the other gun. You can lower that one, get Buchanan's mobile and call the police."

"They *are* the police," I say. "They took a good job, a noble job—"

Wheeler laughs. I raise the gun and Max says, "No! Please, Riley. I won't fight you for that gun. Not after Aaron. But I'm asking you to put it down. Please, please, please put it down."

"He killed them! All of them! And he doesn't give a damn. They're dead and he's smirking and laughing and—"

"And it's wrong, Maximus," Wheeler says, imitating my voice. "It's just wrong. All those worthless idiots he mur-dered, and he doesn't care, and I just want to cry. I want to cry and feel sorry for myself and—"

"*Shut up*," I say.

"He's a bad person, Maximus," Wheeler continues. "A very, very bad person, and I want to kill him, but I don't have the guts, because I'm just a scared little girl. A coward who hid under a bed, and I really wish I had a bed right now, because all I want to do is hide and thank God I'm alive, because that's what matters. As bad as I feel about those others, what matters is that I'm alive. Yes, Miss Riley, you're alive. You know why? Because you have the brains to run. To hide. To get out of the way. Cowardice saved you.

The others? They were just too stupid to live. Literally, it seems. Morons who stumbled into their own deaths—"

"Shut up."

"—and got themselves killed. Through misguided bravery or abject stupidity. They deserved—"

"Shut the hell up!"

I shoot. The bullet hits him in the shoulder. He staggers back but doesn't fall. Then, through clenched teeth, he says, "I believe you need to work on your aim, Miss Riley."

"My aim is fine. That's your right shoulder. If I were trying to kill you, at least I'd have hit your left side."

I shoot again . . . and hit him in the leg. He goes down. As I advance on him, Max breaks from his shock and runs in front of me.

"No, Riley."

"I want—"

"I know what you want, and I'm asking you—begging you—not to do this."

"He deserves—"

"A life in prison. That's what he deserves. A life in prison as a cop who killed kids. That's what he's trying to avoid. You know it. Deep down, you know it."

"I don't care."

"Then I do." He touches my left arm, carefully. "He'll say anything now to make you kill him. You don't deserve that. You don't deserve to wake up in the night and see his face. To be walking down the street and see his face. To keep seeing his face, everywhere, and remembering what you did. Please, please, please. Do not do that to yourself. You've incapacitated him. That's good. That's enough. Anything more . . ."

Anything more is murder.

Murder.

Wheeler is talking. I don't hear him, because I know Max is right. Wheeler will say anything—however hateful—

to make me kill him. He deserves to die, but I don't deserve to live with killing him.

Max doesn't deserve to live with knowing he couldn't stop me.

I look up at Max, and I hand him the gun.

# CHAPTER 37

It's over. Yet it isn't. Three days have passed, and I don't see an end in sight, but Max is free and Wheeler is in prison and neither of those things is going to change, and I am satisfied with that.

I've barely seen Max in three days. We've tried, but it's like two ships passing in the night. No, two ships passing in a storm. We catch sight of each other or we manage to pop off a text and then we're pulled off in our separate directions, by our separate obligations.

We start ending our texts with "Soon." Every last one of them. Our version of goodbye, a closing that isn't a closing but a promise. This will all pass, and we'll see each other soon, and nothing and nobody will stop us.

The process of exonerating Max and charging Wheeler went more smoothly than I'd dared hope. It helped that Predator—who was an ex–military buddy of Wheeler's—was still alive, lying low and waiting for his friend, and when the police showed up at his door, he treated his good buddy the same way they'd treated their colleague—Cantina—and Predator's girlfriend, Aimee. He turned on him in a flash. The only thing rarer than honor among thieves? Honor among killers.

As for what happened that Friday night, we'd correctly

figured out most of it, including Mr. Highgate putting a hit on his son. Wheeler learned of the job and incorporated it into his plan. But it didn't actually start there. It started with Maria. Yes, Maria, the girl with the smile and the defiant T-shirt. Her stepmom didn't want to be a stepmom. Didn't want to share her new husband with his daughter. So she convinced him to take out a life insurance policy on Maria. Then she went looking for a killer. Wheeler caught wind of the job, learned Maria was in therapy, thought of Aimee's failure to coax anything incriminating from me, and he hatched a plan to get rid of me and make a little money at the same time. Then he found out Highgate was looking for a hit on his son, and the pieces fell in place for something much bigger, much more lucrative. A grand scheme to combine two paying hits with silencing two witnesses—me and Brienne—and blaming a schizophrenic eighteen-year-old. As for Sandy and Gideon? They just happened to sign up for the weekend. Collateral damage.

I'll never understand that. I'll especially never understand how any parent could want his own child dead. That will haunt me forever. Change me forever.

What I do understand is that Wheeler was wrong. I didn't run in that warehouse and leave the others to their fate. Because if I did, then so did Max, and I know Max did not. Maybe that's the wrong way to look at it. Maybe I should be able to analyze my own behavior more objectively, but I can't. I need to look at the guy who was by my side the whole time, and when I do, I can say, unequivocally, that he was not a coward.

We did the best we could. We tried to help others. We tried to *get* help for others. Our failure to do so will never stop hurting. That's what I've taken from this. The understanding that there are events and situations that you'll always second-guess, always think you could have done better.

The rest hasn't gone away either. I know people some-times say that if you're depressed and anxious, you just need purpose, something to take your mind off your problems. I have plenty of purposes now—making sure Wheeler goes to jail for life, helping Max and Brienne, putting my own life back together. I'm doing all that . . . and I still wake every night, shaking and drenched in sweat. I have flashbacks that stop me cold. I have moments—just random moments, with no apparent cause—when I'm seized by the overwhelming urge to go to bed, cover my head and stay there. I don't, but I still have to fight that urge every single time. But I will cope with that. I'll cope with all of it. I know now that I can.

Right now, though, coping feels like as impossible a goal as getting time with Max. I'm spending a third of my days recuperating from injuries, a third talking to police and a third dealing with the media. Same for Max, though in his case his injury is less severe and the media attention is worse. I want to say he's been branded a hero—a guy with a misun-derstood condition that led to hateful accusations. There's some of that. But there's also uncertainty and whispers. Last night I overheard two nurses wondering if Max was really as innocent as they said, speculating that while he clearly wasn't behind all the murders, the death of Aaron Highgate was a little suspicious, wasn't it? And Max was, you know, crazy.

Sloane had to drag me away from them. Then I listened as she stalked back and told them off for me. My sister isn't what I thought she was. I'm still not sure what she is, who she is, and that's uncomfortable, because I've lived with her my whole life—I should know her better than anyone. I don't. I'm looking forward to rectifying that, though.

I'm with Brienne now. She's awake. The damage to her spine . . . I want to say that she's fine and everyone was over-reacting, but life isn't like that. The fact she survived is a miracle, and I can't ask for more. Well, yes, I can *ask*, but I can't expect it. The doctors don't know the extent or permanence of the damage. Right now, she can't move her legs. She has some feeling, though, and they say that's a good sign, so I'll take it.

Brienne doesn't bounce back in any other way either. She almost died. Her brother is dead. Her parents? Her parents told the press that River had always been impossible to control, that they knew something like this would happen, that he'd go bad, and it wasn't their fault. Brienne says she'll never forgive them for saying that.

When her parents told the media they needed money to care for her properly, she shut them down. Said she's not going home. She's talking to a social worker. Mom has offered to be her temporary guardian. Brienne's not sure she wants that. However it works out, I'll be there for her. She was brave for me. She risked her life to save me. I will repay her for that, in every way I can.

Max joins us partway through my visit. That is not coincidental. I'd texted to say I was going to see her. We visit Brienne together for a while. Then we leave, still together, and he says, "Do you have a few minutes?"

"I texted Sloane to say I don't need to be picked up for another hour."

He smiles. "Good."

He takes my hand and leads me through the hospital without another word. We're moving fast, ducking down side corridors, tensing every time we hear a voice, and, yes, I do flash back to the warehouse. Like I said, that doesn't go away. But it's a quick flash, pushed aside quickly with a wry observation that these last few days I do feel a little bit hunted, in need of escape. Everyone wants to talk to me, it seems.

*I'm so glad you survived that.* Um, yep, I am too. *It must have been terrible.* Yes, yes it was. *Really and truly terrible, all those kids dying.* Yes, and thank you for reminding me. I'd forgotten for three seconds. *How are you holding up?* I'm vertical. It's a start. *If you need anything . . .* Quiet. Right now, I need peace and quiet, and I know you're trying to help, and I appreciate that, but I just need a little time to myself, okay?

Max takes me to the one place where we can find that peace. The rooftop. It's not easy getting there, but he's scoped out a route that only requires sneaking through two Do Not Enter doors. When we step into the sunshine, the first thing we both do is turn to the huge ventilation system, making enough noise that I swear my teeth are vibrating.

"Hmm," he says. "Not quite as quiet as I hoped."

I laugh and tug him across the roof until the noise of the ventilation system fades behind us. We find a spot on the far side and sit on the edge.

"Much better," he says.

"As long as no one needs that," I say, hooking my thumb at the helipad behind us.

He smiles, and we sit in comfortable silence, our legs dangling over the edge as we look out at the city, dappled with sunlight, and I savor that sight, because it reminds me how close I came to never seeing it again.

We're still sitting in silence when something taps my hand, and I look down to see him holding out a jeweler's box. I take it without a word and open it to find a necklace with a drop-shaped pendant.

"It's a raindrop," he says. "Not a teardrop. I realized after I bought it that might require clarification."

I notice etching, and I lift it to read *Right as rain*, and my eyes fill with tears.

"I wish I could tell you I really am right as rain," he says, his voice low. "That everything's fine now, and things are never going to get that dark for me, and I'm stronger than that, because I want to be stronger than that, I want to show you I can be, but . . ." He takes a deep breath. "For now, I'm

— 335

as close to being all right as possible. Much, much closer than I have been in a very long time. It's not where I want to be, but—"

I turn and throw my arms around him. "I know."

We hug, and I feel . . . I feel everything. I'm scared for him and I'm scared for me. Worried for him. Worried for me. Worried for what's going to happen, and feeling a little bit helpless because I know it's not up to me, but that I'll do my best, for both of us, and he'll do the same, and that's where it starts. With understanding and with trying and with wanting. And it's not all fear and worry and anxiety. There's more. So much more.

I hug him, and I'm happy. That's what it comes down to. He makes me happy, and he makes me a better person, and he makes me stronger, and I can only hope that I do the same for him, and if I do, then the rest doesn't matter.

I pull back, and then I take out the necklace and he helps me fasten it.

"I looked it up, you know," I say. "Where the phrase comes from."

He smiles. "Of course you did. And?"

"No one has a bloody clue."

He throws back his head and laughs. "In other words, it's utter rubbish."

"No," I say. "In other words, it means whatever we want it to mean. So I say that we are, in our own very special way, right as rain."

"We are indeed," he says, and leans over to kiss me.

# MAX: INCREDULITY

Incredulity: *the state of being unable to believe something.*

That is what Max felt, sitting in class, catching a glimpse of Riley waiting outside the window. Incredulity. Not that he is surprised to see her there, considering she drove him and will take him home again. No, the incredulity is more a general sense of wonder, that she is there, that she is *still* there, that she might continue to be there, and that nothing he has said or done in the past six weeks has changed that.

He looks at the instructor, wrapping up class with a note about the assignment. Would Max have imagined himself here a few months ago? Dreamed of it, yes. Believed it possible? No. It was Riley who had brought him registration information for a creative writing class, just something to get him out of the house. His mother had not been pleased. Not at all. She'd told him, in no uncertain terms, that she would not allow it until they were completely certain his medication was working and maybe next fall . . . a full year away.

That's when Max realized he had to take a stand. That his mother thought she was doing her best for him. That Mum hated the suggestion that this "girl" knew better, but this wasn't about Riley—it was about him. Riley was suggesting two hours a week in a writing class, which she'd drive him to and from. Max wanted it. Max saw no fault with the plan. So Max registered. After three weeks in this class, he signed up for two college-level winter term classes. If those went well, in September he'd be off to uni . . . or college, as they called it here. With Riley, he hoped, though it was too soon to do more than hope. Granted, he'd broached the subject already, as a joke, and she hadn't quashed the idea, which was a start.

Max is not "fixed." Max will never be fixed. What he is, at the moment, is stable, and that's where he needs to stay. He won't, of course. It's like walking a tightrope. There are bound to be wobbles.

The catch-22 of schizophrenia is that if he is slipping, he is no longer in a mental state to see he's slipping. That means he needs someone to watch for him. *Everyone* to watch for him. Everyone in his life to know what to look for and be willing to call him on it, and if they are wrong and it's simply a mood swing, then there can be no hurt feelings, no recriminations, no resentment at being under a microscope. He needs to deal with the scrutiny as he deals with the side effects of the meds. This is the price for stability. It's the price for life too, because his alternative is not house arrest—it's writing another suicide note and maybe, just maybe, doing more than writing it.

Class ends, and he's first out the door. First down the hall and through the exit, and then she's there, waiting for him.

"Good class?" she asks.

"It was. I worked out my plot problem."

"Oooh, nice."

He takes her hand and leads her around the building. "I've decided my protagonist—who is not really you, as I've said . . ."

"Of course."

"Despite looking and acting and even sounding like you."

"Mere coincidence."

"It is. Because modeling my protagonist after you, while

flattering, might imply that I am utterly and absolutely smitten."

"Mmm, that would be wrong."

"It would be." He tugs her into an empty doorway and backs her up to the wall. "Because if you knew that, you could use it to do something alarming, like convince me to enroll in that first-aid class with you."

She sputters a laugh. "I do believe you *asked* to join me."

"Only because you'll need a partner for practicing mouth-to-mouth resuscitation, and naturally you'll want me."

"Naturally." Another laugh, and he revels in the sound, so pure and happy.

He did this. He made her happy.

*Yes, Maximus. You did. Now stop gloating and kiss her.*

Which he does. He pulls her to him and he kisses her, a deep and delicious and wondrous kiss, and this is what matters, not just the kiss but every little moment with her, every kiss and every look and every laugh. This is what he holds on to, what helps him believe—truly believe—he can do this, have a life, a real life, because Riley gives him those kisses and those looks and those laughs, and says he's worth them, that he's worthy of a girl like her, and the rest doesn't matter.

Yes, he'd told himself this was *a very bad idea*, but that hadn't actually stopped the flirting or the hand-holding or the kissing, and eventually—well, all right, it only took a week—they came to the conclusion that, bad idea or not, it's what they want. Sometimes, that's what matters most, that if you want something badly enough, you'll find a way to make it work.

He wants a life. He wants a future. He wants Riley. His parents raised him to believe he could achieve anything he put his mind to, and as much as that made it harder to accept the diagnosis—to accept that maybe, just maybe, there's more to life than putting in the effort—it still holds true that at the very least, if he wants something, he can put his mind to it and put his everything into getting it and, in the end, cross his fingers and hope.

When the kiss breaks, Riley says, "You never told me what you decided with the story."

"Ah, yes. You distracted me."

"I did not—"

"Completely did, but I forgive you." He eases back, his arms still around her. "I decided to let my protagonist be happy. In the end, she will be happy."

"So she wasn't going to be before?"

"I hadn't decided. One can't give a character a perfect ending, and there's something to be said for the classic literary downer, where she reaches the end of her journey only to discover it was all for naught, that the world is a hard and harsh place, and it will ultimately devour her and all she holds dear."

"Umm . . ."

"I hate those endings."

She laughs. "Good."

"The question was what note to strike for the conclusion, because it can't be perfect, after what she's been through, what she'll still need to go through. In the end, having cleared her name and brought her parents' killers to justice, she will return to her drought-stricken village, and she'll see her sister and her friends and the boy she left behind, and despite everything that's happened, she will be happy. And then it will rain."

She smiles and reaches up, wrapping her hands around his neck. "Of course it will," she says, and kisses him.

# ACKNOWLEDGMENTS

This book is a departure from my usual fare, but it's one I've been wanting to write for a very long time. As a departure, though, it meant I needed even more help than usual.

First, huge thanks to Amy Black and the team at Doubleday Canada for not only taking a chance on this book but embracing it. Your support made this so much easier.

To my agent, Sarah Heller, thanks for not thinking this was a completely mad idea.

To Antonia Hodgson at Little, Brown UK, thank you for your invaluable help getting Max's British-isms right.

To those who read an early draft of this book, thank you for helping me strike the right note with some sensitive topics. You know who you are, and you know I appreciate your reassurances—this is one book where I was even more anxious than usual.

Finally, thanks to Andrew Murray for his last-minute help with the "gun mishap" scene, not only giving me a reasonable scenario but demonstrating it (well, without the actual mishap. . .).

Kelley Armstrong lives in rural Ontario, Canada, with her family and far too many pets. She is the author of over thirty books, including the highly acclaimed Women of the Otherworld series, which begins with *Bitten*. The final three books in the series were all *Sunday Times* and *New York Times* bestsellers.